GUARDIAN
MISSION NORTHERN ATLANTIC

GUARDIAN
MISSION NORTHERN ATLANTIC

A NOVEL BY
FEYZI ÇELIK

"One man's past may determine the fate of nations."

Guardian
Mission Northern Atlantic

© Copyright 2025 Feyzi Çelik

US Copyright Office Registration Number TXu 2-515-259

This is a work of fiction.

PRINTED IN THE UNITED STATES

979-8-9935656-1-3 (Second Edition)

Cover design and layout: Ron McDougall, HM Design

For Jill, Ayla, and Alex
my safe harbor in every storm.

And to my parents, Lale and Ahmet
my origins, my compass, and the unwavering
hands that shaped the person I am today.

A signal is a promise:
someone is alive enough to be heard.

COAST GUARD OPS, MIDNIGHT LEDGER

Foreword

Over the past twenty years building OnePIN, I have traveled to more than forty countries—meeting people, bridging cultures, and gaining perspectives that shaped both my work and my life.

On the morning of July 5, 2025, two days before my scheduled flight to Ankara, Turkey, I awoke from a vivid dream. In it, I was on that very trip—seated in 4K, my actual seat assignment—crossing the Atlantic toward our Ankara office via Istanbul. The dream's details were sharp, its emotions intense. It felt less like a dream and more like a premonition.

The impact was so strong that I considered canceling my trip. But after reflection, I chose to move forward with my travel plans. That decision became the bridge between reality and fiction.

Guardian: Mission Northern Atlantic grew from that dream. I kept the protagonist's name as my own because the heart of the story revolved around me—my experiences, my questions, and the blurred lines between memory, imagination, and possibility.

Though the events in these pages are fictional, they are rooted in the emotions and imagery of that morning. In many ways, this novel is my reflection of a journey that began before the plane ever left the ground.

Preface

The world is a set of balances—tidal, ethical, economic—kept upright by countless hands most of us never see.

On calm days, that balance looks inevitable. Airlines rise on time, cargo ships stitch continents, satellites whisper truth and weather across the sky. Hospitals hum, networks route, families make breakfasts and plans. We forget how much invisible skill and care it takes to keep millions of moving parts from colliding. We forget how near the cliff edge always is.

War is never far. It doesn't always announce itself with banners; sometimes it arrives as a pattern—quiet pressure applied to the hinges of the world. A corrupted data stream here, an "anomaly" there, a rumor sharpened into a wedge. When power decides it prefers fear to consent, it tests the scaffolding we trust: laws, alliances, shared facts. It looks for the seam between what is possible and what is permitted.

This book begins when that seam is pulled.

An alliance of China, Russia, and North Korea believes technology can tilt history—that if you can blind the right sensors and bend the right signals, you can unmake the Free World without ever planting a flag. They gamble on darkness: that a coordinated strike across sea, sky, orbit, and story can make democracies hesitate long enough to lose the initiative.

They miscalculate one thing: the human tendency to stand up.

The first man to stand is an unlikely one. He is an engineer and a builder, a husband and father, a leader who thinks in systems and second-order effects. He is also, unbeknownst to almost everyone, a man with a sealed past—an old NATO designation that once meant: if the worst night comes, this is a person you can trust. He does not wear a cape. He does not ask to be found. When the attack tears open an airliner over warm Atlantic water and the world tilts, he surfaces into a new kind of duty.

What follows gathers itself around a hidden base on the ocean floor—Echo-7—where dolphins trained to rescue and robots shaped for impossible depths share a mission room with sailors, analysts, pilots, medics, coders, linguists, and logisticians. Here the story widens into a coalition: not only admirals and ministers, but air traffic controllers, Coast Guard watchstanders, search-and-rescue crews, airport station managers, data-fusing analysts who drink cold coffee at 3 a.m., and a reporter who keeps reading a log because getting it right still matters.

There are people who guard the systems built to protect us. As machines grow smarter—and sometimes fall into the wrong hands—the balance can tilt toward those willing to use them without restraint. Yet smart machines and humans can live in balance; it simply requires responsibility. The dark side may try to seize technology to smother democracies and the free world. When that happens, guardians appear. They are ordinary people like you: the technician who signs off on a repair because safety isn't negotiable; the controller who keeps a calm voice when the scope goes wild; the parent who steadies a household through the longest night. The Free World endures because such people keep showing up, choosing duty over noise.

This is also a love story. Not only the love between partners who have built a life of shared breakfasts, long drives, and hard good-byes, but the stubborn love of teams for one another; the loyalty of crews who say "my ship, my squad, my watch," and mean it; the fierce affection of people who choose service over spectacle. Love is not a side plot here. It is the reason strategies stay tethered to what is worth protecting. It is the force that stops cleverness from curdling into cruelty.

You will see how technology can be used to confuse and to save, how a whisper can topple a tower if no one counters it, and how truth still travels, even in headwinds. You will walk through rooms where the lights stay dim to keep eyes on screens, and across decks where salt air scours everything false. You will meet a coalition that is both geopolitical and deeply human—NATO officers and Turkish civil servants, American sailors and European controllers, engineers who think like mariners and mariners who think like engineers. They build something together that tyrannies always underestimate: trust.

At the end, the good wins. Not easily, and not without cost. Victory in the modern world looks less like a parade and more like the quiet restoration of normal: planes land again, ports reopen, markets stop holding their breath, children fall asleep without asking why the adults are whispering. The villains in this story have powerful tools. The heroes have something stronger: a belief that free people can coordinate in daylight, accept limits, correct mistakes, and still move forward.

If you read these pages for suspense, it is here. If you read them for wonder, it is here too—in the ocean's hidden corridors, in machines that learn, in animals that choose, and in the way a single message can cut a channel through noise and call a city to attention. But most of all, read them for the reminder that balance is not an accident. It is daily work. It is maintained by people who measure twice and care enough to get it right when getting it right is hard.

On the worst night, light arrives because someone carried a small one faithfully for years.

This book is for them—builders and guardians, colleagues and kin—and for the love that steadies their hands.

Author's Note

This novel is built on a real map, but many of the roads are imagined.

WHAT'S FACTUAL

The setting of the modern world: NATO exists as a defensive alliance; its member nations, basic structure, and collective-defense concept are real. Maritime chokepoints, transatlantic air corridors, coast-guard and search-and-rescue practices, and civilian aviation frameworks are also grounded in reality.

Technology families: Undersea cables, satellite navigation and communication, electronic warfare concepts, cyber intrusion techniques, autonomous and remotely operated vehicles, and human–animal cooperative research programs all have real precedents in open literature.

Institutions and roles: Air traffic control, port authorities, national disaster response, naval tasking, and intelligence fusion centers operate broadly as described, with many professionals doing quiet, expert work every day.

OnePIN: I founded OnePIN, and its history—and the team's civilian technology chops—are real. OnePIN builds mobile software and services for carriers and enterprises; its day-job is squarely commercial. Any suggestion of government or defense tasking lies outside the company's real-world scope.

Çelik Family: My family is real—think of them as the true North on my compass—while the storms that circle them in these pages are fictional seas drawn for the purposes of story.

WHAT'S FICTIONALIZED

Operations, timelines, and capabilities: Specific missions, covert authorities, rules of engagement, and technical performance details are invented or deliberately altered. Timelines are compressed; procedures are simplified to serve the story and to avoid revealing sensitive methods.

People and units: Echo-7, its underwater infrastructure, command arrangements, and composite teams are wholly fictional. So are call signs, unit names, interior layouts, and most interagency coordination depicted at a granular level. Any resemblance to real organizations or individuals is coincidental.

Adversary decision-making: The depicted coordination among China, Russia, and North Korea, including motives, chains of command, and campaign design, is a narrative construct. It reflects plausible tensions and threat models, not insider knowledge.

Incidents and places in time: Commercial flight numbers, specific accidents, dates, and emergency logs (including the catalytic airliner event) are invented. Real locations appear, but their use in the plot—access, security posture, and on-scene responses—is dramatized.

Tools at the edge: Advanced effects—AI-assisted sensing and deception, novel undersea platforms, bio-behavioral interfaces with marine mammals—are extrapolations from open research and industry trend lines, tuned for storytelling.

Near-future systems: "Kazuars," autonomous submarines, and humanoids in this story are fictional constructs—yet they are near-future technologies, arriving faster than most people expect.

OnePIN (story elements): Any defense or military divisions, projects, or roles attributed to OnePIN in these pages are inventions for the narrative.

WHY THIS BLEND

To honor professionals without exposing them: The book aims to capture the feel of how sailors, controllers, pilots, engineers, analysts, medics, maintainers, divers, and reporters actually work—checklists, redundancies, calm under pressure—while changing specifics so no real tactic, vendor, or vulnerability is teachable from these pages.

To keep faith with geopolitics while telling a human story: Strategy is real; the characters are not. Where the novel simplifies statecraft, it does so to keep the focus on duty, friendship, love, and the ordinary excellence that holds liberal societies together.

Accountability: As smart machines grow more capable, responsibility must grow with them; this novel keeps its eye on that balance—how human judgment and accountability should remain in the loop.

ETHICAL GUARDRAILS I FOLLOWED

No classified sources were used; any technical detail that appears sensitive has been altered or synthesized.

No real private individual is portrayed; composite characters draw on common professional archetypes.

When in doubt, I chose caution over fidelity—if a detail could plausibly aid misuse, it was changed, blurred, or removed.

A FINAL WORD

The most "true" element here is the spirit of the people who keep the world in balance. Their names aren't in this book, but their habits are: measure twice, sign your work, back your teammate, go when called. If the story rings true, it's because of them. If it takes liberties, that's on me—taken in service of a good tale and a safer world.

Dramatis Personae

Principals

Feyzi Çelik
President and CEO,
OnePIN, Inc.

**Commander
Rebecca Hart**
Head of Marine
Biology & Rescue
Operations, Echo-7

Jill Çelik
Feyzi's Wife

Echo-7 (Undersea Joint Operations Base)

Commander Grant Rourke: Director, Naval Tactical Operations
Chief Warrant Officer Lena Morano: Head of Cybersecurity &
 Comms Integrity
Dr. Sienna Patel: Chief, Project ARES, AI & Robotics Enhanced
 Strategy
Lt. Cmdr. Sofia Barrera: Director, Subaquatic Environmental Vectors
Captain Everett "Hawk" Remington Monroe: Commanding
 Officer, USS *Kentucky*
Maj. Arman Reyes: Director, Special Forces Detachment Echo
Col. Jacob S. Vance: Space Command Liaison, Orbital Threats &
 Surveillance
Lt. Noah Reiser: Weapons Officer
Lt. Sandra Coen: Sonar Lead
Lily Ng: Sonar Chief Petty Officer

USS *Missouri*

Capt. Joshua E. Monroe: Commanding Officer, USS *Missouri*
Lt. Alyssa Kane: Weapons Officer

U.S. Second Fleet (Atlantic)

Admiral Michael Lansing: Commander of the U.S. Second Fleet

U.S. Seventh Fleet (Pacific)

Admiral Theodore "Theo" Langston: Commander of USS *Ronald Reagan* and the U.S. Seventh Fleet
Commander Raquel Ibarra: XO of USS *Ronald Reagan*
Lt. Commander Reiko Sato: Weapons Coordination, USS *Ronald Reagan*

United States Coast Guard (First District – Boston)

Commander Rebecca Alden: Officer of the Watch, First Coast Guard District, Boston, MA
Commander Vic Tran: Operations Officer
Lieutenant Dana Reyes: Intelligence Analyst

Newton PD

Officer Megan O'Neill

Air Turkey: Flight XT84 & Corporate

Capt. Murat Kaya: Captain, XT84 (A350-900)
First Officer Selim Kurt: First Officer, XT84
Hakan Demiral: Chief Executive Officer, Air Turkey
Kemal Günay: Boston Station Manager, Air Turkey

U.S. Government (Executive & National Security)

Daniel T. Keaton: President of the United States
Dr. Marshall Kline: National Security Advisor

Government of Türkiye

Kemal Arıkan: President of Türkiye
Halil Şen: Minister of Transportation of Türkiye

US Space Command

Lt. General Marissa Zhao: Strategist at Vandenberg Space Force Base, California
Lt. Colonel Devina Rusk: Mission Lead for Orbital Kinetic Engagements

OnePIN, Inc. (Corporate/Engineering)

Ethan Gagnon: Chief Operating Officer
Adam Kowalczyk: Chief Technology Officer
Laura Whitman: VP of Products & Marketing
Evan Brooks: Chief Financial Officer
Ben Carter: Vice President of Finance
Terry Moreau: Director of IT & Cloud
Gülce Demir: General Manager, Ankara Office
Daniel Mercer: Director of Solutions
Chiara Moretti: General Counsel
Natalie Santoro: Controller
Arda Yalçın: Head of Engineering
Ankit Verma: Director of Technology
Barış Aksoy: Senior Software Engineer
Kemal Özdemir: Senior Software Engineer
Elif Aydın: Senior Test Engineer
Ece Yaman: Senior Software Engineer
Jane Daniels: Senior Finance Associate
Berkay Çetinkaya: Software Engineer
Erhun Kaya: Software Engineer

Media

Rachel Lin: Reporter, *The Boston Globe*

DRAMATIS PERSONAE

Adversary Cells (Russia / China / DPRK)

General Wei Liang: Chief Strategist of Submarine Warfare, Joint Naval Command Division Qingdao, China

General Bao Xinjian: Head of the Central Military Cyber Division

Major General Yuri Sokolov: Russia's Covert Naval Arm

Colonel Alexei Voronov: Head of Joint Russian Chinese Naval Cyber Ops

Aleksey ("Alek") Zubarev: Operations Commander of Unit GRU

Captain Yuri Melnikov: Russian-built, Chinese-enhanced Submarine Kazuar 1

Lt. Alexei Morozov: Weapons Officer of Submarine Kazuar 1

Lt. Zhang Yuwei: Second-in-command of Submarine Kazuar 1

Lieutenant Tomas Neves: NATO Liaison Officer (Russian and Chinese Spy)

Efe Tunçel (a.k.a. Erhan Toprak): Istanbul Airport Operations Desk (Russian and Chinese Spy)

Çelik Family

Alex Çelik: Son

Ayla Çelik: Daughter

Ryan Finley: Ayla's fiancé

Echo-D2 Advanced Dolphin Rescue Unit

Mira: Dolphin, Member of Echo-D2

Orion: Dolphin, Member of Echo-D2

Others

Captain Aylin Demir: Turkish Air Force Cyber Intelligence

Agent Levent Kara: Senior Field Data Forensics Officer at Turkish National Intelligence Organization

Dr. Selin Ar: Interrogator at Turkish National Intelligence Organization

Staff Sergeant Miller: U.S. Signal Analyst

Acknowledgments

I owe my deepest gratitude to Jill, my wife and partner for life—your love, patience, and unwavering belief have been my constant source of strength.

To my children, Ayla and Alex, and to my son-in-law, Ryan; you bring joy, perspective, and meaning to every chapter of my life.

To the OnePIN Team, many of whom have been by my side for more than two decades—you are not just colleagues, but lifelong friends. Together, we built more than a company; we built a family and a legacy.

I am also deeply grateful to the Albert family for welcoming me into their lives and making me a part of their family here in Boston. Jill's and my life would not be the same without your incredible support, kindness, and generosity. You have been a constant source of warmth and encouragement, and I cherish the bond we share.

And to my parents, Ahmet and Lale—my anchors in life. You shaped me into the person I am today and taught me that no obstacle is insurmountable. Your lessons, love, and example have guided me through every storm and toward every horizon.

Explore More

Thanks for reading. Want to go deeper—tech, characters, and behind-the-scenes notes? Scan the QR codes below to explore the world of *Guardian* and meet the people who bring it to life.

ENTER THE GUARDIAN WORLD

 Explore the world of *Guardian*
Concept art, technology & systems, and theme visualizers

TheGuardianSeries.com

MEET THE CHARACTERS

 See the characters—photos, videos & bios

TheGuardianSeries.com/characters/

Scanning these codes opens the book's official website in your browser. No app required. Standard data rates may apply.

Contents

CONTENTS

GUARDIAN
MISSION NORTHERN
ATLANTIC

CHAPTER 1

Moon Line

Altitude 31,000

The cabin lights of Air Turkey Flight XT84 dimmed to a quiet dusk, and the Atlantic unfurled below like a sheet of hammered glass. In seat 4K, Feyzi Çelik tightened the shoulder harness across his chest and let the window frame the world he knew—Boston's jeweled shoreline falling away, the moon riding impossibly close.

He had flown this lane a hundred times. Not like this.

On the map, their arc skimmed New Brunswick and bent toward empty ocean. The flight crew moved with unhurried choreography, clearing trays, sequencing cabin checks. A comfortable silence wrapped the aisle. It should have felt routine. Instead, the air felt tuned—like an instrument held just off-key.

He texted Jill.

"All good. Love you."

He leaned back and watched the moon. It felt near enough to touch, a pale coin pressing against the window.

The sensation tugged a half-formed thought forward: "proximity changes judgment."

A lesson from business, from war rooms, from life. You see more when you're closer—and sometimes the wrong things.

The mind strays on long flights.

3

His drifted to a threadbare set of facts he rarely said aloud: a Turkish boy who learned discipline on a wild inland lake; an engineer shaped by METU, sharpened at BU, weaponized by an MBA at Babson College when he realized ideas were only as strong as the systems that carried them.

Feyzi Çelik founded OnePIN, Inc., a Boston-based mobile technology company. A company born in the seams of the mobile world and scaled—quietly—to a billion pockets. Enough patents to make headlines, if headlines were the point. They weren't. Building was the point. Guardrails, not glory. OnePIN wasn't another flashy startup; it was a precision outfit with staying power in a shifting digital world.

A chime sounded. Somewhere a galley latch clicked shut.

The aisle lights thinned to blue. The captain made a short announcement. Nothing notable. And yet a small muscle in Feyzi's jaw stayed tight.

He checked the seat belt again. Under Armour's SlipSpeed shoes tugged firm against his heels. Phone zipped deep, not loose where the seat's machinery could swallow it. The habits of a man who believed preparation steals from chaos.

The moon held its ground.

He exhaled and let his eyes close for a count of ten, then opened them again.

No sleep tonight.

He searched for something ordinary—a movie, the map—but his thumb hovered above the screen and never settled.

A faint tremor lifted the glass of water on his armrest.

He glanced down the aisle.

Nothing.

The tremor faded. The moon brightened.

Somewhere forward, metal ticked as if cooling from heat it never should have felt.

Feyzi straightened, not sure if he'd heard it at all. He pressed his palm to the armrest, felt the aircraft's long body talk through the frame.

So much order condensed into a single machine, hundreds of souls inside a flying statement of trust: rivets, rules, and human hands will hold.

He looked back to the moon and felt the old intuition rise—the one that had saved deals, teams, and once or twice, lives.

"Something is off."

He didn't know that in a chapters' time the world would rip open. He only knew the water's surface below gleamed too warm under that lovely, watchful moon—like a secret keeping itself.

A chime again.

Then, the slightest, almost polite, shudder.

He tightened the harness and let his eyes find the moon one last time.

"Witness this" he thought.

And the aisle went quiet enough to hear the breath you take before a storm.

Settling into his thirteen-hour flight to Ankara via Istanbul, Feyzi allowed himself a rare moment of reflection.

So much had been built.

So many lives touched.

Yet something stirred—a quiet intuition that the next chapter wouldn't just test his intellect or leadership.

It would demand all of him.

Summer Haze
Forty-eight hours ago

Biddeford Pool wore its July light like gossamer—soft, bright, a veil over the Atlantic's shoulder. The Daniels house breathed with familiar noise: screen doors thumping, grill lids clanging, a bocce ball clacking off a ridge the tide had carved into the sand.

Jill's family did this every year. So did Feyzi. Tradition was a kind of anchor you choose for yourself.

They had two children: Ayla, twenty-six, engaged to Ryan; and Alex, sixteen, fresh off tenth grade. Jill's New England family stayed close—her father Steven and stepmother Claire in Marion, her sister Susan and husband Jonathan in West Roxbury, her brother Bill and wife Helen in Millis—and traditions kept everyone knitted together.

The day glowed—bright but hazy.

A long stretch of beach became the bocce court.

Cousin Ken and Bill traded good-natured jabs as seasoned players. Alex and Ayla learned fast.

Feyzi and Jonathan teamed up to challenge the veterans, laughing as balls caromed off tide-cut ridges.

The beach itself was the unpredictable opponent.

Ayla and Alex traded jokes with cousins between throws.

Ken and Bill argued about a close call that wasn't close at all. Susan turned the corn with a practiced wrist.

Somewhere inside, a photo of Jon Daniels—the meteorologist whose calm voice had read New England its weather for a generation—watched over the room where people still came when the air promised thunder.

Feyzi paused at the top of the dunes and squinted toward the horizon.

Haze flattened the distance into a watercolor wash.

Beautiful. Wrong.

He checked the marine report on his phone.

"Record-breaking sea surface temperatures in the North Atlantic. The Gulf Stream running in the low seventies."

"An anomaly," the article said.

A red band snaking across a map like a warning someone had colored too strongly to be mistaken for anything else.

He slid the phone back into his pocket and let the sounds of his life drown the thought: Alex's shout as a throw kissed the jack; Ayla's laugh; Jill's steady smile across the lawn—the one that said, "we made this."

The day moved in clean chapters: a long swim, a last volley, a quiet walk along the water where the sand held heat longer than it should have.

The wind barely bothered the dune grass.

No sunscreen sting, no salty sting in the eyes. A gentleness that didn't match the ocean's reputation.

At dusk, fireworks stitched color into the haze and left it stitched there, like the sky refused to let the light go.

People clapped. Children shrieked. Adults leaned into each other and called the show "perfect."

Feyzi watched the late smoke drift low and thought of systems again—how warmth can hide where it shouldn't, how pressure can build out of sight until all at once it doesn't.

He looked back at his family, stamped the thought down, and let the night close over them the way a good story closes: with a promise for tomorrow.

Beyond the horizon the Atlantic held its breath.

And Feyzi, intuitive as ever, could feel that change was coming.

Hopkinton, MA
Twenty-four hours ago

Sunday broke over Hopkinton in a clean rectangle of light across the kitchen tile. While the kids slept, Feyzi brewed tea and set out a small breakfast, then moved through the rituals that kept chaos tame: mow the lawn in straight, problem-solving lines; charge what needs charging; pack the same way every time.

This was the work he loved: make order, build systems, trust them.

He always flew with a backpack—tools of the trade: encrypted gateways, hardware tokens, field devices. Each week he and One-

PIN's tech lead, Terry Moreau, reviewed security upgrades. Obsession shared: defense in depth.

Joining the "billion club" took decades. Only a few hundred tech companies reach that scale. OnePIN stayed modest in headcount yet formidable in reach by deploying software directly to SIMs—the heart of the mobile experience. It was a position of trust, earned through reinvention, patient investors, and careful dances with telecom giants.

He packed laptop, tablet, headphones, adapters, snacks, a compact med kit. Summer meant no suits—just shirts and pants. Simple. Efficient.

Ayla drifted down first. They shared tea and a quiet laugh about wedding planning and impossible florists. Later, Jill returned from Maine with salt still in her hair. Dinner was easy.

Goodbyes were harder in houses like theirs because they were honest.

Airbus A350-900
Present Day

Monday carried its own clock. A black Able Limousine pulled up ten minutes early.

Black technical Tshirt. Waterproof pants. Sweater in the carry-on. Shoes you can run in if you have to.

At the door, Jill kissed him; Alex hugged hard, hiding what goodbyes cost him. Feyzi slung the backpack, rolled the carry-on, and waved off the driver's help. He believed in doing things himself.

The ride east was the usual slide of Massachusetts through glass: horse farms, Route 9, the Pike.

Check-in. TSA Precheck. Lufthansa, Star Alliance lounge. A glass of water, an email answered, a call not made because some things deserve to be said in person when you land.

Terminal E at Logan welcomed the Star Alliance faithful with efficient signage and a line of wheelchairs at Gate E8 that promised early boarding to passengers who didn't need them. Feyzi smiled. His people improvised; no judgment in that.

Boarding for Air Turkey Flight XT84 began on time, then not quite. Fourteen minutes late, the bridge clicked to the door of an Airbus A350-900, and Feyzi stepped into the familiar hush of business class, where light and noise and movement are designed on purpose.

Seat 4K held what he needed: room to think, a clean sight line, a window that made the world small enough to understand. He slid the backpack into its cave, set the iPad where it couldn't wander, and buckled the shoulder harness that most people ignored because they hadn't needed it yet. His favorite shoes stayed snug—he knew emergencies demanded mobility.

He texted Jill. "Pushing now. Will ping before sleep."

"Love you. Safe flight," Jill texted back.

He skimmed the map, chose a light meal. Preparation again—calories that won't argue with sleep and a seat layout that won't trap a phone when turbulence turns a cabin into an engine of gears.

When the wheels left the runway and Boston rolled beneath them like a model city on a perfect table, he looked right and saw the moon waiting.

On the climb, he let a different inventory run in the background.

Forty-two countries. A billion devices. OnePIN, Inc. built to last because it builds what other companies stand on.

He thought of the quiet lesson his father taught by building large-scale water projects where there wasn't any and the way he'd replied by building software where no one looked. In his eyes, mobile technology was the infrastructure of the future.

While tech giants dominated headlines, Feyzi focused on overlooked spaces—the niche layers that power the mobile ecosystem.

With discipline and an eye for emerging trends, he grew OnePIN into a global leader and let results speak for themselves.

He thought of Babson College and Boston University and METU and the day the math of his life added up to Jill.

He also thought of Ankara—of his parents, ninety-four and eighty-five, of a government program that needed a signature in person, of younger engineers at OnePIN who still believed in the clean click you hear when the right idea meets the right design.

The cabin settled into the long-haul rhythm. Feyzi adjusted the seat a notch and watched the flight path creep past Newfoundland into the nothing that is not nothing at all—just air and water and the busiest, loneliest corridor on earth.

And then, The Moon.

Full. Bright.

Impossibly near.

He wasn't a man given to omens, but he accepted information wherever it offered itself. The ocean below ran too warm this summer, the way a system runs hot when a fan fails in a rack you can't reach without bringing the whole data center down. You note it. You decide if it matters now or later.

He zipped the phone into his pocket and set both hands flat on the armrests, a small ritual to mark the end of day one and the start of day two—the stretch between.

A mild tremor rolled under the floor and was gone. He felt it more than heard it. The crew moved easily. The aisle stilled.

Feyzi glanced at the map, then back at the window.

The moon held its perfect, impossible distance.

He drew a breath, slow through the nose, out through the mouth, and tasted salt that shouldn't have been there.

Then the glass of water on his armrest quivered, and somewhere forward a metal latch ticked again, like a clock counting to a number no one wanted to name.

He tightened the harness another click and lifted his eyes.
The cabin dimmed. The moon remained.
Feyzi stared at it.
Something stirred inside.
The Moon, silent and steady, wouldn't just watch over the flight.
Tonight, it would bear witness.
And perhaps, become a guide.

CHAPTER 2

Sudden Descent

Two hours into Air Turkey Flight XT84, the business class cabin was winding down. The four crew members were clearing dinner trays, moving with calm precision between the rows of drowsy travelers.

The soft clinking of silverware was fading, replaced by dimmed cabin lights and the occasional rustle of seatbelts being loosened.

Feyzi checked the flight map. They had just entered the third hour of flight, having recently passed over New Brunswick, Canada—the home province of OnePIN's COO, Ethan Gagnon. Smiling at the coincidence, Feyzi shot off a quick:

"Just flew over New Brunswick. Weather looks amazing. Hope you enjoy the family trip."

Ethan had planned a visit with his wife and kids to see his parents. It was late in Boston; Ethan would read it in the morning.

The map displayed their current position: 500 miles east of St. John's, Newfoundland, and 750 miles south of Greenland, smack in the middle of the North Atlantic.

There was no land in sight. Only the transatlantic corridor, filled with invisible threads of flight paths and cargo ships cruising far below. The path was the shortest route between North America and Europe, and one of the most traveled.

As Feyzi traced the route with his eyes, a memory surfaced. He chuckled softly, remembering former President's strange suggestions that Canada and Greenland should join the U.S. While they were ridiculed at the time, from 30,000 feet the geopolitical logic was strangely visible. Greenland was a strategic gateway to the Arctic, a potential corridor for future conflict.

The U.S. military had long relied on it for surveillance and early warning systems. The growing Russian and Chinese naval presence, especially China's fast-expanding fleet, was a reminder that the future of warfare wasn't just cyber—it was physical, territorial, and contested.

But now wasn't the time for geopolitics. Feyzi shook off the thoughts and texted Jill:

"Dinner's done. Love you."

No reply.

She was likely asleep.

He zipped his iPhone into his pocket—securely. He had seen too many passengers lose their phones under the complex business class seat mechanisms on long-haul flights.

The cabin dimmed further.

The crew completed the last of the dinner service.

Feyzi reclined slightly, watching the final scene of *Iron Man 2*.

That's when it happened.

Pilot's Cockpit – Air Turkey Flight XT84

The aircraft jolted violently.

Captain Murat Kaya was sipping black tea from his thermos when the dashboard lit up in red. A shrill alarm pierced the cockpit.

"Structural breach, left fuselage."

"Oh my god" First Officer Selim Kurt muttered, eyes wide.

An explosion had just torn through the mid-section of the A350-900. Instrument panels blinked with fault readings: cabin decompression, electrical failure, fuel pressure drop.

"Mayday, mayday, mayday. XT84, explosive decompression, un-controlled depressurization. Attempting emergency descent," Kaya called out on the radio, hoping someone, anyone, could pick it up.

They began a controlled dive, the autopilot disengaged, and the oxygen masks deployed throughout the aircraft.

"Dropping to 10,000 feet. Maintain attitude," Kaya barked. His hands were steady, but his gut told him the aircraft was bleeding fast.

Back in the cabin, the blast had hit like a sledgehammer.

A deafening bang.

A blinding flash.

Smoke. Chaos. Suction.

A gaping hole had torn open on the left side of business class. The pressure differential pulled passengers and crew through the fuselage breach. Screams were swallowed by the void.

Feyzi, buckled in, was one of the few still in place. His instincts kicked in. He reached up and grabbed the oxygen mask, slipping the band over his head and breathing deeply. It was nearly impossible to see—fog, wires, insulation, debris. The alarms screamed.

He glanced left. Where there had been seats—people—was now just sky. Cables and metal dangled from twisted walls.

The plane began to plummet. Rapidly.

His mind raced.

"Ten minutes," he thought.

That's how long the emergency oxygen would last at this altitude.

And then, the plane leveled slightly. The vibrations lessened. The descent was controlled.

Somehow, the pilots had held it together.

But then Feyzi saw it: fuel leaking from the wing. The sea gleamed silver under the moonlight. They were going to attempt a ditching.

He looked out the right window. The moon hovered just above the Atlantic. It was beautiful—and terrifying.

As the aircraft skimmed toward the ocean, Feyzi felt a brief flicker of hope. The approach was steady. The tail flaps adjusted.

Then, disaster struck.

A crosswind hit from the right. The plane tilted sharply. The right engine clipped the water first—too hard. The impact twisted the aircraft violently, wrenching it into a deadly spin.

The business class section, already structurally weakened, snapped away from the fuselage.

Feyzi blacked out.

He awoke underwater.

Cold. Confused.

Still strapped into his seat, sinking fast. He thrashed, trying to orient himself. His lungs burned.

He reached instinctively for the harness release—on the right side, same as in the car.

Click. Free.

He kicked upward.

He had to survive.

Feyzi burst through the surface, gasping. He was alive. The water—strangely warm, almost 75°F enveloped him—overheated Gulf Stream.

The moon illuminated the chaos: shattered debris, floating seat cushions, no sounds except the soft splash of drift.

Nearby, the tail section of the aircraft slowly sank.

A large piece of fuselage floated beside him. Feyzi clambered atop it, exhausted but alert.

His survival instincts kicked in.

Eğirdir Lake had trained him for this. Growing up in Isparta, Türkiye, he had spent summers on that vast freshwater lake, Türkiye's fourth largest, covering over 482 square kilometers (larger than Lake Tahoe in California). He had faced fierce storms, rowed boats in whipping winds.

He respected water. And now, it respected him back.

He ran a check:

Injury—Bleeding left shoulder. Likely from the seatbelt during impact. Not deep.

Phone—Still in pocket.

iPhone. IP68-rated. Water-resistant, not waterproof.

He powered it on. No bars. Of course. No towers. Middle of the ocean.

He didn't panic. He opened the iOS Connection Assistant.

It guided him to connect to a satellite.

The connection established. A brief signal appeared.

Then, he sent:

"Flight XT84 destroyed. Middle of Atlantic. Feyzi Çelik. Alive. Immediate rescue needed."

The message pinged.

Sent.

Then—A sound.

A cry.

A baby.

Far off to his left.

Feyzi froze. A dream? A hallucination? No.

Another cry. This time to his right. A third one.

Three crying babies.

His brain reeled. Could infants have survived?

Cats, maybe? But it was unmistakable—babies.

He tore off a piece of fuselage and used it like a paddle, guiding his floating raft toward the sound.

Another cry pierced the night.

Then silence.

Then, another cry, even closer.

Feyzi, bruised, bleeding, floating in a shredded sea under a radiant moon, knew one thing:

This was no accident.

The explosion had been precise. The hole surgical. It must have been a surface to air missile.

He wasn't supposed to survive.

And yet—he had.

And now, perhaps, so had others.

His mission, once a business trip, had just become something else entirely.

Something deeper.

Something destined.

He would survive.

He would uncover the truth.

And someone, somewhere, would pay.

CHAPTER 3

Rescue Mission

Two hours and twenty-one minutes into Air Turkey Flight XT84's journey, the transponder signal disappeared from radar.

At that moment, the aircraft was cruising over the central North Atlantic, deep within the boundaries of Gander Oceanic Control, a critical segment of international airspace managed from Gander, Newfoundland and Labrador.

The Gander Automated Air Traffic System had been tracking XT84's eastbound progress along a standard transatlantic corridor. At approximately 30 degrees West longitude, it would have been handed off to Shanwick Oceanic Control, which monitors the northeastern Atlantic.

But it never reached Shanwick.

Gander is one of the world's most important oceanic control centers, sharing responsibility for the North Atlantic with the U.K.'s Shanwick. Unlike continental airspace, most of the NAT (North Atlantic) has no radar; controllers rely on satellite surveillance, automation, and GAATS/GAATS+ to build a radar-like picture and move aircraft with procedural separation and data link.

The NAT is the busiest oceanic airspace on earth. In 2023 there were about 580,000 flights between Europe and North America, an average of 1,590 per day, with organized track systems switching direction by time of day (eastbound at night, westbound by day), underscoring the scale of operations.

Gander Oceanic Control – 12:10 a.m., Tuesday, July 8

The controller on duty, Derrick MacAllister, a seasoned professional with over 20 years of transatlantic experience, had just logged a routine update on the XT84 flight track. He looked up at the screen, puzzled by a blinking status alert. Then the headset in his left ear crackled with static—followed by panic.

"Mayday, mayday, mayday. XT84. Explosive decompression—uncontrolled depressurization. Attempting emergency descent..."

The voice was strained.

Captain Murat Kaya. Breathing hard.

Then came a brief burst of what sounded like coughing and alarms in the background.

"XT84, confirm altitude. Do you have control?" Derrick asked quickly, snapping upright in his chair.

No response.

"XT84, Gander Control. Say again, do you have flight control? Nature of the emergency?"

Silence.

Derrick's fingers flew across the console, logging the call and tagging the flight's last known coordinates:

Latitude 51.8N, Longitude 36.4W, altitude approximately 31,000 feet.

"Gander, this is TK256. We heard a mayday from XT84. Nothing visual on radar, no contact," another flight chimed in, crossing the same airspace 20 minutes behind.

"Roger TK256, maintain heading, advise if you see anything unusual."

Derrick turned to the duty supervisor.

"I've just lost XT84."

A deep silence fell across the control room. Then chaos.

Canadian and U.S. Coast Guard® Mobilize

In under 10 minutes, standard emergency protocols were triggered. The Canadian Coast Guard was notified, and the Boston Air Traffic Control Center, the origin departure hub for XT84, was looped in.

Simultaneously, Gander issued alerts to Shanwick Oceanic Control, which relayed updates to flights under their watch.

Crews began scanning the skies, checking radar scopes, and initiating emergency radio calls on guard frequencies.

In Boston, the First Coast Guard District, headquartered at the Captain John F. Williams Coast Guard Building, received a flash alert.

First Coast Guard District, Boston, MA

The First District covers New England and much of the Northeast coastline, with 12,000 active duty, reserve, civilian, and auxiliary personnel supporting missions from SAR to maritime security. In a typical year, the district conducts 2,400 SAR cases, saves 427 lives, assists 4,500 people, and safeguards $115M in property at sea.

The Captain John F. (Foster) Williams Coast Guard Building is a 160,000-sq-ft waterfront facility in downtown Boston that supports 24/7 operations; its namesake commanded the first commissioned Revenue Cutter, Massachusetts in 1789.

Officer of the Watch

Commander Rebecca Alden, Officer of the Watch, was called in from her on-base quarters at 12:19 a.m. She arrived at the ops center within minutes, already dialing direct lines to the Canadian Coast Guard Halifax Station.

Commander Alden was respected not only for her razor-sharp decision-making but for her ability to inspire confidence in crisis. Formerly a Navy® helicopter pilot, she'd logged hundreds of hours in Arctic conditions and knew firsthand the brutal indifference of the North Atlantic. Educated at the U.S. Naval Academy, oceanography/polar focus, and the National SAR School, she's certified as an Aircraft Commander and Maritime SAR Mission Coordinator.

Now, seated before a multi-screen console surrounded by real-time radar, sonar overlays, and satellite feeds, she snapped into action.

By 12:30 a.m., a shared SAR (Search and Rescue) task force was being formed between Boston and Halifax.

"We've got a long zone and a cold ocean,"

"Mark that negative-return corridor in 4C; expand coverage five miles to the south."

Alden said grimly, marking a 400-mile radius from the last ping.

"I want full thermal scans from NOAA satellites and acoustic net activation from the Naval Undersea Warfare Center."

The U.S. Second Fleet Reacts

The call to the U.S. Second Fleet came just past 12:40 a.m. From their base in Norfolk, Virginia, the re-established fleet, reactivated in 2018, after a seven-year stand-down, was built to deter and fight in the North Atlantic amid renewed Russian undersea activity from the GIUK Gap to the Barents. Its remit runs from the U.S. Eastern Seaboard to the High North, integrating closely with NATO's Joint Force Command Norfolk to protect sea lines of communication.

Admiral Michael Lansing, the duty commander, was briefed immediately.

"The transponder dropped while they were still descending. That plane could've glided 150 miles," Lansing said, calculating rough trajectories.

"And if they ditched... we'll be lucky to find anything by sunrise."

He dispatched a liaison to the U.S. Space Command to check for infrared plumes, debris scatter signatures, or flash events.

"If this was an external hit, I want eyes from orbit," Lansing instructed.

Satellite reconnaissance teams were alerted. NOAA provided real-time ocean current models. Two nearby U.S. Navy vessels, USS *Porter* and USNS *Comfort*, were rerouted and ordered into emergency search grid posture.

International Aviation Agencies Notified

Within an hour, the National Transportation Safety Board (NTSB) and Federal Aviation Administration (FAA) were formally notified.

A joint incident code was created: "Atlantic Air Loss – XT84."

At the NTSB headquarters, Chief Investigator Dr. Eleanor Kranz prepared to dispatch a multidisciplinary team to Istanbul, where the flight had been scheduled to land. Meanwhile, the FAA's Office of Accident Investigation & Prevention (AVP) initiated their parallel track—focused on regulatory compliance, systems checks, and satellite telemetry correlation.

Dr. Kranz was a veteran of multiple aviation incidents, including the Air France 447 tragedy. Cool under pressure and renowned for her cross-agency coordination skills, she began assembling an expert team—airframe analysts, human factors specialists, and black box recovery engineers.

"We treat every missing signal as a solvable mystery," she told her staff.

"Assume nothing."

An emergency virtual command room was created. Data streamed in from Air Turkey, Airbus HQ, satellite companies, and NATO air surveillance networks.

Despite the mobilization, a chilling sense loomed among the senior officers on both sides of the Atlantic:

They had lost a plane.

Search and Realism

By 2:00 a.m., the scale of the problem had crystallized.

The last confirmed contact had occurred at cruising altitude.

No emergency beacon had yet been detected. No other flights had seen debris or smoke.

Weather was clear. No storms. No turbulence.

In short, nothing made sense.

The working theory became: massive structural failure or external impact. The possibility of a missile strike, while improbable, could not be ruled out. Intelligence agencies were quietly alerted.

NSA taps were ordered on regional communications networks, and submarine cable monitoring was initiated from Fort Meade.

The size of the search area was daunting. At cruising altitude, a plane with partial glide capability could cover over 100 nautical miles before impact. But the descent had been rapid. Violent. Possibly uncontrolled. The window for survivors was shrinking.

"This may become a recovery operation within 24 hours," Commander Alden admitted in a secure U.S. Coast Guard conference call.

But still, they launched.

The Atlantic Ocean

The Atlantic is the United States' economic bridge to Europe and Africa. U.S.–EU goods trade alone topped $975 billion on a yearly basis, with services trade adding $501B, trade flows that ride heavily on ships despite the rise of air cargo.

Globally, over 80% of goods move by sea; by value, shipping carries 45% of U.S. goods trade with Europe.

U.S. goods trade with Africa totaled $72B each year, plus $33B in services trade, much of it seaborne across the Atlantic.

The Port of New York/New Jersey, the largest on the East Coast, handled 8.7 million containers yearly, with East Coast ports collectively receiving thousands of containership and tanker calls annually. Federal port statistics track not just boxes but vessel calls, berth times, and throughput across North and South Atlantic port ranges, numbers that explain why any Atlantic disruption instantly ripples through U.S. food, autos, metals, and consumer goods.

These are not abstract figures: the East Coast's grocery aisles, car lots, and construction sites depend on uninterrupted Atlantic shipping lanes. That's why U.S. maritime, Coast Guard, and Navy commands treat an incident in the central Atlantic as more than a rescue, it's a strategic problem touching commerce, alliances, and deterrence.

Silent Hope

Out in the Atlantic, beneath a nearly full moon, one man floated alone on a broken piece of fuselage.

His left shoulder bleeding, his clothes soaked in saltwater, his breath steady.

Feyzi Çelik was alive.

The world did not know yet.

But the rescue wheels had begun to turn.

And somewhere across the sea, ships were already racing toward him.

CHAPTER 4

A Signal from Nowhere

Since the launch of the iPhone 14, Apple's partnership with Globalstar had quietly changed the rules of survival. Satellite-based Emergency SOS services allowed users to connect with first responders even without cellular or Wi-Fi coverage—revolutionary in theory, miraculous in practice.

Feyzi Çelik's iPhone 16, soaked but sealed in his zipped waterproof pocket, had somehow survived the ocean impact. Saltwater glistened on the screen, but the phone remained functional.

His fingers trembled as he pulled it out—half from the cold, half from shock. Blood mixed with saltwater dripped from his knuckles as he tapped the screen, trying not to panic. Each breath was a conscious effort.

He stared at the interface, willing the device to respond. When he initiated the Connection Assistant, he wished for the best. Against all odds, the emergency message was picked up by a Globalstar low-orbit satellite. It routed through Apple's emergency relay system and automatically forwarded to a 911 center based on his home area code—617.

Emergency SOS via Satellite

On the other side of the sky, machines did the human thing: they listened.

Feyzi's phone aligned to a fast-moving Globalstar satellite, the iPhone fed short bursts of encrypted text and telemetry, and Apple's relay system decrypted and passed the message to the right emergency contact point, a human staring at a console.

In low bandwidth, seconds stretch; each packet is a heartbeat. The relay centers exist for nights exactly like this: no towers, no Wi-Fi, just the thin line between silence and survival.

Newton, Massachusetts
Police Department Dispatch Center
1:47 a.m., Tuesday, July 8

Newton is Boston's leaf-lined cousin; thirteen distinct villages stitched together by trolley tracks, the Charles River's slow curves, and streets that remember the first mills and railroad stops. There's no single downtown; instead, there are little hearts: Newton Centre's café glow, Waban's quiet greens, Nonantum's stubborn pride, West Newton's brick-and-timber corners. By day the Green Line rattles through, and Route 90 throws a silver ribbon east to the city; by night the villages fold into porchlight and sprinklers and late-shift sirens that pass and fade.

The Newton Police Department dispatch room lives above that hush. It's the city's narrowest aperture, where every alarm bell and whisper must choose what happens next.

In this room, maps breathe; blocks and cul-de-sacs, school zones and river bends. Tonight, it summoned Megan O'Neill.

It had been a quiet summer night.

Officer Megan O'Neill, an eight-year veteran of the Newton PD's Emergency Dispatch Unit, sat sipping lukewarm coffee while scanning routine traffic reports. A former paramedic, Megan had transitioned to dispatch after a back injury and was known for her composed demeanor under pressure. Megan knew these villages by sound; tires on brick at Newton Centre, the hollow thud over the Commonwealth Avenue carriage road in Auburndale, the long, lonely train horn drifting up from the river at Upper Falls.

Her shift had been uneventful—until her screen suddenly flashed red.

"Flight XT84 destroyed. Middle of Atlantic. Feyzi Çelik. Alive. Immediate rescue needed."

A single card blossomed across Megan's dashboard—metadata stacked like ribs:

Source: Emergency SOS via Satellite (Apple/Globalstar)

Origin: Device registered to 617... (home region)

Forwarding: Emergency relay center to local PSAP (Newton PD)

Payload: compressed text + GPS uncertainty ellipse (open ocean)

Priority: CRITICAL — aircraft distress keyword detected

In training, this is where you breathe twice. In life, there's only once.

She'd dealt with hoaxes before, but this message had the weight of truth.

She quickly keyed in a search for "XT84."

The Air Turkey flight from Boston to Istanbul. Scheduled departure at 9:35 p.m. Confirmed departure at 9:49 p.m., with a 14-minute delay.

But there were no media alerts.

No chatter from aviation trackers.

Nothing.

Still, something in her gut stirred. The phrasing and metadata were precise.

Direct.

Not the style of a prank.

She pulled the secure line and dialed the Boston field office of the FBI.

"Boston FBI. Agent Perkins speaking."

"This is Officer Megan O'Neill from Newton Dispatch. We've received a Globalstar satellite emergency message. States Air Turkey Flight XT84 was destroyed over the Atlantic. Passenger named Feyzi Çelik claims to be alive."

A pause.

"Repeat the name and flight number."

"Feyzi Çelik. XT84."

Perkins didn't waste time. "Forward the message now." The line went dead. Megan sat back and exhaled.

Five minutes later, her phone rang again; Logan Airport's Air Traffic Control patching her directly to the U.S. Coast Guard's First District Command Center in Boston.

U.S. Coast Guard Command Center, Boston

Commander Rebecca Alden stood over a digital map displaying overlapping SAR grids in the North Atlantic. A Naval Academy graduate and decorated SAR veteran, Alden had built her career on precision and nerves of steel. She had just wrapped a call with the Canadian Coast Guard when her assistant rushed into the room.

"Ma'am. Incoming from Newton PD. Emergency satellite message tied to XT84."

She took the call without hesitation.

"Commander Alden."

"This is Officer O'Neill. Newton Dispatch. We received a Globalstar relay message from a functioning iPhone. Sender identifies as a survivor from XT84. Message says: Flight XT84 destroyed. Middle of Atlantic. Feyzi Çelik. Alive. Immediate rescue needed."

It was the first real clue. Alden's mind snapped into place.

"Copy that. Thank you, Officer. Stay on standby. I'm escalating this now."

She slammed down the phone and spun to her operations officer.

"Get Logan ATC on the line, check if Feyzi Çelik was on the flight manifest."

Thirty seconds later, a voice confirmed:

"Affirmative. Çelik, Feyzi. Seat 4K, Business Class. Checked in, no baggage claim, carry-on only."

It was real.

The Boston Coast Guard control room went silent, watch floor tilted; not physically, but in mood. Voices went low and fast, the way crews talk when the clock acquires gravity. Screens divided into quadrants: orbital tracks, sea states, thermal layers, and a blinking SAR overlay that pulsed like a lighthouse.

Someone killed the fluorescent hum over the central table; the room went to pools of light and the sound of keyboards.

"He made it..." someone whispered.

Immediate Escalation

Commander Alden radioed Admiral Michael Lansing, still co-ordinating ship deployments with the Second Fleet out of Norfolk.

"Admiral, we have confirmed satellite contact from a named passenger. Location: still unconfirmed. But the message was routed via Apple's Globalstar system. That means a functioning mobile device. It's real."

Lansing exhaled slowly. "We've got a live one."

Alden's voice turned hard.

"And Admiral... the message said destroyed. Not crashed. Not downed. Destroyed."

That word changed everything.

A pause. Then Lansing responded, voice firm.

"Copy. Task satellite recon. Bring NOAA imagery forward. Prioritize new signal triangulation. I'll notify Joint Intel."

Admiral Michael Lansing, a forty-year Navy veteran, was known for his unshakable calm and cerebral approach to crisis. A graduate of the Naval War College and former commander of multiple carrier strike groups, Lansing had spent his career navigating the unpredictable politics of global security. Unlike many in his rank, he had spent years on the deck rather than behind a desk. His experience with Arctic rescue operations and joint NATO missions made him uniquely suited to handle the escalating unknowns of the XT84 situation.

His office walls were adorned with tokens from his deployments—pieces of hull plating from decommissioned ships, framed dispatches from successful operations, and a faded photograph of the USS *Theodore Roosevelt* from his first tour. Lansing had seen his share of chaos, but something about this event felt different.

He recalled the Black Sea intercept in 2017, when radar ghosts turned out to be a rogue drone swarm—his call then had saved lives. He had ordered the carrier group to hold fire despite immense pressure from Washington. It turned out the swarm had been experimental U.S. hardware gone off-course. The restraint had prevented an international incident. That memory still haunted him. This felt like that night all over again, unknown, high-stakes, and on the brink of spiraling.

Race against Time

A soaked mobile handset is a dying lighthouse, but for a while it can still send store-and-forward bursts to passing satellites even when pointed clumsily; attach compressed Medical ID and battery status, clues for triage and urgency, broadcast a Find My beacon via satellite at longer intervals if enabled.

Back in Boston, Alden turned back to her team.

"Trace every Globalstar satellite within range," she ordered, her voice crisp.

"Triangulate and overlay sea current models. Cross-check with last NOAA current sweeps and airborne infrared."

Her command center, a circular war room ringed with real-time monitors and digital maps, hummed with renewed purpose. A junior lieutenant snapped to action at the communications console, while a pair of analysts leaned into their terminals, pulling telemetry archives and overlaying satellite pass predictions.

"Get Naval intelligence in the loop. And tell them we need real-time access to NATO surveillance feeds. Eyes in the sky, full spectrum," Alden continued, her tone resolute.

Her operations officer, Commander Vic Tran, nodded. "Yes, ma'am. Tasking now."

He moved like a man wired to her cadence; the kind forged through joint deployments and mutual trust. The team's focus sharpened, and a wave of urgency rippled through the room.

The operation was no longer a theoretical exercise. It was a race against time.

Question of Intent

She knew what came next—of intent. Aircraft didn't just vanish. And survivors didn't emerge from nowhere with intact phones unless something bigger was at play.

Was it a mechanical failure?

Or... something more sinister?

Was XT84 downed by a missile?

Commander Alden tapped her pen on the desk; eyes fixed on the red pin marking the last known coordinates on the map.

"Who is Feyzi Çelik?" she whispered to herself.

"What kind of man survives that?"

Her voice, though quiet, did not go unheard.

One of the junior intelligence analysts nearby, a young officer named Lieutenant Dana Reyes, looked up sharply from her console. She didn't say anything; just exchanged a glance with another operator and started a silent query on her terminal, searching for every file connected to the name.

The ripple had begun.

CHAPTER 5

Encircled

Feyzi had no idea how profoundly his satellite message had changed the situation thousands of miles away. He couldn't know that rescue operations had been mobilized across the U.S., Canada, and the North Atlantic Command. He didn't know his name had triggered a tri-nation alert or that ships were already moving into position.

He had his own problems.

Big ones.

For the last ten minutes, he had been straining to identify the source of the cries—those strange, soft wails that had pierced the darkness.

At first, he had thought they were infants. Then perhaps wild seabirds or echoes from the wreckage. But now, even that sound was gone.

Silence returned; deep, damp, and suffocating.

Above, the Moon, his only companion, hung low in the sky. Its pale silver light shimmered on the black water like fractured glass.

He tapped the screen of his iPhone and checked the battery: still nearly full. He had worried about preserving power, but in that moment, visibility mattered more than longevity.

With a swipe, he turned on the flashlight.

The beam cut through the darkness, illuminating only a narrow radius around the piece of fuselage he was floating on. Saltwater stung his eyes. He scanned in slow, deliberate motions, trying to pierce the moving waves. Debris bobbed around him—shredded seat cushions, bits of insulation, a piece of cabin lining shaped like a fin at first glance.

Then... something moved.

He froze.

Just beyond the edge of his light cone, the water rippled unnaturally.

Then he saw it.

A tail.

Then another.

And another.

Feyzi's heart sank.

"Sharks," he whispered.

He counted four dorsal fins, slowly carving semi-circles around him. Their movement was measured, controlled—curious, not yet aggressive. But they were circling. The classic hunting pattern.

His floating platform—a twisted, jagged section of fuselage—suddenly felt painfully thin. It offered no real protection. There was nothing between him and them but a few inches of aluminum and sheer will.

He felt his breath shallow.

He inhaled slowly through his nose.

Exhaled slowly from his mouth.

Don't panic.

He reminded himself that sharks were not mindless killers. They were apex predators; but usually cautious, especially when uncertain. Still, the metallic smell of blood from his shoulder could be attracting them.

He quickly removed his shirt, tore a strip from it, and tied it tightly around the gash. The bleeding had slowed, but the saltwater made it burn with renewed intensity.

The sharks swam closer now, more confidently.

He could make out the sleek shapes just under the surface—powerful, muscular, indifferent to his fear.

Suddenly, he remembered something from his youth.

"Don't ever thrash," his grandmother once told him while teaching him to swim in Lake Eğirdir. "If you ever meet something in the water stronger than you, don't act like food. Float like a piece of wood. Let them wonder."

That memory calmed him.

Lake Eğirdir, Türkiye's fourth-largest freshwater lake, had been his childhood playground—20 miles long, nestled among mountains, and home to fierce winds and deep water. It wasn't the ocean, but it taught him respect for nature.

And survival.

Feyzi adjusted his body slowly, keeping movement minimal.

He turned off the flashlight. The light, he realized, may be drawing too much attention. The Moon gave him just enough vision to watch for movement.

The sharks were still circling.

Slower now.

Waiting.

A distant noise interrupted the night. A subtle vibration in the air. Feyzi lifted his head.

A soft, rhythmic hum—far off, barely perceptible—grew steadily louder.

Could it be... a plane?

No. It had a different pitch. Lower. Mechanical.

A helicopter?

He stood slightly, carefully balancing on the floating debris, trying to raise his visibility. But he could see nothing. Only sea. Only shadows.

The sharks tightened their circle.

His mind raced:

If they attack, do I dive and swim to confuse them?

Do I stay still?

Could I fight one off with that metal rod?

Would a helicopter even see him at night?

The helplessness hit him all at once.

"This can't be it," he said aloud.

"This isn't how my story ends."

Not like this. Not after everything.

He stared down at the fins cutting through the moonlit water.

Then he stared up at the moon.

Still there.

Still watching.

Feyzi clenched his jaw. "Not yet."

And somewhere inside, something shifted. From fear... to resolve.

He would survive the ocean.

He would outwait the sharks.

He would endure the night.

And when the morning came, he would be ready.

CHAPTER 6

The Awakening

Istanbul, Türkiye – 7:20 a.m. (GMT+3)

The sun was just rising over Istanbul when the message came in. At the Istanbul Air Traffic Control Center, nestled on the city's outskirts with a panoramic view of the Black Sea, a routine morning shift was underway.

The control tower rose like a tulip of glass and steel, its curves catching the sunrise as if the building itself were turning to look east, north, and west at once. Inside, duty controllers worked a 360° sweep of the world's newest super-hub, their displays stitched to a network that now choreographs triple-independent runway operations, a first in Europe, pushing peak capacity from 120 to 148 movements per hour.

The radio was calm, the cadence precise, the choreography relentless. Beyond the panes, the Black Sea haze burned off as arrivals crossed the shoreline and the departures line snapped forward, three at a time.

Operators moved through checklists, sipping strong black tea and listening to the rhythmic hum of inbound flights from across Europe and Asia when a coded alert arrived from Gander Oceanic Control in Canada.

"Possible aircraft incident, Air Turkey XT84, Boston to Istanbul, signal lost over Atlantic."

Controllers could feel the tilt of the room change; subtle, like pressure dropping before a storm. Someone dimmed the house lights over the central table. Istanbul's tower went from routine to ritual.

The control room fell silent. Coffee cups stopped mid-sip. Operators glanced at each other, waiting for someone to break the stillness.

The shift supervisor, Erhan Kartal, stood slowly, picked up the red-line phone, and made his first call—to Air Turkey's operations headquarters across the airport campus.

Air Turkey Headquarters – Istanbul

The CEO of Air Turkey, Hakan Demiral, was already reviewing early morning reports when his secure line rang. A former pilot turned executive, Demiral had an almost obsessive memory for aircraft tail numbers and routes.

His secure phone buzzed.

"Sir, we've lost contact with XT84. Last signal from Gander Control in the Atlantic. No confirmation of crash—yet."

Demiral froze. XT84 was a long-haul pillar of their North American operations. The aircraft, an Airbus A350-900, was only three years old. Impeccable maintenance record. No issues reported at takeoff.

"Get me Boston. Now."

Boston – 12:35 a.m.

The Air Turkey Boston station manager, Kemal Günay, was sound asleep when his phone rang.

The vibrating ringtone pulled him out of bed.

"Kemal, it's Hakan. We have a possible emergency with XT84. Wake your entire team. I need a passenger manifest, crew names, and contact details. You're establishing our U.S. response center."

"Understood. I'm on it." Kemal replied, already halfway into his uniform.

Kemal's wife stirred beside him. "Everything okay?"

He didn't answer.

Air Turkey's model runs on banked waves, arrivals cresting before departures, to let a single Istanbul morning pulse launch dozens of long-hauls to Asia and Africa and pull overnight westbounds from the Americas into tight connections. Pull one thread, XT84, and planners must re-time crews, swap tails, and protect bank integrity so hundreds of downline passengers still make their day. The Boston station chief knows: a glitch in Massachusetts becomes a kink in Mumbai by noon.

Air Turkey, The Flag That Went Global

The airline Demiral led was Türkiye's proud standard-bearer, young in spirit and young in fleet, built on an audacious idea: connect more countries than anyone.

Recently that boast became official; Air Turkey is recognized for serving the most countries on Earth. The map looked like a net thrown over the hemispheres: over 400 destinations across 150 countries, a lattice that turned Istanbul into a true tri-continent hinge.

Ten years earlier, the carrier was already big; now it was among the world's giants.

Passenger totals climbed year after year; the fleet modernized in waves; and the airline unveiled plans to add 200 Boeings, over 80 Dreamliners for long-haul growth and 150 737-8/10 for the continental mesh, on top of a large Airbus widebody and narrowbody backbone.

Deliveries are slated to 2030, with a strategy to transition to an all new-generation fleet by 2035.

Public fleet trackers peg the average aircraft age in the single-digits, a hallmark of a young, efficient fleet, and industry tallies put current metal in the high-hundreds, with orders to spare. A growth plan this bold only works if the network can drink it: Istanbul's triple-runway regime is the straw.

Turkish Government – Ankara

Across the country in Ankara, Minister of Transportation Halil Şen had just stepped out of his front door. As his car pulled out of the residential compound, his secure mobile buzzed.

He listened in silence. Then, calmly:

"Take me to the Presidential Complex. Call ahead. I want the situation room open in ten minutes."

Two black police escorts merged onto the road ahead of his vehicle. Two more followed behind. The motorcade surged through the morning streets of Ankara, cutting through commuter traffic with lights flashing.

Within thirty minutes, Kemal Arıkan, the President of Türkiye, along with Şen and the Minister of Foreign Affairs, convened in the basement-level situation room—where military, civil aviation, and intelligence briefings are typically held.

A secure video call was immediately placed to the Turkish Ambassador in Washington, D.C., the Consul General in Boston, and the Air Turkey liaison embedded at Boston Logan Airport.

"We need confirmation," the President Arıkan said sternly.

"And pressure, maximum pressure, on the United States to assist immediately in rescue operations."

What they didn't yet know was that rescue efforts had already begun hours earlier, coordinated between the U.S. Coast Guard, the Canadian Coast Guard, and the U.S. Second Fleet.

But in the fog of uncertainty, every minute felt like hours.

The Ankara Situation Room

The Ankara situation room ran cool: porcelain cups; a muted wall of maps. Ministers spoke softly, not for secrecy but stability. Outside, motorcades stitched across ring roads; inside, the President's instruction cut clean: confirm, pressure, assist. On another screen, IST's tower camera showed a sky paling from copper to blue and a field of tails, red crescents lined like chess rooks.

Some nights diplomacy is posture; this morning it was pace.

Media Storm – Istanbul and Beyond

By 8:15 a.m., every Turkish television morning program had broken into live coverage. The scrolling headline was chilling:

"AIR TURKEY FLIGHT XT84 – SIGNAL LOST OVER
ATLANTIC – RESCUE UNDERWAY"

At a hastily organized press conference, CEO Hakan Demiral addressed the nation:

"We have received an unconfirmed emergency transmission from Flight XT84, en route from Boston to Istanbul. Rescue coordination is currently active. At this time, we are awaiting further updates and cannot confirm the status of the aircraft."

He looked shaken.

Professional.

But behind his composure, a storm was brewing.

Family Response Centers – Istanbul and Boston

Air Turkey immediately activated its Crisis Response Protocol.

A dedicated Passenger Family Center was opened at Istanbul Airport, cordoned off from media and the general public. A mirrored facility was established in Boston, staffed with Turkish and American Airlines personnel. Trained psychologists, grief counselors, and cultural liaisons were dispatched within the hour.

Only immediate family members were permitted entry. Each family was escorted to private rooms. Phones were silent. Eyes filled with questions no one could answer.

Digital displays in the airport quietly changed.

Where it had once said "Arriving on Time", the screen now read:

"Call Air Turkey."

Inside a small office at the Istanbul terminal, a junior airline attendant wiped tears from her eyes and whispered:

"Allah korusun..." (May God protect them).

No one corrected her. Because in that moment, faith was all they had.

Down a corridor away from arrivals, the Family Center breathed in low tones and paper cups. A wall display showed time zones instead of news. Counselors kept pens ready but didn't write much; they listened.

Every few minutes a door cracked open, and an attendant whispered a name, and the room turned as one—hope, then gravity.

CHAPTER 7

Shockwave at OnePIN

Ankara, Türkiye – Tuesday, 9:00 a.m.

The morning at OnePIN's Ankara office began like any other. The sprawling OnePIN office in Ankara, a modern glass-and-steel structure nestled within the tech corridor outside the city center, was already humming with life.

Early sunlight poured in through floor-to-ceiling windows, casting golden streaks across ergonomic desks and server monitors blinking in rhythm. Coffee brewed in the communal kitchen, its rich aroma weaving through the corridors like an unofficial morning anthem.

Arda Yalçın, Head of Engineering and a seventeen-year veteran of the company, was the first to arrive. He liked the quiet of the early hours—ideal for addressing complex bugs that had been flagged overnight by the Boston team. This was his sacred window before the world logged in, when clarity and focus reigned.

Arda glanced across the office, proud of how the team had grown. From a five-person crew to a world-class engineering squad tethered to the pulse of OnePIN's global platform. Every bug squashed overnight in Boston was a ripple he and his team tackled with precision each morning in Ankara.

One by one, his team trickled in:

Ece Yaman, Senior Software Engineer, dropped her daughter at school before heading in, her earbuds still playing a parenting podcast.

Kemal Özdemir, another seasoned engineer, settled in with a cup of strong Turkish tea and a new bug report open in front of him.

Elif Aydın, Senior Test Engineer, was already reviewing QA logs from the latest sprint, her brow furrowed in concentration.

They gathered around Arda's desk, discussing patch priorities, performance regressions, and test coverage. Kemal cracked a joke about AI-generated logs being smarter than their intern from last summer, prompting a round of chuckles.

By 9:30 a.m., Berkay Çetinkaya and Erhun Kaya, both Software Engineers, had arrived. They transitioned the conversation to the glass-walled conference room. Two team members working remotely, Derya Koç, Senior Account Manager, and Barış Aksoy, Senior Software Engineer, joined via Teams from the field. The meeting moved quickly. Everyone was deep in discussion, moving cards on the sprint board, juggling release timelines.

Arda looked around the table with quiet pride. They were a machine—precise, efficient, bonded. The kind of team you could build a future with.

The Breaking News

Gülce Demir, General Manager of the Ankara Office, arrived late; caught in traffic on Atatürk Boulevard. She entered briskly, coffee in hand, ready to catch up. Her office was a minimalist haven: clean desk, wall-sized whiteboard, and a desktop filled with dashboards.

She booted up her laptop.

Her homepage—set to a national Turkish news outlet—immediately displayed a flashing headline:

"BREAKING: Air Turkey Flight XT84 Missing – Last Contact Over Atlantic"

"Flight departed from Boston, believed to have crash-landed. Rescue underway."

Her eyes scanned the subtext. Her breath caught in her throat.

Boston. XT84.

"That's Feyzi's flight," she whispered.

She blinked again, hoping it was a mistake. Her breath caught.

For a moment, the letters blurred.

She blinked hard. It couldn't be—Feyzi was on that flight. He had messaged just yesterday. Then her fingers flew to her phone.

She grabbed it and ran to the conference room.

"Stop everything," she said, out of breath, her voice edged with disbelief.

"Look at this."

Elif dropped her pen. It clattered loudly on the conference room table. Berkay's tea cup paused mid-air, trembling slightly in his hand. Over the Teams call, a sharp inhale was audible from Barış.

The room froze, the weight of the moment anchoring everyone in place.

Arda paused mid-sentence. The room fell silent.

He switched the Teams call screen share to Gülce's browser. The headline now stared back at every face—remote and in the room.

"This can't be right."

"Maybe it's a false report..."

"He's on XT84. It says Boston to Istanbul. That's the one."

A beat passed.

Then another.

"No way," Erhun whispered.

"Is this real?" Barış asked over Teams.

It was.

Crisis Mode

Gülce didn't hesitate. She dialed Terry Moreau, Director of Technology, at his home in Upton, Massachusetts. It was 2:30 a.m. in Boston.

Terry answered on the second ring. "Gülce?"

"It's XT84. Feyzi's flight. It's missing. It's on the news."

Terry didn't respond for a moment. Then, quietly: "Understood. Initiating protocol now."

The Business Continuity Plan was activated immediately. Within minutes, Terry accessed OnePIN's system management console. Feyzi's digital credentials were suspended. His laptop, if ever powered on again, was programmed to automatically wipe itself. Security required it.

This wasn't his first 2 a.m. call. During the pandemic cyber-attack of 2021, he had pulled three straight nights safeguarding OnePIN's cloud perimeter.

But this—this felt personal.

Terry hesitated before touching anything related to Feyzi's phone. That was different. It could still be traceable. It could still be... useful.

He took a breath, then composed messages to Ethan Gagnon, Chief Operating Officer, and Laura Whitman, Vice President of Marketing and Products. Ethan was now the acting head of One-PIN. Laura became the #2 ranking officer.

By 2:30 a.m. Eastern, the internal chain of command had shifted.

Terry glanced at a framed photo on his desk; OnePIN's last leadership offsite. Feyzi smiling, arm around Ethan, pointing to a whiteboard scribbled with wild ideas.

Now, silence.

The Personal Impact

Back in Ankara, the team sat stunned. "Should we call Jill? Ayla? Alex?" Ece asked softly.

The silence was heavy. "Not yet," Terry said on Teams. "Let her sleep. It's the middle of the night there. There's nothing we can do until morning. She'll need her strength."

Nobody objected. Elif reached for her phone, then stopped.

Gülce nodded, then turned to Arda.

"You're in charge of engineering here until we know more. Keep the team focused. Nothing speculative. We wait for real information."

Arda gave a short nod. His hands were clenched on the table, knuckles white. A flash of anxiety gripped his chest. The weight of responsibility, normally shared in long Slack threads and casual shoulder taps, now rested squarely on his shoulders. He swallowed hard, forcing calm. He had to project confidence—for the team, for Feyzi, for himself.

Gülce stood, grabbed her bag, and walked out without another word.

A Personal Call

On the way to her car, Gülce called Mertcan Uslu, Feyzi's cousin and Vice President at Tisan, the construction company founded by Feyzi's father, Ahmet Çelik. He picked up immediately.

"Gülce?"

"I'm coming to you. We need to go to Feyzi's parents together. They shouldn't hear it from the news."

Ahmet and Lale Çelik, now 94 and 85, were home in Ankara. They had no idea what was unfolding. The news hadn't reached them yet.

Mertcan exhaled sharply. "I'll get the car ready."

"This is different," Mertcan replied quietly. "This time, we don't know if we'll have good news."

It was going to be a difficult conversation.

She closed her eyes at a red light, bracing herself.

They had to be strong now.

Outside, the streets of Ankara moved on; buses groaned, horns blared, pedestrians crossed without looking up.

But inside the car, there was only silence and the knowledge that the next knock on a door would change everything.

CHAPTER 8

The Riders Beneath the Waves

Feyzi stared at the circling fins. They had been moving around him for nearly ten minutes; methodically, persistently.

They weren't leaving. He had been preparing himself for the worst; mentally rehearsing what it would take to survive a shark attack with nothing but a floating piece of fuselage and a wounded shoulder.

His arms trembled from the effort of staying afloat. Saltwater stung his eyes, and the chill gnawed at his resolve. Alone in the vastness, disoriented and fatigued, a creeping sense of hopelessness began to take hold.

Then he heard it.

A cry—not from a human, but something that echoed eerily like a baby's wail. It came from behind him.

He turned slowly, cautiously.

Splash.

A gray body burst out of the water with a powerful splash, sending shimmering droplets into the moonlight.

Its whistle was sharp and resonant, slicing through the quiet night like an electric current.

Feyzi flinched instinctively, his heart leaping before his mind could process what he saw.

The moonlight reflected off its smooth skin.

A dolphin.

Feyzi exhaled with a mix of disbelief and relief. It had been dolphins circling him—not sharks. Now that he looked more closely, their curved dorsal fins and familiar whistles made it obvious. But he had never been this close to one in open water.

More heads surfaced—six, then eight—bobbing and diving, surrounding him in synchronized motion. Each seemed to pause and turn, meeting his eyes directly, as if assessing him.

Then they began making animated, almost urgent chirping sounds.

Baby cries were dolphins.

"What is going on here?" he murmured aloud.

One dolphin swam forward and leapt partially onto the fuselage next to him. Half its body emerged from the water.

Feyzi leaned back slightly—startled.

Behind its dorsal fin, he saw something unexpected.

A saddle.

His pulse quickened. He turned on his iPhone flashlight again and scanned the others. Each dolphin wore one.

He suddenly remembered military-trained dolphins, used by navies around the world for underwater surveillance, search-and-rescue, and even mine detection. He also knew of programs attempting nonverbal communication training; a quest to understand dolphin intelligence more deeply.

Now here they were.

Alive.

Trained.

Present.

The dolphins circled him again, more actively this time. One nudged his leg gently. Another swam in tight loops beside the fuselage. A third tapped its nose against the saddle, then looked directly at him again.

"They want me to ride them," Feyzi whispered.

"They want to take me somewhere." It was an insane thought. But then again, everything that had happened since the explosion defied reason.

He looked around. The night was still, the sea endless, the Moon pale above. There was no sign of human rescue.

No ships. No aircraft. Just him and a pod of impossibly intelligent dolphins.

He made a decision.

Feyzi slid slowly into the water, careful not to make sudden movements. The first dolphin swam alongside him and stopped. Feyzi grasped the saddle with both hands and eased himself onto its back.

The dolphin chirped, then another one tapped his shoulder gently with its nose—twice—and dove below the surface. Feyzi took a deep breath, tightened his grip, and followed.

What followed was surreal. The dolphin glided quickly through the dark water—10, maybe 15 miles per hour.

Feyzi held his breath for as long as he could. When his lungs began to burn, he tapped the dolphin's back, and it instantly brought him to the surface. He gasped, then resumed.

The rhythm continued. Underwater speed, surface breath, switch dolphins.

Again, and again.

They moved as one, like a choreographed rescue team.

After about 30 minutes, they slowed.

Feyzi could now see dark rock formations jutting from the sea around him. He thought they had reached a coastline, but when he tried to approach, a dolphin swam in front of him and gently blocked his path.

Another nudged him to turn. They weren't there yet.

Feyzi felt his limbs aching with exhaustion, his grip on the dolphin's saddle loosening. His vision blurred slightly as the saltwater stung his eyes and every muscle in his body begged for rest.

A whisper of doubt passed through his mind; how much longer could he last? The pod swam forward again, for another 200 feet.

Then they stopped.

One final tap. They wanted him to dive again. He inhaled deeply. They dove.

This time, they entered a submerged tunnel—a narrow corridor between jagged rock walls. The current was gentle, but the space was tight. Artificial light began to illuminate the water ahead.

The tunnel widened into a glowing chamber. The water shimmered with an otherworldly glow, casting fluid, wavering patterns on the stone walls. A warm current brushed past Feyzi's skin, tinged with a scent reminiscent of sea salt and ozone.

The light seemed to breathe, pulsing like a heartbeat, illuminating columns of gently rising bubbles and translucent tendrils of underwater flora that swayed like ghostly curtains in the deep.

Feyzi felt his heart race, not in fear, but awe. It was as if he had crossed into a place untouched by time, a sanctum of mystery hidden beneath the sea.

Bioluminescent coral-like structures lined the walls. Strange, humming lights pulsed gently in shades of aqua and violet. And then they surfaced.

They had reached a massive underground cavern, half-flooded and lined with glowing panels and carved stone. The space was alive with energy. Dozens of dolphins swam in circles below a series of elevated walkways and ledges.

A woman stood waist-deep in the shallows, her long blond hair trailing behind her. She was tall and athletic, dressed in a streamlined wetsuit. She was making hand gestures, nonverbal communication. The dolphins responded with clicks and spins.

Then she turned. She saw Feyzi. Her eyes widened in surprise.

She held up her hand and signaled him upward.

Her brow furrowed, not in confusion but recognition; as if something, or his sudden presence here, stirred a memory. Her lips parted slightly, though no words escaped. There was something more behind her eyes—a flicker of anticipation, or perhaps dread.

Feyzi paddled weakly toward a ledge.

The dolphins helped, gently lifting him from below with their snouts until he reached a flat platform.

He collapsed forward; exhausted, soaked, bleeding.

He passed out.

When he awoke, two humanoid figures stood over him.

They weren't people. Not exactly.

To Feyzi's foggy vision, they looked almost human; until they moved. Their joints pivoted too smoothly, their balance too exact. Something in their eyes, or what should have been eyes, shimmered with an artificial gleam.

He blinked again, trying to reconcile the impossible. Was this real? Was he dreaming? A cold spike of adrenaline surged through him, and his breath hitched in his throat. These were not figments of a hallucination.

They were here. Real. And watching him with unmistakable intent.

They resembled Boston Dynamics' most advanced robotics; but more refined, smoother, quieter. They moved like humans but with calculated precision.

One knelt beside him and spoke in clear, neutral English:

"Are you feeling stable, Commander Çelik?"

The voice was synthetic, but oddly gentle. Feyzi blinked. Confused. Disoriented.

Commander?

He hadn't heard that title in nearly thirty years.

The word echoed like a ghost from a forgotten life; one buried beneath layers of corporate titles, parenthood, and civilian routine.

In a flash, he saw himself in military fatigues, standing on a coastal outpost in Izmir, receiving a sealed envelope from a NATO courier.

The name printed on it:

Feyzi Çelik. Top Secret.

He hadn't dared open that mental vault in decades—and now, somehow, it had found him again.

He opened his mouth to reply, but the words never came.

His mind went blank.

He passed out again.

CHAPTER 9
Base Echo-7

Feyzi awoke to a faint mechanical hum; low, rhythmic, and oddly soothing. His limbs felt weighted, as if gravity had deepened. Each breath was slow, heavy.

Memory clung to him in fragments—the dolphins, the tunnel, the crash—but none of it felt real. Was he dreaming? Had he died?

He blinked, slowly adjusting to the clean, artificial light above him. The ceiling was smooth, reinforced steel with embedded luminopanels that shifted from soft white to a cool blue hue. He was lying on a medical cot inside a circular glass-walled chamber.

The cot beneath him was firm and sterile, and the air carried a faint scent of ozone. Light pulsed in subtle rhythms across the walls—too smooth, too clean to be ordinary. This was no hospital.

Outside the glass, a humanoid stood still, monitoring a wall of touchless digital displays.

Another floated past the door; silent, efficient, precise.

Feyzi sat up. His shoulder was bandaged. His body ached, but he was alive.

"Welcome to Base Echo-7" said a calm, human voice.

He turned toward the source.

The woman with the long blond hair stepped into view. Now in uniform—black, with dark gray accents and a minimalist shoulder patch that read only: Echo-7.

"I am Commander Rebecca Hart."

She had deep blue eyes; deeper than the ocean, striking against her fair complexion. Her face was arrestingly beautiful, not in a delicate way, but sculpted with strength. She carried herself with a tall, elegant posture, her athletic form accentuated by the sleek lines of her uniform.

There was a sharpness in her presence, not of ego but of focus. The kind of person who had made a career in places others feared to tread.

"Where... am I?" Feyzi asked, his voice cracked and dry.

"You're beneath the North Atlantic. Approximately 400 miles southeast of Greenland. What you experienced last night; was the outer perimeter of a Level 9 classified U.S. military facility."

The Origin of Echo-7

Construction on Base Echo-7 began in late 2018, in direct response to the re-activation of the U.S. Second Fleet, which had been decommissioned for nearly a decade before rising Russian naval aggression and Arctic expansionism forced a strategic reevaluation. The timing was no coincidence.

Officially, Echo-7 didn't exist.

Ops Floor

Hart's earpiece chirped. "Hydrophone ring H-12 reporting a zero-delta seam at sixty to ninety meters."

"Tag it watch and widen the sample window to one-five minutes," she said without looking away from Feyzi.

It wasn't just hidden; it was forgotten by design. Only seven people on the planet had clearance to speak its name aloud. And now Feyzi was one of them.

From the surface, it looked like nothing—just a rocky islet barely large enough to host a drone weather station and a solar panel array.

But beneath that facade was one of the most advanced underwater military installations in existence.

Carved into the seafloor and reinforced with carbon-hardened alloys, Echo-7 extended nearly 2.3 kilometers across and 600 meters deep, housing:

A submarine dry dock system capable of hosting up to four U.S. nuclear submarines.

A crew capacity of 400, including Navy operators, submarine teams, analysts, and special operatives.

Missile defense systems—both anti-submarine and anti-destroyer—embedded into the cliffside architecture.

A tethered vertical launch tube array, hidden under foldaway rock shields, capable of high-velocity tactical missile launches.

"Constellation handover in ninety seconds," Comms whispered in Hart's ear.

"Freeze non-essentials. Record at full fidelity. No gaps," she replied.

A status tile for USS *Missouri* winked green in the corner of the glass. No one exhaled.

Currently, one Virginia-class nuclear submarine, the USS *Missouri*, was stationed within the main dry bay, operating with a full crew of 150. It was on a classified strategic deterrence mission in support of NATO operations; a mission so secret that even many at Echo-7 didn't know its full parameters.

"*Missouri* maintains emission control," Ops confirmed.

"Keep her dark," Hart said. "Eyes only."

Technological Superiority

Echo-7's strength didn't lie only in firepower. It was a cognitive fortress.

At the center of the command module sat ARES (Advanced Reasoning & Engagement System), a quantum-cooled supercomputer capable of processing petascale-equivalent for classified workloads; more than 10,000 times the speed of any known civilian-grade processor.

ARES lifted a narrow gray corridor on the overlay, then hesitated—as if thinking.

The fusion board shuffled priorities—three sectors slid to the top of the stack.

ARES controlled real-time satellite fusion imaging from 37 orbital units, oceanic submarine tracking algorithms fed by hydrophone networks across the Atlantic Ridge, deep-space monitoring inputs in coordination with U.S. Space Command, autonomous defense coordination with AI-assisted decision trees for triage, defense, and retaliation protocols.

"We're at eighty-seven percent ingest," Comms winced.

"Don't compress," Hart said. "If we lose edges, we lose the ghost."

ARES could predict the movement of every vessel—military or civilian—across the entire Northern Atlantic, including under-ice submarines, stealth drones, and commercial shipping. Its primary purpose: situational dominance without detection.

An amber tile trilled once, then flattened to green. No one relaxed.

Dolphins, Humanoids, and Bio-Tech

Echo-7's marine division was unlike any other in the U.S. arsenal.

The pool feed bloomed in the glass: Echo-D3 surfaced, painting the water with clean clicks.

At its core were 22 genetically enhanced dolphins, part of a decades-long evolution of naval bio-research. These dolphins had been bred and trained for:

Mine clearing, submarine detection, stealth escort missions, underwater rescue retrievals.

"D3 flags a pattern mismatch two grids north," an analyst called.

"Cross-correlate with H-12. Keep it quiet," Hart said.

They could receive and interpret up to 124 distinct hand signal patterns, perform autonomous decision-making, and exhibit behaviors closely resembling emotional intelligence. Some had been trained in phoneme-mimicry; the early stages of interspecies verbal exchange.

It was these dolphins that had found Feyzi, read his distress, and delivered him to Echo-7.

Supporting them were 11 humanoid robotic units, internally known as SEVs, Subaquatic Environmental Vectors. Built for tasks no human body could endure, SEVs could dive to depths exceeding 3,000 meters, operate for up to 96 hours underwater, integrate with small tactical submarines, perform independent patrol, surveillance, and intercept missions.

In the SEV bay, unit 4 cycled pumps to ready.

"Hold launch posture," Hart said. "Passive only."

The SEVs had no remote operator. Each ran on local AI, trained on millions of hours of situational simulation and capable of evolving its mission logic mid-operation.

A soft alarm pulsed—amber, not red.

"False positive?" comms whispered in Hart's ear.

"Treat it as a question," Hart answered. "Leave it on the wall."

Special Forces and Shadows

In the last six months, Space Command had placed 20 covert operatives into Echo-7 under the guise of "Oceanic Intelligence Liaisons." Their true purpose remained classified even to Commander Hart. Rumors among base personnel spoke of counter-satellite sabotage, deep-sea installations, and non-terrestrial monitoring protocols.

Even as Feyzi stirred in the medical chamber, ARES had already scanned and logged his vital signs—heart rate variability, oxygen saturation, neural activity spikes. But it hadn't stopped there. In the milliseconds that followed, it had compiled and processed his entire digital footprint: encrypted NATO biometric archives, military service records marked "eyes only," and dormant metadata fragments scattered across decades of secure networks. It was watching him; not with malice, but with a precision too exact to feel benign.

A lens somewhere irised wider. ARES made another tiny decision about him.

For the first time since waking, Feyzi felt the chill of being truly known by something not human.

The overlays faded; the glass returned to medical blue as if nothing had been there at all.

As Feyzi absorbed all of this; his mind still groggy—Commander Hart sat across from him and said:

"You weren't found by accident."

He looked up, eyes narrowed.

"The dolphins didn't just rescue you. They recognized you. Your biometric signature is in the archive. You're tagged under a decommissioned file... one that hasn't been touched in thirty years."

She paused.

"Welcome back, Commander Çelik."

He had buried that chapter long ago; severed ties, burned records. That anyone still had access to those files meant someone had been watching. Waiting.

Feyzi didn't respond. Not yet.

His mind was still racing—memories fragmenting, reforming. But one thing was clear:

He had just been pulled into something far bigger than survival.

As the glass walls closed again and Hart disappeared down a corridor, Feyzi realized the world above no longer knew he existed.

And yet, someone down there had never forgotten.

CHAPTER 10

The Call to Norfolk

Naval Station Norfolk, Virginia
Office of Admiral Michael Lansing
Tuesday, 6:45 a.m.

Admiral Michael Lansing leaned over his cluttered desk, staring at a silent tactical screen displaying a 1,000-mile radius over the North Atlantic. His coffee had gone cold. His second night without sleep.

His eyes were bloodshot, the lines on his face deeper than usual. The silence of his office, broken only by the hum of electronic displays, mirrored the stillness he felt creeping into his bones.

Years of crisis had hardened him—but something about this one felt different. Something quieter. More surgical.

The official log had already confirmed the disappearance of Air Turkey Flight XT84, and Echo-7's satellite telemetry now estimated its crash radius with a five-mile margin. Subsurface sonar buoys had detected dispersed fuselage remnants; but no large debris field.

That, alone, was strange. But nothing was stranger than the call he was about to receive.

He rubbed the back of his neck and stared again at the tactical screen. Still no movement. Just a blue-black void with scattered pings of sonar returns.

No signatures. No heat blooms. Only questions.

Then—his gut clenched. The encrypted console flickered.

INCOMING CALL – ECHO-7 COMMAND

He answered with a swipe.

"Lansing."

"Sir, this is Commander Grant Rourke, Base Echo-7."

"Go ahead." Lansing sat up straight.

"Sir... we've recovered a survivor from the Atlantic. Identified by our dolphin search unit."

"A survivor? From XT84?"

"Yes, sir. Though... the dolphins weren't searching for the commercial airliner. They were deployed for something else entirely."

Lansing narrowed his eyes. "Explain."

Echo-7 Debrief

"Sir," Rourke began, voice steady, "tonight, a custom-modified Black Hawk helicopter—tail #439—was inbound from Ramstein Air Base, transporting eleven highly specialized software engineers. Their mission was classified Tier 1-C. They were being embedded into Echo-7's Quantum Division."

"Their arrival was covert. No flight plan on civilian logs. The helo was flying under radar, 150 feet over the Atlantic. Rough seas, low ceiling."

"We lost contact at 04:06 Zulu. No explosion, no crash beacon, no radar profile. It simply disappeared."

"We initiated an internal SAR using SubTeam Bravo and deployed our advanced dolphin rescue unit to sweep the quadrant."

Lansing interrupted:

"And instead of your engineers... you found someone else."

"Yes, sir. At 05:19 Zulu, dolphin team Echo-D3 made contact with a male survivor. Facial ID confirmed: Feyzi Çelik. Civilian with a military rank, Commander. Confirmed U.S. citizen. No match in defense contractor database. But..."

Rourke hesitated.

"Our facial recognition hit a match in the NSA's biometric vault; under Command-Level Asset Archive. The classification is extreme."

"How extreme?" Lansing asked.

"Sir, the file is tagged: President's Eye Only."

Lansing had only ever seen one other file with that designation; and it had required direct sign-off from a sitting President and two Supreme Court justices.

For a civilian survivor to carry such a tag... that was either a clerical error or a geopolitical fuse waiting to be lit.

The Implications

If two unconnected aircraft—one military, one civilian—were brought down in overlapping airspace without radar or missile telemetry, the implications were chilling. Either someone had developed undetectable strike technology... or the North Atlantic had become a covert war zone.

There was a long pause. Lansing leaned back slowly, mind racing.

"Was he listed as a passenger on XT84?"

"We verified with Air Turkey Boston manifest. Seat 4K. Business Class. We believe the Black Hawk and XT84 were struck by the same unknown foreign force—possibly a misfire, possibly intentional. Two aircraft, very different altitude profiles, downed in proximity. Possibly coordinated."

"Jesus..." Lansing muttered.

"Sir, I must emphasize: the dolphins recognized Commander Çelik as a friendly. They brought him to us unaware he was a commercial passenger."

"Understood."

Directives from Norfolk

Lansing rubbed his forehead.

"Commander Rourke—listen carefully. You will maintain absolute radio silence regarding this matter outside Echo-7. I want zero outbound communication from Commander Çelik. No satellite relays, no secure uplinks, nothing."

"I don't care if the President himself calls for an update," Lansing said. "This doesn't leave your bubble. Until we understand what we're dealing with… we treat it like it doesn't exist."

"Understood, sir."

"Put the base into Level 3 lockdown protocol, red-tag all logs connected to this incident, and restrict knowledge to your core command team only."

"Yes, Admiral."

"And Rourke…" Lansing lowered his voice.

"Don't let him out of your sight."

Lansing hovered his finger over the comms panel, hesitating before disconnecting. He glanced back at the tactical map; still clean.

But his instincts screamed otherwise.

Someone out there knew exactly who Feyzi Çelik was.

And they might be watching.

CHAPTER 11

The White House Call

As soon as the call ended, Lansing opened a secure terminal, his jaw clenched and his mind racing, the weight of uncertainty pressing down on him like ballast in deep water.

He bypassed the Joint Chiefs and dialed the National Security Advisor, Dr. Marshall Kline, a former Army intelligence general turned chief geopolitical strategist.

"This is Kline."

"General, it's Admiral Lansing. You need to inform the President immediately. We have a survivor from XT84—an individual tagged under your office's biometric archive."

"Who?"

"Name is Commander Feyzi Çelik, Turkish American."

Kline went quiet.

"He was recovered by Echo-7. Facial scan authenticated. File locked: President's Eye Only. He's alive. And he's talking. What do you want us to do?"

"Stand by."

"General—do I have authorization to detain him?"

Kline's response was cool, precise—a shallow intake of breath betrayed by a twitch of his jaw, followed by a glance toward the far wall where a secure cabinet hummed faintly.

"Admiral Lansing, hold him. But do not interrogate. Do not extract. Do not inform NATO. Do not contact Turkish intelligence.

Until the President reviews the file..."

A pause.

"You will treat Commander Çelik as either the greatest asset or the greatest liability we've never accounted for."

Lansing exhaled sharply, the words echoing in his ears like a sealed order—irreversible, absolute. He felt the pulse in his temple quicken, his instincts alert to the invisible chessboard already taking shape.

As the call ended, Lansing stood by the window of his office, the rising sun casting a pale orange hue over Norfolk Harbor.

In his gut, he knew this was no coincidence.

One helicopter.

One airliner.

Two downed vessels.

Each event an anomaly on its own.

One man survives—with a file only one person on Earth is allowed to read.

"Who the hell are you, Commander Çelik?"

He turned back to his desk, already drafting the sequence of secure notifications, alert codes, and contingency protocols required to mobilize the White House Situation Room within the hour.

It was time to brief the President.

CHAPTER 12

The Breach

Admiral Michael Lansing sat alone in his office, lights dimmed, his shoulders heavy with the weight of sleepless hours and unanswered questions, a faint tremor in his fingers betraying the pressure he kept hidden, the digital glow of his secure console washing across his face. The call with National Security Advisor Dr. Marshall Kline had ended, but the questions it left behind echoed louder than ever.

He stared at the classified incident report blinking on his screen.

Black Hawk down. XT84 down.

No prior radar detection. No sonar ping. No heat plume.

No alert from Echo-7.

Impossible.

The entire raison d'être of Base Echo-7—it's very construction— was to prevent this exact scenario.

Surveillance drones. Acoustic hydrophone grids. Quantum AI-powered pattern anomaly detectors. Advanced missile plume tracking. SEVs in rotational deployment. Underwater drones with persistent sonar pings. A fleet of genetically enhanced dolphins.

And still... Nothing.

Lansing blinked, his breath shallow. His mind reeled against the silence—the absence of explanation where there should have been warnings, signals, alerts. He felt a sudden spike of disbelief, chased quickly by dread. Was this the moment they'd all feared—the moment the system they trusted had been rendered blind?

Lansing clenched his jaw. He knew what others would soon ask.

Was it internal sabotage? Was the system blinded from within? Could a foreign actor have developed a weapon system Echo-7 wasn't built to detect?

The most advanced underwater base in the U.S. arsenal—blind to a missile launch or strike happening right in front of it.

If Russia had developed stealth submarine technology, the geopolitical balance would shift overnight—allowing them to deploy undetectable vessels along the U.S. eastern seaboard, threaten NATO supply lines, and operate within first-strike range without triggering a single alarm. But Russian stealth capabilities—while advancing—were not believed to be that mature.

Not by a long shot.

And China? Their naval power was growing rapidly, but deep-water launch stealth from this range. Unlikely. But not impossible.

And what if it wasn't a nation-state? What if it was something else—an ultra-clandestine consortium, a rogue AI system gone dark, or a technology so advanced it defied current military frameworks? Something—or someone—with knowledge of Echo-7's blind spots and the precision to exploit them without leaving a trace. That thought—that chilling alternative—was the one Lansing didn't want to put into words.

He stared again at the blinking red pin on the North Atlantic map.

Two aircraft. Two types of passengers. Two missions. Both hit. Within miles of the most secure undersea base on Earth.

Lansing whispered to no one but himself:

"Someone got past Echo-7."

The words hung in the air like a charged current. His hand hovered momentarily above the edge of the desk, fingers twitching slightly.

Behind his eyes, a storm gathered—calculation, fear, and a trace of awe. Whatever had breached Echo-7 hadn't just slipped through their defenses; it had done so with surgical precision, as if to leave a signature.

He stood up, walked to the window, and stared into the gray dawn beyond Norfolk.

And then, even quieter:

"Someone wanted us to know they could."

A technical annex slid onto his screen, half of it black bars.

VISIBILITY GAP: THERMOCLINE SEAM ...
ANOMALY CLASS: "OCEAN-NORMAL / ZERO-DELTA" ...
CLASSIFIER BEHAVIOR: AUTO-DOWNWEIGHTED ...
LIKELY VECTORS: [████████████] ...
RISK: REPEATABLE.

Lansing stared at the redactions.

Blindness would have been easier to explain.

This was worse—the ocean had agreed with the intruder and told Echo-7 nothing was there.

CHAPTER 13

The Call to Izmir

May 1993 – Burdur, Türkiye

Feyzi had expected a quiet end to his short-term military service—just a temporary interlude before returning to civilian life in Boston. He harbored a quiet hope that the time away would offer clarity, a break from the pressure of high expectations, and maybe a glimpse into the life his father once lived in uniform. Two months of basic duty under Türkiye's program for citizens living abroad.

No special treatment. No shortcuts.

He reported to Burdur Infantry Training Center, blending in among other conscripts without a single favor requested, even though his father, Ahmet Çelik, was a well-known contractor building a large dam and hydroelectric power plant, just kilometers away.

Unlike many sons of privilege, Feyzi didn't flinch at discipline or demand leniency.

He trained.

He listened.

He followed orders with precision.

It didn't go unnoticed.

Colonel Alparslan Demir, commanding officer of the Burdur base, had quietly run a background check after noticing Feyzi's composure. Not only was Feyzi disciplined and athletic—he also held a master's in mechanical engineering and had just graduated from Babson College, one of America's top business schools.

He also discovered Feyzi's uncle: Emin Çelik, a legendary strategist within the Turkish defense community, known for his work on cross-border radar systems and early-stage drones. He was the head of one of the largest quasi-government Turkish defense companies. He once disarmed a rogue military plot using only field surveillance data and a two-hour briefing to the Prime Minister—a feat whispered about in elite military circles.

Still—no one from the Çelik family had asked for a single favor. And that, more than anything, impressed Colonel Demir.

Then the call came—from NATO Command in Izmir.

They needed a native Turkish speaker, fluent in American English, with technical and military comprehension, and—most importantly—someone completely trustworthy.

Colonel Demir called Emin Çelik directly.

"Would you trust Feyzi with a NATO mission marked Top Secret?" he asked.

"With my life," Emin replied.

Within hours, Feyzi's clearance was fast-tracked to Level 6 – NATO Special Operations Access.

Colonel Demir summoned Feyzi to his office.

"Are you ready for something far outside your original plans, Çelik?"

Feyzi stood tall and nodded.

"Yes, Commander."

The steady rhythm of rotor blades cracked the morning stillness as a matte-black Black Hawk helicopter descended from the cloud-streaked sky. Dust and gravel spiraled outward from the helipad as soldiers shielded their eyes. The downdraft thumped against Feyzi's chest as he stood tall, unmoving.

The aircraft landed with surgical precision—its doors already open, rotors still spinning. The thump of boots on concrete and the hiss of hydraulics made the scene feel more like a special operations insertion than a routine transport.

Feyzi saluted sharply and jogged forward, boarding without hesitation. As the helicopter lifted off and veered west toward the Aegean coast, he felt a shift inside—something irreversible. With every mile, the world he thought he knew faded behind him.

Izmir – NATO Operations Center

Police escorts awaited his arrival.

He was driven directly to the NATO regional headquarters, where he was escorted past multiple security gates into a soundproof, no-electronics command room deep underground.

Inside sat Major General Haluk Sancar, representing Türkiye, and Major General Robert K. Hastings, representing the United States.

They were mid-argument.

Flanking them were two rising stars from each side:

Colonel Emre Öztürk, Turkish Special Forces Liaison

Lieutenant Colonel Daniel Pierce, U.S. Intelligence Division

Feyzi stood at attention, quietly observing. He had expected to translate. Instead, he found himself mediating.

For three days, tensions flared. The subject was a classified multinational operation in the Middle East with the potential to destabilize regional alliances.

Türkiye refused involvement—concerned about its neighbors. The Americans pushed hard. Intelligence was at risk. Billions in military assets were already mobilized.

Feyzi did his job.

Calm. Precise. Neutral. Yet behind the steady exterior, his mind whirred with the weight of each demand and counterproposal, every power play and bluff. He wondered whether any of these generals had noticed the fault lines their words were carving into an already fragile region—or the quiet opportunities still hiding beneath the noise. And all the while, he listened—absorbing every element of the mission's strategic and logistical framework.

By the third night, the delegates had reached a dead end.

Feyzi didn't sleep.

Alternate Solution

He spent the night in a spare office with a map table, a stack of mission dossiers, and his engineering mind in overdrive.

By dawn, he had built a third-path strategy—one that satisfied both security objectives and political sensitivities. It required fewer assets, eliminated civilian risk zones, and saved an estimated tens of billions of dollars in operational costs.

He approached General Sancar at 7:00 a.m.

"Sir, may I show you an alternate solution?"

The general reviewed it silently for fifteen minutes, then looked up and smiled.

"You're not just a translator, are you?"

He waved Feyzi forward.

"Go. Present it to them. In your words."

Feyzi walked into the American briefing room. Three hours later, the room was silent.

Both sides were in full agreement. The strategy offered NATO a decisive maritime edge—one that could anchor naval supremacy for the next century, shifting the balance of global power and rewriting future doctrine.

Pierce and Hastings asked about his future plans.

"I'm going back to Boston," Feyzi replied. "Going to ask a woman named Jill Daniels to marry me. Build a life together."

"No military career?"

"Not in the plan."

That night, a covert joint directive was signed. The mission would proceed—under Feyzi's design.

But there was a catch.

They wanted him there. On the ground.

Feyzi hesitated for a breath—his instincts reminding him of the danger ahead, of what he might be walking into. But there was no doubt in his mind. This wasn't just a mission; it was a calling, and he knew he had to see it through. Embedded—not as an operator, but as a live strategist.

"If it goes sideways," Hastings said, "we'll need your brain. Not your gun."

Feyzi agreed.

The operation became one of NATO's most delicate, and most successful, covert missions in its history.

After the mission succeeded, one of NATO's most difficult in decades, the delegations prepared a joint commendation.

The Integrator

Feyzi thought he had proven himself. He knew this might be his best chance to propose an idea, an innovation that had been weighing on him for months. He requested a secure and top-secret meeting with Major General Haluk Sancar and Major General Robert K. Hastings.

The meeting took place in a sealed operations chamber below Izmir HQ. What they discussed was recorded under the highest level of secrecy—accessible only to the Presidents of the United States and Türkiye.

No aides were present. No summaries were allowed to exist outside direct oral briefings.

They spoke without slides, without paper—only a grease pencil and a steel tabletop that would be wiped down to bare metal when they were done.

Feyzi drew three concentric rings and labeled them only in concepts: matter, mind, mandate.

"Not a weapon," he said. "A posture."

He outlined a program that braided disciplines no one had dared to knot together: life systems tuned for resilience, cognition that could learn across domains in real time, and governance that could keep both on a leash.

The examples were sketched, never named—precision edits that strengthened bodies against extremes without altering who they were; a learning engine that adapted like an immune system rather than a spreadsheet; control scaffolds that guaranteed human veto at every boundary. Thirty years ahead on paper. Centuries, if built as one organism.

The generals waited for costs and headcount.

Feyzi offered something else: compartmentalization as design. No single lab would ever hold more than a fragment. Protocols would move like sealed ciphers, air-gapped, couriered, timed to expire. Hundreds of researchers would tackle clean, narrow problems—enzyme stability here, low-noise sensors there, training data hygiene somewhere else—each believing they were optimizing a mundane subsystem.

Only one person would see the curve the fragments drew when assembled. He did not intend to write that curve down.

Access would be the bargain. He requested doors into America's most advanced research corridors—public and private. University centers and national facilities. Medical institutes for benign trials that looked like ordinary therapeutics. Defense labs for materials that resembled next-gen avionics. Civilian compute for "logistics forecasting." Each cover story true in its smallness. None revealing the whole.

Safeguards came next: tripwire ethics; two-man integrity on every irreversible step; red-team cells empowered to halt work cold; a standing rule that capability must never outrun control. He described a sanction that mattered to him more than prison—erasure of the blueprint from every medium but memory.

Sancar watched him the way a sapper watches a fuse. Hastings listened like a man hearing the shape of a century.

Neither asked for a name. They asked for an outcome: a world where free nations could remain free without announcing how.

Feyzi nodded once. "Then it must stay small," he said. "Invisible. Built as a series of harmless truths."

He left the room with nothing in his hands and everything on his back: a quiet mandate to architect the unbuildable.

Over the following years, doors opened. He walked corridors where keycards had no labels and clocks had no faces. He met hundreds of brilliant people who never knew they'd shaken hands with the integrator. Their parts fit because he made them fit. The whole remained a rumor shared by three men and a grease pencil that had long since been wiped clean.

When the chamber was finally resealed, there was no handshake—only the scratch of pens on a final line authorizing access and silence in equal measure. The work would change the future of humankind. Its existence would be denied until the day it was needed—and perhaps long after.

The Pentagon® and the Turkish Armed Forces issued him an honorary rank of Commander upon his release from duty—an extraordinary distinction for a non-career soldier.

A civilian with military standing—a man marked "Friendly" in both Turkish and American NATO files.

Both nations needed him and had to protect him when time comes.

The Seal of Secrecy

Given the geopolitical volatility of the mission, and Feyzi's unexpected role in it, and his proposed technologies involved, both countries agreed to bury the details under the rarest classification:

President's Eye Only.

His biometric profile, identity, and field history were encoded into NATO archives, tagged only for retrieval by high-clearance security officials in both governments. His file was classified not to be opened without bilateral presidential authorization.

It was signed by President Bill Clinton and President Süleyman Demirel.

When Feyzi became a U.S. citizen in 2000, it was Clinton himself who handed him the naturalization certificate during a private ceremony at the White House.

Feyzi told Jill it was just a lottery win—a fun story to tell their children one day.

But it wasn't luck.

It was legacy.

And no one—not even Jill—knew.

CHAPTER 14

The Day Everything Changed

The Knock at 7:30 a.m.

The New England sky was painted in soft pinks and grays as dawn broke over Hopkinton. A slight breeze rustled the pine trees surrounding the Çelik home near Saddle Hill Road. It was 7:30 a.m.

Three vehicles pulled into the driveway in solemn coordination. Ethan Gagnon, Chief Operating Officer at OnePIN, who lived nearby in Hopkinton, stepped out first with his wife, Diana, close behind. Moments later, Adam Kowalczyk, Chief Technology Officer at OnePIN, and his wife Hanna arrived from Westborough, followed by Terry Moreau, Director of IT at OnePIN, and his wife Emily from Upton.

None of them spoke.

Their faces were pale, drawn tight by the weight of what they had to do.

They had rehearsed this moment a dozen times on the drive over, but still—none of it felt real.

Ethan hesitated for just a moment before ringing the doorbell, his hand hovering near the button as a flood of memories rushed in—Feyzi cracking jokes during board meetings, guiding the team through crisis, always the anchor in a storm. His chest tightened. What if this time, their anchor was gone?

Inside, Jill stirred from sleep. She glanced at the clock and frowned. Too early for visitors. Her heart picked up pace. She slipped on a robe and made her way downstairs. When she opened the door, the sight of the entire OnePIN leadership team—along with their wives—stole the breath from her lungs.

"Jill..." Ethan began gently, his voice low and careful. "Can we come in?"

She nodded slowly, sensing something was very wrong.

They stepped inside without a word. Jill sat on the edge of the couch, her hands clenched tightly, her pulse drumming in her ears.

A cold sweat gathered at the base of her neck as dread coiled in her chest. Her mind raced ahead of the moment, imagining every terrible possibility—but refusing to give voice to any of them. The silence in the room only amplified the roar of her thoughts.

Ethan and Adam sat across from her. Diana and Emily quietly moved to the kitchen. Hanna hovered close, offering silent comfort.

"Jill," Ethan said, "there's been an incident."

She didn't blink. Her body tensed.

"Feyzi's flight... Air Turkey XT84... went off radar over the Atlantic a few hours ago. It was en route to Istanbul when something happened."

The words hit like ice water. Jill's lips parted, but no sound came.

Terry added, "We don't have all the details yet. The authorities haven't made a full statement. The plane lost communication just past Canadian airspace. No one knows what happened."

"We don't know... if there are survivors," Adam added, carefully.

Jill sat frozen. Her breath shallow. Her knuckles white.

"We are here," Diana said softly, setting down a glass of water. Her hands trembled slightly as she glanced toward Jill, then exchanged a quiet look with Emily—a look that held both sorrow and strength, as if silently promising they'd help carry whatever came next.

"For anything you need."

Ethan leaned in, his voice breaking slightly. His shoulders drooped as he clasped his hands together, his eyes brimming with unspoken memories of Feyzi—the time he rallied the team through the economic downturn, the laughter they shared during strategy offsites, the fierce loyalty he always showed.

"Feyzi is the strongest, most resilient man I've ever known. Whatever happened out there, if there's a way to make it back— he'll find it."

Adam nodded. "He's been through impossible situations before. He's always come back."

Jill's eyes welled, but she remained composed. "I just... I just need to know something. Anything."

"We'll know more soon," Terry said. "We're in close contact with people who are following the situation."

"Has Alex—?" Jill started to ask.

"Still asleep," Ethan said. "We wanted to tell you first."

They all sat in silence for a moment. The weight of uncertainty pressed down like a physical presence.

Upstairs, faint movement suggested Alex was stirring.

Jill stood.

"I will tell him," she said quietly.

As she climbed the stairs, the team remained downstairs, holding their breath.

Terry looked at Adam and Ethan.

"This... is going to be the hardest thing we've ever done."

"And we've done a lot," Adam whispered.

But this—this was personal. This was family.

They would wait.

Together.

A silence passed between them—an unspoken vow, sealed by years of shared battles, loyalty, and love for the man they lost.

In that moment, they were more than colleagues.

They were his chosen family, and they would hold the line for him now.

CHAPTER 15

Eyes in the Deep

Echo-7 Underwater Command Base, North Atlantic

Commander Rourke paced across the sealed glass floor of the command hub, his boots echoing with each step. Deep lines etched across his sleepless eyes, and the stubble on his chin betrayed two nights without rest. He clenched and unclenched his fists, occasionally pausing to glance at the tactical maps floating holographically above the central table—though his gaze passed right through them. His thoughts were drifting—uncomfortably—toward the weight pressing on his conscience, a burden growing heavier with every unanswered question.

Twenty-five years in uniform had prepared him for war, chaos, diplomacy, and deception—but not for this. He had built a life around loyalty: to his country, to the Navy, and now to Echo-7, the crown jewel of his career. They had trusted him to command it. He would die to protect it. And perhaps that's why they put him here.

Rourke was a "Yes" man—reliable, precise, mission-oriented. He didn't question orders. He executed them. Maybe that's what they needed at Echo-7—not a visionary, but a loyal custodian of silence.

The events of the past 36 hours were shredding his chain of logic.

Breach One: They had lost the specially equipped Black Hawk, carrying 11 of the most valuable software engineers assigned to Echo-7's top-secret submarine program. No wreckage. No signal.

Breach Two: XT84, a commercial airliner, shot down at 30,000 feet, right under Echo-7's detection envelope.

Breach Three: Whoever launched the attack, got away clean. No sonar signature. No thermal residue. No satellite trace. Not even a ripple in the damn water.

Breach Four: A civilian survivor picked up by genetically enhanced dolphins, now sitting in the most secure installation in the Atlantic, with a mysterious NATO "Friendly" tag and a buried classification file that said: "President's Eye Only."

Rourke exhaled slowly.

This was not just a security failure. It was a direct insult to Echo-7's very purpose:

Detection.

Defense.

Denial.

He couldn't protect his assets. He didn't see the attack. He didn't stop the escape.

And now he was harboring a wild card.

Unresolved

He met with Commander Rebecca Hart on the observation deck above the dolphin intelligence pool. The chamber shimmered with blue light, echoing with soft aquatic clicks and sonar pulses.

Hart's posture was composed but alert, her arms crossed tightly over her chest. Her gaze lingered on the dolphins below, but her mind clearly ran deeper.

A flicker of conflict danced in her eyes—was she defending Feyzi, or trying to convince herself to trust him? She turned to Rourke, jaw tight, as if bracing against unspoken doubts.

As second-in-command at Echo-7, she had always been the emotional compass of the base—the one to raise questions, to challenge assumptions, to serve as the conscience in a world of cold military logic. But Rourke rarely gave her the space to lead. He was a traditionalist, a man shaped by rigid command hierarchy. Her instincts, though respected, were often sidelined.

And yet, she had never seen anything like Feyzi.

"He won't talk about the military," Hart said quietly. "I've spent time with him. No signs of mental instability, but he won't even acknowledge his clearance."

"What does he talk about?" Rourke asked.

"OnePIN, his company. Family. He's lucid—smart. But evasive."

"Or trained," Rourke muttered.

Hart looked at him sharply.

"He's a U.S. citizen, sir. We pulled his immigration file. Clean. No red flags."

Rourke rubbed his temple. "We need Washington to move faster."

The Confrontation

Rourke met Feyzi in the conference chamber. The air felt taut, electric, as if charged with the weight of decisions yet unspoken. A single camera blinked steadily in the corner. Microphones buzzed faintly—live, watching.

There were no aides. No guards. Just two men and a truth that neither was sure the other would accept.

Rourke shifted his stance, an edge of doubt creeping into his normally steady posture. Orders from above were few, and time was slipping.

He didn't like uncertainty—and Feyzi was nothing but.

"I know you want to contact your family," Rourke began. "But you walked into a very complicated situation."

Feyzi nodded slowly. "I didn't walk in. I was pulled in."

"That's not an accident," Rourke said, leveling his gaze. "And XT84 wasn't the only aircraft that went down. There are... other operations. Still unfolding. You've witnessed things most civilians don't even know exist. I can't let you leave. Not yet."

Feyzi thought "Not yet" is the most dangerous phrase in a locked room.

"I understand," Feyzi replied calmly. "But let me be very clear, Commander—I'm not your enemy. And I'm not your asset."

Feyzi thought "Assets are owned. Survivors owe nothing."

Rourke stared. "Then, what are you?"

Feyzi's reply was steady.

"I'm someone who can only discuss his background with the President of the United States. And by the look on your face, you already know why."

Rourke clenched his jaw.

"This guy isn't bluffing, what the hell did he do for this country?" he thought.

Limited Access

Rourke handed over a silver access badge.

"You're confined to Level 1 and the aquatic wing. You won't see any other personnel. No data terminals. No comms. And everything you do is on camera."

"I'd expect nothing less," Feyzi said, taking the badge.

"And one more thing," Rourke added, softer this time.

"Don't make me regret this."

The Pool

Feyzi stepped into the massive dome housing the dolphin teams. The air was humid and filled with a soft, echoing resonance—clicks, whistles, and distant splashes composing a living symphony. Light filtered in through reinforced acrylic panels above, casting undulating reflections across the water. The scent of salt and sterile metal mingled in the air.

Commander Hart stood waist-deep in the pool, her expression focused, lips slightly parted as she issued a precise series of hand signals to the dolphin units. Her presence was commanding yet fluid, as if she were part of the aquatic rhythm herself.

One of the dolphins responded with a high-pitched chirp and a barrel roll, causing a cascade of ripples that shimmered like liquid silver. Feyzi paused on the platform's edge, momentarily awed by the grace and intelligence on display before stepping forward.

When she saw Feyzi, she smiled.

"You're cleared for dolphin socialization?" she teased.

Feyzi grinned. "Apparently that's the only company I'm allowed."

Hart waved the team over. "This is Echo-D3. Your rescue squad."

Feyzi thought "They found me in a black ocean. Why do I feel safer with them than with the cameras?"

Six dolphins circled the platform. Feyzi crouched and placed a hand gently atop each head.

"Thank you," he said softly.

Hart translated in clicks and hand motions. The dolphins responded with squeals and synchronized leaps.

One dolphin lingered behind, swimming close. It poked its head above the waterline and mimicked the baby cries Feyzi had heard the night of the crash.

Feyzi murmured "So I didn't imagine it. Someone wanted those cries carried."

Hart turned to him, translating: "Now you have six new friends."

Feyzi laughed, a real, unguarded moment.

"I can't believe I'm thanking dolphins for saving my life."

But inside, a darker thought surfaced—a chilling knot of fear, betrayal, and defiance tightening in his chest.

His heartbeat faster, not from the memory of the crash, but from the realization that the real danger might now come from the very country he had once served.

"Let's hope I don't get shot by my own country before I get the chance to thank anyone else," Feyzi whispered.

CHAPTER 16

The Unseen Strike

Flashback – 20 Hours Earlier
Low Altitude, North Atlantic
112 Miles Northeast of Echo-7

The modified UH-60M Black Hawk skimmed silently over the open ocean, blades slicing the air with clinical precision.

Black Hawk, Blue Water, was a UH-60M at the bones, but the airframe wore ocean gear like armor. ESSS stub wings carried auxiliary ferry tanks, with two more internal bladder tanks lashed to the cabin floor, bringing range into fixed-wing country. A retractable IFR probe sat folded against the nose; insurance for tanker hookups if weather closed. The rotors were de-ice wired, the intakes sand- and spray-screened, and the landing gear carried pop-out emergency floats, the kind that give crew a fighting chance if steel meets sea.

Inside the nose cone, a maritime weather radar painted squalls and sea clutter. The avionics stack had been gutted and rebuilt: dual INS/GPS, HF + SATCOM for when VHF dies at the horizon, and a low-probability-of-intercept data link that whispered Echo-7's corridor updates in bursts.

The cabin smelled of hydraulic fluid and aluminum, with survival rafts, immersion suits, and waterproof hard cases cinched in a grid of restraint straps that creaked with every gust.

From the outside, she was just a Black Hawk. From the inside, she was a knife built for the Atlantic.

The night was clear. Stars dotted the sky like pinpricks in velvet. Below, the Atlantic stretched smooth and still—a vast pane of polished black glass under a crescent moon. No clouds. No turbulence. Just calm.

Inside, 15 people sat in total silence. One of them, Dr. Kimberly S. Johnson—a quantum encryption expert whose name had never appeared in a public database—clutched the corner of her seat with white knuckles. As the rotors hummed above, her mind drifted briefly to the encrypted message she'd left behind for her daughter, a failsafe she never thought she'd need.

Across from her, a former DARPA coder traced circles on his wrist with his thumb, a quiet tic born from a lifetime of debugging code under impossible deadlines. Each of them carried the weight of classified knowledge—and the quiet awareness that not all of them might live to deliver it.

Four crew members—two pilots, one flight systems specialist, and one tactical officer—kept the aircraft on course and within Echo-7's covert ingress corridor.

Four Minds, One Machine

Briggs flew the sea-skimming profile, ninety feet AGL when he could steal it, two-hundred when cloud decks forced him, trading noise for invisibility. Zhang handled systems and sensor fusion, trimming for fuel, cycling de-ice, and nursing the ferry tanks down in sequence. The flight systems specialist ran the power management and bleed-air choreography, eyes swinging between torque, temps, and the fuel page. The tactical officer watched the silence: emissions control (EMCON) tight, transponder dark, comms in micro-bursts every ten minutes—enough to prove they were alive without drawing an audience.

The remaining 11 were civilians... at least by appearance.

But every one of them was an elite software engineer under deep classification. Their combined résumé could rewrite the future of cyber warfare: DARPA veterans, former NSA contractors, AI theorists from MIT's black programs, and quantum encryption architects whose work didn't appear on any university registry.

They were handpicked for a reason.

The Island – A Dot That Eats Helicopters

Echo-7's island was a stone knuckle in the North Atlantic, just too small for runway lights, big enough for a single helipad inset into basalt and armored with sacrificial grating for rotor wash.

At night the pad glowed low-observable blue; a wind cone and TACAN beacon slept behind blast shields until a Hawk called short final.

The rule was simple: land clean, leave cleaner. No hover shows. No wasted seconds.

The sea punished poetry.

The Mission

Their destination: Echo-7, an underwater command base that didn't officially exist.

Waiting below was USS *Missouri*, a next-generation Virginia-class nuclear submarine outfitted for something extraordinary: Project STRATUM, a fusion of neural networks and AI-driven battlefield decision systems, designed to transform underwater combat and threat interception forever.

But the code wasn't finished. Not yet.

That's why the engineers were flying in to integrate STRATUM's final layer, a live decision-making lattice that would allow US Military fleet to analyze, adapt, and respond to hostile engagements in real-time—without human lag.

The idea was simple. Execution was anything but. If STRATUM malfunctioned—or worse, was compromised—it could turn an entire nuclear fleet into a rogue element. The thought had crossed more than one mind on board, but none dared speak it aloud.

This wasn't an upgrade.

It was an arms race.

Code That Weighs More Than Metal

The crates didn't look dangerous: shock-isolated modules, sealed resin bricks, cold packs around a prototype whose name only existed in codenames. But the weight of them was strategic.

If you listened closely, you could hear gyros settle when the cabin went smooth, and the faint tick of a thermal controller stepping half a degree.

No one said it, but everyone knew: if STRATUM thinks wrong once, fleets die right.

Cockpit – 00:02 midnight ET

In the green wash of the MFDs, numbers made a promise: torque 79%, TGT well under redline, fuel feed balanced, ETA eight-oh-three to the island edge. The ferry tanks burbled through their transfer pumps like distant kettles. A radalt ribbon crawled along the bottom glass, the most honest friend a sea-flight ever has.

Chief Warrant Officer Taylor Briggs leaned forward, eyes scanning the horizon. Everything was clear. The skies were perfect. Instruments showed no anomalies.

Lieutenant Monica Zhang, his co-pilot, rechecked their encrypted channel to Echo-7.

"Still green. Guidance holding. ETA eight minutes."

Briggs nodded, keeping his tone light.

"Let's drop the cargo, shake hands with the ghost crew, and get home before breakfast."

In the back cabin, the engineers double-checked ruggedized cases strapped to the floor—each one containing drives, models, and one prototype module sealed with tamper-evident resin.

They had rehearsed it until it was muscle: four-point harness release, visor down, hand finds raft lanyard, knife to strap if jammed.

"Out and up," Briggs had said in the brief, "never back into the cabin."

Immersion suits were unzipped to the sternum for speed.

The tactical officer moved down the line, tapping shoulders, counting eyes.

No one talked about the black lesson: that at night, in winter water, the clock pries fingers from metal faster than courage does.

None of them spoke.

They didn't need to.

They were between weather systems, night smooth as lacquer. The radar showed nothing with a tail; the RWR was quiet; the HF net hissed like a sleeping cat. The only oddity was a half-second stutter in the SATCOM keep-alive; too short to log, too long to fully ignore. Zhang looked at it, frowned, and let it go. The sky above the ocean can be a room with a trick wall; sometimes signals fall in.

The Hit

It happened in silence.

The air had been still—too still. A sharp static crackled in the headsets for a half-second before vanishing, as if the sky itself had exhaled. Then came a gut-punch jolt, the kind no simulation ever captured. Inside the cockpit, Briggs' fingers tightened on the controls instinctively, but it was too late—far too late. Every hair on Zhang's arms stood on end as the cabin lights stuttered in a seizure of sparks and shadows.

No alarms. No warnings. No incoming alert on any system.

Just a jolt—so violent it felt like the Earth had reached up and grabbed them. The Black Hawk pitched sideways, then downward. Lights flickered. Sparks erupted from the ceiling panels.

Briggs didn't even get a mayday out.

The tail section buckled first. Then the electrical systems went dead. No flame. No sound from the outside. Just instant mechanical failure and a violent spin.

Inside the cargo bay, bodies slammed against fuselage walls. Equipment tore loose. Screams, grunts, the shriek of metal folding under invisible pressure.

Whatever hit them didn't make a sound.

What Kills Without a Signature

Maybe it was non-kinetic; a high-power microwave lance that reached into circuitry and turned order to noise.

Maybe an air-launched glide pod with no hot plume, riding a passive seeker on the Hawk's rotor harmonics. Or a surface effect; a buried emitter on the waterline that waited for the right silhouette to pass and then punched the bus.

Briggs would never know which story was true. The result was the same: physics with its finger in the breaker box.

It left no radar trace. No heat plume. No visible trail.

And it struck with surgical precision—mid-air, mid-route, over a flat and featureless ocean.

Then came the crash.

Gone Without a Ripple

Six seconds is nothing and everything. In six seconds, you can lose hydraulics, cavitate a pump, roll past the critical blade angle, and let the world rearrange the cabin. The tracking grid blinked dumbly because there was no burn, no debris fan, no transponder squawk, just a line that stopped where it should have curved.

Somewhere hundreds of feet beneath them, something shifted; a shape, a shadow, but no sonar pinged it. No one saw it move. No automated alert was triggered at Echo-7.

The entire aircraft disappeared from Echo-7's tracking grid in under six seconds.

From the perspective of Echo-7's command center, the Black Hawk was there one moment—stable, transmitting—and gone the next. In those tense seconds, red warning lights blinked uselessly on untouched consoles.

Technicians froze mid-sentence.

The Only Ladder Is the Sea

Commander Rourke's voice cracked over the intercom—"Confirm telemetry!"—but there was nothing to confirm. The screen simply faded to static. It was as if the aircraft had never existed at all.

The order for Echo-D3 went out before anyone could debate it. On the surface, two RHIBs were already slapping through chop toward the last good fix, towing acoustic beacons like breadcrumbs. Below, the base's listening wall woke, filters spun for rotor hub harmonics and power-train shrieks. The ocean answered with whale song and trawler screws and then, finally, something else, a human cadence, far from where math said it should be.

No wreckage surfaced.

No distress signal ever reached them.

Commander Rourke deployed Echo-D3—the genetically enhanced dolphin rescue team—as a last hope.

They never expected to return with a civilian.

Return to Present – Echo-7 Base

Frame by frame, the flight became a disappearing trick. Voltage rails wobbled, buses cross-talked, one inertial reference hiccupped and then reported everything normal a tenth of a second before everything wasn't.

No blast signature.

No thermal spike.

Just coherence, then none.

In a secure data room four decks below sea level, encrypted logs from that flight were being studied by intelligence analysts one frame at a time.

The engineers were gone.

The mission compromised.

And somewhere in the deep—something had acted with precision and intent.

Not just against one aircraft.

But two.

XT84 and the Black Hawk had both fallen... within moments of each other.

And the mystery only deepened.

Target or Collateral

Feyzi stood alone in the observation tunnel that overlooked the pool. Blue water shimmered as dolphins swam their circuits.

A question returned like an echo in his own mind:

Was I the target—or just collateral?

The thought stabbed through Feyzi's mind like a blade of ice. His pulse quickened as his eyes followed the rhythmic patterns of the dolphins below.

A bead of sweat traced down his temple, though the tunnel was cool. If someone had orchestrated all this—two strikes, two aircraft, perfect silence—then this wasn't random.

And if it wasn't random, then he was either the survivor of a miracle... or the only piece that still mattered to whoever had pulled the trigger.

The Island Remembers

Far above the command decks, the helipad waited under salt and stars. Wind scraped the grating like a match across stone.

A single blue light pulsed at the edge of the circle, the kind you can see through rain if you're lined up right, the kind you miss if you're not.

The sea kept its secrets.

The island kept its promise: Only helicopters can land here.

And only the living.

CHAPTER 17

The Message That Broke the Silence

The Paper That Outlasts the Night

The Boston Globe had been Boston's metronome for a century and a half; founded in 1872, steady through wars, recessions, and the kind of winters that bury headlines under ice. From a startup sheet on State Street to a digital powerhouse, it earned its reputation the hard way: by getting it right and getting it first when it mattered.

Its Spotlight Team became legend, those quiet obsessives who pried open doors no one else could, winning Pulitzers and changing institutions, most famously with a 2002 investigation that shook the Catholic Church worldwide.

To the city, *The Globe* wasn't just a paper; it was a promise that the truth would be printed even when it hurt.

Boston, Massachusetts – 7:14 a.m.

Rachel Lin had a ritual. While most reporters scoured breaking headlines and social feeds, she dove into the overnight 911 logs— looking for anomalies, absurdities, or overlooked tragedy.

The Newton Police Department's overnight dispatch log wasn't glamorous, but over the years, it had gifted Rachel a handful of bizarre, beautiful, and sometimes tragic leads that had turned into page-one stories.

Rachel's ritual wasn't romance; it was forensics. She read the overnight like a detective: CAD numbers, call types, the cadence of a dispatcher's keystrokes. An inconsistency here, a timestamp there; she could feel a story the way a sailor feels weather. *The Globe* taught her that: start small, then verify, then move. In a newsroom famous for patience and precision, speed only mattered after the truth showed up.

This morning, she scrolled lazily through the log, sipping luke-warm coffee.

Then her eyes stopped cold.

Incoming satellite communication from iPhone 16—Message received at 01:47 a.m.:

> "XT84 destroyed. Middle of Atlantic. Feyzi Çelik. Immediate
> rescue needed."

She didn't tweet.

She checked. First: cross-reference the Newton incident number; second: confirm the device pathway, Apple's satellite SOS relay can route to local PSAPs by home area code; third: look for a federal echo—FBI or Coast Guard inquiries always leave a faint magnetic trace on the local line. If the dots connected, the story lived. If not, it died on her screen, not in print—That was *The Globe* way.

Her reporter's instinct jolted her awake before the caffeine even had a chance.

She recognized the name: Feyzi Çelik—CEO of OnePIN, Boston-based tech entrepreneur, husband and father. He had boarded XT84. The flight was now the center of a global tragedy.

But no survivors had been reported.

Yet here was a message.

A name.

Logged publicly.

Survivor?

Rachel's hands flew across the keyboard.

In the background, the newsroom warmed from quiet to hum; assignment editors riding headsets, copy editors laying tripwires for style and law, the metro desk taking shape like a storm front. Somewhere up the chain, an editor who'd come to Boston to chase truth over trendlines would ask the only question that mattered: Can we stand on it in court?

The Globe had the scar tissue, and the Pulitzers, to prove why that question comes first.

Newton Police Department – 8:07 a.m.

"Rachel Lin, *Boston Globe*," she said to the desk sergeant. "I need to speak with the officer who logged the 1:47 a.m. satellite emergency call."

Within minutes, she was led into a back office where a young woman in uniform sat, clearly rattled but composed.

Her name tag read: Officer Megan O'Neill.

Rachel turned on her recorder.

The office smelled of copy paper and coffee; a clock ticked too loudly. Rachel set her phone down where O'Neill could see the recording light. Trust was a currency here, and *The Globe* didn't counterfeit. She asked short questions and let silence do work, another old Spotlight trick.

"It came in like any 911 text," O'Neill explained.

"Except it wasn't local—it was flagged as a satellite transmission through Apple's Emergency SOS system. The system identified the sender as Feyzi Çelik and flagged the XT84 message as extremely high priority. It said he was alive and needed rescue."

"Did you assume it was real?"

O'Neill nodded slowly.

"At first, no. But once I cross-checked XT84, I called the FBI. They didn't question it. They asked for the metadata and told me to stay quiet."

"Then what?"

"The Boston FBI field office looped in the Coast Guard, Logan ATC, and I think even the FAA. I was told to follow standard protocol. The rest… I don't know."

Rachel closed her notebook.

She had enough.

As Rachel stepped out into the morning light, her phone already in hand, she could feel the weight of the story building. If this was real—and it felt real—it would be the kind of story that changes everything.

On the ride back, the city slid by in morning steel; bridges, a river, a skyline that remembers shipyards and printing presses.

Rachel thumbed a message to Metro/Investigations: 911 log verified; FBI escalation likely; Coast Guard looped.

In the newsroom, a slot editor spun up a legal read while the audience team warmed a breaking banner that wouldn't publish until the last fact clicked into place.

The Globe's creed was simple: be first to be right.

She wasn't chasing headlines anymore.

She was chasing truth.

The Report That Sparked a Fire

Since 1872, the paper had been Boston's institution of record; privately owned today but publicly judged every morning. Digital transformed the press run into a pulse; hundreds of thousands of subscribers refreshed screens like porch steps once held bundled broadsheets. A single push alert could tilt a city's day.

Rachel knew this power wasn't a trumpet; it was a tuning fork. Hit the wrong note and the whole town hears it.

After verifying the log's authenticity, Rachel was able to confirm—off the record—that the FBI had flagged the message as genuine and immediately escalated the matter to multiple federal agencies.

But Feyzi Çelik's name had not been released to the public. No statement. No leak.

Why hide the only known signal from a possible survivor?

Rachel wrote:

"EXCLUSIVE: Satellite Emergency Message Suggests Possible XT84 Survivor—Tech CEO Feyzi Çelik Sends Plea for Rescue."

"A satellite emergency beacon from an iPhone registered to Boston-based technology executive Feyzi Çelik was received by Newton Police early Tuesday morning. Çelik, a confirmed passenger on Air Turkey Flight XT84, was believed to have perished when the flight disappeared over the North Atlantic. His message—received minutes after the crash—indicates he may have survived and is awaiting rescue. But his name has not been acknowledged by authorities. Why?"

The draft hit the editing stack. Standards asked for one more off-record confirmation; Legal flagged a line about "destroyed" versus "downed"—Copy tightened verbs; Audience mapped the national pickup.

Rachel didn't bristle; this was the forge.

When *The Globe* prints your byline over a story like this, they make sure the page can carry the weight.

The Globe Newsroom – 11:41 a.m.

The office hummed like a server room. On the glass wall, a city map pulsed with engagement heat—Jamaica Plain bright, Newton brighter, New York and DC kindling. Editors called sources by first name, the kind earned over twenty winters and a dozen snow emergencies. Caldwell's doorway became a turnstile—lawyer, investigations, comms—each nod a green light Rachel had earned.

Editor-in-Chief Maureen Caldwell stood in her office doorway waving the draft.

"Rachel! This is explosive. This headline is going national. You're going to be on CNN before lunch. Let's go."

Rachel nodded, adrenaline rising.

Her pulse throbbed in her ears. The weight of what this story meant—both professionally and personally—settled into her chest like a stone. Somewhere out there, a man was either waiting to be found... or being hidden.

Çelik Residence – Hopkinton, MA
12:11 p.m.

The house was packed.

Ethan, Diana, Terry, Emily, Adam, Hanna, and Laura. Jill's brother Bill and sister Susan were there too. The entire OnePIN inner circle had quietly gathered.

Alex sat in the living room, nervously scrolling through social media. Ayla paced the kitchen.

Then the screen blinked—just once.

A notification. A shift.

A live headline slicing through the silence.

"BREAKING: *The Boston Globe* Reports Satellite SOS from
XT84 Passenger Feyzi Çelik."

The anchor was speaking fast. Graphics flew across the screen.

And then—a live press conference cut in from Boston Coast Guard HQ.

CNN Live Coverage – 12:13 p.m.

A tall, uniformed officer from the U.S. Coast Guard stepped up to the podium, surrounded by flags and microphones.

"Hello, I am Commander Rebecca Alden, Boston Coast Guard. We can confirm that at approximately 1:47 a.m. Eastern Time, our partners at Newton Police Department received an emergency satellite message attributed to Mr. Feyzi Çelik, a passenger aboard Air Turkey Flight XT84. The message indicated he was alive at that time and requested immediate rescue."

"We do not currently know his location. We have not found the wreckage. The search and rescue zone is vast—hundreds of miles wide—stretching across one of the most remote parts of the North Atlantic. The U.S. and Canadian navies, supported by aerial and satellite reconnaissance, are actively engaged."

"We hope and pray that Mr. Çelik—and possibly others—are still alive. Every asset is being deployed. But this will take time."

For a brief moment, it felt as though the entire nation had paused—united by a signal from the deep.

Inside the Çelik home, the silence was deafening.

Then a single sob broke out. Jill covered her face with both hands and collapsed into Ayla's arms.

He was alive. Or had been.

And that was enough—for now.

Alex stood frozen, eyes fixed on the screen, whispering one word. "Dad..."

Ethan stepped forward and wrapped his arms around Jill. Terry squeezed Alex's shoulder. Laura and Adam held hands, their eyes glassy with relief.

Why *The Globe* Moved the Needle

It wasn't the headline; it was the paper behind it.

A publication that had weathered centuries of Boston skepticism and still landed Pulitzers on the mantel doesn't cry wolf.

When *The Globe* wrote "possible survivor," the city didn't just read it; they believed it enough to act, to call, to look outward toward the Atlantic and imagine a single human in a wide cold sea.

That's the work.

Outside – 12:45 p.m.

News vans began to stack up at the end of the driveway. Satellite dishes rose. Lights flicked on.

A camera crew adjusted a tripod on the lawn.

Jill glanced out the window and murmured, "Feyzi would've hated this." Her voice cracked with exhaustion and defiance.

Cameras, speculation, noise—it all felt wrong.

But behind that defiance, a fire was building. If the world wanted to watch, let them.

Let them witness his return.

And yet... she smiled.

"Whatever it takes," she whispered. "Come home."

Because maybe, just maybe, the world finally knew what she always did—Feyzi never gave up.

CHAPTER 18

Echoes of Loyalty

Base Echo-7 – Tuesday, 12:21 p.m.

Commander Rebecca Hart sat alone in the off-duty observation room, her posture rigid, fatigue visible in the tight set of her shoulders. A faint bruise darkened her left temple—a souvenir from two sleepless days navigating a base on edge. Her eyes, though heavy, remained locked on the muted CNN broadcast flickering across the wall-mounted screen. The red ticker at the bottom looped over and over:

"BREAKING: Tech CEO Feyzi Çelik Believed to Be Sole XT84 Survivor – Satellite SOS Message Triggers Global Response."

A soft smile curved across her face.

Not a smile of satisfaction.

A smile of vindication.

She looked over her shoulder toward the sealed corridor, the silence behind it pressing against her like a held breath—no footsteps, no hum of machinery, only the faint vibration of distant ocean currents reverberating through the walls—the one that led to the isolated sector where Feyzi Çelik had been confined since his unexpected arrival.

"They'll never be able to erase him now," she whispered to herself.

Hart had served for two decades, one of them buried inside the classified heartbeat of Echo-7. She had trained super-intelligent, genetically enhanced dolphins. She had reviewed top-secret strike plans. She had coordinated black ops missions few would ever know existed.

And yet, she had never seen anything like Feyzi.

Not just his calm under pressure—like when he stood barefoot on the observation deck, scanning sonar logs with quiet resolve, or when he refused pain meds after his rescue, insisting on clarity instead of comfort—his humility, or his refusal to panic after surviving a mid-air catastrophe.

Not even the fact that the dolphins—themselves bred to detect lies, malice, and danger—had instinctively protected and delivered him.

It was something deeper.

She remembered his eyes when he touched the dolphins' heads. Gratitude. Reverence. He had treated them not as animals—but as comrades.

"They chose him," Hart thought. "And that means something."

She turned back toward the screen. Now the Coast Guard Admiral was speaking live. Behind the official updates, she saw what the world didn't:

The U.S. government had just lost the option to quietly make Feyzi disappear.

He was now a public name. A face. A story.

And Commander Hart? She was the closest thing to a witness the media didn't know existed.

They couldn't bury this man.

Not with her still breathing.

She folded her arms and leaned back in the chair, thoughtful, her mind wrestling with the quiet shift she hadn't admitted to anyone— not even herself. Somewhere between briefing files and sonar logs, she had started believing in him. Not because of orders, but despite them.

"Who are you, Commander Feyzi Çelik?" she murmured.

And then, with a quiet chuckle:

"You saved people once... didn't you? Maybe a lot more than we'll ever know."

Hart stood and looked down toward the dolphin pool below. Team Echo-D3 swam silently in a synchronized ring. The lead dolphin nudged the water's surface, waiting.

She tapped on the glass and smiled again.

"They love you, you know," she whispered, her hand lingering a second longer on the glass.

"That first night—they wouldn't leave your side. Even when Rourke tried to pull them away. They chose you, over protocol." She whispered.

"And so do I—just a little."

Then she turned and walked back toward the command level.

The corridor leading out of the observation room was dim and cool, lit by soft LED strips that ran like veins along the curved walls. Hart walked slowly, her boots quiet against the carbon-fiber decking.

She passed through Sector Theta, the marine telemetry wing, where dolphin biometrics scrolled across translucent screens. A technician raised his eyes briefly but said nothing. Wordless tension hung in the air.

Her pace quickened as she entered Operations Tier 2—the old warroom level, now used mostly for autonomous drone coordination. Rows of consoles flickered with encrypted chatter from unmanned subs patrolling hundreds of miles out.

She heard whispers—operators speaking in hushed tones. No one had been briefed fully on Feyzi Çelik, but rumors traveled fast in steel corridors.

At the hydroacoustic surveillance dome, she paused. A glass wall revealed the sonar projection chamber—pulse maps rotating slowly in 3D, lit with ghostly blue echoes.

Hart stared at the last known coordinates of XT84 and the Black Hawk.

Still no pings.

Still no source.

Whatever hit them was smarter than anything they'd ever seen. And quieter.

Hart pressed forward, passing the personnel rec wing, where off-duty crew members sat in silence around muted vid-screens. A few glanced up at her—curious, exhausted.

They were trained for deep-sea survival, cyber defense, and zero-visibility conflict.

But this? This was different.

This wasn't warfare.

It was something colder.

Invisible.

As she reached the sealed lift to Command Tier Alpha, Hart hesitated.

She remembered her last conversation with Rourke. His jaw tight. His tone absolute.

"No more questions, Commander," he had said. "Not about Çelik."

She had nodded.

But inside, something had fractured.

She stepped into the lift, her reflection splitting across the brushed steel walls.

For ten years, she had followed orders. She had defended Echo-7 with a loyalty bordering on faith.

But today… she wasn't so sure who was defending who. Because now, Feyzi Çelik was no longer a secret.

And nothing inside Echo-7 would ever be the same.

CHAPTER 19

The File

Türkiye – The Hinge of Continents
The Gate Between Seas

To outsiders, Türkiye is a map-painter's delight: one country laid across two continents, a bridge of cities and mountains that runs from the Balkans to the Caucasus and the Levant. But to strategists, it is a choke point with a heartbeat.

Whoever sits in Ankara watches the Turkish Straits, the Dardanelles and the Bosporus, the only saltwater doors between the Black Sea and the Mediterranean.

Since 1936, the Montreux Convention has given Türkiye the authority to regulate military traffic through those narrows, a legal lever that can raise or lower the temperature of a region with a signature.

A NATO ally since 1952, Türkiye anchors the Alliance's southeastern flank, its air bases, ports, and armies pointed toward pressure lines that run through the Black Sea, Syria–Iraq, and the Eastern Mediterranean. The United States and Europe have relied on Turkish access; most famously İncirlik Air Base, for decades of operations and deterrence.

Trade makes the geopolitics tangible. Türkiye joined a goods customs union with the EU in 1995, stitching factories in Anatolia to showrooms in Berlin and Milan.

Energy flows too: oil from the Baku, Tbilisi; Ceyhan pipeline finishes its journey at Ceyhan on Türkiye's Mediterranean coast, while gas from the Southern Gas Corridor (TANAP/TAP) crosses Anatolia toward Europe, routes that only matter because Ankara keeps them open.

When war blocked Ukrainian ports in 2022, Istanbul hosted the Black Sea Grain Initiative, the UN-backed deal that let ships thread safe corridors to inspect points in Türkiye and feed the world again, proof that the state guarding the Straits can still bend history at the conference table.

Then there is scale: a nation of 85 million people with a defense industry suddenly exporting drones and systems across dozens of countries; a state that hosts millions of refugees, absorbing regional shocks so others don't have to.

Strategic yesterday; strategic today.

Europe calls it a partner; Washington calls it an ally; the map calls it a hinge.

On the Straits, freighters queued like beads on a wire; the night current pulled them past palaces that had seen a dozen empires come and go.

Ankara, Türkiye Tuesday, 9:42 p.m. (GMT+3)

The Ministry of Transport building, a blocky monolith in the heart of Ankara, hadn't slept in twenty-four hours.

Minister Halil Şen sat in his high-ceilinged command room, its walls lined with live news feeds and tactical monitors, the air heavy with the smell of coffee and tension. Advisors circled like satellites, whispering updates, their faces worn and hollow from sleepless hours. A cold draft blew from the marble floor, only intensifying the anxiety.

He had just concluded another round of emergency briefings about XT84 when a single phrase froze him mid-sentence:

"Sir, CNN is reporting the name of a possible survivor... Feyzi Çelik."

He turned sharply to the aide who delivered the report.

"Say that name again."

"Feyzi Çelik, sir. Boston-based technology executive. Turkish American dual national. His name appeared in an SOS message sent via satellite, apparently from the crash site."

Minister Şen didn't waste a second.

"Find out who he is. Everything. Immediately."

National Intelligence Center, Ankara

By midnight, the search had escalated.

Military databases, diplomatic registries, and intelligence logs were scoured. The existence of a 'President's Eye Only' designation suggested implications that could ripple through military alliances, exposing buried intelligence operations and shaking the foundation of NATO-Türkiye covert coordination. But each query led to the same result:

Classified – Access Denied – Level: Cumhurbaşkanı Gözleriyle (President's Eye Only)

A junior officer finally escalated the dead-end up the chain.

Within an hour, two sharply dressed officials from the National Intelligence Organization arrived at the Ministry.

They carried a sealed black dossier with crimson lining, transported in a reinforced briefcase clutched tightly between them as they moved through the sleeping city in a black convoy of armored SUVs.

The convoy swept through Ankara's rain-slicked avenues under escort, slicing through red lights with impunity, headlights illuminating startled pedestrians and shuttered storefronts. Every turn of the wheels carried a deeper urgency, the kind known only to those at the heart of national secrets.

A file stamped "Cumhurbaşkanı Gözleriyle", President's Eye Only, doesn't just live in Ankara.

The alliances stitched to it do. NATO logistics, U.S. access rights, EU trade corridors, Straits control under Montreux, and Black Sea navigation norms, they all share the same spine. If a name inside touches any of those nerves, phones ring from Beştepe to Brussels to DC.

Stamped across the front in bold capital letters:

GİZLİ: CUMHURBAŞKANI GÖZLERİYLE – NATO /
TÜRKİYE ORTAK DOSYA (Top Secret: President's Eye Only –
NATO / Türkiye Joint File)

Beneath the cover sheet, a redacted memorandum peeked through:

RECOGNIZED AS CIVILIAN COMMANDER.
OPERATION [REDACTED].
ENDORSED BY PRESIDENT CLINTON AND PRESIDENT
DEMIREL. STATUS: PERMANENTLY PROTECTED
INDIVIDUAL.

The ink was faded but unmistakable. Authority from both nations, sealed in silence for decades, now exposed by a crash in the Atlantic.

The agents handed it silently to Minister Şen, who immediately understood its significance.

"I'll take this myself."

Presidential Palace, Ankara, 2:17 a.m.

On one wall: Bosporus traffic scrolling like a pulse; on another: Black Sea radar plots; at the center: feeds from İncirlik and the NATO network.

112

The staff knew the choreography—if grain moves, prices ease; if ships stop, ministers wake—and tonight every dial was tapped to listen for a single life in a cold ocean.

President Kemal Arıkan was still awake in the Situation Room; a subterranean command chamber buried deep beneath the Presidential Palace; its modern walls fortified with both steel and silence. Banks of screens displayed everything from global satellite feeds to Turkish airspace control. The overhead lights were dimmed to a bluish hue, casting the faces of his inner circle in a ghostly glow.

The staff had never stayed this late before.

Whispers bounced along the curved walls as junior aides exchanged uneasy glances.

"There must be something big happening," one muttered.

Another replied: "Is it about flight XT84? It must be... what else could stir the President at this hour?"

One of the staff whispered "İncirlik Base is green."

Translation—the alliance still had its runway.

Arıkan sat alone at the central command desk, his expression unreadable.

He looked up from a sea of information as Minister Şen entered the Situation Room and handed him the sealed folder.

"Sir," Şen said quietly. "It's about Feyzi Çelik."

The President raised an eyebrow. Then, without another word, he waved everyone out of the room.

Aides, generals, translators—gone.

Alone in the silence, he opened the dossier.

Fifteen Minutes Later

For generations, the West measured Ankara by where its runways pointed. Lately they measure it by what its factories build. Turkish drones—TB2, Akıncı—and other systems have lifted Ankara's leverage, adding export power to the old geography.

A partner with ports and airspace is useful; a partner that also manufactures capability is indispensable.

The President closed the folder slowly and exhaled.

"Straits, steel, and silicon; that's our leverage now," he whispered to himself.

The weight of history lingered in his hands. Inside was a legacy buried under layers of allied secrecy—Feyzi's role in a joint NATO mission decades ago, his unconventional command title, the fingerprints of President Süleyman Demirel and U.S. President Bill Clinton... and the rare bilateral agreement marking him as a "strategic civilian asset" under permanent protection.

Only a few individuals in the world had ever earned such a distinction.

And now, one of them had fallen from the sky into the world's view.

He recalled a quiet morning years ago when a young Feyzi had briefed NATO staff in Brussels. Even then, his insight had turned heads—particularly Arıkan's, who had been Türkiye's defense attaché at the time.

The young man had vanished from official records shortly after, and Arıkan had assumed he'd been folded into one of those operations no one ever talks about.

Now, decades later, here he was again—emerging from the shadows. Arıkan's eyes moved slowly across each line, disbelief tightening in his chest. The scale of Feyzi's past—his authority in the technology he had built, his embedded role in one of NATO's most covert missions—was staggering. He had suspected something unusual back then, but nothing could have prepared him for this.

Now, the President finally understood why the file bore the highest level of secrecy—why even his own access had been restricted until this moment.

The Turkish President smiled to himself.

"Ah, Feyzi... we meet again," he said softly.

He walked to the encrypted red line on the far wall.

"Get me the White House," he instructed, his gaze fixed on the red line.

"If the Americans still remember who he is... then we may no longer control the next move."

"It's time for the President of the United States and I to talk. Our nations owe this man more than silence."

Ankara's lights bled into the rain; somewhere beyond the hills a pipeline hummed toward the sea.

CHAPTER 20

The President's Desk

The White House
West Wing Washington, D.C. – 7:33 p.m.

The West Wing at night runs on carpeted thunder; footsteps swallowed by wool, whispers ricocheting off framed photographs of handshakes and hurricanes. Kline paused under a brass sconce where the air smelled faintly of printer ozone and lemon oil.

Two Marines passed with faces like sealed envelopes. Beyond the door lay the room where history pretends to be simple.

National Security Advisor Dr. Marshall Kline stood outside the Oval Office, a sealed black dossier in his hands—marked. His knuckles were white from the pressure of his grip, the file slick against his palm from a thin layer of sweat.

A muscle twitched along his jaw as he stared at the door, rehearsing what he would say, knowing the balance of global diplomacy might shift the moment he spoke. in bold red:

PRESIDENT'S EYE ONLY
NATO BLACK VAULT FILE
SUBJECT: ÇELİK, FEYZI
CLASSIFICATION: STRATEGIC CIVILIAN ASSET

He hadn't read it. He wasn't authorized to.

But he now had something even more pressing to share.

He knocked once.

The folder didn't weigh much, but some papers bend light. Kline felt it: the peculiar gravity of documents stamped so high that even the curious learn to look away. He had carried combat medevac casualties with steadier hands.

Inside the Oval

The Oval is a trap and a stage. The Resolute Desk throws a low gleam; the rug's compass rose points every conversation toward its center, and the drapes drink the light until the television owns the room.

On quiet nights the clock ticks loud enough to cross the carpet. The portraits have opinions.

President Daniel T. Keaton was lounging behind the Resolute Desk, the soft glow of the television casting flickering shadows across the dark-paneled room. Only the muted hum of the screen filled the air. The scent of leather and old paper lingered in the dim light, and the room—usually bustling with aides and advisors—felt eerily still.

Keaton flipped through cable news with a mixture of irritation and boredom, the isolation amplifying his sense of detachment from the whirlwind outside. The room was dimly lit.

On the screen, CNN was looping the Coast Guard press briefing—a quote glowing in the banner: "We have a message from Feyzi Çelik, but we do not yet know his location..."

Keaton shook his head and grunted.

The chyron writhed: SEARCH WIDENS; SURVIVOR POSSIBLE. Stock footage of gray ocean rolled under the words.

Keaton watched the b-roll waves instead of the anchor; like every elected human, he stared at the metaphor and not the storm.

"Coast Guard's on live TV speculating about a ghost message? What a mess."

Kline stepped inside.

No aide ever walks into the Oval at night with good news and a sealed file.

Kline closed the door with the soft click that means: this conversation leaves a bruise.

"Mr. President, we need to talk—now."

Keaton didn't look up.

"This about the Turkish flight?"

"Yes. And more. Much more."

Kline placed the sealed file on the desk, then added:

"And... we found him. He's alive."

Keaton's head jerked up.

"What?"

"He's been rescued, sir. He's currently being held at Echo-7."

Keaton sat up straight, his mood changing instantly.

Echo-7 wasn't a line item; it was a shadow budget and a handshake. If you pulled up the carpet of the Potomac, you could trace it: NCR sites, NMCC loops, WHCA channels, a lattice of quiet wires trained to wake the republic without waking the neighbors.

"Echo-7? Are you telling me a civilian survived a transatlantic shootdown and got pulled into one of the most classified underwater facilities on Earth—and I wasn't told?"

Keaton's voice rose, caught between incredulity and wounded pride. His brow furrowed, and for a beat, he looked genuinely rattled—not by the news itself, but by the fact that he hadn't been the first to know.

The idea that something this monumental had occurred without his immediate involvement grated against his instincts. His ego bristled like a struck chord.

Kline stiffened.

"Admiral Lansing was following protocol, sir. The moment we confirmed his identity and the nature of his file; I brought this to you."

The flowchart had teeth: confirm, contain, notify. If a name pinged in the very top tier, some calls went sideways; to places with fewer calendars and more safes. It wasn't personal; it was physics. Kline knew that explanation never helped.

Keaton stood, furious.

"What the hell are we running here, a silent movie? Who else knows?"

"Commander Rourke. Commander Hart. Admiral Lansing. No one else at the base has full knowledge of his background."

Keaton glared at the file on the desk.

"This guy—the tech CEO? The one who sent the satellite message?"

"Yes, Mr. President. And according to NATO's archive... far more than just a CEO."

Keaton opened the file slowly, scanning the opening paragraphs. His scowl began to soften.

Not operations. Arrangements. Not orders. Obligations. Paragraphs that spoke in the language of "forbearance" and "mutual custodianship," stamped by the antique machinery of state. Names that live in footnotes, seals that no press secretary can explain on camera.

"This... is real?"

"Yes, sir. Confirmed by both Turkish and NATO intelligence. His identity and role were buried under dual executive signatures—Clinton and Demirel. President's Eye Only."

Keaton leaned back in his chair, flipping further through the dossier, each page casting deeper shadows across his face. His eyes narrowed as he scanned the pages—what he found wasn't what he'd expected.

There were no operations, no alliances, no troop movements. Just vague references, code-level acknowledgments, and archaic diplomatic seals. The implications were unspoken but undeniable.

It wasn't about missions—it was about something far older, deeper, and disturbingly beyond his reach. His fingers slowed, then stopped.

He sat still, stunned.

This wasn't just a tech CEO with a lucky survival story.

This was someone folded into a legacy of silence—his name shielded not by redactions, but by ancient arrangements and invisible structures no one had dared revisit. Even the presidency, it seemed, was too recent a lens to fully understand what Feyzi Çelik represented. A civilian, yes—but tied to something far greater than any uniform or title.

He could hardly believe it.

Keaton felt the Oval contract; like the air had thickened a degree. He set the papers down and listened to nothing for two full breaths. Somewhere past the Rose Garden a helicopter dragged a ribbon of sound across the sky. On nights like this, even the lawn hums.

These documents had been locked away for over three decades— sealed behind layers of international protocol, double-signed by Clinton and Demirel.

It was bigger than him. Bigger than any presidency.

Keaton exhaled slowly and forced his posture into calm. Whatever this was, it wasn't something to control—it was something to navigate.

He closed the folder.

"This guy was a ghost."

He looked back at Kline.

"And now, he's sitting in Echo-7, probably sipping water and petting dolphins?"

"Yes. Confined to a secure section of the base. But his name is already in the media. The news is spreading like wildfire."

Keaton pressed his thumb and forefinger to his temples. He took a breath, exhaled, then snapped the file shut.

"I don't like this story being written without me, Marshall."

He turned to his desk phone and hit the secure line.

"Get me Admiral Lansing. And patch in the President of Türkiye."

Then to Kline:

"We're going to flip this. Make it our story."

The Moves – Three Calls and a Curtain

Kline walked out of the Oval with three tasks:

WHCA to open a SVTC (secure video) with Admiral Lansing, Second Fleet, and Boston Coast Guard; NMCC on silent read. State Ops to line a leader-to-leader with Ankara in fifteen; protocol says thirty, crisis math says half. Press Secretary drafts a holding line that can walk on one leg: "We are coordinating with allies; we can confirm a message; we can't yet confirm a location."

Behind the curtain: Legal starts a privilege wall, Counsel drafts a finding no one will quote, and the Chief of Staff builds a squeeze box so information leaves the building only in authorized shapes.

Elsewhere...

Far from flags and carpets, a windowless room kept its own weather: stale air, cold coffee, monitors set too bright. The operator wore headphones that had outlasted two contracts and one ideology. The incoming header flashed PRIORITY RED, and the temperature of the room seemed to drop. He didn't say anything; he flattened his hands on the desk like he was steadying a boat.

While military aides scrambled behind encrypted channels and global leaders prepared their next moves, a separate alert pulsed into life across an offshore relay system—its signal a jagged flicker of crimson on a black terminal screen.

The message appeared as a string of encrypted code, but its header glowed unmistakably: PRIORITY RED.

Packets unfolded like origami; checksum true, signature misread, an old key breathing in a new machine. The line that was supposed to go one way split into two thin wires: one back to a sponsor who seldom signed emails, the other to an asset who hadn't been needed in years.

The plan hadn't planned for survival. Plans almost never do.

Somewhere in a dimly lit command post, a lone figure leaned forward as the notification expanded, eyes narrowing. Whoever had built the plan hadn't prepared for this outcome—Feyzi Çelik was alive, and with that one truth, the entire board had shifted and global leaders prepared their next moves, a separate alert pinged quietly across an offshore relay system.

Not from Washington.

Not from Ankara.

Not from NATO.

But from someone else—someone whose plan hadn't accounted for Feyzi Çelik still being alive.

A cursor blinked. A second monitor woke. Somewhere in that network a script elected to begin again; sleeping nodes stirred, a listener woke on a buoy, a handset in a locker pinged a tower it shouldn't, and a failsafe that was meant to bury a problem started counting down instead.

The ocean, indifferent as stone, held the cables like veins.

And now, everything had changed.

CHAPTER 21

Silent Currents

Unknown Location
Secure Intelligence Facility People's Liberation Army
Joint Naval Command Division Qingdao, China

In a windowless war room buried beneath reinforced concrete and layers of digital encryption, the air was cold and dry, tinged with a faint metallic scent from humming processors lining the walls. Fluorescent lights buzzed overhead, casting sterile light onto polished steel floors.

Dozens of analysts moved with mechanical precision behind banks of monitors, each displaying silent satellite feeds, encrypted radar telemetry, and real-time data streams.

The war room didn't breathe so much as tick. Every console ran a private weather system—cooling fans, tiny whirlwinds of dust, the static crackle of synthetic fibers. Teacups sat on anti-vibration mats next to keyboards arranged with parade-ground geometry.

No one raised their voice; the only loud thing allowed underground was certainty. A floor runner in soft-soled shoes passed behind the analysts, swapping encrypted thumb drives the way a nurse changes IV bags. Above them, the big board exhaled numbers as light.

A massive digital heat-map of the North Atlantic glowed crimson across the main wall, pulsing with oceanic activity. Along the red-hued coastline, a single marker blinked with persistent regularity—Echo-7.

Qingdao's picture of the Atlantic was stitched from stolen seconds: commercial AIS ghosts, weather scatter, fringe returns from satellites with innocent names, and the quiet kindness of undersea microphones that don't officially exist. An AI triage layer; trained on decades of ship habits, repainted chaos into intent.

Echo-7's marker pulsed like a lighthouse seen through fog, a beat that said: Here, then not; here, then not. The rhythm was a dare.

General Wei Liang, Chief Strategist of Submarine Warfare, leaned forward with a rare smile—the kind that barely touched his lips but glinted in his eyes. For years, he had operated in the shadow of American naval superiority, quietly orchestrating war games and simulating counter-strike doctrines.

Wei believed wars were written in logistics long before they were spoken in steel. He collected other people's mistakes like art—Admiral's memos, fuel spreadsheets, the travel times of tugboats in winter.

His private mantra: Quiet water wins. He had made a career of forcing loud navies to sail in quiet water.

This moment, the fruition of decades of strategic vision and clandestine cooperation, was personal. It wasn't just a tactical success—it was a vindication. The smile came not from triumph alone, but from the quiet satisfaction of proving his skeptics wrong. To his left, a Russian liaison officer adjusted his headset.

"Operation Echo Phantom is complete," General Wei said flatly. "No radar signature. No sonar trace. Zero detection."

The operation's spine wasn't a missile; it was a rhythm; gaps in radar sweeps, legal traffic lanes turned into blindfolds, surface weather that made satellites squint. Decoys lived one sea-mile away, breathing the same sea as their predators.

Power stayed low, like a hunted animal. When they had to speak, they whispered into the ocean's bones.

Across from him, Major General Yuri Sokolov—of Russia's covert naval arm—responded with a slow nod, his expression unreadable. Though his words were calm, there was a flicker of restrained pride behind his eyes—a quiet assertion that Russia's contribution had been the linchpin. General Wei caught it. The nod, the tone, the silent implication. Their alliance was effective, yes—but neither man truly trusted the other. Strategic necessity had made them partners, not comrades.

"We told you the integration would work. The 'Yurevich-class' hull was the final piece. Without it, the stealth systems would have failed."

The Yurevich-class: Russia's next-generation stealth submarine platform. Angular, matte-skinned, and completely silent in low-speed cruise. Its development had been stalled for over a decade—until China intervened.

Angular plating broke returns into useless corners. A thin, compliant skin drank vibration until even cavitation sounded pastoral. The propulsor wore a hush like velvet. At loiter speed, the hull's heat profile blurred into the water around it; at sprint, battery banks carried it across danger like held breath.

The boat was not a machine.

The boat was a decision: arrive unseen, leave unproven.

China had the engineers. Russia had the physics. And both shared a common obstacle: U.S. maritime dominance.

Sokolov never smiled with his mouth. He smiled by removing a problem from his eyes. He turned his headset just enough to reveal the nape scar he never spoke about and said nothing that wasn't weighed on both sides.

Their partnership was built on arithmetic: two distrusts equal one result.

Strategic Fracture

Thirty years ago, China's naval ambitions ran aground, literally, on a battlefield design penned by one man: Feyzi Çelik.

On a grainy simulation display buried within an old PLA strategic archive, a handful of officers stood in stunned silence as the maneuver played out again. The setting: post-Gulf War, early 1990s. American and Turkish naval assets executed a staggered redeployment of frigates and oilfield tankers, forming a pseudo-blockade that rerouted oil traffic through choke points dictated by NATO interest.

From the Persian Gulf to the South China Sea, the algorithmic outputs showed the same result: strategic containment. For China, it meant fuel dependency, increased transit vulnerability, and maritime deterrence—without a single shot fired.

General Wei had seen the simulation years ago. It had circulated under code name "Gorgon Loop," a classified war game modeled after Çelik's design. Every time they ran it, the result was the same: American naval supremacy, Chinese paralysis.

The archived sim ran with the mercy of old software; blocky ships, pixel seas, a clock that stuttered in the corner. But its math was modern cruelty: choke a strait here, tilt insurance premiums there, let fuel queue at the wrong harbor until industry flinches.

Çelik hadn't waged war; he had priced it out of reach. It was an algorithm that tasted like salt and copper to every planner who watched it end.

Since then, China's navy had grown to match the U.S. in size—but not in capability. Its warships remained gas-turbine powered. Its aircraft carriers, non-nuclear. The U.S. Navy operated indefinitely in blue water. China could not.

The chokehold route, from Hormuz through Malacca, remained the noose. And Feyzi Çelik had tied the knot with surgical precision.

Now, China's ambitions to invade Taiwan hung in the balance. USS *George Washington*, the Seventh Fleet's crown jewel, was deployed in the Philippine Sea as of May 2025. U.S. destroyers regularly patrolled the Taiwan Strait—an unbroken line of control.

If China was to win the war before it began, it needed one thing: invisible dominance beneath the waves.

The Taiwan Strait was a long coin toss. Everyone knew its odds, no one trusted its wind. Wei had no interest in tossing coins.

He wanted a table that leaned just enough so that anything round rolled the right way.

The Target

Project STRATUM. STRATUM did not "track" as humans do. It listened to decisions before they happened; subtle correlations between power draws, trim changes, and the way a commander breathes when he chooses audacity over caution. Fed years of fleet telemetry and the folklore of war, it built countermoves like a tide: not fast, not slow, simply inevitable.

China's cyber infiltration had uncovered it buried deep inside Echo-7's operational blueprint.

A fusion of AI neural networks, real-time submarine combat protocols, and predictive threat interception; STRATUM was not merely a system; it was an awakening.

In one classified simulation, a virtual fleet of Chinese stealth subs disappeared from the board within ninety seconds; each movement predicted, each evasion countered before execution. The AI adapted in real time, anticipating human decisions before they were made.

If activated, STRATUM wouldn't just reveal their presence—it would dismantle their doctrine. It was the technological equivalent of omniscience beneath the sea. And it would make Chinese and Russian underwater fleets obsolete overnight.

No admiral says this out loud, but Wei did in his head: If the sea learns to think, the bold drown first.

This technology could not be allowed to mature.

And so; Echo-7 became the test field.

A chance to validate their new Yurevich-class stealth submarine— and simultaneously cripple America's most secretive weapons lab.

Two critical events aligned with surgical precision:

A Black Hawk helicopter carrying 11 top-tier software engineers was scheduled to arrive at Echo-7.

XT84, a flight carrying Feyzi Çelik, was transiting 30,000 feet above the same airspace.

Only a handful of elite operatives knew what was in motion. Deep inside a high-security cyber operations bunker in Chengdu, a young Chinese operative named Lin keyed in the final lines of code with trembling fingers.

His screen pulsed with warning flags from U.S. Army helicopter diagnostics, each one meticulously crafted to simulate a minor but mission-critical fault. Across the globe, these false maintenance flags registered automatically, grounding the Black Hawk and delaying its launch by exactly 47 minutes.

Half a world away, another handler working undercover at Istanbul Airport gave a quiet nod to a ground crew supervisor. The pretext: an unscheduled baggage scan. XT84 was delayed by 14 minutes in Boston. Neither operative knew the full scope of the mission. But both executed their roles with clinical precision.

The result: two targets intersected in the same Atlantic corridor, above and below, at the same time.

On the big board, two vectors slid toward each other like ingots on a tilted table. Beneath them, the Yurevich exhaled no sound at all, a ghost beneath a page.

Perfect Execution – Almost

Whether it was a cold beam, a clever field, or something with fins and a conscience, the strike read like a typo in physics; one line of reality simply didn't print. The helicopter shuddered into a new equation and fell through it. XT84 entered a kind of silence that isn't quiet; it's removal.

The Yurevich-class submarine moved undetected, its new hull absorbing sonar like silk. The missile—or whatever delivery method was used—left no radar trail, no acoustic bounce, and no trace. Echo-7 never saw it coming.

The Black Hawk was hit. XT84 was hit.

Two downed aircraft. One catastrophic moment.

The mission succeeded.

Almost.

On a secondary monitor three seats from the aisle, a pixel went the wrong color for half a second; battery telemetry that shouldn't exist, an SOS pathway that shouldn't be alive. No one saw it.

Machines did.

Machines remember.

Unintended Consequences

Back in Qingdao, a data stream came through—a satellite relay from a U.S. emergency beacon.

Victories are loud even in quiet rooms. This one ended with a beep. The relay didn't even merit the word "alarm."

It was simply truth, discovered.

Then, a name appeared in news alerts:

"Feyzi Çelik – Potential Survivor."

Wei's hand missed the teacup on the first try.

The words pulsed on the monitor like a heartbeat. For a full second, no one in the room moved. Then, the soft clink of a teacup being set down broke the silence. General Wei's hand hovered above the desk, trembling slightly before forming a tight fist. The analysts glanced at one another, uncertain if they should breathe.

Wei stepped forward, eyes locked on the screen. The sterile hum of machines seemed louder now, the room shrinking around the gravity of a name. His voice, when it came, was hoarse—almost reverent.

"Run it again," he said.

But the message didn't change.

The room froze.

Wei's smile vanished.

"You said he was aboard," he growled at the Russian officer.

"He was. XT84 is gone."

"He wasn't supposed to survive."

Survival breaks cover stories, timetables, theology, and carefully measured escalations. A living witness is a metronome that forces everyone to keep time.

The Russians knew it.

The Chinese knew it.

The ocean did not care.

Worse—U.S. military command had not flagged Çelik's presence as operational. They'd assumed the airline crash was collateral—not coordinated.

"Do they know who he is?"

"No."

Wei's jaw tightened. His voice dropped into a whisper.

"They will."

And when they did, they would see the connections. The oil blockades. The war game simulations. The STRATUM system's foundations.

Wei did not shout. He lowered: Sanitize the Chengdu chain; burn the logs, bury the backup, move Lin to a desk with windows and thank him. Flood the infosphere: three decoy survivors, one false wreck line, a dozen anonymous experts who will confidently say the sea does not return names. Put a hand on Sokolov's shoulder and remind him gently that shared triumphs die when partners write history alone. And most importantly, listen—not for sonars or satellites, but for the click when Washington's narrative changes key.

When the orders were done, the war room returned to its habit of not existing.

Tea cooled.

The big board resumed its red breath.

Down a side corridor, Lin stood under a fluorescent light and watched his hands shake—useful hands yesterday, dangerous hands today. He pressed his palms together until the tremor stopped.

On the wall, a framed photograph of the sea looked like carved granite.

He tried to remember if the ocean had ever been blue.

They would realize that Feyzi Çelik predicted all this three decades ago.

Feyzi wouldn't just recognize what was coming.

He would stop it.

CHAPTER 22

Two Presidents' Talk

White House – West Wing Situation Room
03:12 a.m.

A secure red-line transmission linked Washington to Ankara, bridging two fortified nerve centers of global power. In the White House Situation Room, dim lights cast long shadows across polished oak surfaces, where digital maps pulsed in cold blues and reds. Aides lined the perimeter, some standing at attention, others hunched over terminals, their faces pale in the glow of LED displays.

The line itself had a temperament. It preferred certainty, punished hesitation, and amplified every intake of breath across three thousand miles of copper, fiber, and willpower. A duty tech in the corner watched a latency counter hover under 400 milliseconds and relaxed by a fraction; diplomacy lives in half-seconds. Somewhere under the Potomac, a relay cage hummed like a beehive wrapped in velvet.

The scent of burnt coffee lingered in the air alongside the quiet hum of filtered air systems. At the far end, the President sat flanked by advisors, every eye fixed on the large display slowly connecting to its Turkish counterpart.

Thousands of miles away, Ankara's Situation Room mirrored its American twin in austerity and tension—walls paneled in dark wood, Turkish flags illuminated beneath overhead projectors, and a security detail braced near a sealed entry door. Despite the hour, no one had left their post. Everyone in both rooms understood: this was no routine diplomatic call. The world was shifting.

National Security Advisor Dr. Marshall Kline stood behind President Daniel T. Keaton, carefully silent as the encrypted video call came online.

Chairs were set two inches off the table; enough to look engaged, not enough to squeak. Name placards faced inward; titles faced the cameras. A small clock with no numbers pulsed amber in the rear wall, counting classified minutes that would never appear on any schedule. A protocol officer moved a glass of water half an inch closer to Keaton's hand; presidents should never reach.

Across the screen, in the dimly lit Situation Room of the Turkish Presidential Complex, stood President Kemal Arıkan, sharply dressed, composed, and equally burdened.

The rooms did what rooms do when the center holds: they got smaller.

Arıkan's room was cooler by design; cold air for hot decisions. An aide at his left elbow ran a whisper channel on an earpiece—simultaneous translation, threat updates, energy flow summaries. Every thirty seconds, a slim folder appeared at his fingertips, one page only, typed in a font chosen for speed, never beauty. He did not break eye contact with Washington to read them; he read with a blink.

Beneath the tailored suit and formal poise, his mind raced. The name Feyzi stirred more than political concern—it awakened memories. He remembered the young strategist's calm voice during a NATO debriefing decades ago, the way he'd held a room of generals in rapt attention.

Arıkan's shoulders eased slightly, a subtle shift from President to compatriot. He remembered the Brussels briefing room that smelled of copier toner and raincoats, the way a young Feyzi had sketched a strait on a napkin and explained how to move ships by moving ideas first. Generals had argued about missiles; Feyzi had argued about momentum. The room had gone still because someone had finally shifted the floor. For a brief moment, the weight of office gave way to something more personal: the quiet hope that perhaps, against every odd, the right man had returned at the right time.

Keaton didn't waste time.

Titles evaporated for a beat. It was a human exchange; one leader telling another that a name had defied statistics. In both rooms, shoulders dropped an inch. Around them, the war maps didn't change, but they felt different, like coastlines after rainfall.

"President Arıkan," he said. "We found him."

There was a pause.

"Feyzi?" Arıkan asked.

Keaton nodded slowly.

"Alive. Safe. At one of our black sites. I've just read his file."

President Arıkan exhaled in deep relief and stepped back from the screen.

"We feared the worst."

"So did we," Keaton said. "But this changes everything."

Unseen Threads

Both leaders knew this wasn't about one man anymore. As the implications settled over them, their expressions shifted. Arıkan's jaw tensed—not just from the gravity of the moment, but from the realization that the geopolitical landscape was unraveling faster than his military advisors had warned. In his mind, he ran through potential strike patterns, regional destabilization risks, and economic shockwaves that could ripple across Eurasia.

Keaton, meanwhile, leaned back slightly, eyes narrowed as if seeing a chessboard stretching across the oceans. The revelation of a Sino-Russian alliance operating in stealth wasn't just a tactical threat—it was an existential one. He glanced briefly at the live map feed behind Kline's shoulder, red clusters indicating known submarine routes, and for a moment, the weight of his office pressed visibly on his brow. This was a storm, and they were already in the eye.

"This was no accident," Arıkan said. "Your Black Hawk. Our airliner. Targeted at the same time, in the same quadrant. Our intelligence is connecting Russian deployment with a stealth platform that didn't exist six months ago."

Keaton nodded.

"They didn't build it alone. Our intercepts suggest Chinese neural design signatures in the control systems. They've partnered."

There was silence.

Then Arıkan said quietly, "They're moving faster than we thought."

Partnerships born of pressure don't shake hands; they share blind spots. The silent calculus was obvious: one side brings hull and habit; the other brings pattern and code. Put them together and you get speed where caution used to live.

"Too fast," Keaton replied.

"And we didn't see it coming."

On the far screen behind Kline, layers of the Atlantic sat like stacked glass: commercial lanes etched in pale blue, subsurface patrol boxes in faint red, and a constellation of "maybe" marks; the honest color of intelligence.

Anyone who'd stared at oceans for a living could see it: something had taught the water a new trick.

Opportunity Through Crisis

Keaton leaned forward.

"I'll be blunt, Kemal. Our countries haven't exactly been close."

Kline slid a thin binder into the light: a decade of frost distilled to bullet points; sanctions that taught factories to scavenge, drills can-

FEYZI ÇELIK

celed and replaced with parallel exercises, speeches that burned hotter than the facts behind them. At the bottom of the list: three lines in ink, not toner. The handwriting was careful. Bridges we can rebuild in an hour; bridges that need a season; bridges that must never have existed.

"You speak truth," Arıkan said with a respectful smile.

Keaton continued, "We drifted apart. Distrust. Sanctions. Politics. The fallout from the 2016 coup attempt had triggered waves of suspicion, with Ankara accusing Washington of harboring dissidents. In return, the U.S. tightened military export controls and froze bilateral energy deals. Joint exercises were suspended.

Then came the S-400 crisis—Türkiye's defense purchase from Russia that upended NATO protocols and shattered decades of alignment. The friction deepened with regional competition in Syria, each side backing different militias, each speech more barbed than the last. Trust eroded, quietly but steadily. But thirty years ago—one man, your citizen—helped secure the entire Middle East. Oil lanes. Economic corridors. Trade stability. That mission... was a masterstroke."

The Turkish President straightened.

"His mind stabilized regions. Without him, we would have lost decades of progress."

"Now we need him again," Keaton said. "Same vision. Same clarity. Only this time, the stakes are global."

Arıkan nodded. "And this time, Türkiye must be part of the answer."

He paused. Then added, "As Atatürk, our founding father, once said: Yurtta sulh, cihanda sulh. Peace at home. Peace in the world."

Keaton cracked a rare smile.

Keaton allowed the smile because the line deserved it. Arıkan allowed the proverb because memory deserved it. Between them, staffers wrote the moment into two different histories that would eventually rhyme.

"Beautiful words."

"They still guide us," Arıkan said.

136

Orders from the Top

Then, both men locked eyes; two Presidents facing the storm of a new world.

No one said the words aloud, amnesty for old frictions, but they signed it anyway with posture.

The rooms tipped from recollection to direction.

Pens cleared holsters.

Feet planted.

Cameras adjusted gain to catch the whites of eyes.

"He's the only one who can architect our response," Keaton said. "From a hidden base, Echo-7."

"Agreed," Arıkan replied.

"We grant full NATO clearance, effective immediately."

Keaton turned to Dr. Kline and gave a single nod.

Kline tapped his tablet, the screen illuminating with a pale blue glow as biometric verification flickered across the surface.

A soft, mechanical chirp confirmed the authentication.

Instantly, the encrypted message deployed—traveling through hardened fiber-optic relays, jumping across military satellites, and tunneling through NATO's quantum-secure grid.

The instruction ran a gauntlet: hashed at the edge, split like a river through redundant paths, wrapped and rewrapped until it looked like harmless noise. In a satellite that wore a weather name, a packet prioritized itself without admitting why. In an underground node near Mons, a flag that never shows turned green. Miles away in Norfolk, a junior watch officer glanced at a console, then pretended he hadn't seen history arrive as a pop-up.

In a dimly lit command post, a red strobe pulsed above Admiral Michael Lansing's terminal.

The words "PRIORITY ONE – PRESIDENTIAL OVERRIDE" blazed across the display, accompanied by a high-pitched ping that pierced the room's silence.

The ping wasn't loud, just immovable.

Lansing's officers stilled the way sailors do when the sea makes a new sound. The directive text came on in clean lines, no rhetoric, no adjectives, as if the letters knew the fewer the words, the larger the wake. Someone reached to silence the room alarm and missed the button on the first try.

Officers glanced up from their stations, momentarily frozen.

Lansing's jaw tightened. He reached for the console, already knowing the name that would appear.

FEYZI ÇELIK

Released.

Reinstated.

Reactivated.

DIRECTIVE: RELEASE FEYZI ÇELIK.
REINSTATE RANK – COMMANDER.
ASSIGNMENT: NATO STRATEGIC ADVISOR – ECHO-7.
SECURITY LEVEL: PRESIDENTIAL OVERRIDE.

Somewhere below decks, a mag-locked door acknowledged a new name. Access paths rewrote themselves the way tide rewrites shoreline. A man with a clipboard lost his authority and didn't know it yet. The base exhaled and took a different shape.

President Keaton looked back to the screen.

"I'll take care of Jill and the family," he said.

"They'll know soon. But this is the start of something bigger."

A staffer in the West Wing picked up a quiet phone that never rings twice. In Hopkinton, a porch light would stay on long enough to outlast the broadcast cycle. The message script on the staffer's tablet had four paragraphs and no adjectives. It ended with an offer most families never get: we will carry the noise for you.

Arıkan nodded.

"Then let history remember this moment," he said, his voice steady but layered with meaning.

Decisions rarely end with applause. They end with air handlers and the feeling that the room is one chair lighter. Aides knew not to fill the quiet. History needs space to sit down.

For a long beat, neither man spoke. The video connection held in a frozen frame—two leaders staring across time zones and histories, each measuring the cost of what was to come.

In both rooms, aides remained still, sensing the gravity of something larger than orders or alliances.

No closing remarks.

No signatures.

Just a quiet nod shared across continents, heavy with consequence.

"When East and West rejoined. Not in war—but through a man who saw the future long before we did."

The call ended.

And the world quietly began to change again.

In Washington, the meeting log captured a string of initials and a time stamp with no verbs. In Ankara, a leather folio closed on a single page with one signature and a pressed corner—a private habit to mark a turning.

Two cities wrote the same bar of music in different keys.

CHAPTER 23

The President's Call

The Çelik residence was crowded with family, close friends, and OnePIN colleagues. The living room, typically warm and lively with Pottery Barn decor and framed family memories, now felt tense—thick with unspoken dread. The lights were dimmed low, casting long shadows across bookshelves lined with photographs of better times.

People were clumped into quiet corners, whispering anxiously, fingers tapping smartphones for updates. Someone had left a tray of untouched tea glasses on the marble counter. Even the fireplace, once a source of comfort, sat dark and cold. The silence between updates was unbearable, stretching out like static in the air.

The Çelik home had a way of recording days like this. The grandmother clock in the living room ticked too loudly; the rug under the coffee table remembered every foot that crossed it. Someone's jacket still hung on a chair back; sleeves folded like hands at a bedside. On the counter, a single spoon rested in a teacup—its handle pointed north, as if trying to find true.

Then, Jill's phone rang. It wasn't a normal ring.

It came through a secured number—private, unlisted, and labeled only as "U.S. Government: Priority Call."

She answered.

"This is the White House switchboard. Please confirm this is Jill Çelik."

Her heart froze. "Yes, this is Jill."

"The President of the United States would like to speak with you and your immediate family. Please ensure that only you, Alex, Ayla, and Ryan are present. The discussion is confidential and must remain private. We'll initiate the secure video link shortly."

Jill stood motionless for a moment, the phone still gripped tightly in her hand, its weight suddenly unbearable.

Her mind reeled—what could this mean? Was it confirmation of her worst fear, or hope clawing its way back from the abyss? Her breath caught in her throat, and for a heartbeat, she considered not speaking at all. But then she looked around at the anxious faces, some avoiding her gaze, others looking for answers in hers.

She drew in a breath, straightened her spine, and with a trembling voice, asked everyone to give them the room. Confused, yet respectful, the OnePIN team, family members, and friends quietly filed out.

Only Jill, Alex, Ayla, and Ryan remained in the Çelik family room.

There was the soft choreography of leaving without looking: chairs scooted in, chargers unplugged, murmured apologies for stepping on memories. In the foyer, a cousin pressed a half-hug to Jill's shoulder and slipped away like a good secret. The door clicked; the house grew smaller.

Ryan grabbed the Apple TV remote, opened the app, and cast the incoming link onto their 72" Sony television.

The screen washed to blue, then black as velvet, then bled into the gold of the Seal. A latency counter in the top corner blinked out of sight; someone, somewhere, decided the family did not need to know what milliseconds were worth tonight.

In a few seconds, the Presidential Seal appeared.

Then—he was there.

The President of the United States, in the Oval Office.

The camera sat slightly low, human on purpose, so the Resolute Desk didn't loom. A glass of water was placed just within frame, a detail only staff notice, and families later remember.

Behind the President, the drapes held their breath.

Jill instinctively reached for her children's hands, her fingers trembling as they wrapped around Alex's and Ayla's.

Ayla's face was pale, lips pressed tight, eyes already glassy with emotion.

Alex stood rigid, his jaw clenched, eyes darting toward the screen as if trying to make sense of what was happening.

Jill's thumb traced a small circle on Alex's knuckle; the same motion she'd used when he was five and afraid of deep pools. Ayla's shoulder trembled under Ryan's palm, the tremor that lives between sob and laugh. This is how people brace for impact: with hands.

Jill felt the heat of their skin, the pulse of fear and hope beating just beneath the surface. She gave a gentle squeeze—an anchor for them, and for herself—as they faced the unknown together.

Ryan placed a hand on Ayla's shoulder. They stood side by side— together for whatever was about to come.

The President took a moment before speaking. His eyes scanned the screen and paused on Jill. He saw strength in her eyes. He knew she had held the line for her family while the world waited. She had no idea how powerful an image this was—a united, dignified family on the brink of relief or devastation.

"This is not a typical call," the President began.

His tone carried the weight of unrehearsed truth. No cadence, no campaign. Just breath, then words; the way doctors speak, or captains do when the ocean has had its say.

His voice was quieter than usual, less showman, more human.

"I just finished speaking with President Kemal Arıkan of Türkiye. I'm calling you on behalf of both of our nations."

Jill's knees went weak.

"I have good news," he said. "Feyzi is alive. He's been rescued. He's in U.S. military custody and receiving medical attention."

Jill broke.

Her chest heaved as the President's words pierced through the protective shell she had worn all day. Her heartbeat thundered in her ears, and a warm rush flooded her face as tears welled in her eyes.

Her breath hitched, shallow and fast, vision blurring as she instinctively covered her mouth. The tears came, unstoppable—silent at first, then shuddering.

The sound Jill made was not a sob so much as air remembering lungs. Ayla folded at the waist and stood again without moving her feet. Alex's jaw loosened like a knot finally unpicked. Ryan's exhale shook the picture frames.

For a day, she had stayed composed—managing the grief, the unknown, the house, the guests. But now, hearing those words, the walls crumbled. Ayla grabbed her, sobbing. Alex looked stunned, blinking hard. Ryan exhaled sharply and clutched both women close.

"He's injured," the President continued, "but his injuries are not life-threatening. He's in stable condition and being treated at a secure U.S. facility. He won't be able to come home immediately—but you'll speak with him soon."

The sentence had three promises tucked inside it: alive, treated, soon. The mind grabs the first two and wrestles the third. Jill filed soon beside doctor's lobbies and airport gates—rooms where time changes shape.

The room was frozen in disbelief.

"I wanted to tell you personally before this goes public. The U.S. Coast Guard will be making a statement shortly. But I needed to look you in the eyes and deliver this message first."

A staffer off-screen lifted a hand to slow a countdown that only screens can see. Someone in the West Wing breathed into a fist, willing the clock to linger on this room before it moved to the world.

There was silence—then Jill, through her tears, found her voice.

"Thank you," she said simply.

Ayla, Alex, and Ryan echoed her sentiment.

The President smiled slightly.

"I know you didn't vote for me," he said with a grin, "but I hope I earned a point or two tonight."

Jill gave a reluctant chuckle, still wiping tears from her cheeks.

"Please," the President added, "keep this conversation confidential. What Feyzi's been part of... it's larger than any of us. There are sensitive international implications that are still unfolding."

He ended the call with a final nod.

"Thank you for your husband's service to this country."

'Service' nested in Jill's ear and would not move. It was heavier than rescued, more deliberate than survivor. It carried rooms with no windows and corridors where badges buzzed doors open.

Only Jill caught the weight of that last sentence.

"Service?"

Her mind raced. What happened on that flight? What exactly was Feyzi involved in?

When the screen went black, she looked at her children and Ryan.

"We're not out of the woods yet," she said. "Let's stay quiet about this—for now."

Jill smoothed her short hair with both hands, then didn't recognize the gesture as her own. The hallway seemed longer, the carpet deeper. The living room's low murmur rose as if the house itself were asking a question. She answered it with six words that rearranged every person in the room.

Then, she turned to the hallway and walked back into the living room, where the muffled quiet had given way to anxious rustling. Whispers floated like smoke, subtle and speculative. A few hopeful glances turned toward her, eyes brimming with cautious optimism.

The hush in the room carried the weight of collective expectation, every heartbeat synchronized to the rhythm of her footsteps. The emotional current pulsed stronger than any words could convey where the rest of the family and OnePIN team waited in silent anticipation.

"He's alive and rescued," Jill said.

The room erupted.

Cheers. Cries. Hugs.

People clung to one another, laughing and weeping.

Laughter crashed into tears and back again. Someone dropped a phone and didn't pick it up. Two engineers from OnePIN hugged in a way they'd never hug at work, then stepped back embarrassed and hugged again. In the far corner, Heather, a neighbor, pressed her hands to her mouth and prayed with her eyes open.

Jill stayed grounded.

There was joy, yes. But uncertainty too.

She slipped her phone into her jeans' back pocket.

Any moment now... Feyzi might call.

The house discovered new units of time: a notification long, a spinner long, a glance-at-the-doorway long. The grandmother clock took to striking half-minutes Jill could hear in her bones. On the mantle, a school photo looked newer than it had that morning.

Fourteen Minutes Later

Satellite trucks exhaled generator breath. A traffic cop held a palm up to a river of late-morning cars and the river obeyed. Above the crowd, a camera operator stood on a milk crate like a lighthouse, swinging his lens through a sea of faces.

Commander Rebecca Alden stood at a podium, flanked by the seal of the U.S. Coast Guard and a wall of muted flags.

Alden's thumb tapped the inside of the podium once, twice, then stilled. No teleprompter. A single page. The corner folded not for place, but for courage. The wind picked up enough to lift a flag just shy of snapping.

The press conference buzzed with tension; camera shutters clicked in staccato bursts, reporters jostled for a clear view, and whispered speculations filled the air.

The morning sun glared off camera lenses, and the faint echo of helicopters overhead reminded everyone that this was more than a human-interest story—it was a national event.

Alden's posture was straight but tense, her eyes betraying the weight of what she was about to say.

She gripped the sides of the podium briefly before beginning, the silence that followed sharper than any shout in front of the U.S. Coast Guard Base in Boston. The press conference was being broadcast live on CNN, ABC, CBS, NBC, and every major network.

"This morning," Alden began, "we received a confirmed emergency beacon signal from Flight XT84. The message was traced to Mr. Feyzi Çelik, a passenger on board."

The crowd hushed.

Even from the dais you can hear it when a story lands; the hush that isn't silence; it's recalculation. Alden let it settle for half a breath, then proceeded, a captain steering into new water.

"At approximately 11:48 a.m. Eastern Time, U.S. Air Force pilots conducting reconnaissance with the USS *Porter*, USNS *Comfort*, and Coast Guard vessels USCGC *Escanaba* and USCGC *Tahoma*, located Mr. Çelik approximately 370 nautical miles northeast of Bermuda."

There were gasps in the press row.

"He was the sole survivor. There are, tragically, no other confirmed survivors from XT84 at this time."

The first rows bent over their notebooks as if the act could shield them from the sentence. A veteran reporter put his pen down and closed his eyes. A young producer mouthed, "oh my God," to no one.

Murmurs and the sound of frantic typing rippled through the press corps.

"Mr. Çelik was recovered alive but injured. His condition is stable. He is currently undergoing treatment at a secured U.S. military facility. He will remain under care until he is medically cleared for release."

There were other sentences on the page: the grid reference, the recovery timeline, the weather ceiling at dawn. Alden did not read them; she gave the country what it needed first: life, place, path.

Commander Alden paused.

"This is a miracle. And we ask the public to join us in praying for Mr. Çelik's full recovery."

When she stepped away, microphones leaned after her like hungry birds. Questions fired—How found? Why alone? Where now?—but the line held: investigation, ongoing, families first.

A lieutenant gathered the papers with hands that finally shook.

Back at the Çelik Residence

The entire room stared at the screen, tears streaming down faces, but joy finally breaking through the long night.

He was alive.

Relief arrived in ripples. Someone refilled the untouched tea glasses. Someone else texted I'm coming over and then remembered they were already here. In the hallway mirror, Jill saw a different woman; one whose face could hold joy and strategy at the same time.

But Jill couldn't shake the final thoughts that stirred in her heart:

Why wasn't he coming home? What condition was he in? What had he endured?

And just beneath that...

What did the President mean by service?

Why not discharge? Why a secure facility? Why the word 'service' when the man wore no uniform? Jill folded those doubts carefully and put them on a mental shelf next to spare linens; ready, reachable, not forgotten.

She would wait for Feyzi's call.

Something inside her whispered that the truth ahead wasn't simple—that beyond the joy of survival lay a story tangled in secrecy and consequence.

She felt it in her bones: this call would not just reunite them—it would change everything.

And this time, she would get the answers.

CHAPTER 24
Orders from the Top

Commander Rourke stood silently at his desk in Echo-7's command center, a spartan but high-tech room tucked deep within the facility's fortified walls. Holographic displays blinked on the surrounding walls, cycling through threat assessments and classified updates in pulsing amber light.

Echo-7 taught its people a new alphabet: amber for maybe, red for now, blue for breathe. The displays didn't scroll; they tided, information washing in and out, so eyes never drowned. A thin strip along the bulkhead pulsed to the heartbeat of the base—power draw, oxygen mixture, hull stress—an honest metronome that told you if the ocean outside was calm or considering you.

A low hum from nearby servers filled the air, mixing with the faint vibration of submarine currents echoing through reinforced metal floors. On the wall behind him hung a digital NATO insignia and a vintage photo of Rourke's own graduating class from Annapolis—faded, but proudly framed.

The servers weren't loud; they were present; a cat sleeping on a chest. Cooling flowed through floor grilles in a constant, body-temperature breeze. Somewhere beneath the deck, pumps murmured the sound of decision: open one valve, close another, keep a city alive in a cylinder of steel.

The room was dim, deliberately so, to keep personnel sharp and focused. Under the desk's soft under glow, the sealed envelope in Rourke's hand glinted faintly—a crimson Presidential Seal catching the ambient light like a quiet explosion. In Echo-7's command center, the weight of a single envelope pressing against his palm like a ten-ton slab.

Stamped with the Presidential Seal. Hand-delivered via encrypted channel from Admiral Michael Lansing.

He didn't open it right away.

The paper was heavier than it looked, embossed like it could bruise. Under the seal, a second watermark shimmered when he tilted it; the kind you only see in rooms where names grow smaller as the stakes get big. Rourke rubbed a thumb along the fold and felt the tooth of the stock.

Some orders arrive as pixels. The old ones arrive so you can feel them. He already knew what it was. Rourke exhaled and looked up.

"Get me Commander Hart. Now."

Moments later, Hart entered, her face tight with tension. Rourke met her eyes.

She clocked everything without moving her head: the folder's placement at a 45° angle, two chairs pulled a half-inch from the table (hasty, respectful), and the comms light over the door set to discreet green—privacy engaged, recording quarantined. A choice had been made elsewhere; here, they would make it real.

"We're going to see Commander Çelik," he said simply.

Hart's stomach dropped.

Her training kicked in—muscle tension, shallow breath, mental triage—but it didn't dull the dread rising in her chest. A memory surged forward, unbidden: the day she watched a colleague escorted from a black site, never to return.

Her fingers twitched near her thigh as if reaching for a sidearm out of instinct.

Her breath caught.

"This is it," she thought. "Quick orders are never good. They're going to erase him. And they want a witness."

Panic scratched the edge of her composure.

"I need to find a way to walk away from this," whispered to herself. But she didn't walk away.

They walked side by side down the hallway toward the temporary quarters where Feyzi had been resting.

Echo-7's spines ran in arcs, not right angles—curves that kept pressure honest and footsteps quiet. Bulkhead labels read like music: B-3 MED - B-3 COMM - B-4 WETLOCK. As they passed the wetlock, a bead of seawater crept along the gasket like mercury, then vanished back into the ocean's breath.

When they entered, Feyzi was lying flat on his back, beneath the sterile glow of recessed LED panels embedded in the low ceiling. The room smelled faintly of antiseptic and metallic air—standard-issue recycled ventilation in Echo-7's lower decks.

Some rooms have gravity; this one had vector. No curtains, no flowers; just purpose. A ceiling panel showed a false dawn to keep circadian rhythms from unraveling. On a side shelf: sterilized shears, a pressure band kit, two half-read printouts of drift models with tea rings on the corners. The monitor's tone was not a beep so much as a polite knock every second.

A soft monitor beeped rhythmically in the background, tethered to sensors at his temple and wrist. The sheets on his cot were taut and white, but a thin blanket had been pulled aside, revealing the outline of bruised ribs under his hospital-grade shirt.

He turned his head slowly as they entered, his eyes open, calm, almost expectant.

Rourke gave a short nod.

"Commander Çelik," he began—this time using the title deliberately. He held up the sealed folder and broke it open.

The use of "Commander Çelik" shifted the air by a degree. Rooms like this understand rank the way the sea understands depth; the word changed the buoyancy of everyone in it. Hart straightened because you always straighten for continuity; the kind that keeps ships pointed bow-first into weather.

"By Presidential Order," Rourke read aloud, "your honorary NATO commission is restored and reactivated, effective immediately."

The language was spare; rank restored, authority delegated, chain clarified. A separate slip bore a time hash and a two-word countersign only the issuing office knew, the verbal skeleton key Rourke could use if anyone topside tried to slow-walk compliance. This wasn't ceremony. It was clearance transposed into oxygen.

Feyzi didn't react. He simply stared, listening carefully.

"You've also been granted full operational authority to lead NATO coordination efforts regarding current events. You will be reporting directly to a joint U.S.–Turkish command center."

Rourke then handed Feyzi a secondary slip—a message personally forwarded from Ankara.

"The President of Türkiye extends full support and instructs you to proceed with full authority. Your judgment is trusted."

He paused.

"And I have been ordered to follow your lead."

Orders are wind; rooms are sails. The change tugged at everyone's posture. Hart felt an odd relief bloom behind her ribs; the sense that the base had been holding its breath and had finally decided what to be.

Hart gasped softly.

Feyzi sat up slowly. His body ached—each movement triggering a dull reminder of the crash—but his eyes were sharp, scanning the room with renewed focus.

He wore pain like a well-folded map—visible only when opened.

Pain wrote its footnotes along his side, but his gaze moved like a mapmaker: door, cams, drip rate, oxygen line, watch cap on the locker, Hart's stance (protective, forward), Rourke's thumb flattening the corner of the order (tension, ownership). He collected the room, then let the room collect him.

Beneath the calm exterior, his mind surged with questions, old instincts coming back online.

He pressed his hand lightly to his ribs and steadied his breath, his expression unreadable.

Disbelief and duty churned just beneath the surface, but he gave away nothing—except for the slight tightening of his jaw, a subtle tell that something deeper was stirring inside him.

"Thank you, Commander," Feyzi said quietly. "That escalated faster than I expected."

Rourke lowered his gaze.

"I want to apologize," he said. "For the confinement. For the silence. I was following orders. My duty is to protect this base at all costs. You were an unknown variable."

Echo-7 wasn't built for apologies; it was built for results. The apology arrived anyway and sounded like the one thing the base couldn't automate.

Hart watched Feyzi receive it with a nod that said we'll move faster if we forgive each other now. "I understand. If I were in your shoes, I would've done the same."

Hart, standing beside them, said nothing—but her thoughts were loud:

"No. He wouldn't have done the same. He wouldn't have followed stupid orders. That's exactly why he's here now—and why they need him."

She hadn't seen Feyzi's records—none of them had. His file had been locked away in levels of clearance she would never touch. But now, standing in the same room with him, she didn't need a dossier. Her instincts told her everything she needed to know.

This man radiated quiet authority, the kind that couldn't be faked.

More than that—her dolphins had brought him here. Not by accident. The genetically enhanced dolphins had trusted him, surrounded him, protected him. Creatures who could detect the subtlest irregularities in a human's neural and emotional patterns had chosen Feyzi. That trust meant more to her than any badge or rank.

The dolphins' logs read like poetry to Hart; click trains and signature whistles that put names to shapes. They had circled Feyzi with low-amplitude burst pulses, the acoustic equivalent of a hand on a shoulder. They had towed him only when his breathing pattern fell into cold-water danger. Animals don't do metaphors, she told herself. And yet.

For someone who had built her career on logic and control, she found herself doing something new: believing.

She felt an unexpected flush of pride. This chapter, the waiting and second-guessing, was finally closing.

But her mind couldn't let go of the puzzle:

"How did this move so quickly? How did the Presidents of the two most powerful NATO countries bypass military protocol and respond within hours? Who exactly was Feyzi Çelik?"

On B-2, the Ops Table accepted a new login that opened closed corridors on the tactical overlay. In Comms, a sat path reserved for contingencies woke and rolled three degrees to lock on a colder bird. In Supply, a warrant officer pulled a sealed pelican case he'd been told to forget and placed it by a lift with a sticky note: For CDR C. A place learns a name the way a harbor learns a hull shape.

Before the silence thickened, Feyzi leaned forward.

"I need to call home," he said. "Jill. Alex. Ayla. Ryan. They need to know I'm okay."

Rourke held up a cautioning hand.

"Fair warning: the public line is that you're being treated at a U.S. military hospital and recovering from surgery. It's true enough, and it

154

buys us time. So, keep your words simple. Ask your family to lay low. No media. No details. Everything you say may have ripple effects."

Feyzi nodded.

"Understood."

Covers work best when they borrow true pieces: a surgery that cleaned and set, a doctor's name that exists, a facility whose windows nobody outside ever sees. The story could survive daylight because it had bones—and bones survive.

Rourke stepped aside and handed him back his phone.

"Dial this number first. It'll route you through a secure, encrypted military satellite relay. Then, you can call Jill."

The number routed to a hardened gateway, split into redundant paths, then reassembled as a voice that would sound like it was next room. A tiny icon at the top of the screen—a symbol no consumer phone ever shows—told Feyzi a whole network had decided to pretend to be ordinary for him.

Feyzi took the phone with both hands, his grip firmer than expected, as though anchoring himself with its familiar weight.

For a beat, he hesitated—thumb hovering over the screen, breath shallow, heart pounding. The cold metal of the device bit against his palms, and he blinked hard to steady his vision.

His thumb hovered over the screen and found the small tremor he didn't feel in his chest. He remembered the sound of his kitchen, the weight of morning light on the table, the click of Jill's ring against a mug.

This wasn't just a call.

It was a lifeline.

A bridge back to the world that believed he was gone.

"Thank you," he said.

Commander Hart met his eyes.

"No," she replied. "Thank you, Commander."

Rourke stepped back a pace—not out of deference, but to clear the lane. Hart shifted to give the wall cam a cleaner profile—security and mercy in the same movement. Outside the door, someone pretended not to stand guard.

Above them, an operations strip-light flicked from amber to a steadier blue. It was cosmetic, meaningless to anyone who didn't live here. To Echo-7, it said what the envelope had said in older words: Orders received. Vector set. The ocean pressed its palm to the hull and waited.

Feyzi exhaled deeply and tapped the keypad.

He was calling home.

He pressed Call and felt the base itself seem to listen.

CHAPTER 25

The Press Conference

The news crowd outside the Çelik residence had grown into a full-blown media encampment. News vans idled up and down a quiet Hopkinton street, their satellite dishes scanning the sky in slow, mechanical arcs.

A yellow POLICE LINE ribbon sagged between mailbox posts like a tired smile. A town cruiser idled with its windows down, the officer inside timing the chaos by battery swap; every ninety minutes, new packs for cameras, new caffeine for crews. A drone hovered until a hand from the cruiser pointed it down. On the curb, a producer wrote "HOPKINTON, MA—LIVE" on a whiteboard with a squeaky marker, as if the street needed reminding it had become a proper noun.

The scent of gasoline and heated rubber clung to the humid air, mixing with the crisp tang of freshly mowed grass now trampled underfoot. Cameramen stepped over flowerbeds and crunched past ceramic lawn gnomes, their boots leaving muddy imprints on the meticulously cut 2.5-inch lawn—Feyzi's lawn.

A sprinkler head, still damp from the morning schedule, lay tilted and unmoored. A trampled hydrangea tilted its blue face skyward like a witness. Someone had dropped a lav mic windscreen in the grass—it looked like a small, gray bird that had forgotten how to fly.

Children's sidewalk chalk drawings had been scuffed away by tripod legs. The hum of generator engines and the murmur of impatient journalists filled the space where silence once reigned. Neighbors peeked nervously from drawn curtains, shaking their heads at the chaos. He would have hated this. His sanctuary now buzzed with camera clicks, shouted questions, and the electric tension of a waiting world.

Across the street, a teenager kept a tally in pencil on a ruled notebook—networks spotted, states represented, anchors recognized—until a parent pulled him away and gave the look that means enough. A runner slowed to a walk and pretended to stretch, counting seconds between live hits by the way a producer raised three fingers, then two, then pointed.

Laura Whitman, OnePIN's Vice President of Products and Marketing, was the designated spokesperson for both the family and the company. She stood just under 5'9" tall, with a graceful posture and intelligent brown eyes that scanned every detail with purpose. Her blond hair was pulled into a sleek chignon, and a discreet gold pendant glinted just above the lapel of her tailored navy suit.

With her MBA from Harvard Business School and a BS in Engineering from MIT, she was the team's Ivy League force—sharp, composed, and compassionate. She had once delivered keynote speeches at global tech forums and navigated crisis communications during product outages, but this moment was heavier than any boardroom pitch. This time, the stakes were personal.

She built a message map on a single page: Life (confirmed, stable), Loss (310 + 22), Thanks (rescuers, agencies), Ask (privacy). On a second page, she wrote the sentence she hoped she'd never need: Stop the feed. She tucked it behind the first like a spare parachute.

She had spent the last two hours working nonstop to prepare a public statement. She printed a copy and sat with Jill in the kitchen.

"You don't have to say anything," Laura said softly. "But the press won't stop. We need to give them something—otherwise they'll spin it all on their own."

Jill scanned the statement. She nodded once and whispered, "Do it."

Laura had rushed down from her home in Maine the moment she heard about Feyzi. She hadn't left Jill's side since. For nineteen years, she had worked with Feyzi across continents, late nights, and hard decisions. They built technology together. They built a company. She had followed his lead since the day they met. He was the kind of leader that people wanted to follow.

Laura could still hear his advice from a night long ago when a server cluster failed and the world felt tilted: We hold eye contact. We speak one sentence at a time. We never guess. She folded that memory and slid it into today like a steel bookmark.

Laura knew Jill wouldn't speak, not today. But her presence—and the presence of the family—would matter. It would humanize this story. It would reflect something bigger.

Jill stood just behind Laura, flanked by her children—Alex, Ayla, and Ryan. Jill wore a soft gray sweater over a white blouse, her face pale but composed, lips pressed tightly together. Alex stood tall in a dark blazer, trying to project strength though his eyes darted nervously between reporters. Ayla clutched Ryan's hand, her other arm wrapped protectively around her mother's waist, while Ryan held himself steady, shoulders squared.

They stepped onto the walkway as one, moving with quiet coordination, stopping behind a small podium hastily placed at the edge of the driveway. As the cameras clicked, the sight of them was striking: a strong Turkish American family, bonded by love, touched by tragedy, and holding on to hope. Their posture, expressions, and quiet dignity spoke louder than any words.

A handful of microphones wore station flags like bright teeth. A boom pole dipped and rose, searching for breath like a fishing rod for current. Somewhere behind the crowd, far away, a neighbor's wind chimes tried and failed to be heard over the generators' purr.

Laura waited for the crowd to quiet down. She looked calm but commanding—tall, poised, and resolute in a smart navy-blue blazer.

She placed her notes low, where only she could see them, and set her phone face down—the screen a dark square that could swallow focus. She touched the pendant at her throat, once, like pressing save on courage.

She took a breath, then began.

"Good afternoon, everyone. My name is Laura Whitman. I am the Vice President of Products and Marketing at OnePIN, and I have the honor of speaking today on behalf of the Çelik family and our entire company team.

"With me today are Jill Çelik, Feyzi's wife... their daughter Ayla, their son Alex, and Ayla's fiancé, Ryan.

"We are here today because of a tragedy that has shaken the world. Flight XT84, bound for Istanbul, disappeared over the Atlantic Ocean with 310 passengers and 22 crew members aboard. It is a moment of profound loss and sorrow.

"Before I say anything more, we ask that we all pause for a moment of silence in honor of every soul lost."

A long pause. Silence falls over the press corps.

The silence landed. The only sound was the tick of a camera's shutter as a reflex a photographer could not unlearn. The officer by the cruiser removed his hat without looking up. Someone on a live feed held a mic to nothing and let nothing speak.

"Thank you. Jill and her family know how incredibly fortunate they are to be among the few who have reason for hope tonight. They also know the weight of that hope."

Jill's left hand slid to the small of Ayla's back; Ayla leaned a half-inch closer without stepping. Alex kept his chin level the way men do when they're learning how to be watched. Ryan stood a half-step behind and to the side, the position of shield and witness.

"We have been informed that Feyzi Çelik has survived the crash. He is currently under medical care and is being monitored closely. The family has not yet spoken with him, but we've been told his injuries are not life-threatening. We are deeply thankful to the brave rescue teams and to the agencies coordinating this effort.

"But I want to be clear—Jill and her family understand what this moment represents. While they feel relief, they are also carrying grief—for every family who is still waiting for answers, and for the countless lives lost."

Journalists don't cry on duty; they change posture. Two did—shoulders rounding in the universal, human way that means heard. A producer made a slashing motion under her chin to kill a b-roll package: the words were enough.

"Feyzi will forever carry the weight of this tragedy with him. He survived, yes—but he will carry those souls on his shoulders for the rest of his life.

"At this time, we ask the public and media for one thing only: privacy. The Çelik family is still processing what has happened, and they need space to breathe, to grieve, and to heal.

"We will continue to provide updates as Feyzi progresses in his recovery. We know that the world is watching, and we are thankful for the outpouring of support from across the globe.

"On behalf of the family and our OnePIN team, thank you for your understanding, your compassion, and your respect."

Laura lifted her eyes from the page.

"No doorstep interviews. No calls to the schools. No footage through the windows."

She didn't raise her voice; she raised stakes.

"We're grateful. Please let the house be a house."

Laura stepped back.

No questions. No clarifications. The message was delivered with dignity—and finality.

The first shouted question never came. A microphone lowered, then another. The pause felt deliberate, almost ceremonial; like stepping back from a flag. Laura nodded once as if accepting a treaty signed without ink.

Her hands trembled slightly as they dropped to her sides, hidden from the cameras. She kept her posture firm, but inside, a wave of exhaustion and cautious pride swept through her. The weight of responsibility had been immense, and for a moment, as she met Jill's eyes, Laura allowed herself to feel it.

She had delivered the message with the strength Feyzi would've expected—and she hoped it would give the family room to breathe.

The crowd didn't cheer. They didn't shout.

Instead, they stood quietly, respectful. The Çelik family turned and walked back into the house, leaving a line of flashing cameras behind them. For now, that was all the world would hear.

As the family turned, a cameraman lifted his rig slightly—to make the frame lighter—and a correspondent squeezed a producer's shoulder: "Good." A satellite tech muted his feed and, for a second, the street became a street again.

Inside, Jill exhaled—a long, shaky breath that seemed to drain days of fear from her bones. She wasn't sure how long she'd been holding it, but the release came with an odd mixture of weight and relief.

The door latch gave a soft thunk, the kind a house makes when it has your back. Shoes came off with the small scrape of rubber on tile. On the console table, a stack of sympathy cards leaned like a snow drift in slow motion.

The silence in the house was different now, deeper, punctuated by the distant hum of a refrigerator and the muffled shuffle of feet in the hallway.

For the first time in days, the press was outside, and she was inside—alone with her thoughts. She looked around the room, eyes pausing on the empty couch, the half-drunk cup of tea still warm on the coffee table, and the framed photo of their last family vacation.

Somewhere, across a secure line, her husband was alive.

Upstairs, a charging cable glowed with a tiny, patient LED. On Jill's phone, the ringer slider sat at half, exactly where she'd left it when the calls became too much and too necessary at the same time. She turned it up one notch and slipped the phone into her back pocket—the posture of someone who wants good news to arrive as sound.

Not a rumor. Not a whisper. Alive.

And soon, she hoped, he would call.

The refrigerator hummed its low vow. A floorboard settled like a sigh. Through the window, the press lights dimmed two clicks for a top-of-the-hour reset. On the mantle, the family photo softened with dusk.

The house learned a new skill: holding hope without spilling it.

She needed to hear his voice—not just to know he was okay, but to be reminded that they were still tethered to the same world.

CHAPTER 26

The Call

Jill's back pocket buzzed.

She had been standing near the kitchen island, nervously fidgeting with a tea bag, the strings looping and unlooping between her fingers. The kitchen was quiet, bathed in soft morning light filtering through the blinds. A half-eaten piece of toast rested on a ceramic plate beside her, untouched.

The air smelled faintly of lemon dish soap and cinnamon from the tea box left open. The rhythmic hum of the refrigerator provided a background drone, punctuated by the distant murmur of reporters beyond the front lawn.

The whole kitchen seemed tuned to a single frequency. The pendulum clock over the living room wall swung like a metronome for nerves; the ice maker coughed once, then thought better of it. Outside, the media's murmur swelled and faded like tide over gravel. Inside, lemon and cinnamon braided the air into something that almost passed for calm.

Her bare feet shifted restlessly on the cool tile floor, grounding her against the tension that gripped the rest of the house. She tried to distract herself from the circus unfolding outside. The vibration was firm and deliberate—unmistakably different from any typical alert. She pulled the phone out, and the screen lit up:

Secure Government Line – Caller ID: Feyzi Çelik

It wasn't a ringtone so much as a tone of permission; three soft pulses, evenly spaced, followed by a small green shield where a name should be. Under it, a line read End-to-end session established. Jill could see her reflection in the glass: eyes too bright, jaw set, a woman rehearsing how to receive a life.

Her breath caught, and for a moment her world stopped spinning. A thousand thoughts raced through her mind—was this a final goodbye? Had something changed? Was he alive but broken beyond recognition? Was it really him? What if it wasn't? What if it was someone else calling on his behalf? Her hands trembled, the screen seeming to pulse with the weight of it all.

Her heart stopped.

Then raced.

Her fingers trembled slightly.

She stared at the screen for a beat too long.

Should she turn on the camera? What condition would he be in? Was he bandaged? Broken? Was this a goodbye?

She pulled herself together, took a steadying breath, and pressed the green button.

For a half second the screen showed geometric snow—blocks aligning, lines interlacing—then the picture opened like a curtain. A tiny padlock icon waited in the corner, then dissolved.

Somewhere under the ocean, a switch decided they were allowed to be human for a few minutes.

The screen flickered.

And there he was.

Feyzi.

Alive.

Looking back at her.

His familiar face appeared—rugged and warm, still the same sharp cheekbones, the salt-and-pepper hair perfectly tousled as always, darker with deep streaks of gray on the sides. He looked tired, yes, but clear-eyed.

Strong.

Alive.

Handsome as ever.

He wore a dark navy-blue uniform, the fabric crisp and official, with the unmistakable Echo-7 insignia over his heart.

Behind him, a soft-status strip glowed along the baseboard: oxygen 21.0, hull load nominal, comms green. On a side console, a ceramic mug sat on a fiber pad that kept tea at not quite hot—the temperature of long conversations. A folded gray blanket rested on the bunk, square corners like a promise he meant to keep.

For a split second, Jill's breath caught again—this time not out of fear, but out of awe. Seeing him like that, formal and sanctioned by a world she hadn't yet understood, made her realize how much more was at stake.

He wasn't just her husband anymore. He was something larger.

Something seen now by governments and commanders as essential. It stirred something unfamiliar in her: pride mixed with dread. His role had changed—and perhaps, so had their future.

Behind him was a simple yet futuristic room; sterile but comfortable. The walls were matte gray, embedded with silent air filtration vents. Sleek, recessed lighting cast a soft halo over polished aluminum surfaces. A transparent screen floated in one corner, blinking softly with data lines and infrared schematics, some kind of operations command system.

"Hi, love," he said gently.

Jill choked on her first words, trying not to cry. She managed a smile that crumpled almost immediately.

"You made it. You always make it."

He nodded slowly, then exhaled.

"I almost didn't."

He leaned forward slightly.

"I think I was ejected. My seat detached from the fuselage just before the plane hit the surface. I must have been knocked out on

166

impact—don't remember anything for a while after that. But I think the seat absorbed most of the force. It saved my life."

His eyes flicked sideways, the way they do when a moment reels in unbidden: the belt pyros popping, a white flower of foam where ocean met metal, the sudden quiet that feels like space.

He didn't describe it. He didn't have to. The silence between sentences held what words shouldn't carry.

Jill wiped her cheek. "Where are you?"

"I'm in a secure U.S. base. I can't say more about the location, but... it's safe. Very safe. The Navy has me covered. There are some... complications."

He chose his words like stepping stones across a fast river. Jill heard what wasn't said: classification, timelines, names she wouldn't be given. And yet his voice never drifted. It lived on the safe bank and invited her to stand with him.

Her eyes narrowed.

"There's strong evidence this wasn't an accident. Other foreign governments were involved," he continued. "I don't have all the answers yet, but I promise you—I'll help them find out what really happened. For the innocent people we lost. They deserve justice."

"Will you be in danger?" she asked, her voice tightening.

Feyzi looked directly into the camera, steady as stone.

"Jill, I am in one of the most secure locations on planet Earth. Literally. Nothing's going to happen to me here. I promise."

The camera picked the light out of the Echo-7 pin and threw a small star across his chest. Jill watched that gleam as if it were the second hand on a clock, proof that time still moved forward and not only down.

He held her gaze. That was the moment she fully believed it. Not because he said it. But because it was him.

"Can I talk to the kids?"

Jill nodded instantly, turning her head.

"Alex! Ayla! Ryan! It's Dad!"

They came running—Ayla was first, skidding slightly on the hard-wood floor as she turned the corner, her hand catching the edge of the doorway. Alex followed close behind, wide-eyed and breathless, nearly bumping into her. Ryan trailed a beat later, dropping the TV remote onto the couch in his rush. Their footsteps pounded like heartbeats echoing off the walls.

Ayla's sock slid on the hardwood, a laugh hiccupping through tears as she caught herself; Alex's shoulder brushed the doorway and he apologized to it, to the house, to fate; Ryan's phone hit the couch and bounced once like a joyful heartbeat. They crowded the frame the way people crowd lifeboats—not from fear, but from instinct.

No one spoke at first—they simply froze, as if the screen had turned them to stone. Then came a collective exhale, a tearful gasp, and the sudden rush to the screen, crowding together without a second thought, shoulder to shoulder, each of them desperate to take in the face they feared they'd never see again.

Ryan quickly mirrored the call onto the Sony TV, and within seconds, the family filled the room—Jill, Alex, Ayla, and Ryan—all squeezed onto the couch, facing the screen, hands touching, hearts bursting.

On the big screen, pixels gave up trying to be technology and surrendered to being face. Jill adjusted the throw pillow under her knee; Ayla tucked a strand of hair behind her ear and left it there, forgetting. Alex took a breath he didn't realize he'd been holding since last night and let it out like a benediction.

One by one, they spoke to Feyzi.

Alex, ever the quiet one, smiled with misty eyes and simply said, "I knew you'd survive."

Ayla couldn't stop crying. She didn't even speak at first—just placed her hand on the screen and whispered, "We love you."

Feyzi's mouth shifted at the corners, a smile learned in harsher rooms. "Ben de sizi." He didn't translate. He didn't need to. The living room filled with understood.

Then he turned serious.

"I'll be away for a while. This stays confidential. Everything we said. Don't share it, not even with friends. There's more going on than I can explain right now. But I promise—I'll call daily. Every evening, same time."

Jill nodded once—we know how to be quiet—and reached for a small notebook she kept for impossible days. She wrote three words and underlined them: alive, secure, later. Alex lifted his chin: "We'll run interference." Ayla pressed her palm flat on the coffee table: "We can do hard things." Ryan said nothing and locked down the Wi-Fi guest network without looking.

They all nodded. They had been raised this way.

Privacy.

Loyalty.

Trust.

When the call ended, Jill stepped away from the group, her phone still warm in her hand.

Jill stood by the sink and let the sun stripe through the blinds warm the back of her hand. She wasn't eavesdropping; she was holding the house; turning the kettle, straightening a coaster, making space for a second miracle in one morning.

Parents

There was one more call that needed to be made.

Feyzi. To his parents.

Feyzi stared at the blank screen for a long moment, his thumb hovering over the dial button. The adrenaline from speaking with Jill and the kids had worn off, leaving behind a raw ache in his chest. He thought of his mother's voice, warm and fragile—his father's quiet strength. What would they say? How would they react? Would they sense the strain in his voice, the weight of secrets he couldn't yet share?

He scrolled to Anne and Baba and waited for the ship of courage to dock. The room behind him hummed in its quiet way. A pulse on the status strip crept one notch and back again. He pressed call and let the ocean carry the sound.

He hesitated—not from fear, but from the wish to shield them a moment longer. But that moment had passed. They deserved to know.

With a quiet inhale and a steadying exhale, he tapped the number.

From the secure room, he dialed his mother and father in Ankara. The connection crackled once, then steadied.

A lace curtain moved in a breeze from a window just out of frame. A wall clock with a calligraphic numeral 12 ticked louder than physics should allow. His mother's eyes gathered tears the way air gathers light; his father's jaw did what jaws do when the world reorders itself and men must let it.

His mother answered, her voice breaking the moment she saw his face. His father, silent beside her, wiped tears away with a trembling hand.

"Anne... Baba... I'm okay."

That was all they needed.

His mother touched the screen with two fingers, then her heart— old superstition, new technology—and kissed the air. His father tried to say "çok şükür" and only the second word emerged. Across the world, time closed its parasol and let them stand in the same weather.

Across continents, a family was whole again—though oceans apart and still tethered to shadows of uncertainty. Feyzi placed a hand gently over his heart, exhaling as his parents smiled through tears.

Massachusetts

Jill, back in Massachusetts, clutched the phone to her chest, eyes closed, whispering a silent thank you to the universe. In these quiet, fragile gestures, their hearts aligned across time zones—unspoken truths binding them together.

She set the phone down face-up beside the toast now gone cold, the tea bag steeped to amber resolve. On her phone screen was a grocery list that suddenly felt like a contract with normal life: milk, eggs, batteries, hope.

But for the first time in days… there was peace.

And hope.

Outside, news trucks dimmed their mast lights one notch. Somewhere in the house a floorboard remembered how to creak like a floorboard and not an omen.

In the Echo-7 room, Feyzi closed his eyes for six counted breaths, then opened them to a workstation that had waited patiently for the man to return to the work.

CHAPTER 27

Echo-7 Team

Echo-7, Atlantic Ocean
Classified Location – 600 feet below sea level

Feyzi sat across from Commander Hart and Commander Rourke in the Command Briefing Room, a circular chamber ringed with high-resolution tactical displays and ceiling-mounted projectors.

The walls pulsed faintly with LED status indicators—green for now, but ready to turn crimson at the first sign of a threat. A world map glowed on the far wall, dotted with moving icons representing naval assets, while beneath their feet, the subtle vibration of the ocean-fed generators reminded them how deep they were below the surface.

A digital table in the center displayed real-time data streams— encrypted message logs, sonar traces, and a synchronized feed of Echo-7's internal systems. Overhead, soft recessed lighting cast a sterile glow, giving the room a sense of eerie calm beneath the storm of rising tensions.

Though he trusted Hart, Feyzi's eyes lingered on Rourke, evaluating the man not just by rank or decorum, but by the subtle cues of judgment and instinct. Something about Rourke's mechanical precision and unreadable expression made Feyzi wary. It reminded him of senior intelligence officers he had once briefed decades ago—men who followed protocol to the letter but missed the soul of the mission.

Rourke was respected, yes. But instinct? Instinct required deviation, and Feyzi wasn't yet sure if this commander knew when to break the rules. This installation didn't need a rule-follower—it needed someone who could see beyond them. Echo-7 wasn't just any installation. It was a covert hub at the heart of a shifting global storm.

"I want a full division briefing," Feyzi said.

"Everyone who leads a key operation on this base. Special Forces, submarine command, SEVs, ARES, marine ops, Space Command, cybersecurity—everyone."

Hart stood without hesitation. "I'll gather them immediately."

Rourke shifted uncomfortably in his seat.

Feyzi turned to him.

"While she's preparing the team, walk me through the Black Hawk."

Rourke exhaled. "At 0417 hours Zulu," Rourke began, tapping a series of keys on the console, "the Black Hawk UH-60, call sign Nightshade, carrying 11 software engineers and 4 crew, lost contact with operations command."

The screen behind him flickered, displaying the chopper's flight path—its green traceline ending abruptly in a red 'X'.

"They were en route from Naval Air Station Lajes, Azores—our nearest above-surface logistics support base—to Echo-7. The chopper was bringing sealed software payloads for the final phase of Project ARES integration."

Feyzi stared at the screen, his body frozen. He'd met some of those engineers in the past—bright minds, idealistic, often working late into the night. Faces now blurred by memory flashed before his eyes.

He clenched his jaw. "Do we have names?" he asked quietly.

Rourke hesitated. "We do. I'll share them privately."

Feyzi nodded slowly, pushing down the wave of guilt that tightened in his chest.

"They didn't stand a chance, did they?" he asked, voice tight.

"No," Rourke said.

"Telemetry cut off right here—over Echo-7. Exact same time XT84 vanished from civilian radar. We think the Black Hawk was hit first. Whatever happened—airborne or orbital—it was synchronized."

He tapped a console. A map appeared, showing a flight path overlay, then a blinking red mark.

"And the safe?" Feyzi asked.

Rourke nodded.

"Waterproof, biometric lock, titanium casing. It went down with the chopper. We believe it's lying at roughly 2500 meters, south-southeast of the base."

Just then, Hart reentered.

"They're ready in the main briefing room," she said. "All section leaders present."

Echo-7 Command Briefing Room

Feyzi stepped into the room, pausing just past the threshold. The Echo-7 Command Briefing Room was a marvel of military engineering—half subterranean fortress, half space-age nerve center.

LED-backlit maps of the Atlantic rim curled across the digital display walls, while biometric authentication terminals blinked softly at each workstation.

The light was cool, almost bluish, casting sharp silhouettes along the angular command desks. A subtle hum of filtered air and distant sonar pings gave the impression of being aboard a deep-space vessel rather than a naval installation.

A full ring of high-ranking officers stood at attention, flanking the perimeter. Their stances were disciplined, though several exchanged subtle glances—curiosity, skepticism, perhaps even relief. Some stood rigid in their pressed uniforms, while others shifted slightly, betraying the strain of long shifts and growing uncertainty.

At the head of the room, Commander Hart raised her voice. stood at attention.

"Everyone, this is Commander Feyzi Çelik. Survivor of XT84. Effective immediately, he is assigned supreme operational command of Echo-7 by direct Presidential order, under joint NATO U.S.–Turkish authority. Commander Çelik was a key figure in a high-impact NATO operation thirty years ago and has now been reactivated."

Feyzi scanned the room as Hart led introductions by starting with herself:

"Commander Rebecca Hart, Head of Marine Biology & Rescue Operations"

"Commander Grant Rourke, Director, Echo-7, Naval Tactical Operations"

"Captain Joshua E. Monroe, Commanding Officer, USS *Missouri*, Virginia-class nuclear submarine"

"Major Arman Reyes, Director, Special Forces Detachment Echo"

"Dr. Sienna Patel, Chief of Project ARES (AI & Robotics Enhanced Strategy)"

"Lieutenant Commander Sofia Barrera, Director of SEVs or Subaquatic Environmental Vectors"

"Colonel Jacob S. Vance, Space Command Liaison, Orbital Threats & Surveillance"

"Chief Warrant Officer Lena Morano, Head of Cybersecurity & Comms Integrity, Echo-7"

The ring of officers held, but the room itself seemed to lean in. Echo-7's ventilation hushed to a low hymn. Somewhere below, the pool clicked with distant dolphin chatter—like rain on metal from another world.

Feyzi didn't fill the silence. He measured it.

"Before we move," he said, "I need five seconds from each of you—your real edge, not your résumé."

They went clockwise.

"Monroe," the submarine captain said. "I can hold a nuke boat on a thermal seam for twelve hours without a whisper. Your ghost shows up, I'll be the shadow behind it."

"Reyes," the Special Forces major said. "We break locks no one admits exist."

"Patel," the ARES chief said, almost reluctant. "My machine doesn't guess. It narrows futures."

"Barrera," the SEV director said. "I put steel where lungs can't go."

"Vance," the Space Command colonel said. "I make orbits confess."

"Morano," the warrant officer said. "If the leak breathes, I'll hear its lungs."

Hart didn't add a tag line; she simply met Feyzi's eyes. The message was clear: You lead. I'll help the room follow.

Rourke's jaw flexed once, a tell that he heard the shift in gravity and didn't like it. That was fine. War rooms don't need unanimity. They need velocity.

Feyzi nodded. "Then let's earn the hours we don't have." Feyzi stepped forward.

"We are now operating under wartime conditions," Feyzi began, his voice calm but weighted with the gravity of what was coming.

His mind flashed to the classified Gulf simulation briefings he'd helped construct three decades earlier—back when scenarios like this were theoretical, hypothetical exercises sketched on war room whiteboards. Not anymore.

He glanced across the room, noting the posture of each officer—some with arms clasped behind backs, others with crossed arms and furrowed brows. A few exchanged looks, their eyes flickering with unease.

No one interrupted.

Feyzi took a step forward. "We don't have the luxury of diplomacy or delay. This team—this room—is the firewall between global escalation and containment," he began.

"This team will determine the outcome of a global confrontation in its opening phase. The world doesn't know it yet—but the war has already started."

He let the weight settle in the room.

"I do not believe in coincidences. XT84 and the Black Hawk were targeted within the same three-minute window. I was meant to die. And now, I know why."

He tapped the control console. A map of global energy transit routes appeared behind him.

"Thirty years ago, after the Gulf War, a covert U.S.–Turkish operation reshaped oil chokepoints between the Persian Gulf and Southeast Asia. That maneuver secured U.S. naval leverage over energy corridors. China's navy grew in size—but not endurance. Gas turbines. Non-nuclear carriers. Limited reach."

He pointed to Taiwan on the map.

"The Seventh Fleet—led by the USS *George Washington*—patrols the Philippine Sea. China needs a way to neutralize American reach without firing a single shot. They've partnered with Russia and built something we never expected."

He walked to the center of the room.

"I believe they created a stealth submarine, likely a Type 096-R with Shihè cloaking tech. After the XT84 crash, I could feel it in the water. So did the dolphins."

"I'm not a career soldier—I'm a tech CEO. I solve problems. But I can't do this alone."

He looked each person in the eye.

"This is a team effort. I trust you. And I'm asking you to trust me. We're not fighting for medals. We're fighting for our children's future."

Commander Hart stood quietly and thought:

"This is why he's always on the winning side."

Mission Directive
Immediate Operational Priorities

Feyzi clicked the digital control. A tactical schematic appeared.

Mission 1: Internal Compromise – Echo-7

"Our communications—both encrypted and open—are being intercepted. There is foreign spyware in our systems. First objective: isolate, trace, and neutralize the leak from within Echo-7. Assume nothing. Verify everything."

As Feyzi finished, Chief Warrant Officer Lena Morano tensed slightly. Her fingers hovered over a tablet as red diagnostic overlays flickered to life behind her.

One screen pulsed with blinking lines of code—unusual traffic patterns feeding from auxiliary uplinks.

The room dimmed briefly as Hart keyed in a local lockdown protocol. An uneasy murmur passed among the officers.

Morano pinched open a capture on the wall-screen: a ribbon of traffic, all green until one slender thread fractured into off-timing bursts.

"Aux uplink Charlie-4 is clean," she said, "but the timing gate is wrong by 21 microseconds. That's not drift; that's mimicry."

"A tap?" Hart asked.

"Worse. Glasslark." Morano's tone went flat. "It forges silence. Px-level beacon that rides the ACKs on internal service calls, then stutters at the thermocline seam in our cable trunk to look like ocean noise."

"How long?" Feyzi asked.

"Long enough to learn us," she said.

"Not long enough to reach greed. It's still sampling."

"Cut it," Rourke said.

"Not yet," Feyzi answered.

"Starve it first. Re-route noncritical services to air-gapped edge nodes. Kill DNS hints. Swap MAC tables every ninety seconds. I want it hungry and visible."

Morano's fingers flicked. The room lights dimmed a shade as nonessential systems slipped to manual. ARES threw a faint amber crescent against the glass, then recalibrated; quiet, curious.

"Also," Feyzi added, "no personal wearables, no passive badges, no idle Bluetooth anywhere on this deck. If it can handshake, it can hemorrhage."

A half-dozen officers patted at pockets like people suddenly remembering old sins. Hart was already collecting devices in a steel tray.

"White Static is live," Morano said. "If it's inside our walls, it just discovered it's alone."

Mission 2: Spy at Lajes Air Base

"The Black Hawk departed from Naval Air Station Lajes in the Azores. There's a mole on that base. Someone coordinated departure timing and altitude to align XT84 and the Black Hawk. Counterintelligence must begin immediately."

Colonel Vance's brow furrowed. "That's a NATO-aligned station," he muttered under his breath. His arms crossed reflexively, as if bracing for political fallout.

In the meantime, a NATO counterintelligence cell worked under red lights; photos hung with magnets on a portable whiteboard. Fuel bowser logs. Catering times. A clipboard in a mechanic's fist. So ordinary it hurt.

"Find the human cadence," the lead investigator said. "Movements that made sense for a day but not for a minute."

A junior analyst circled a code in blue: a maintenance flag that didn't match the aircraft tail's service cadence. The same anomaly had appeared two hours earlier on a stateside Army diagnostic server, then vanished. Two continents. One hand.

"Mirror accounts," the lead said. "Or a ghost with keys."

Mission 3: Air Turkey Security Breach

"XT84's Boston departure clearance was manipulated. A traitor was involved. Turkish intelligence must investigate flight logs and internal communications. This was a coordinated strike."

Commander Hart's jaw tightened.

She glanced at Feyzi, remembering how the dolphins had circled him right after he reached the surface.

"He was marked," she whispered to herself.

In parallel, three Turkish cyber officers replayed the departure window frame by frame. An innocuous SMS to a ramp supervisor appeared for exactly four seconds, then rewound itself out of the archive like a magician reclaiming a card.

"Not deletion," the youngest officer said, stunned.

"Preclusion. The log believes it never saw it."

"Which means," her chief said, "they tested this on us before today. We were a rehearsal. And someone told them we passed."

She tapped the table.

The lights over Istanbul's map hardened into a grid.

"Pull analog backups. Handwritten. Radios. Eyes. We reassemble a story they couldn't eat."

Mission 4: Enemy Stealth Submarine

"A stealth submarine, likely Russian-built with Chinese enhancements, is operating near us. This is no longer theory. They destroyed the Black Hawk. We must locate and destroy it."

Captain Monroe's hand instinctively went to the data feed on his wrist monitor.

"USS *Missouri* is ready for pursuit," he said, his voice low but resolute.

Captain Monroe lifted his wrist display and painted an invisible box over the Atlantic rendered on the far wall.

"Type 096-R with exotic cladding, as Commander suggests, gives us one chance," he said. "They can't cheat buoyancy or heat forever. They'll hide in a density step or ride our prop wash."

He glanced at Hart. "Can your team stitch a mammal net across grid Juliet-Four?"

Hart nodded. "We'll run a counter-singing pattern—misleading applause. They'll push the target off its favorite seam."

"Good," Monroe said. "I'll drag a false wake at three knots and invite our guest to follow the wrong whale."

Rourke folded his arms. "And if we spook it?"

Monroe didn't blink. "Then it makes a mistake. Mistakes make echoes."

Mission 5: Orbital Laser Weapon Platform

"XT84 wasn't downed by a bomb or missile. It was sliced—cleanly—by a satellite-based laser. I saw the light. We must identify, track, and eliminate this weapon before it strikes again."

Colonel Vance keyed in a new orbital telemetry scan.

Above him, the schematic updated with a glowing red arc labeled UNKNOWN ORBITAL SIGNATURE.

He looked up and locked eyes with Feyzi.

"That explains the ion burn traces we logged earlier."

Vance pulled up an orbit stack ARES had already tasted: sun-synchronous birds, commercial swarms, defense birds that don't officially exist. He slashed all the obvious suspects and let the residue hang like dust motes in a church.

"We're not looking for a satellite," he said. "We're looking for a pass-through. A bus with a rental payload; laser package hot-swapped at perigee, fired once, then handed off."

Dr. Patel frowned. "Power budget?"

"Borrowed," Vance replied. "Induction from a visiting tanker in high inclination, then bled through a rapid-discharge lens. One cut. No plume. The signature looks like the ionosphere got embarrassed."

ARES drew a thin red thread across the dome. A timing window. Short. Precise. Mean.

Feyzi's eyes hardened. "Name it."

Vance hesitated. "Working codename only. Kazuar."

The word hung, cold and efficient.

"Then we break the perch," Feyzi said.

"Spoof its star trackers. Feed it a sky it can't navigate."

Patel was already there.

"ARES can forge a celestial lattice and project it through our up-link masts and partner dishes. It'll see a sky offset by arcseconds. It will miss its own mirror."

"Good," Feyzi said.

"Make it blind without telling it why."

Mission 6: Deep Recovery

"The ARES modules are still sealed in a safe onboard the Black Hawk. Once the area is secure, SEV teams will retrieve the safe. That software is our technological edge."

Lt. Commander Barrera gave a sharp nod.

"My SEVs are already calibrated for the dive. We'll be ready at first light."

Lieutenant Commander Barrera walked the line of eleven SEVs; matte-bodied, jointed like patient predators. Engineers laced fiber bundles along collar rings; electrolytic packs slid home with a muted thunk.

"Dives two by two," Barrera said. "SEV-4 and -7 lead; -3 and -9 trail. We maintain a triangle around the safe. If the enemy nudged it, there'll be a pressure bruise on the silt."

A tech raised a hand.

"Currents at depth are messy. You'll get salt ghosts."

Barrera smiled thinly.

"That's why we brought our own ghosts."

She tapped the deck twice.

Two dolphins answered from the adjacent channel with low, rolling clicks—ready.

Human.

Machine.

Mammal.

One team.

Mission 7: ARES Deployment Fleetwide

"Once retrieved and finalized, ARES must be deployed across our fleet—subs, carriers, and destroyers. It is our decisive counter to stealth threats."

Dr. Sienna Patel's eyes lit up, but her expression quickly sobered.

"We were days from completing simulation testing. I'll lead the integration effort personally. I will need a high caliber software engineering team."

Patel keyed a sequence and opened the isolation bridge. The room smelled like new snow and copper. In the windowed slab sat ARES' cognitive edge; an array that didn't look like a brain and thought better because of it.

"Fleetwide deployment is not a push," she said. "It's an adoption. We teach each ship's systems to request the right slice instead of swallowing the core."

"Fine," Feyzi said.

Feyzi paused. The room remained frozen in silence, broken only by the rhythmic blink of the mission schematic and the soft hiss of the pressurized vents overhead.

Then Feyzi added, firmly:

"Effective immediately—no electronic communication enters or exits this base until Mission 1 is complete. Every line of code, every device, every node will be verified."

He turned to Commander Hart. "We begin now."

Hart stepped close enough that he could hear the whisper of neoprene against fabric.

"You need buy-in," she said softly. "Not compliance."

Feyzi glanced at the ring of faces—skepticism, curiosity, loyalty at different temperatures. He touched the console. The map blinked out. What remained was the room: thirty people, one air, one purpose.

"Echo-7," he said, quieter than the machines, "we'll bleed for the right reason or not at all. So, here's the promise: I won't waste you. I won't lie to you. And when this ends, I will carry the blame if we're wrong."

He lifted two fingers.

Hart mirrored the gesture.

Reyes, then Monroe, then Patel followed, an improvised oath that didn't need a name.

From somewhere beneath their feet, a dolphin answered with a clean, rising whistle. It sounded like agreement.

Rourke didn't move for a long heartbeat. Then, slowly, he raised his hand, too.

The room exhaled.

"Now," Feyzi said, voice steady, "let's make the ocean tell the truth."

CHAPTER 28

The First Breach

Echo-7 Cyber Command Center

Warrant Officer Lena Morano stood behind a wall of transparent holographic displays, the cold hum of electromagnetic shielding brushing past her ears like a subtle electric breeze.

Her boots were planted on carbon-fiber flooring etched with fiber-optic sensor nodes, which glowed faintly beneath the layered glass. The temperature was a steady 62 degrees Fahrenheit, engineered to preserve processor efficiency, and the air carried a faint, sterile bite—part ozone, part machine oil.

Reflections from cascading code snippets shimmered across her visor as her eyes darted between diagnostics and threat matrices. She stood upright, shoulders squared, her posture honed from years of midnight breach drills and code red alerts that never made the headlines. The room pulsed in dim, cool blue—every surface designed for signal shielding and zero RF interference.

"Confirming anomalous outbounds from Node G-12," she called out. "Data bursts every 37 minutes, each using onion-layered encryption with embedded quantum key hopping."

Lieutenant Bryce, her deputy, turned—his tone focused, but his expression bore a trace of admiration. He and Morano had worked together through three prior breach alerts, each forging a rhythm between their roles.

Bryce, with his knack for tracing rogue telemetry patterns, now stood slightly behind her, his trust implicit but his curiosity piqued.

"All telemetry routes point to the SEV logistics subnet," he said.

"Maintenance routines... or something mimicking them."

Morano narrowed her eyes.

"SEV-07. A maintenance drone assigned to bay three. That unit hasn't run a deep-sea mission in four days. Why is it pinging telemetry headers with 256-bit asymmetric encryption?"

She touched a panel, zooming in on the signal trail—and froze.

"It's beaconing," she said quietly.

"To a passive relay buoy outside our security perimeter. This is how they've been listening."

Echo-7 Command Center Briefing

Feyzi stood with Commander Hart and Commander Rourke, Morano's findings now displayed in full behind them.

"We believe the buoy is located approximately 3.4 kilometers southeast of Echo-7," Morano explained.

"Depth: 160 meters. Camouflaged and likely pressure resistant. It's intercepting compressed intelligence leaks and transmitting them via deep-sea burst modems."

"Which SEV drone was compromised?" Feyzi asked.

"SEV-07. Tampered firmware. Likely at the hardware supplier level. Shenzhen subcontractor."

She looked up. "That buoy has a direct line to whoever attacked XT84."

Commander Hart turned to Feyzi.

"I'll take a retrieval team. I want that buoy out of the water before our next data cycle."

Feyzi shook his head, then smiled.

"You'll have company. I'm coming with you."

Hart blinked.

"Commander—with respect, we're 600 feet down and heading deeper."

A flicker of memory flashed through her—those haunting hours when the XT84 alert came in, when her dolphins insisted on diving toward a signal she couldn't explain. She had trusted them, and they'd led her to him.

That same instinct told her now—this man belonged.

Her protective instincts clashed with her discipline, but beneath it all was a rising conviction: Feyzi Çelik wasn't just another mission variable. He was a fulcrum. And maybe, just maybe, she had been waiting for someone like him. This isn't a press event.

"Exactly. Which is why I need the team to see that I'm not giving orders from behind reinforced glass. I was rescued by Echo-D3. I want them to see me as one of them."

Rourke hesitated, then gave a silent nod.

Echo-7 SEV Bay

Inside the prep chamber, two elite divers joined Hart and Feyzi. Their names—Chief Diver Anika Zhao and Petty Officer Marco Torres—were stitched into the graphite-black exosuits that shimmered under the prep bay's sterile overhead lights.

The suits, a marvel of engineering, felt like second skin, molded from graphene-infused smart polymers that flexed with breath and thought. Internal heat-regulating membranes adjusted to body temperature while advanced haptic sensors delivered tactile feedback even through pressurized gloves.

Zhao, quiet but surgical in her precision, checked over her HUD systems with the calm demeanor of someone who'd logged over 400 dives. Torres, broader and more expressive, gave Feyzi a respectful nod, his mirrored visor temporarily retracted to reveal a short beard and a streak of confidence.

The chamber smelled faintly of disinfectant and ocean salt, and the low hiss of air scrubbers filled the silence between suit diagnostics and last-minute checks. Around them, diagnostic panels blinked amber-to-green, confirming oxygen levels, pressure equalization, and encrypted mission telemetry links.

They were clad in next-gen exosuits: graphene-infused smart polymers with reactive buoyancy control, heat-regulating membranes, and advanced haptic response layers. Their HUD visors displayed oxygen metrics, sonar overlays, and encrypted tactical readouts in real time.

Feyzi slid on the helmet and tightened the seal. Hart stepped into her suit with seamless confidence.

"You ever dive in one of these?" she asked.

"First time," Feyzi replied. "But I learn fast."

They entered the pressurization tube, dolphins from Echo-D3 pod swimming just beyond the reinforced glass.

One of them—the leader who had circled Feyzi during the XT84 rescue—approached and hovered. It clicked gently against the glass.

"That one remembers you," Hart smiled.

"She's waiting for you to prove you belong."

The hatch opened.

Underwater Mission Zone
Southeast Quadrant T

They dropped into the dark, swallowed by an abyssal world where sunlight had never reached. A pressure shift coiled around their suits like an invisible serpent, while tiny bioluminescent organisms blinked past in erratic patterns—fireflies of the deep. Echoes from their sonar pings danced across jagged stone formations and dense kelp forests drifting like ancient sentinels.

Water pressed against their bodies like cold steel, and every exhale felt amplified by the gravity of their mission. Feyzi's ears rang slightly, not from the descent—but from the sheer magnitude of what they were about to recover.

He glanced at Hart, who glided ahead with practiced fluidity, her silhouette merging with the ghostly flashes of marine light. Even through his visor, he could feel the tension—adrenaline, purpose, and the unspoken understanding that they were not alone in the deep.

Sonar pings illuminated the ocean in ghostly monochrome bursts. The buoy's estimated location appeared as a blinking marker on their HUDs.

Hart took point, Feyzi followed, and the divers flanked them. The dolphins flitted alongside like spectral guardians.

"Visibility at 60 meters. Watch the thermocline," Hart said over encrypted comms.

Feyzi could feel it—a low hum beneath the sea's silence. Not sonar. Not propulsion. But something...

"Contact," one diver called out.

"Buoy in visual. Anchored to rocky outcrop. Confirming relay dish... blinking infrared. It's active."

As they approached, the lead dolphin let out a high-pitched warning trill.

Hart immediately scanned left.

"Movement. Bearing 093. Something large just changed depth fast."

"Stay tight," Feyzi said, shifting position. "Cut the relay. Bring it back."

Chief Diver Anika Zhao detached the buoy, sealed it in an EM-locked bag. The team turned back.

Then another vibration hit them—stronger. The dolphins darted around them, tightening the formation.

Hart looked at Feyzi. "That wasn't a whale."

Her voice was low, edged with certainty—not speculation, but instinct. The sound, the movement, the way the dolphins had reacted—it all confirmed what she felt in her gut.

These creatures had saved him once, and now they were warning her. It wasn't just sonar or sensor feeds—it was something primal, something she'd learned to trust beneath the surface. As the lead dolphin circled tightly, its behavior sharpened Hart's focus.

She turned her gaze back toward the shadowed water beyond and added quietly, "And they want us to know they're close."

He nodded slowly.

"They're watching us now. Let them. We're not prey."

Echo-7 SEV Bay – 40 Minutes Later

The dive team breached into the airlock. The buoy was intact. Immediately rushed to Cyber Command.

Feyzi peeled off his helmet, drenched but focused. Salty droplets clung to his lashes, and his breath came in steady, controlled draws as he adjusted to the bright fluorescence of the SEV Bay. His fingers ached slightly from gripping the dive controls, but there was a renewed light in his eyes—an electric pulse of purpose.

Around him, the chamber hissed with depressurization valves and filtered oxygen vents, wrapping the moment in a cocoon of mechanical rhythm. He glanced toward Hart, who gave him a quiet nod, the kind exchanged by those who'd crossed an invisible threshold together.

Morano was already routing the buoy's burst data to secure analysis.

"We'll extract the relay logs in less than two hours," she said.

"If it holds origin signatures or encryption fingerprints, we'll have something to triangulate."

Commander Hart turned to Feyzi as the rest of the dive team exited.

"You earned more than trust down there," she said. "You earned a place in their world."

She didn't mean the team. She meant the dolphins—the Echo-D3 pod who had risked their lives for him, who had circled and steadied him in the depths, and now hovered with a trust that even Hart couldn't fully explain.

That trust wasn't earned through protocol or rank.

It was primal.

Instinctual.

And Hart, standing in the filtered glow of the SEV Bay, felt it just as fiercely. These creatures, bred for intelligence and empathy, had recognized something in Feyzi before she had.

And now she understood: their world had already chosen him.

The rest of Echo-7 just needed to catch up.

And Feyzi knew it.

CHAPTER 29

Full Sweep

Echo-7 Subcommand: Task Force Polaris

After the successful neutralization of the enemy's surveillance buoy, tension across Echo-7 had shifted to a razor-sharp sense of vigilance. The mission had proven Feyzi Çelik was not just a desk-side commander, but a man willing to face the deep unknown. He had earned respect, and now it was time to act.

Feyzi and Commander Hart returned to their respective quarters, soaked and chilled, still high on adrenaline. The artificial daylight in Echo-7 had shifted to "evening mode," casting everything in bluish hues. The metal hallways—normally vibrant with operational foot traffic—were quieter now, reflective. A subtle hum from the central power core reverberated through the titanium beams of the base.

In the privacy of his quarters, Feyzi pulled off the last of his wetsuit, toweled off, and changed into dry fatigues. He tapped the wall console and called an emergency session. Within minutes, the leadership team—now known as Task Force Polaris internally—gathered again in the command center.

The command center's lighting had dimmed to red alert readiness, interspersed with blinking diagnostic panels and live satellite overlays. The air smelled faintly of ozone and recycled air scrubbed clean through layered filtration. Senior officers assembled around the oval war table, their faces worn but alert. The tension was palpable—every officer had a story behind their eyes, but tonight, they shared one mission.

"Great job, everyone," Feyzi began, his voice still rough from the pressure masks.

"What we accomplished today proves Echo-7 isn't just surviving—we're fighting back."

The war table's inlaid map dimmed to a low-sea blue, and for a heartbeat the only sound was the breathing of the base; air handlers, coolant loops, hull stress monitors clicking like distant metronomes. Around the oval, sleeves rolled and ranks receded; this was now a room of craft, not ceremony. Hart stood half a step to Feyzi's right, the unspoken geometry of joint command. Rourke's hands were flat on the table—yielding posture, calculating eyes.

He turned to Chief Warrant Officer Lena Morano.

"Chief, your call on the buoy's transmission was crucial. You've exposed the enemy's tether point. But I suspect they planned for redundancy. Please scan the base again—and this time, don't overlook old-school methods. Bugs. Cables. Routers. Let's not underestimate simplicity."

Lena nodded sharply, tapping lines of encrypted command onto her tablet. Around her, her team began spreading out toward subsystem clusters, their body language tense but precise.

Full sweep rules implemented immediately.

No Assumptions: Anything that can carry charge or memory is suspect: door controllers, scrubbers, UPS inverters, label printers, exercise bikes.

Power-Down Audit: Cycle every subsystem cold; log boot jitter to the microsecond. Anything that "wakes with a limp" gets benched.

Analog Intercept: Sweep for pressure tubes, passive inductive coils, optic taps in legacy cable trunks.

Human Vectors: Randomize badge routes and mess hours; compromise hunts start with habits.

RF Silence Windows: Thirty-minute dead-air blocks base wide; no internal BLE, NFC, or passive telemetrics. If a device still speaks, it sends a confession.

Morano's team peeled off like a practiced orchestra; one to environmentals, one to legacy training bays, one to wetlock controls, and a fourth with resin seals and a bag of old-fashioned wax crayons for tamper lines.

"Understood, Commander. We'll run another full diagnostic. Everything with a circuit gets powered down and back up. We'll measure for anomalies in reboot. But it'll take time. Give me a few hours."

"You'll have it," Feyzi replied.

He dismissed the team for a short break.

As he walked back to his quarters, he passed the med bay, where a recovering crew member gave him a quiet salute. Feyzi returned it with a small nod, the moment lingering as a silent acknowledgment of shared purpose.

Once inside, he sat on his bunk and finally let his head fall back. His body ached from the dive, and the adrenaline was wearing off.

For the first time since the XT84 crash, Feyzi allowed himself to rest.

He set his watch for forty minutes, the length of a good lie and a bad nap, then slipped under a sleep that felt like anchorage rather than escape.

When the chime touched his ear, the room was where he'd left it; the fight had politely waited.

Hours Later: Command Center

The dim red glow of operational lighting painted the command center in a somber hue. The low hum of machinery merged with the soft clicks of keyboards and the occasional murmur of status updates.

Commander Hart gently knocked on Feyzi's door, then stepped inside. Hart's knock was two beats, then one: Echo-7's version of sirens under a blanket.

"Time to get up, Commander. Chief Morano has findings."

Feyzi rose, stretching his back and legs as he grabbed his jacket. Together they headed to the command center where Task Force Polaris was already assembled.

As they walked, she passed him a squeeze pouch of electrolytes and a one-line update in her handwriting: "Base breathing steadier."

It was not medical; it was moral.

Lena Morano stood in front of the main diagnostics panel, her face composed but eyes sharp with alertness. Around her, a few junior cybersecurity officers tapped at auxiliary consoles, rechecking their signal simulations and hash reports. A steaming thermos sat on the corner of her station, untouched.

"Commander, we found two more transmission nodes," Lena announced.

Feyzi leaned in. "Where?"

"First was inside a wall-mounted CO_2 scrubber in the west SEV equipment bay," she said.

"Perfect cover. It used the environmental system's low-frequency electromagnetic field to piggyback bursts of data. We had to isolate the power unit to find it."

Morano pulled the scrubber's schematic up.

"They tuned a rogue coil to resonate against our fan motor at 48.3 kHz, just outside our standard sweep. The fan becomes the antenna. We found it by comparing phase drift across three identical units. Two breathed like lungs. One breathed like a liar."

Rourke let out a long breath through his nose.

"It survived three inspections." Morano said. "We killed that first."

She tapped the screen, flipping to another diagram.

"The second was embedded inside an old-generation training simulator console in the Special Forces prep wing. It had a piggyback chip soldered directly to the backup BIOS. It survived the last software purge because it triggered only on specific handshake requests."

"Piggyback chip was lacquered under the backup BIOS with thermal paint," Morano continued.

"It only woke when it heard an old handshaking word; a training phrase that instructors still use out of habit. We were compromised by nostalgia."

Hart's jaw flexed. "Kill the phrase."

"Already retired," Morano said. "New call is Quiet Sea. No legacy words on this base."

There was a moment of silence. Hart's brows furrowed slightly, the implications spreading like static across the command table. Behind her stoic expression, a flash of anger burned, a violation buried so deep inside their systems it had almost evaded them again.

Feyzi finally spoke. "Are we secure?"

"I can't say 100%," Lena replied.

"But I can say this: we swept every pathway. We filtered every signal band from subsonic to terahertz. We scoped every ground line and thermal node. Unless they invented something from a sci-fi film, we're clean."

Feyzi nodded once. "Good. Now we stop being prey." He tapped the console.

"Morano, seed three canary credentials into dead-end service accounts and an exfil decoy with telemetry that looks almost valuable—fleet power curves, a believable flaw, one step from truth. If they bite, we want a route home."

"Copy," Morano said. "Bait smells like lunch. We'll watch who eats."

Feyzi nodded, absorbing her words with a glance toward the war map behind her. A flicker of pride stirred inside him; not for what he had done alone, but for the team now rallying around him.

"Then we move to Mission 2. Activate surveillance on Lajes Air Base. Notify Turkish intelligence to proceed with Phase One on Istanbul Airport comms chain. We need to flush this network," said Feyzi.

Phase Lines—Operation North Lantern

Hart slid a palm across the tabletop and the map split into three pulsing lanes.

"North Lantern goes in three acts," she said. "We don't announce it—we perform it."

Phase A—Lajes.

Rourke leaned in. "Cover story?"

"Maintenance," Hart replied. "Two-person audit team. Orange vests. Clipboards that actually work."

Morano flicked up a checklist. "Analog first. Fuel chits, catering slips, ladder truck logs—paper that can't be backdated by a clever database. We match it to digital manifests and look for time slippage and repeat hands."

"And the mirror accounts?" Feyzi asked.

"Frozen on contact," Morano said. "Any badge that clones, closes. No drama. Just a door that doesn't open."

Phase B—Istanbul Chain.

The screen pivoted to a grid of gates and runways; Turkish call signs ghosted the audio.

A voice joined by secure link; calm, edged in Ankara steel. "MIT online," the liaison said. "We will scrape tower phraseology, pull gate cameras, and harvest ramp whispers."

"Parked vans?" Hart asked.

"We cross-check radio relay vans that linger longer than coffee," the liaison answered.

"Interviews on paper only. No phones in rooms; grief is leverage, and we will not give them a wire to pull."

Feyzi nodded. "Good. Build the story the machines can't erase."

Phase C—Echo-7 Shield.

The Atlantic rose on the wall, a breathing thing.

Hart pointed at the thermocline like a conductor calling strings. "Echo-D3 patrols every four hours—net pattern, low and wide."

Captain Monroe's icon pulsed from the *Missouri*. "We'll drag a false wake at three knots inside the seam," he said over the internal net—voice steady as ballast. "Either they show hunger, or they burn patience."

He paused just long enough to let confidence do its work. "*Missouri* copies. Running the seam in five."

Feyzi met every eye around the table. "We don't swat what we can follow, and we don't follow what we can't bring home. North Lantern isn't a memo; it's a move. Execute."

Colonel Vance slid an orbital overlay into the corner of the main display.

"Kazuar window reopens in thirty-one hours. We can dirty the sky by three arcseconds with our partner dishes and tie its star trackers in knots. Dr. Patel, prep ARES for celestial forgery. Low amplitude first: don't spook the beast."

Patel: "Copy. We'll teach it a sky that doesn't exist and let it miss with dignity."

Hart gave a faint smile. "We're moving, Commander."

Each watch change, sixty seconds of still; no typing, no speaking, just the sound of the base. You can't defend a place you don't hear.

The eleven engineers from Nightshade and the XT84 crew roll on the med bay skylight frame; handwritten, not etched. Sunlight will never touch it; respect will.

Every brief ends with two sentences anyone could carry up a ladder in a storm. Tonight's: "We close our leaks. We hunt theirs."

Feyzi gave her a look of gratitude, then turned back to Task Force Polaris.

"Good work. We're winning. And the world doesn't even know it yet."

A technician stared at a diagnostics bloom that refused to behave. The Echo-7 buoy line still blinked, dutiful as ever; only now its timing carried a human heartbeat he didn't recognize.

He rubbed a thumb across the scope and told his commander what all frightened men tell power:

"Still normal."

He muted the channel and whispered the thing power never likes to hear.

"...until it isn't."

He didn't know the word for it, but he felt it just the same: the ocean had chosen a different center.

CHAPTER 30

The Silence

Undisclosed Location – Russian Federation

Inside a reinforced underground command center near Severo-morsk, north of the Arctic Circle, an array of screens flashed with pulsing red alerts, bathing the room in a cold, ominous glow.

The air was thick with the sharp tang of ozone, mingled with the sterile scent of recycled ventilation. The low-frequency hum of subterranean turbines underscored every heartbeat. Banks of holographic consoles projected shifting telemetry streams and encrypted signal traces across the angular walls.

Operations Commander of Unit GRU—Aleksey ("Alek") Zubarev—sat forward in his steel-backed chair, the metal creaking faintly under the tension in his frame. His knuckles pressed into the brushed alloy surface of the command desk, white from strain.

The quiet in the room was more unsettling than any alarm. Engineers, dressed in standard-issue black fatigues with GRU emblems stitched on their shoulders, moved swiftly but silently, their fingers dancing over transparent control panels. Muted keystrokes, clipped whispers, and the occasional beeping alert punctuated the room's fraught atmosphere.

"Report." His voice cut through the room like a gunshot.

"Sir," said Lt. Petrov, wiping sweat from his brow.

"We've lost telemetry from all three Echo-7 infiltrations. The relay buoy is inactive. No pings received in the last three hours."

Zubarev turned slowly. "All three?"

"Da, Comrade Colonel. The primary underwater buoy, the secondary ping-back line embedded in Echo-7's internal router matrix, and the tertiary piggyback drone on their command uplink—all went silent within a two-hour window."

Zubarev stood, fists clenched behind his back. The room seemed to shrink.

"This is not accidental."

"No, sir," replied Petrov. "It was surgical."

The stillness had temperature. It wasn't peace; it was a freezer burn that bit the lungs. Zubarev let it linger a heartbeat longer than was kind. He believed in silence the way other men believed in saints. Silence tells you who can breathe under it.

"Petrov," he said at last, "say it without the theater."

"We were seen," Petrov answered. "Not on camera. In behavior."

Zubarev's gaze slid over the rows of faces. He didn't raise his voice. "Then we become smaller than our own noise."

A slim Chinese officer across the table stood—Major Zhao Liyang, of the PLA Strategic Reconnaissance Bureau. His black uniform was crisp and decorated with minimalist insignias denoting cyber warfare and orbital surveillance command. A faint scar traced his jawline, partially hidden by his neatly trimmed goatee.

His Mandarin-accented Russian was precise, clipped, and utterly devoid of emotion. Though calm in demeanor, Zhao's presence carried a quiet authority, his reputation preceding him as one of Beijing's most elusive data warfare tacticians.

"Feyzi Çelik," Zhao said flatly.

Zubarev grunted. "Of course. The civilian wildcard becomes the center of the board."

Zhao didn't hurry, didn't posture. He set a hand on the console as if greeting an old friend and spoke like a professor removing a rumor from the room.

"You threaded them. Then they learned the thread. Çelik doesn't chase anomalies. He recasts the baseline and lets anomalies chase him."

Zubarev gave a half laugh with no humor. "You quote him like scripture."

"I don't quote ghosts," Zhao said. "I design for them."

Zhao activated a secure line on the console and brought up recent surveillance data. It showed a fuzzy sonar echo of the dolphin squad exiting the underwater sector. It also displayed digital forensics logs—connection attempts from their own tools being denied at root security levels.

"We were overconfident," Zhao admitted.

"The software implants were working for months. We underestimated their response time."

"We underestimated him," Zubarev snapped, but the words were laced with something deeper than frustration.

"Because you gave them patience," Zubarev said, turning slightly.

"Patience makes predators."

He stepped closer, voice dropping into something intimate and dangerous.

"Tell me where patience ends."

"When the pattern starts to imitate us," Zhao replied.

A thin smile cut across Zubarev's face. "Good. Then we stop imitating."

Zubarev felt the weight of his mistake.

This wasn't luck.

This was chess.

And Feyzi had always been three moves ahead.

"He wasn't supposed to survive XT84. That laser shot was supposed to vaporize the fuselage. We synchronized perfectly with the Lajes departure... and he still survived."

The memory drummed through the floor; the moment their timings kissed at altitude, the moment the world should have broken cleanly in two. Zubarev had felt it in his bones, that engineer's certainty that math had finally cornered luck. Now luck sat across the ocean, putting on a uniform and answering to Commander.

"Fate is laziness with an alibi," Zubarev muttered. "We don't hire fate here."

"We should have used redundant satellites," muttered Petrov.

Zubarev spun and slammed his fist on the table.

"Do not blame hardware! This is a man problem. One man. A NATO ghost with a civilian face."

The room fell silent again.

Zhao sent an encrypted burst transmission to a dual-channel relay point in Xinjiang. Moments later, a confirmation came through.

"Moscow and Beijing have been informed. They agree. We proceed to Phase 2."

The room seemed to breathe again, machines inhaling on someone else's cue. Zhao keyed a second channel no one else could see; the line flattened to a single unblinking green.

"Beijing acknowledges," he said. "No speeches."

"Good," Zubarev replied. "Speeches are how men forgive themselves in advance."

He didn't sit. Men who sat missed turns.

Zubarev raised an eyebrow. "Is Beijing ready?"

"They activated the stealth fleet 48 hours ago. The new prototype, Haixia-X, is near operational status."

"Near is a distance," Zubarev said. "Does it cough?"

"It whispers," Zhao answered. "Low signature, adaptive hull. It drinks heat it doesn't want to show."

"And if it meets the *Missouri*?"

Zhao didn't blink.

"Then our field test finds religion."

Zubarev walked toward the global map on the wall, which spanned nearly two meters wide and emitted a soft, pulsating glow.

The surface shimmered with adaptive liquid crystal overlays, each region annotated with real-time satellite feeds and pulsing telemetry threads.

Red digital overlays highlighted Echo-7's estimated location, XT84's crash zone, the Black Hawk's trajectory, and projected NATO fleet movements, complete with animated vector arrows and threat probability circles.

The system's speakers emitted low tonal pings—sonar echoes, data callouts, and encrypted network handshakes. The map wasn't just a visual tool; it was a living, breathing interface.

Zubarev studied the Atlantic as if it might apologize. Vector arrows flexed and settled, haloed in the cold light. His reflection overlaid the ocean like a watermark.

"You feel it?" he said quietly, almost to himself.

"Feel what?" Petrov asked.

"Their confidence," Zubarev said. "It has frequency. They've moved from defense to appetite."

Zhao folded his arms. "Then we starve them."

As Zubarev studied the projection, his reflection shimmered faintly across the glass. A quiet rage brewed beneath his stillness, but his expression was focused, surgical, as if watching a chessboard tilt out of balance.

"Then we escalate. Deploy a worm into the Lajes Base network. Set it to passive until triggered. We'll need a failsafe if they trace the ground leak."

"Not the old song," Zubarev added.

"I want a worm that sleeps like furniture. It wakes only when someone says a word they shouldn't. Pick a word they love."

Petrov frowned. "Such as?"

"'Routine,'" Zubarev said. "People die under that word all the time."

Zhao tilted his head. "We will sew it into their comfort."

"And when they find it?" Petrov asked.

"They will," Zubarev said. "Let them think it's the only one."

"Understood."

"And tell the Kazuar to move north by 30 clicks and await orders. No active pings. No risk. We only get one more shot before NATO scrambles the entire Atlantic."

Zhao's eyes flicked to the orbital pane. Star fields drifted like polite strangers. "We nudge trackers with noise, not force. If they're faking the sky, we agree with the lie and then change the clock. A blind man can still tell noon by heat."

"And if they cut the mirror?" Zubarev asked.

"Then we switch to constellations they don't own," Zhao said, almost bored.

"There are still stars no one has branded."

Zhao stared at the sonar image of the now-quiet Echo-7.

"They have ARES now, or they soon will. If we don't neutralize that software."

Zubarev rolled his shoulders, metal whispering under his jacket.

"I don't fear machines that think. I fear people who think with them."

He looked back at Zhao. "Can we misteach it?"

Zhao considered. "We can show it a fight that never begins and end it a hundred times. If it learns the wrong lesson, it will be very clever at losing."

"Good," Zubarev said. "Let their genius get tired in the wrong direction."

"They'll end our advantage before it even starts," Zubarev finished.

For a long moment, neither said anything.

"Then we must not fail again."

The room accepted the sentence like a contract. Screens steadied. People resumed being necessary. Petrov's hands found their work.

Zhao's cursor wrote permissions no one else would ever read. Zubarev stood still long enough to feel fear arrive and just long enough to let it leave.

"We do this clean," he said.

"No boasting on the wire. No signatures in the ash."

He lifted his chin toward the ceiling he could not see.

"They built a refuge under an ocean. Fine. We'll change the water."

Far beneath them, the icy rock of the Russian north groaned faintly under tectonic stress—a subterranean reminder that even the most ancient forces were stirring.

Zubarev stood at the map's edge, fists still clenched, watching the silent pulse of Echo-7 flicker on the wall. Zhao remained behind him, unmoving, eyes narrowed.

Neither spoke.

In that lingering silence, it wasn't just strategy that settled into the room—it was inevitability.

Far above Severomorsk, midnight wore a thin aurora like a rumor. South and west, a slab-sided transport lifted off a remote strip with its lights out and its intentions tidy. In orbit, a bus that didn't have a name slipped twenty-nine degrees north and pretended it had always meant to be there. In the Philippine Sea, Haixia-X flexed her skin and swallowed a degree of heat she could not afford to show.

Zhao watched the Atlantic pulsing on the wall and finally broke the silence with a sentence that was not for the room.

"Ghosts don't die," he said softly. "They're replaced."

Zubarev didn't answer. He closed his eyes for a count of three and saw the neat geometry of a plan with no blood on it yet. When he opened them, the board had not moved. It just looked different.

"Begin," he said.

The turbines under the granite answered like a distant choir, and somewhere in the cold, careful dark between continents, the first counters began to slide.

Somewhere beyond the digital overlays, in the abyssal pressure of the Atlantic, a war was no longer brewing.

It had already begun.

And in the darkness, war continued to whisper forward.

CHAPTER 31

The Hidden Signal

Lajes Air Base, Azores

The morning fog clung stubbornly to the tarmac at Lajes, wrapping the airstrip in a gauzy veil that made every shadow stretch unnaturally long. Ground crew moved like silhouettes through the mist, and the distant whine of jet engines sounded eerily muffled. Inside the nearby operations center, walls of reinforced glass enclosed rows of terminals glowing faint blue, and the floor vibrated subtly from the hum of backup generators cycling power.

The space smelled faintly of burnt circuitry and antiseptic—evidence of a long night spent scanning for ghosts in the system. Inside the base's operations center, the atmosphere was anything but calm. The hum of fluorescent lights and the aroma of over-brewed coffee saturated the air, as if tension had permeated the very walls.

A joint intelligence team—composed of U.S. Air Force cyber specialists, Portuguese counterintelligence, and embedded Turkish operatives—was camped inside a sealed data forensics lab adjacent to ATC Command. The room was sterile, save for cables snaking across the floor and server diagnostics humming in intervals. A hint of ozone clung to the cooled air, a byproduct of ionized equipment operating at full capacity.

At the center of the operation was Captain Aylin Demir, Turkish Air Force cyber intelligence, seconded to NATO for joint ops. Her olive-drab uniform bore no rank insignia—a deliberate choice for deep recon tasks.

Her posture was that of a coiled spring—alert, precise, and unwavering—echoing the countless high-stakes missions she had run under darker skies.

There was no wasted motion as she moved through the lab, and even in silence, she commanded attention—standard for deep recon tasks. She had a reputation for precision and had been hand-picked by Ankara for one reason: to find the breach that enabled the coordinated strike on XT84 and the Black Hawk.

"Go back to the flight control logs from the week before the incident," she ordered.

Staff Sergeant Miller, a U.S. signal analyst with a thick Boston accent and three tours behind him, brought up the patch history overlay on the primary screen.

"There it is," he said, pointing to a small software push timestamped 48 hours before the Black Hawk's final flight.

"Patch ID: Delta-V422," Demir read. "Access level: high. Sign-off credentials... Lieutenant Tomas Neves."

The room froze for a moment.

Lt. Neves wasn't just a liaison. When he walked through the corridors of Lajes, junior officers straightened unconsciously. He carried himself with quiet authority, the kind that came not from rank but from earned trust.

His decorated history in Kosovo and Lebanon had cemented his role as a bridge between NATO command and local Portuguese forces. His calm demeanor and perfectly timed humor had made him a staple of the base culture—he remembered birthdays, sent flowers when someone's spouse was hospitalized, and never raised his voice.

That's what made the discovery all the more chilling. He was one of the most trusted NATO integrators on the island. Decorated for his coordination work during joint airlift missions to Kosovo and

Lebanon. A man with roots deep in both the Portuguese military and NATO command.

Demir's eyes narrowed. Something in Neves' recent behavior—his uncharacteristic avoidance of the team, those rushed locker visits—clicked into place.

"Do we arrest?" Miller asked.

"No," Demir said flatly. "Not yet. We track him."

She stepped aside and keyed in her secure tablet, composing a Level-5 encrypted message.

TO: Commander Feyzi Çelik
RE: MISSION 2 – INFILTRATION POINT IDENTIFIED
Patch origin confirmed. Lt. Neves. Request permission to trace all outgoing comms before engagement. Target unaware. Surveillance initiated.
—A. Demir

Feyzi's response came within minutes:

APPROVED. DO NOT CONFRONT. IF HE'S REAL, HE'S NOT ALONE.
—FC

Three Hours Later

A new subroutine flagged activity on Neves's assigned workstation. A portable military-grade satellite phone had initiated a burst transmission from his locker, routed through a spoofed weather station uplink.

"That's not normal," Miller muttered.

Demir's team launched a decryption tool. The packet was small—but not idle. It was targeted, directed to a node buried in a server stack in Kaliningrad Oblast, a heavily militarized Russian exclave.

They ran an AI-decoder pass. Inside the message, embedded in signal modulation frequency, was a single word: "STRATUM."

Demir's face paled. She tapped her secure comms line.

"Ankara, this is Echo Trace-1. We have confirmation. STRATUM keyword used in covert outbound. Origin Lajes Air Base. Target confirmed."

Kaliningrad, Russia – SVR Cyber Command

Inside a steel-and-concrete command block, the SVR Cyber Command nerve center buzzed with quiet intensity. Server racks lined the walls, emitting a low, steady hum punctuated by the occasional flicker of diagnostic LEDs.

Fiber-optic cabling crisscrossed beneath reinforced glass floors, glowing faintly like veins of data pulsing through the facility. Surveillance monitors displayed satellite overlays, electromagnetic spectrum charts, and live-feed intercepts from global hotspots.

The air was crisp and faintly metallic, scrubbed dry by industrial filters. On one wall, a red-lit holographic insignia of the Russian Federation shimmered like a warning.

This was no ordinary bunker—it was a digital battlefield cathedral, designed to wage the new kind of war: invisible, immediate, and global. The chamber was silent save for the occasional metallic echo of bootsteps and the hiss of filtered air. Buried 70 feet beneath the Kaliningrad coast, an alert tone pinged the main operations terminal.

Colonel Alexei Voronov, head of joint Russian-Chinese naval cyber ops, leaned forward.

"Comrade, one of our ghost assets just used the STRATUM keyword," the aide said.

Voronov's expression didn't change, but his mind raced. He remembered the word's origin—an experimental AI command stack created for multivector misdirection.

If NATO had caught it...

"They've found something," he said slowly. "Pull up the node routing."

"Too late. Their counter intel just went active," the aide replied. "The backdoor's gone dark."

Voronov cursed under his breath and typed a brief summary.

TO: MoD Moscow / CC: Beijing Naval Liaison
SUBJECT: STRATUM ASSET COMPROMISED

LAJES BASE STRATUM keyword detected in monitored burst transmission. NATO counter-surveillance active. Feyzi Çelik is operational. Echo-7 not neutralized. Enemy now aware. Asset burned.

RECOMMEND PHASE SHIFT TO DISRUPT STRATUM
MODULE RECOVERY.
—Col. A. Voronov

Within seconds, confirmation arrived:
"Phase Shift Approved."

Back at Lajes

Demir's tablet buzzed again. A second message from Feyzi.

STRATUM CONFIRMED. LOCK DOWN COMM PATHS.
MOVE TO SECURE INTERCEPT. THEN GET TO BOSTON. I
WANT YOU ON SITE.
—FC

Demir nodded to Miller, her expression carved from steel. Her breath slowed deliberately, anchoring herself for the next phase.

The distant murmur of the operations center seemed to fade, replaced by the pounding of her own pulse—a quiet war drum inside her chest. She could almost hear the soft thud of her boots as she turned sharply on her heel, the sound echoing down the corridor like the countdown of a fuse.

"Let's go pick up a traitor," she said, her voice low but unshakable.

If STRATUM was what Ankara feared it was—an AI-assisted coordination module—then its exposure was only the first round in a much larger war.

The trap was set.

But the battlefield was expanding.

And the war was just warming up.

CHAPTER 32

Face of the Moles

Lajés Air Base, Interrogation Room 3

The concrete walls of the interrogation chamber were painted with bland NATO beige, interrupted only by a flickering overhead light and a wall-mounted camera with a blinking red indicator.

The air smelled faintly of disinfectant and recycled air. The space was intentionally sterile—designed to exhaust, not comfort.

Lt. Tomas Neves sat restrained, hands cuffed to the metal table. His uniform was crisp, creased perfectly down the sleeves and pant legs, as though he were clinging to order. But his eyes were bloodshot—somewhere between anger and regret. His jaw twitched now and then, his foot tapped in a syncopated rhythm beneath the table—tells of a man unraveling slowly.

Across from him sat Captain Aylin Demir. She wore civilian clothing now—black sweater, slacks, and a sidearm holstered low at her waist. Her dark hair was tied back in a tight braid, and her expression was unreadable. Her calm demeanor did not match the adrenaline flooding the room, but it mirrored her years of training. She looked composed, but inside, she burned with urgency.

She slid a file folder across the table. Inside were still images: a packet dump from his satellite phone transmission, a heat signature map of his workstation, and the one that made his shoulders sag—a shot of the word STRATUM encoded in his encrypted burst to Kaliningrad.

"We know," Demir said. "You were burned the moment that signal left this base."

Neves didn't flinch. He stared at the table; lips pressed into a hard line. A muscle in his neck tensed, then relaxed.

"You were good," she continued.

"A NATO integrator with twenty years of clearance. Kosovo. Kabul. Beirut. And you blew it all for one word. One mission."

He raised his eyes at last—flat, depthless. "You think this is my first room?"

His voice was quiet, almost bored.

Neves had been taught by two masters who never shared a doctrine but loved the same outcome: silence. Moscow gave him the old craft—SVR tradecraft etched like scripture: no admissions, no corrections, no help.

Beijing added discipline: breath control, micro-movements, and the long patience of a winter campaign. Together they built a man who could hide in plain sight and starve a conversation to death.

Demir worked him hard. Hours bled into one another—lights up, lights down; temperature dropped a few degrees; white noise rose and fell like a tide. Rapport, then rupture. Calm questions that went nowhere; sudden challenges that hit like hammer blows.

He gave her nothing. He asked for water once, drank deliberately, and set the paper cup down with the rim aligned to the table's edge. The metronome tap of his shoe never lost count.

She tried silence—the kind that makes an untrained source fill the void. Neves recited Os Lusíadas in his head, keeping cadence with the whir of the ventilation fan. When she disrupted rhythm with random bangs on the door, he drifted to a different anchor: Mandarin aphorisms drilled into him in Shenzhen—quiet controls motion. His pupils stayed small. His pulse, steady. He even smiled once at the camera, a thin crescent that said he recognized every tactic.

Eleven hours in, Demir called a pause and stepped into the corridor. The glass in the door reflected a woman who had exhausted the playbook without breaking the subject.

She needed weight—something he couldn't deadlift with discipline.

They found it in his file. Emily Neves, twenty-three. A master's student at a California college. Apartment, campus, study carrel—a life arranged with the precision of someone who never expected to be a lever.

Demir made the call. The move would be clean and legal: protective custody, not harm. But optics would do what pressure could not. She coordinated with the stateside team, set parameters down to the second, and returned to the chair as if she had merely gone for coffee.

Minutes later, the wall screen hummed awake. A camera angle snapped into focus: an interrogation room a continent away—cinderblock walls, a stainless table.

Emily sat at the center, hands bound in front with soft restraints, eyes darting to the lens. Three armed figures in dark masks stood behind her, silent and still.

The syncopation under the table stopped. Neves tried to rise, the chain at his wrist snatching him back into the chair. The muscle in his neck went rigid.

Emily blinked into the light.

"What is happening, Dad? Who are these people?"

A Portuguese curse slipped out before he swallowed it. He turned his head slowly toward Demir.

The calm was gone, replaced by a hard shine.

"This is a line you do not cross."

Demir didn't blink.

"She's safe—for now. Protective custody. But your double life put her inside the blast radius. You can end this."

"Prove it's today," he said, voice gravel.

"Prove it's California."

She nodded once.

The stateside operator panned to a wall clock, then to a news feed running muted in a corner monitor. The angle widened; the three masked guards shifted just enough to reveal standardized plate carriers—clean, non-military. The picture-in-picture flicked to a hallway where a deputy U.S. marshal passed with a clipboard. The time code burned in the lower corner.

Neves slowed his breathing, fighting to re-enter the bunker in his head. Count four in, hold four, four out. He murmured in Mandarin under his breath—do not rage at counterintelligence. But Emily's voice cut through the routine, thin with confusion rather than fear.

"Dad?"

His foot found the rhythm again, then lost it. The training held for one more long minute. Then his gaze drifted to the corner speaker, to the faint hum behind it. For the first time, he looked tired.

Demir leaned in, voice low.

"Talk. She walks out of that room today."

Neves stared at the screen as if he could pull her out by will alone. When he finally looked back at Demir, the fight hadn't left his eyes—but it had changed shape.

Finally, he spoke. His Portuguese accent came through slowly, carefully.

"You don't understand what STRATUM is."

Demir leaned in, arms folded, elbows on the table.

"Then, tell me."

Silence.

She tapped the microphone embedded in her collar and signaled the security team outside. They began replaying a looped feed from inside Echo-7—the moment when Feyzi Çelik addressed the Echo Command and described the coordinated attack on XT84 and the Black Hawk.

Neves's eyes twitched at the sound of Feyzi's voice.

"He lived," he muttered.

Demir nodded.

"Yes. And you're going to help us understand why they wanted him dead."

Neves closed his eyes, took a breath, and began to speak.

What is STRATUM?

"STRATUM isn't a weapon," Neves said. "It's worse."

He paused.

"It's a decision engine. An autonomous battle brain. Designed by NATO's deepest AI think tanks. Decentralized learning. Pattern prediction. Real-time threat coordination."

Demir frowned. "ARES?"

Neves shook his head. "ARES is the platform. STRATUM is the soul."

He continued:

"It was developed to integrate threat data from orbital, surface, subsurface, and cyber domains—ingested, interpreted, and acted upon in seconds. No human latency. It predicts enemy intent before it happens. STRATUM would make stealth submarines obsolete. It would kill cloaking technologies. It would know where your enemy is before they even issue orders."

Demir exhaled slowly.

"And the modules the Black Hawk was carrying..."

Neves nodded. "Three of them. Neural clusters, trained on Eastern naval tactics. STRATUM was being born. And they were flying it to Echo-7 to complete training and activation."

Who Ordered the Strike?

Demir kept the interrogation calm, but her voice was icy now.

"Who coordinated the strike? Russia? China?"

"Both," Neves replied.

"China provided the stealth sub tech. Russia inserted the orbital laser prototype into the commercial satellite grid. But neither of them made the decision alone. That came from a joint shadow command structure based in Vladivostok. I don't know the names."

He looked up.

"But I know this—they're afraid of one man. They didn't care about Echo-7 at first. Until they realized he was still alive."

Demir stared at him. "Feyzi Çelik."

"Yes," Neves said. "They've feared him since his Middle East play 30 years ago. STRATUM is his endgame. They thought they could bury it with him."

Fallout

As guards entered the room, Demir received a ping from her secure line. It was from Commander Çelik:

> GOOD WORK. CONFIRM INTEL. BRING NEVES TO
> BOSTON FOR JOINT DEBRIEF. WE'LL MEET FACE TO
> FACE.
> —FC

She looked down at Neves.

"You're going to Boston."

Neves blinked.

"Will I make it?"

Demir holstered her sidearm.

"Depends on whether you keep talking."

She stood and nodded to the guards.

As they unlocked Neves from the table, he looked once more at the looping feed of Feyzi's speech still playing on the corner monitor.

His jaw tensed again.

Somewhere behind his eyes, something shifted—whether it was fear, respect, or something darker, Demir couldn't yet say.

Outside the interrogation room, the corridor lights dimmed to operational red.

The war was coming closer.

But now, they had a face for the betrayal.

And Boston was waiting.

CHAPTER 33

The Gatekeeper

Istanbul Airport – Air Turkey Operations Center
03:14 Local Time

The operations floor was unusually quiet for a global hub that never slept. Normally, this time of night hummed with gate clearances, last-minute luggage tags, and transit coordination. But tonight, it had been purged—swept clean by a covert detachment of the Turkish National Intelligence Organization (Milli İstihbarat Teşkilatı – MİT), operating under full blackout.

The room held a strange stillness, broken only by the soft ticking of a wall-mounted clock and the distant whir of luggage belts halted mid-cycle.

The faint smell of aviation fuel clung to the filtered air, mixing with the sterility of wiped-down plastic and ozone from recently disconnected monitors. Even the fluorescent lights seemed subdued, their low hum absorbed by the eerie emptiness that now filled the space.

In a glass-walled side room overlooking the main tarmac control screens, three intelligence officers hunched over a matrix of departure logs, gate assignment records, and biometric swipe data from the past 72 hours.

The hum of fluorescent lights buzzed over their heads, casting a pale wash across the aluminum desks. Cold air hissed from ceiling ducts, making the window glass vibrate faintly.

Commander Feyzi Çelik watched remotely from Echo-7 via a secure uplink. Turkish officials had granted him full visibility, under Presidential authority.

The Timing Anomaly

Agent Levent Kara, MİT's senior field data forensics officer, circled the timeline of XT84's final Boston activity. A scar ran from his left temple down to his cheek—an old shrapnel wound from Mosul—and his jaw tightened as he registered the timestamp.

Kara had seen patterns like this before—in Baghdad, in Aleppo—where delays meant more than logistical hiccups. They meant design. His fingers lingered over the datapoint a moment longer than necessary, betraying the unease building in his gut. His fingers were callused from years of physical ops.

"Here," he said, pointing to a seemingly innocuous log entry.

"At 02:38 UTC, the flight was delayed by 14 minutes. Not by weather, not by mechanical. The reason field was left blank."

Feyzi's voice crackled through the encrypted speaker.

"Who had authority to make that entry?"

Kara replied, "One name: Efe Tunçel. He's part of the night operations desk—gate and departure queue optimization."

Feyzi asked calmly,

"Is he in custody?"

"No," Kara replied.

"He hasn't reported for duty since the incident."

Feyzi's voice sharpened. "He ran?"

"Looks that way."

The Real-Time Breakthrough

Just then, a junior analyst from the cyber unit pushed a fresh printout into Kara's hands, his breath short, eyes darting between the paper and the live monitors.

"Sir—look at this. Tunçel's login was cloned to another IP address just moments before the XT84 delay edit."

Kara read it aloud, jaw tightening.

"VPN tunnel, routed through Almaty, Kazakhstan. Ghosted through three Russian exit nodes."

A chill settled in his spine—the exact playbook he had once uncovered in Beirut echoed here. One of the younger agents behind him swore under his breath, while another stood up abruptly, glancing toward the exit as if expecting Tunçel to walk through the door.

"Where's Tunçel now?"

"No idea. His apartment was found empty. Passport gone. Border exit records say he never left—but we believe he flew under an alias. He had help."

Feyzi cut in again.

"Was there CCTV?"

"Yes, but someone wiped it. Tunçel knew which sectors had analog backup. We're trying to retrieve VHS reels—actual tapes."

Feyzi took a long breath.

"He was trained."

Back to Echo-7 – The Dossier Builds

Later that morning at Echo-7, Chief Warrant Officer Lena Morano loaded a real-time threat matrix on the curved command room wall, its matte-black surface alive with layered holographics and tactical overlays.

The lights had dimmed to mission-red, casting everyone in crimson shadow as the war table illuminated regions of interest.

The air inside the room was chilled and dry, filled with the faint ozone tinge of recycled air and charged electronics. Rows of consoles blinked silently, while the occasional ripple of whispered coordination passed between officers manning their stations.

Morano's fingers danced over the surface of her command tablet, syncing datasets from Lajes, Istanbul, and orbital scans, feeding the growing neural grid shaping their intelligence picture.

She marked XT84 and the Black Hawk's synchronized window again.

"Tunçel's timing edit lined them up over the same naval grid square."

Commander Hart muttered under her breath,

"Perfectly choreographed."

Feyzi remained still.

"He delayed XT84 by fourteen minutes. That delay put us directly over Echo-7. That made us a target."

He turned to Morano.

"Let's name this for what it is: a military strike disguised as an airline accident."

She nodded grimly.

The Manhunt Begins

Back in Istanbul, MİT deployed special assets to coordinate with Interpol and Turkish border control. The interior of their temporary base at a decommissioned security wing was suffused with high-strain energy—cracked monitors hastily reconnected, phones ringing with terse exchanges, the air heavy with the scent of burnt coffee and overnight tension. Every pair of eyes was alert, every movement sharpened by urgency.

The last known alias Tunçel used—Erhan Toprak—flagged a one-way booking to Belgrade. His seat: 11C. Window. The manifest revealed he had cleared security just minutes after the CCTV blackout began, using a biometric spoofing kit likely smuggled in via diplomatic pouch.

One agent muttered a curse as they traced his boarding corridor.

He had walked past them all.

Cool.

Precise.

Invisible.

Feyzi, now seated in his private quarters aboard Echo-7, typed a quick secure note to Turkish Intelligence:

FIND HIM. BRING HIM BACK ALIVE. WE'RE NOT DONE UNRAVELING THIS.
—FC

He sat back, eyes dark.

Three missions down.

Four to go.

And the clock was ticking.

CHAPTER 34

Polaris Rising

Echo-7 – Polaris Command Center

The command center buzzed with anticipation. Mission 1, 2, and 3 had been executed with precision—spyware purged, the mole at Lajes neutralized, and Air Turkey's internal breach exposed.

Commander Feyzi Çelik stepped into the room where the Polaris Task Force—the operational leadership team of Echo-7—had gathered.

The room was bathed in mission-red lighting, and low hums from consoles echoed like a heartbeat beneath the gravity of what was unfolding. Coffee mugs sat half-finished next to glowing consoles, and a faint, ever-present vibration from the ocean pressure outside reminded everyone they were hundreds of meters below the surface.

He looked around and began,

"Three missions. Three victories. I want to thank each of you. The enemy underestimated us. But now, we know more than they think we do."

Chief Warrant Officer Lena Morano stepped forward, her hair pulled back in a tight braid, dark eyes sharp behind AR-tinted glasses. She exuded a composed urgency; the kind bred from years of handling signal warfare and classified breaches. She rarely smiled—but her voice carried conviction.

"Our cyber division intercepted another packet this morning. The keyword 'Kazuar' was embedded within both encrypted satellite traffic and low-frequency burst data from the stealth perimeter," she said, projecting a hex-mapped visualization of the data spikes onto the wall.

"Kazuar?"

Commander Hart asked, leaning forward, eyes narrowing beneath furrowed brows. Her fingers gripped the edge of the console in front of her, knuckles whitening.

Morano nodded.

"Yes, and here's the interesting part. 'Kazuar' appears to be dual-use. We initially assumed it referred to the stealth submarine. But digging deeper into the packet signatures and hash identifiers, we've determined it's also the codename for the cyber-AI system embedded into the sub. A hybrid warfare protocol—submarine and algorithm."

Feyzi thought "How did I miss this?"

Hart's eyes narrowed.

"So, the vessel isn't just invisible—it's thinking."

"Exactly," Morano replied.

"It's capable of autonomous threat detection, reactive cloaking, and even comm silence simulations. The AI controls evasion paths and communications traffic routing. Think of it as a captain without hesitation and a ghost that learns."

Morano didn't step back from the glass; she stepped closer to the idea.

"It doesn't chase numbers," she said, almost to herself.

"It chases stories. You give it a noise pattern, it asks what kind of animal would make that noise, and then it becomes the water that animal prefers."

She glanced at Feyzi. "If we want it to surface, we don't frighten it. We make a surface it misses."

Hart leaned in, elbows on the console. "You're saying we don't beat the cloak; we invite it to a party it thinks it planned."

"Exactly," Morano said. "It is confident, not arrogant. Confidence can be moved."

Feyzi let that settle. "Then we move it."

Feyzi addressed the room.

"Commander Rourke, please regroup with Captain Joshua E. Monroe aboard USS *Missouri* and Major Arman Reyes from Special Forces Detachment Echo. Prepare defensive protocols. That submarine will attack again. But remember; they lose stealth the second they fire."

Rourke stood with resolve, jaw clenched, voice even. This was his moment to lead.

"Yes, Commander. We'll be ready."

Feyzi met his eyes and gave a firm nod.

"Unleash hell the moment they make a move."

Rourke saluted.

"With pleasure."

Rourke turned his head to the overhead comm and spoke in a tone that made motion feel inevitable.

"*Missouri*, this is Echo-7 Polaris Actual. Your lane is the thermocline seam we drew at Juliet-Four. I want your wake quiet and your patience loud."

Captain Monroe came back without static.

"Copy, Polaris. We'll hum so softly the fish compose poetry."

Hart cut in, a smile that didn't reach her eyes. "Echo-D3 is on net. If the dolphins cut left twice in under ten seconds, that's not choreography—it's concern."

"Understood," Monroe said. "If they're nervous, I'm nervous."

Feyzi nodded once. "That's doctrine now."

As the Echo-7 Polaris Task Force dispersed, alarms pulsed red across the command center.

A low, rumbling alert echoed through the hall like the growl of a submerged beast.

Officers stopped mid-step, and a chill swept through the room.

Enemy Stealth Submarine – 'Kazuar'
15 Nautical Miles North-Northeast of Echo-7

Inside the Russian-built, Chinese-enhanced submarine Kazuar, Captain Yuri Melnikov, a decorated veteran of the Arctic Fleet with a streak of silver in his buzz-cut hair, narrowed his eyes.

The red emergency lighting cast deep shadows across the titanium alloy walls, and condensation dripped near one of the aft coolant vents. Everything inside the Kazuar felt heavy, pressurized—not just by the depth, but by the burden of the hunt.

"Targeting sequence locked. Firing window in thirty seconds," said Weapons Officer Lt. Alexei Morozov, his voice taut.

"Deploy sequence," Melnikov barked. "Fire on my mark."

"Mark!"

Whoosh. Whoosh. Whoosh.

Three torpedoes launched in tight succession, slicing through the deep Atlantic toward Echo-7.

The steel chamber groaned faintly with the release.

The command deck tightened three degrees cooler. Melnikov didn't look away from the scope.

"They're fast and proud," he said. "Kazuar believes in its first idea."

Melnikov turned to his second-in-command, Lt. Zhang Yuwei, whose face was a mask of calm calculation.

"They will retaliate. But we have the cloak advantage. Activate evasive pattern Beta-Seven. Dive hard. Thirty-five degrees down angle."

"Da, Kapitan."

Echo-7 Command Room – Immediate Response

"Three torpedoes inbound!" shouted Lt. Sandra Coen, sonar lead, fingers dancing across the glass interface. Her voice cracked slightly, but she held steady.

Commander Rourke stood at the center platform, posture rigid, eyes locked to the large overhead tactical display. The room dimmed to red-alert settings, casting every officer in a warlike glow.

"Deploy countermeasures! Pattern Delta-Four!" he ordered.

"Yes, sir!" cried Lt. Noah Reiser, weapons officer. His hands moved in swift, memorized motions.

Flash pulses of electric counter-torpedoes launched from Echo-7's side pods. Each scrambled and interfered with the torpedo's acoustic guidance systems.

"Impact in 10... 9..."

A moment of breathless silence. Then—whoomp...whoomp...fizzle.

"All three neutralized,"

Coen reported.

"Countermeasures successful!"

"Return fire," Rourke ordered.

"Five torpedoes. Full spread. Include one airborne missile volley."

Within seconds, Echo-7 retaliated.

The room didn't cheer; it exhaled. Hart's hand landed once on the rail—gratitude without ceremony. Somewhere under their boots, a pipe pinged as pressure settled into a new truce.

Coen's voice softened, almost human again.

"That was clean." Reiser grinned and immediately hid it, as if joy might scuff the paint.

"Don't marry the moment," Rourke said. "It doesn't love us back."

Five torpedoes surged through the black water, followed by two airburst-capable missiles that launched vertically and curved toward Kazuar's last known position.

On the *Missouri*, Monroe stood with his eyes half-closed, the way some men listen to vinyl.

"Let the first pair brag," he told his helmsman.

"The third is the one that decides to be humble. That's our hitter."

The helmsman didn't argue; he adjusted two degrees starboard and trusted physics to keep its promises.

Kazuar Submarine – Combat Room

"Multiple inbound threats!" cried Lt. Morozov.

"Deploy decoys and ECM," Melnikov responded.

"They've found us faster than expected. We are compromised."

Countermeasures flared in every direction. Kazuar twisted into a spiral dive. Lights flickered as they plunged beneath a trench shelf. Bulkheads creaked. The deck shifted under their boots.

Morozov's knuckles went bloodless on the console, but Zhang's voice stayed even.

"We're shedding shapes," she said. "Our ghost looks like four ghosts now."

Melnikov stared into nothing. "Make us the one that regrets it least."

The boat understood. Steel sang once, a low, uncertain note that sailors pretend not to hear.

"Status?" Melnikov demanded.

"Two impacts evaded. Three tracking our wake," Zhang said.

"Take us under the trench shelf—north. Silent running."

As the hull creaked under pressure, Melnikov muttered to himself:

"They'll be coming for us now. Hunted. Alone. If we return to Moscow empty-handed, we're dead men anyway."

Zhang didn't look up.

"Alone is a discipline," she said. "Let them be many. Many is noise."

Melnikov smiled with half his mouth. "Then be the quiet that ends them."

Kazuar dove into the cold abyss of the North Atlantic, wounded but still dangerous.

Echo-7 Command Room

"Torpedoes passed through the decoy field. No confirmed hit," Coen said.

"Last known heading: 347 degrees north," Hart added.

Hart pointed at the display where Kazuar's last sure thought flickered.

"It ran where it would run if it wrote the textbook," she said. "So, let's burn the page."

Feyzi shifted closer to the glass.

"Rourke, draw it toward the seam Monroe is painting. Morano, feed the perimeter a rumor the AI can't resist; an honest lie about a pressure pocket and a wounded signature just outside its comfort. Hart, I want Delta and Echo dolphins at the hinge point. If they blink, we roll right."

Rourke didn't hesitate. "Moving the board."

Rourke exhaled.

"They're still out there. Hiding. But no more shadows. We've drawn blood."

Commander Çelik stepped forward.

"Track them. And prepare the next move."

He turned to Commander Hart.

Feyzi paused, then said:

"STRATUM isn't online. Not yet. The software modules—our only working version—were lost with the Black Hawk. Until we recover that safe, STRATUM is just a theory."

He looked toward the large screen tracking Kazuar's last known trajectory.

"But we can't wait for the tech to save us. Kazuar is still out there, wounded and dangerous. We fight this next round the old-fashioned way—sonar, steel, and tactics. We find it, we finish it."

The room went quiet, each officer processing the gravity of what lay ahead.

The red light worked its slow drumbeat across the room. A chair scraped, soft as a breath.

Morano raised her head from the code and found Feyzi's eye.

"Old-fashioned doesn't mean blind," she said. "Give me twenty minutes and I'll make the water tell better lies than they do."

Hart angled her body toward Feyzi.

"Then let me choreograph the truth. Dolphins read what metal hides. We'll write a path Kazuar thinks it authored."

Rourke rested both hands on the rail. "*Missouri* says the seam is behaving. We can take a swing without losing our balance."

Feyzi nodded, jaw set.

"Then this is the swing. No glory runs. If you don't have a surety, you don't take the shot."

He looked from face to face—their gravity, their fatigue, their refusal to be smaller than the hour.

"We end it because we're patient, not because we're angry."

Somewhere in the base a pump kicked over, and the floor gave a tiny, reassuring shiver. The ocean pressed in, the way a heavy blanket presses a chest, and for a moment it felt like a promise instead of a threat.

"Bring me its last good option," Feyzi said, voice lowering.

"And then take it away."

A faint pulse from the red console lights throbbed like a war drum in the silence that followed.

North of them, where the sea was thick with its own cold, a line of bubbles wrote the shortest chapter in a long book and vanished before anyone could read it.

Far below that, in a trench where light became rumor, something that believed in its own invisibility drifted a fraction off true.

It wasn't much. It was enough.

CHAPTER 35

The Deep Game

Belgrade, Serbia—Midnight

July air off the Danube hung heavy over Zemun, clinging to the Turkish National Intelligence Organization (MİT) agents crouched behind an abandoned tram shelter.

Heat bled from the rusted rails, and shards of broken glass threw back a tired sodium glow; diesel and warm concrete thickened the air.

One agent shifted, sweat beading at his collar, while another quietly flexed his fingers to keep his grip dry and his hands loose.

In the distance, a dog barked once—then silence.

Intel confirmed the target would arrive within the hour. Tunçel Karan, a mid-level logistics officer turned international mole, had slipped through surveillance in Ankara and fled the country using forged diplomatic credentials. But now, he was boxed in—surrounded by shadows and steel.

The sting operation was a joint mission—coordinated through a secure CIA-MİT satellite node under the authority of Polaris Command.

With help from Langley's cyber-ops division, Tunçel's alias was flagged at the Serbian-Montenegrin border. Thermal drones overhead followed his signal, drifting above like silent sentinels in the night. Every heartbeat felt like thunder in the stillness.

They had one shot.

A silent flash grenade cracked through the quiet. Within seconds, Tunçel was on the ground, face-first, wrists zip-tied by black-gloved hands.

"No broken bones," the MİT field commander confirmed to the listening ops room in Ankara.

"Package secured."

Ankara – Interrogation Chamber – 17 Hours Later

Feyzi watched from the Echo-7 command center's secure channel, flanked by Commander Hart, Chief Morano, and the rest of Polaris Task Force.

The room was dim except for the ambient glow of terminal lights and the central monitor, casting shadows across tense faces. Hart leaned forward slightly, her eyes narrowed, arms crossed; Morano tapped rhythmically on her tablet, her brows knitted.

A low hum filled the room, underscoring the weight of the moment. The feed streamed from a Turkish safehouse, where Tunçel now sat, sweating, blinking beneath an overhead lamp—his posture rigid, as if aware that the judgment of an unseen court was underway.

They did not touch him. They did not shout. Tunçel was trained for both.

Hour 1–3: Baseline and Silence.

The interrogator, Inspector Kerem, opened with the PEACE model: calm, note-taking, letting Tunçel talk about nothing. Family names, school cities, weather in Belgrade—the kind of harmless trivia a double-agent refuses to decorate.

They mapped his baseline: blink rate, sip interval, the way he pinched the bridge of his nose before each "No comment."

His pulse never spiked.

He'd been here before.

Hour 4–6: Cognitive Load.

A second interviewer, Dr. Selin Ar, took the chair.

No accusations.

She asked him to recount his last seventy-two hours in reverse order, then middle-out, then by location only. The questions weren't about guilt; they were about bandwidth.

Tunçel maintained cadence, even corrected a city block number she "misremembered."

His breathing stayed even.

He was conserving energy like a diver at depth.

Hour 7–9: The Scharff Game.

Kerem returned with a binder and three quiet assertions presented as facts:

"We already detained your driver at Zemun quay."

"We pulled a micro-SD from the tram shelter bench."

"The Belgrade dead drop used a magnetized drain cap."

Two were true. One was not.

Trained sources correct misinformation reflexively.

Tunçel stared at the table and let the lies hang. He neither confirmed nor corrected. The binder closed.

Hour 10–12: Pride/Ego Up—Then Down.

Selin sketched his reputation—competent, careful, invisible— then called it small.

"Mid-level clerk," she said mildly, "moving pallets in the dark for men who don't learn your name."

He took the insult like a stone, expression flat, but the corner of his mouth tightened.

Ego is a hinge; they didn't pull, just placed weight on it.

Hour 13–15: The Striptease.

Evidence arrived in thin slices, each verifiable on camera: a still of his forged credential at the border kiosk, thermal of the rendezvous path, scraped metadata from a burner handset. Nothing dramatic, just enough to shrink his universe.

Kerem set a glass of water on the table and a single page beside it: a scanned waybill out of Bar, Montenegro, authenticated by a Serbian customs stamp.

"This is not about you," he said. "It's about a shipment you greased. We already have the pallet. We just don't want to miss what was underneath it next time."

Hour 16: The Choice.

Selin slid a pre-drafted agreement across the table—limited co-operation for limited indictment, contingent on actionable, time-bound intelligence.

No threats. No promises they couldn't keep.

Then she offered the only currency that buys men like Tunçel: control.

"A controlled call," she said. "You place it. Your words, our script. We roll your handler early, or we let him walk into a camera. You decide who burns: you, or the man who will replace you in twelve hours and end your usefulness forever."

The room held still. The AC hummed.

Tunçel's training told him to wait them out. His eyes slid to the corner where a neutral clock ticked, and for the first time his respiration pattern shifted—a half-breath hitch.

He was not afraid of pain. He was afraid of becoming irrelevant.

He didn't speak. He reached for the pen.

"Tell me about Kazuar," the Turkish interrogator asked coolly.

Tunçel hesitated, then exhaled, eyes darting. His disheveled hair clung to a sweaty brow, and dark stubble framed his jaw—signs of sleeplessness and stress etched into his face.

"Kazuar isn't just a submarine," he muttered, his voice hoarse. "It's the tip of a trident. A cyber-kinetic strike suite. A brain."

"Go on."

"It's designed to locate and neutralize key decision nodes—military, economic, informational—by injecting stealth payloads and launching both physical and algorithmic strikes. STRATUM was its counter."

Feyzi leaned forward in his seat.

"STRATUM wasn't just an AI," Tunçel continued.

"It was the immune system. It was the only thing NATO was building that could outpace Kazuar's adaptive warfare protocol. That's why the Black Hawk was downed. They weren't targeting engineers. They were targeting the code—before STRATUM could go live."

A long silence followed.

"Who's behind it?" the interrogator asked.

Tunçel's lips curled.

"Russia laid the framework. China built the shell. North Korea fed it the virus. The alliance is already here. You're just late to realize it."

Commander Hart stiffened.

Feyzi crossed his arms.

"So, Ukraine was a warm-up. Taiwan's the prize."

Tunçel nodded once.

"They want a new world. One that isn't run from Washington. Or Brussels. They want the STRATUM buried and the old alliances broken."

The screen flickered as Turkish intelligence cut the feed.

Commander Hart turned to the group.

"We're staring at a new axis—Russia, China, and a rogue tech partner. Possibly Iran, maybe North Korea."

Morano added, "All signs point to coordinated hybrid warfare. Submarines, satellites, deep-state infiltration, algorithmic disruption."

Feyzi stood slowly, absorbing the data. A cold weight settled in his chest, as if the gravity of what he had just heard was anchoring him to the floor. His gaze lingered on the fading screen, jaw tightening.

He remembered Boston—his departure, the time lost, the faces of those who never made it off XT84. Now he saw the threads being pulled together, the outlines of a much larger chessboard. Determination flared behind his eyes, sharper than before.

"They want a new world," he thought. "But they'll have to go through me to build it."

"We need to recover the STRATUM modules before they finish their buildout. If they gain full control of the undersea domain, the Pacific will fall without a war."

Rourke stepped forward.

"Then we go hunting."

Feyzi nodded.

"The hunt continues. But this time—we draw the map."

A soft beep echoed through the command center as a new satellite ping illuminated the global display. The lights dimmed slightly, and somewhere near the comms panel, a relay fan clicked to life.

Around the room, Polaris officers exchanged glances—no words, just silent understanding.

The game was shifting, and they were no longer chasing shadows.

They were setting the board.

CHAPTER 36

The Hunt for Kazuar

Echo-7 Polaris Command Center

Commander Feyzi Çelik stood at the center console of the Command Center, flanked by the Polaris Task Force.

The air was dense with anticipation. A soft, continuous hum from overhead panels underscored the room's focused silence, broken only by the occasional click of a keyboard or the low murmur of side conversations.

Light flickered faintly from the data wall, casting shifting reflections across the polished floor. Technicians adjusted headsets, glancing between holographic overlays and sonar feedback panels.

Every movement was taut with expectation, as if the room itself were holding its breath. The room had witnessed the takedown of spies, the protection of secrets, and the revelation of a superpower alliance.

Now, it was time to strike back.

The room didn't cheer; it leaned forward. That's what belief looks like in places without windows.

Rourke folded his arms across the railing as if steadying the whole Atlantic with his forearms. Hart stood half a step off Feyzi's right shoulder; his weathervane for anything the ocean tried to hide. Morano's hands hovered over her console without touching, as though sound alone might smudge the data.

When Feyzi spoke, the noise of the base thinned until even the turbine hum felt like it was listening.

Feyzi addressed the room.

"Kazuar isn't just a submarine—it's a predator with a brain. And it's invisible to all conventional detection. We can't hunt it like a normal vessel. But we can track its wake. We can feel its shadow."

He turned to Captain Joshua E. Monroe.

"Captain, I want USS *Missouri* out of dock silently. Take her below the sonar baseline. Kazuar must not know we're hunting. Prepare your crew for close-quarters deep-sea engagement."

Monroe nodded.

"Aye, Commander. *Missouri* will make her descent under full silence. We'll be the hammer. Just show us where to strike."

He covered the mic and turned to his XO.

"No hero names on the shots," he murmured.

"Just good work that keeps breathing."

The XO nodded. On boats like *Missouri*, poetry wore coveralls.

Feyzi turned next to Chief Warrant Officer Lena Morano, Head of Cybersecurity & Comms Integrity at Echo-7:

"Chief, we need a detection grid Kazuar won't expect. I want you to partner with Lieutenant Commander Sofia Barrera. Pull every waterproof sensor we have. Reprogram them for maximum motion sensitivity— multi depth acoustic sensing with wide angle sampling. Think in layers."

Morano's mouth quirked, half a smile that didn't try to be friendly.

"Layers are where lies go to live," she said softly, already writing needles through the code.

"Let's give their AI a sea so textured it forgets what smooth felt like."

Barrera slid beside her, the kind of technician who tuned machines like other people tuned violins. "If we randomize spiral descent by a factor that isn't random," she said, "we can look messy and still stitch a pattern only we can read."

"Make the mess beautiful," Feyzi said. "Beauty is memorable."

Lena adjusted her glasses. Her world had always been codes and networks, but this... this was war.

Physical.

Elemental.

"Yes, Commander. I'll write a field update for multi axis drift detection and current shear alerts. We'll blanket the trench. Sofia, you'll need to calibrate their navigation parameters."

Lt. Commander Barrera, a specialist in SEVs, nodded.

"We'll fit the sensors with micro-drones. I'll calibrate their gyros for controlled spiral descents at varying depths."

Feyzi turned to Commander Rebecca Hart.

"Commander Hart, I need your dolphins."

Hart blinked in surprise.

"Can we use them to distribute the sensors from below?" asked Feyzi.

Hart's face lit up.

"Absolutely. We'll pair them with sonar guided drop paths. They'll spread the devices like seeds across the deep. Faster and more randomly than drones ever could."

Hart's eyes brightened in a way the red light couldn't dull.

"They'll understand the work," she said. "Dolphins like problems you can hold."

Feyzi grinned. "So do engineers."

"Then we're in luck," Hart said. "They think you're part of the pod."

Girl Power: The Triad of Strength

Morano paused long enough to sip black coffee that had given up on being hot and glanced over at Hart and Barrera in the prep bay window. The three of them caught each other's eyes through glass and reflection and the messy geometry of a shared job.

No speeches, no slogans.

Just an understanding: if this worked, no one would write it up right. If it failed, everyone would.

That's not why they were here.

As the team prepared, the control center became a hive of coordinated brilliance.

Lena worked furiously with Sofia, converting static defense systems into mobile scouts. Hart prepped her dolphin squad with gesture signals and reinforced tracker harnesses.

Three women—each from vastly different backgrounds—now led the most advanced anti-submarine operation in NATO history.

Lena, the introverted cyber savant who once froze under pressure during the Echo-D3 satellite outage but later rewrote the mission protocol under fire, now moved with calm assurance, found herself facing the ocean with real-world stakes.

Sofia, precise and quietly daring, handled field tech like a musician adjusting an orchestra.

And Hart, empathetic and driven, spoke to marine mammals with silent strength.

Together, they formed the neural web of Echo-7's next great move.

Sensor Dispersal: Operation Netcast

Drones launched from the surface bay. Rourke directed them in formations, watching through tactical overlays as they scattered high frequency sensor pods across a 20-nautical-mile ring.

In the big screen's corner, a navy of blue motes drifted outward like careful constellations, each pod sliding to its mark with the modesty of a tool that didn't want applause.

Rourke watched the formation as a chess player watches a clock. "Hold your edges," he muttered.

"Let the middle feel inviting."

Underwater, Feyzi suited up with Hart.

The second time in a suit, but now, not as a survivor—this time, as a hunter.

The water took them the way deep water always does; politely first, then with opinions. Mira and Orion swam point, bodies reading pressure changes the way musicians read a room.

Hart angled two fingers left and both dolphins answered with a tight roll, harness LEDs blinking once in agreement.

Feyzi felt the suit redistribute warmth across his ribs, a quiet reminder that fear and cold share the same voice.

"You good?" Hart asked over comms.

"Better than good," he said. "Angry in the right direction."

Hart looked at him and smiled behind the helmet glass.

"You always do this? Swim with dolphins before launching counter-submarine operations?"

Feyzi smiled.

"Only when the fate of the free world depends on it."

They plunged into the dark, guided by two dolphins—Mira and Orion—who sliced through the murky water like silent sentinels.

The ocean around them was thick, cold, and black as ink. Bioluminescent plankton sparked briefly in their wake, and the glow of the dolphins' sensor harnesses shimmered like constellations underwater.

The pressure tightened around Feyzi's helmet, and he could feel the subtle pulse of the trench's depth pushing against his chest. Short sonar pings echoed faintly, bouncing between stone walls and coral shelves, creating a ghostly rhythm of sound.

It was not just a descent—it was an invasion into a world of darkness where predators ruled, and silence meant survival. With trained accuracy, the dolphins executed drop-offs, placing sensors into crevices, shelves, and along current seams.

Feyzi followed closely, placing backup sensors by hand.

Near a rock lip that looked like a sleeping jaw, Orion hesitated, hovered, then tapped Feyzi's forearm with a snout nudge that felt like advice.

Hart translated without words, the way you do when you've earned it. "Tighter to the seam," she said softly. "He's telling you the current lies to itself here."

Feyzi adjusted ten centimeters, and the pod chirped back a brighter tone.

"Thank you," he told the dolphin out loud.

"Careful," Hart teased. "They'll start charging you consulting fees."

An hour later, they resurfaced.

Echo-7's screen glowed with a perfect, encircling sensor field. Every pod chirped back, alive and scanning.

Lena exhaled and let a hand drift a centimeter above the console, not quite touching it, as if she could feel the grid in her skin.

"It's not beautiful," she said. "It's correct."

Sofia glanced at the coverage map; the ring was imperfect in the right places, the way a human hand draws a circle when it wants something to find the gaps.

Hart closed her eyes for a beat and listened; even topside, she could tell when the pod voices found their rhythm together. It sounded like a new animal had been born.

Detection and Engagement

Lena monitored from the Command Center.

"We have movement. Displacement ripple at sector Echo-Four. Matching size and vector for Kazuar."

Hart zoomed in.

"That's them. They're moving into torpedo range."

Feyzi opened a comm to USS *Missouri*.

"Captain Monroe. Target within shadow field. You are cleared to engage."

Aboard USS *Missouri*

"Contact confirmed," said Sonar Chief Petty Officer Lily Ng.
"Kazuar within vector lock."

Monroe stood tall.

"Launch Sequence Alpha. Two torpedoes—wide arc. Follow with triangulation burst and decoy pulse."

"Firing!"

The boat leaned into purpose. In Control, no one raised their voice.

A junior sonar tech named Ruiz mouthed along with Ng's cadence without realizing he was doing it, a quiet echo to a rhythm that kept people alive.

Monroe kept one hand on the periscope stand and one on the edge of the chart table as if to remind the submarine it belonged to hands, not ghosts.

When the first pair left the tubes, the boat felt momentarily lighter, like a promise had been mailed.

Two torpedoes launched in a crisscross pattern, followed by two more. A final sonar fog canister launched overhead, emitting a broadband noise burst that blinded Kazuar's sensors for a beat.

Kazuar – Internal Deck

For a blink, the deck had that whispering groan steel makes when it remembers the foundry.

Melnikov looked at the overhead and spoke to the hull like an old friend you've wronged.

"Not yet," he said. "Not for them."

Zhang didn't look up from the board. "We won't," she replied. "But they learned our handwriting."

"Multiple torpedoes inbound!" cried Lt. Morozov.

"ECM failing!" Yuwei shouted.

Melnikov cursed. "Turn! Dive now! Fire our counter torpedoes!"

The stealth hull groaned under pressure.

The Kazuar twisted, wounded and rattled.

Two torpedoes skimmed past.

A third detonated near its propulsion array.

The lights flickered.

Echo-7 Command Room

"Hit confirmed!" shouted Lena.

"Propulsion systems damaged. They're bleeding power," Hart added.

Rourke leaned in.

"They'll try to escape under deep shadow."

Feyzi shook his head.

"They're trapped. *Missouri*, finish the job."

Captain Joshua E. Monroe's voice came through.

"Final shot, sir."

Boom.

The deck of USS *Missouri* vibrated with the force of the launch, a concussive thud that echoed through the steel bones of the submarine.

Back at Echo-7, the command center momentarily froze—no one breathed, no one spoke.

Then, slowly, as the confirmation pulsed on the main screen, the silence broke into cascading reactions: gasps, cheers, the clatter of a coffee mug knocked over by a celebratory fist.

The screen confirmed: Kazuar destroyed.

The cheer rose, broke, and rolled back like a tide, leaving behind the better thing—work.

Hart's arms tightened around Sofia and then let go because there were still dolphins to settle, still gear to stow, still a sea to reassure. Lena sat hard and put her hands under her thighs to stop them shaking.

Rourke didn't smile. He looked at the tactical and whispered to no one, "One down doesn't equal done."

Lena dropped back into her chair, exhausted.

Feyzi looked at the screen.

"One less ghost in the sea," he whispered, his voice barely audible over the rising chorus of relief.

The hum of the command center dimmed slightly as the main lights shifted to a soft, ambient blue.

Around him, the Polaris Task Force began returning to their stations, but Feyzi stood still, eyes lingering on the tactical display.

He thought of the Black Hawk, of the shattered calm that had started this journey.

Kazuar was gone—but the war had only just changed shape.

The ghosts were fewer but not finished.

He turned slowly to Hart.

"Prep the next briefing. We still have a long way to go."

Hart nodded and reached for her slate, but paused when she saw the way Feyzi's eyes had fixed on a part of the map that wasn't lit.

"Where?" she asked.

"The place you feel when you're not thinking about the place," he said.

"Where the trench goes quiet like it's listening."

She stared at that unlit patch and felt the same tug she'd felt the night Echo-D3 insisted they turn starboard toward a sound no machine could hear.

"I know it," she said.

"Good," Feyzi replied. "Then that's where we plan from."

Far to the north, under a lid of sea so cold it kept secrets for centuries, a field of silt sighed as if something heavy had just remembered to breathe.

A minute later, on an unremarkable pier in the Azores, a man in a reflective vest closed a locker and palmed a coin that was not a coin.

He didn't smile. He didn't hurry. He simply chose a different corridor than yesterday.

In Ankara, a light stayed on in a window that should have gone dark two hours ago; the person behind the desk reread a line and underlined a different word this time.

Back in Echo-7, Mira and Orion circled once in their tank and stilled, their bodies pointing toward a patch of water that the map hadn't learned yet.

The ghosts were fewer. The sea was not.

Somewhere in the depths, another shadow stirred.

CHAPTER 37

The Turning Point

Echo-7 Polaris Command Center

Echo-7 was no longer just a covert facility buried in the depths of the Atlantic. It had become the epicenter of a global response effort.

Overhead lights dimmed slightly, replaced by pulsing blue glows from holographic displays that shimmered across the command table. Status screens streamed real-time fleet movements, satellite shifts, and diplomatic channels. The air buzzed with a quiet, purposeful urgency.

After eliminating the stealth submarine Kazuar—one of the greatest threats to NATO's underwater defense structure, Commander Feyzi Çelik stood before the Polaris Task Force with a singular goal: escalate the operation.

The battle had proven one truth. Pentagon protocols were too rigid, too slow.

What the world needed now was swift, coordinated, surgical response—and Echo-7 had delivered.

The room settled into that rare frequency where fear and competence agree to share a chair.

Rourke stood with his hands braced on the rail, body angled like a shield; Hart hovered a half-step behind Feyzi, her attention moving the way a searchlight moves; slow, patient, relentless.

On a side console someone had taped a child's crayon rocket ship—two triangles and a smile—next to a checklist labeled NIGHT OPS.

Nobody mentioned it. Everybody saw it. Echo-7 had stopped being a place and become a promise.

U.S.-Turkish Joint Task Force Meeting

Feyzi opened a secure line to the joint command center, where representatives from the U.S. Navy, Turkish Armed Forces, and NATO Intelligence were waiting.

Across the split-screen feed, anxious faces stared back—Admiral Grayson from Norfolk, General Özkan from Ankara, and Director Dumas from Brussels.

A digital globe pulsed red at its poles.

"Mission 4 is complete," he began.

"Kazuar is neutralized. But this was not a singular threat. It was part of a broader, coordinated campaign to destabilize the alliance. The next phase begins now."

He laid out the entire sequence of missions: STRATUM's development, the Istanbul ground breach, the orbital laser threat. Then, he escalated the briefing up the chain of command.

The faces on the split screen blinked in their different midnights.

Grayson looked like a man who sleeps with his tie on; Özkan's jaw worked as if chewing a sentence he refused to spit; Dumas had the pale, haunted calm of someone who knows how thin silence can be stretched before it tears.

Feyzi didn't posture. He leaned closer so they could see the lines the ocean had drawn into his face.

"This won't be a parade of memos," he said. "It's a choreography. If we hesitate, they write the steps."

Grayson pursed his lips. "And you're certain this is coordinated?"

"Certain enough to stake my name," Feyzi replied. "And yours if you like."

He let the edge breathe, then softened it with the thing they needed more than certainty.

"We can win this if we move like one body."

Commander Hart, standing just behind him, exchanged glances with Chief Morano. Both women nodded subtly—every mission had pushed them harder than the last, but this was the moment they'd prepared for.

Hart spoke without taking her eyes off the board.

"When we pulled Kazuar's shadow off our hull, it wasn't because we shouted louder. We whispered better."

Morano nodded, fingers dancing a quiet staccato over a keyboard.

"And we stopped loving our own assumptions," she added. "Let's keep that romance dead."

Pentagon and NATO Command Activation

Within the hour, a priority transmission was delivered to the Pentagon and NATO General Command in Brussels.

Feyzi issued a formal call to raise the threat level to its highest tier: DEFCON 2 across all U.S. forces and a matching NATO posture—meaning forces must be ready to deploy and fight on very short notice.

This is the second-highest level of alert in the U.S. defense readiness system—signaling that armed forces must be ready to deploy and engage in combat within six hours. It is one step below full-scale war and has only been reached once in history during the Cuban Missile Crisis.

The announcement sent a ripple through Echo-7. Junior officers whispered to one another, tension rising in their shoulders.

Commander Rourke cracked his knuckles instinctively and muttered,

"So, this is it."

Lena Morano glanced at her tactical console, tightening backup communications paths, while biting the inside of her cheek. Hart's fingers tightened around the edge of the display table.

In Brussels, Supreme Allied Commander Europe (SACEUR) convened an emergency session.

In a stone-walled chamber humming with security encryption gear, member states voted unanimously.

The chamber carried the smell of old decisions: varnish, wool, the cold tang of sealed windows.

A translator lifted her headset and rubbed the hinge of her jaw, eyes shiny with the realization that she had just given history its voice in three languages.

When the final yes crossed the room, SACEUR didn't exult; he simply exhaled through his nose and said, "Do not confuse unanimity with safety." The microphones picked it up anyway, turned it into policy.

Somewhere deeper in the base a pump thumped, and the floor answered with a low, reassuring tremor, as if the ocean itself had signed the order.

NATO Command Broadcast – Global
Order of Operations

Echo-7 was granted operational command over Atlantic and adjacent Eurasian theaters. On the command screen, lines darted across the map like nervous currents of light:

United Kingdom: HMS *Queen Elizabeth* strike group ordered to North Sea.

France: *Charles de Gaulle* carrier group redirected from the Mediterranean toward the Suez.

Germany: Frigate FGS *Sachsen* and U-31 submarine repositioned to protect Baltic Sea corridors.

Türkiye: Barbaros-class frigates and Type 209/214 submarines deployed to Aegean and Black Seas.

Air forces were scrambled. Naval bases buzzed to life. Military satellites realigned their coverage grids.

On Echo-7, the buzz turned into a steady rhythm of action.

It was like watching a ship tack into wind.

Techs stopped jogging and started walking quickly. Orders got shorter. Mistakes got louder and therefore rarer. Someone in Comms pulled the lucky coin from under the screen, kissed it once, and stuck it back.

Hart passed the Echo-D3 tank and the dolphins followed her with their eyes; that old electricity sparked in her chest; the one that said animals feel storms before instruments do.

U.S. Fleet Command – Western Pacific Theater

Admiral Theodore "Theo" Langston, commander of the U.S. Seventh Fleet, stood aboard the USS *Ronald Reagan* near the South China Sea when a secure call came through. The night air smelled of diesel and ocean brine, punctuated by the low hum of power across the carrier deck.

He took the encrypted tablet.

"Admiral Langston," Feyzi's voice came through.

"Kazuar has been eliminated. But that was just one head of the hydra. There will be others. We believe China has deployed similar stealth submarines in your theater."

Langston nodded.

"We've suspected as much. What do you suggest?"

Feyzi replied,

"Use what we used. Drones. Dolphins. SEV-compatible sensors. You need to detect their movement, not their heat. We'll transmit the sensor dispersal protocol. And Admiral—no assumptions. If it's quiet, it's hiding."

Langston snorted softly and turned to watch the deck crew move like a single muscle under sodium lights.

"Quiet's a liar," he said. "Always has been."

He tilted the tablet, so the moon threw a pale wash across his face.

"If this works, I send you bourbon. If it doesn't, I send you a list of things I wish I'd said nicer."

"Send both," Feyzi answered, allowing himself half a smile. "I collect contradictions."

Langston looked out at the sea.

"How long until ARES is ready?"

"Fifteen days," Feyzi said.

Langston raised a brow. "That's a bold promise, Commander."

"I know," Feyzi answered. "But we don't have another choice."

Langston chuckled, half admiring, half skeptical.

"Then let's hope you're a miracle worker."

For a heartbeat the Pacific seemed to hold its surf in its mouth.

Langston let the silence measure the promise.

"Fifteen days is a story the sea enjoys ruining," he said at last.

"It's not a story," Feyzi replied. "It's a schedule with teeth."

Langston nodded once, satisfied not with the plan but with the man.

"Then bite."

The call ended.

Feyzi exhaled slowly.

The countdown had begun.

Hart didn't ask if he believed his own timeline; she watched the way he set the tablet down carefully, like a thing that might bruise the table if dropped wrong.

"You know they'll try to take a piece of you on the way up," she said, not unkindly.

"They can gnaw all they like," he answered. "I only need the part that writes."

"Then write the sky," Hart said.

Hart stepped beside him, placing a quiet hand on the table edge.

"They'll be watching us now," she said.

"Every move."

But there was one final obstacle.

Feyzi turned to the Polaris command screen.

"We still have to deal with the orbital laser weapon platform. Before ARES can be deployed, we need to take out that satellite. We'll strike next—high above the Earth."

Morano slid into the conversation with that hush smart people bring to dangerous rooms.

"We've been learning its manners," she said. "It's proud of how quiet it is. Proud things forget they're visible when they admire themselves."

Feyzi turned the holographic overlay of the orbital ribbon with two fingers until the inclination caught light.

"Pride's a lever," he said. "Give me the fulcrum."

"We spoof a star it recognizes, then shift it off course," Morano said. "And then move it."

Hart frowned, thinking it through from water up to vacuum. "And if it refuses the sky?"

"Then it tells us what it really wants," Morano replied. "And we take that away instead."

In the background, the room dimmed slightly, signaling night cycle transition.

The faint pulse of the Earth's orbit, projected as a glowing ribbon on the side wall, reminded everyone that the next frontier wasn't just below the waves—it was overhead, and closing fast.

Across continents, small human scenes adjusted to the pitch of the hour. In Brussels, a custodian paused with a mop at the threshold of the secured chamber and crossed himself without quite knowing why. In Ankara, a field officer folded a photo back into a wallet and tightened the strap on a go-bag he had hoped not to use again. In

Norfolk, Grayson took his ring off, spun it once on the desk, and put it back on a finger that suddenly felt younger.

Back in Echo-7, the night cycle bled the room into cool shades. The map of the world pulsed softly, like a child's nightlight left on for courage.

Feyzi stood very still and let the silence assign him the next sentence.

Hart watched him watch the orbit and realized that command, at its best, is just the art of asking the right thing of people at the right time without stealing their courage to do it.

"Let's take their altitude away," he said finally, almost gently. "One clean move. Then we breathe."

Rourke leaned toward the mic and rolled his shoulders as if he could make the base taller by willing it so.

"Polaris, set for skywork," he said. "Keep the ocean listening."

No one clapped. The lights didn't change. But in the bones of the place, something leaned forward.

Somewhere above the equator, a dull metal shape adjusted its attitude by a degree that no human eye could care about and every instrument would record.

Far below, a wave broke wrong on a beach no one was watching, and a gull screamed like it understood math.

In Echo-7, two dolphins lifted their heads at the same moment and then, as if embarrassed by their certainty, sank back into the water and closed their eyes.

The turning point was not loud. It rarely is. It was a hand on a wheel, a breath taken on purpose, a line of code that chose humility instead of pride. And then the world—stubborn, complicated, beautiful—began to turn.

CHAPTER 38

Strike From the Stars

Mission 5: Elimination of the
Orbital Laser Weapon Platform
Echo-7 Polaris Command Center

The lights in the Polaris Command Center dimmed to twilight mode as the orbital threat grid bloomed to life across the main wall.

A rotating, three-dimensional hologram of Earth was draped in glowing arcs—each an orbital path, each tagged with a string of alphanumeric codes denoting NATO, allied, or enemy satellites.

Among them was an elusive target: the cloaked orbital laser platform.

Commander Feyzi Çelik turned toward Colonel Jacob S. Vance, Space Command Liaison to Echo-7.

Vance was tall, broad-shouldered, with a grizzled edge to his features that hinted at decades of command. He had once served as director of orbital logistics for NORAD and brought a wealth of pragmatic, space-era battlefield intuition.

The air around them vibrated with controlled tension. Technicians whispered across consoles, and the ambient hum of processors filled the space like a low-frequency drumbeat.

"Colonel," Feyzi said, voice calm but resolute, "it's your team's turn to show the power of NATO. We've taken the fight to the seas. Now, we take it to the stars."

Vance didn't posture. He slid a headset on and spoke like a range officer calling wind.

"Rules of engagement stand: no debris cascade, no power-grid spillover, no collateral on civil bands. We do this clean, or we don't do it."

He pointed to a thin line on the globe.

"We're going to catch it between ground radars while it's cold-soaking. When the cloak cycles, it leaves a seam; temperature and attitude drift. That seam is our handle."

Feyzi nodded once. "Then pull."

Vance nodded and keyed in a secure uplink to Vandenberg Space Force Base in California.

On the wall display, the visage of Lt. General Marissa Zhao appeared—stoic, sharp-eyed, and framed by the constellation maps of Orbital Defense Command. Zhao, a former astrophysicist turned defense strategist, was known for her icy precision and a reputation forged in early Space Force skirmishes over disputed orbit lanes. She wore a silver-edged Space Command flight jacket, and her left sleeve bore the emblem of Operation Aegis.

Feyzi addressed her directly.

"We didn't start this war. But we're going to finish it. XT84 was carrying innocent civilians—mothers, children—from fourteen countries. They were murdered in cold blood by a surgical space strike. The weapon used wasn't an accident. It was a precision laser platform designed for orbital decapitation strikes."

Zhao gave a tight nod.

"We believe the platform is operating under adaptive cloaking and low power signaling. But our last triangulation sweep pinned it in a decaying polar orbit. It's moving, but we've got eyes on it now."

"Eyes" meant a patchwork the platform wasn't expecting.

Space Fence returns with glint anomalies, passive RF from oceanic ships acting as opportunistic receivers, infrared bloom off the radiator edges, and a tiny time drift in its two-line element set that didn't match any declared satellite.

Zhao kept her voice level. "We'll spoof a star tracker update packet. If it accepts, it corrects attitude. That correction confirms control. Once it trims, your window opens."

"Good," Feyzi said. "Make it think it fixed itself."

The Weapon of Choice: X-37B

Zhao's ops room tightened. Checklists rolled.

A tech in the back row raised a hand. "Weather?"

Lt. Colonel Devina Rusk—mission lead for orbital kinetic engagements, didn't look up. "We're going upstairs, not across town."

The room moved as one.

Colonel Vance stepped forward.

"We're authorizing the use of X-37B. Orbital vehicle 4-01 is hot and ready."

Vance kept it simple for the room.

"We're not shooting a laser at a laser. We're dropping a hammer on a rifle. Gravity doesn't miss meetings."

He cut a look to Feyzi. "Once the rods go, nobody talks loud. We let physics do the bragging."

A tactical feed unfolded, showing the unmanned, delta-wing craft—a miniature, black-shrouded spaceplane stored in its hangar at Cape Canaveral.

Operated by the U.S. Space Force, the X-37B was a ghost in low-Earth orbit: undetectable, untraceable, and now, armed.

Its payload had been modified under emergency protocols by Rusk.

Rusk, appearing via a separate feed, looked weathered but focused. Her short-cropped auburn hair framed alert eyes and a burn scar traced faintly along her jawline—a remnant of a failed booster deployment during an earlier atmospheric re-entry mission. She was known across orbital command channels for her fearless decision-making and relentless discipline.

Her eyes were locked on telemetry data while her fingers hovered over launch prep diagnostics.

"We'll deploy three kinetic rods," she said from Vandenberg, her voice layered with exhaustion and urgency.

"Solid tungsten. Non-explosive, high-velocity impact. The rods will shatter the platform without creating an orbital debris field."

"We tuned the rods for sectional fracture," Rusk added.

"They'll cut structure and dump heat without turning the sky into shrapnel. Guidance is purely kinetic. No warhead, no signal to jam."

"Window?" Feyzi asked.

"Seventeen minutes wide. We'll use the fifth," she said.

"Why the fifth?"

"Because that's when they think we've given up."

Mission Execution – The Space Hunt

While the X-37B coasted, Morano ran cover from Echo-7; quiet cyber that looked like background weather. She salted low-value telemetry with perfectly plausible errors so the enemy's analysts would chase ghosts a half-orbit behind.

Hart watched the orbital ribbon with the same focus she used on sonar. "Patterns repeat," she said, half to herself. "Water or vacuum. They always do."

After two hours of orbital synchronization, the X-37B reached interception proximity. In a silent ballet 250 miles above Earth, the spaceplane maneuvered with micro-thrusters, guided by AI-assisted targeting systems synced with Echo-7's uplink.

"Target lock confirmed," said Rusk.

"Rod alignment stabilized."

Zhao leaned into her mic. "Confirm we're clear of the ISS and all commercial tracks."

A voice from the deconfliction pit answered, "Green across the board."

Vance folded his arms. "Then send it."

The countdown began.

"Ten seconds to firing solution."

"Five... four... fire."

Three tungsten rods detached from the undercarriage. They fell like spears, gliding through the vacuum, guided by precision kinetics.

The room didn't cheer. It measured.

Guidance thrusters whispered a last trim. Ground tracks ticked. A junior controller whispered numbers under his breath like he was pacing a runner to the finish line.

Rusk's tone never moved.

"Rod one time-to-impact two eight minutes. Two rides the lead wake. Three takes the insurance angle."

She glanced to Zhao. "We'll know from the radiator first."

Thirty minutes later, a silent white bloom flared against the backdrop of space. The flash reflected against orbiting debris fragments, briefly illuminating the dark hemisphere below.

Enemy Satellite—obliterated.

Zhao exhaled through her nose; one second, not more.

"Confirm no fragmentation outside planned cone."

A tech called, "Negative uncontrolled debris. Cone is clean."

Vance rolled a shoulder. "One less switch to pull on us."

Feyzi kept his eyes on the track. "Two more and we close the sky."

Within the next twelve hours, NATO interceptors launched by France's CNES and the UK's Skynet wing destroyed two more using high-altitude drone deployment systems, followed by onboard microwave disruption beams to disable control nodes.

France ran a tight play; high-altitude drone loft, optical handoff, microwave disrupt. The satellite didn't explode; it sighed and went dark. In the UK lane, Skynet's team used a similar approach but cut power through control nodes first, then cooked the bus. It fell asleep with its eyes open and never woke.

On Echo-7, Morano tracked the telemetry go quiet in layers, like lights going out down a hallway.

"That's it," she said. "They can still look. They can't cut."

Echo-7 Polaris Command Room

Rourke didn't move at first. He watched the compliance bands flatten and only then let his hands come off the rail.

Hart glanced toward the Echo-D3 tank; both dolphins had surfaced and were still. It meant nothing scientific. It meant enough.

Cheers broke through the tension.

Lena Morano raised a fist.

Commander Hart turned to Feyzi.

"That was for XT84," she said, voice heavy with meaning.

Feyzi's answer was a small nod that carried weight.

"For them, and for the ones who never get named on a crawl."

He didn't raise his voice. "We're not finished. We just took their fastest tool off the table."

His eyes didn't leave the screen.

"Now we've removed the sky from their advantage."

He addressed the room, voice low.

"As I promised after the crash—this doesn't end here. We're going to hunt the architects of this war. One by one. Until they face justice."

The tension among the command staff didn't entirely dissolve.

Rourke folded his arms, squinting at the map as though trying to predict the enemy's next move.

Morano exhaled hard and sat down, eyes scanning for anomalies that weren't yet visible.

A low alert tone pulsed in the background, reminding everyone that victory in orbit did not mean safety on Earth.

Rourke leaned closer to the plot.

"They'll try to win the next hour on the surface; ports, cables, fuel."

Morano was already moving tabs. "I'm scrubbing maritime AIS for pattern anomalies. We'll flag anything that looks like a tug acting like a frigate."

Hart rubbed a thumb along the edge of the table. "And we keep the dolphins hot. If the enemy pushes underwater to compensate, we'll hear it first."

Feyzi nodded. "We hold altitude denial and water awareness at the same time."

Enemy Command – Kaliningrad and Chengdu

A red light pulsed inside the war room beneath Kaliningrad. Colonel Alexei Voronov stood still, reading the confirmation.

"Loss of three orbital assets confirmed. X-37B engagement verified."

Voronov turned to his deputy.

"Accelerate Phase Two. Reassign remaining assets to the Northern Atlantic, South China Sea and Caspian vector. Inform Chengdu."

Kaliningrad shifted from anger to procedure in under a minute.

Orders split along three vectors: Atlantic probing, Pacific masking, and a quiet push into the Caspian where radar is more rumor than fact.

In Chengdu, the reply wasn't drama; it was logistics; retask two ground stations, stand up a reserve bird in a dusty hangar, move a crew who'd expected a weekend home. The board didn't look broken to them. It looked different. That was enough.

In Chengdu's Aerospace Command, a similar message came through. The Chinese general whispered a single word.

"Understood."

And across the world, in silence, the board reset—the next move imminent.

In the debrief, Zhao's team logged the strike in plain language: find, fix, finish, confirm.

No slogans, no chest-thumping.

On Echo-7, the lights returned to normal, and people went back to the work that keeps a win from evaporating.

Feyzi stood a step back from the map and let the room settle. The sky wasn't safe. It was manageable.

That would do for tonight.

CHAPTER 39

Global Ripples

World in Motion

The world had gone quiet—but not still. Silence from government leaders. Silence from the Pentagon. Silence from NATO. But silence, in this case, was deafening.

Global news outlets were in overdrive. Military correspondents, geopolitical analysts, and defense insiders all converged on one truth: something massive was underway.

The New York Times ran a bold headline across its front page:

"Alliance on the Edge: Unprecedented NATO Naval Mobilization Stirs Global Anxiety."

The article cited anonymous sources who described "unusual command uplinks from Echo-class undersea facilities," suggesting that an off-grid NATO installation had taken operational control of Atlantic assets. A satellite image captured dozens of fighter jets scrambling from Ramstein Air Base in Germany, while ship spotters in Portsmouth tracked the HMS *Queen Elizabeth*'s sudden departure at midnight.

CNN's Anderson Cooper hosted a special segment from the network's global affairs desk:

"This is no exercise. We are witnessing the largest synchronized NATO movement since Operation Desert Storm—perhaps since D-Day. Naval formations in the Mediterranean, Baltic, and South

China Sea are re-aligning. Carrier groups are vanishing from ports. And the White House? Silent."

Markets moved first. Futures spiked in thin liquidity; crude jumped on talk of convoy protection premiums; insurers started revising war-risk clauses before sunrise in London.

Container lines issued advisories that read like weather reports; new routes, new speeds, "out of an abundance of caution." Flight radars showed transatlantic crossings nudging south by a few hundred miles, then back again, as dispatchers tried to thread a path between rumors and fuel margins.

In Brussels, a short NOTAM appeared and disappeared inside fifteen minutes, long enough for pilots' group chats to fill with screenshots and questions that had no answers.

From satellite feeds, BBC World News confirmed that Germany's FGS Sachsen and U-31 submarine had moved from Kiel toward the Danish straits.

French media reported that the *Charles de Gaulle* had bypassed its scheduled port call in Naples, moving east toward the Suez with full escort.

CNN Turkey showed Turkish Type 214 submarines submerging out of Gölcük Naval Base, flanked by Barbaros-class frigates.

In Moscow, evening news anchors spoke of "routine exercises" with a tone that suggested anything but routine. Beijing's primary channels ran archival footage of ship launches on loop and kept the lower-third banners bland. Neither capital admitted to movement; both tightened the message discipline inside ministry corridors. Off the record, defense attachés traded the same sentence in different accents: watch the cables, not the press releases.

In Japan, NHK broadcast footage of joint drills between U.S. and Japanese destroyers in the East China Sea suddenly being suspended—both fleets turned toward combat formation without explanation.

Civil aviation felt the tremor. Dispatch centers in Frankfurt, Doha, and Montreal pushed quiet guidance to long-haul crews: top up fuel, carry alternates that made no sense yesterday. An FAA hotline briefed airlines on "possible space-based interference" without naming a source. A handful of business jets diverted to Shannon with no mechanicals declared, only a notation; "operational prudence."

And in Washington D.C., *Politico* published a scathing editorial:

"The President has not spoken. The Pentagon has refused comment. And yet global mobilization is happening in full daylight. The question is no longer whether something is happening—it's who's calling the shots."

Energy desks started calling each other instead of the screens. Traders who had never heard of Echo-class facilities now said the word like it had always been on the map. A Baltic cable operator reported "elevated maintenance activity" and then stopped answering calls. In the North Sea, a survey ship went AIS-dark for three hours and came back on the grid twenty miles east with no comment from the owner. Shipping lawyers began drafting addenda and left the signatures blank.

Reactions Across the Globe

In Berlin, Chancellor Kühn gathered her security council in a closed-door session at the Reichstag. Satellite feeds flickered across the room, and aides exchanged grim nods.

A staffer slid a single page to the Chancellor with three colored bands: cyber, power, water. She circled cyber and handed it back. "Start here," she said.

"If it's quiet, it's because we haven't looked hard enough." Across town, a rail control room ran a backup protocol usually reserved for strikes and storms. Trains still moved. The operators spoke less.

"Activate our cyber defense layer," she ordered. "And prepare for incoming coordination from Echo-7."

In Seoul, the Minister of National Defense called an emergency summit.

"If the Atlantic has mobilized," he warned, "the Pacific cannot sleep."

In London, Defense Secretary Aisha Ocafor addressed Parliament behind closed doors.

"We are no longer in the age of conventional deterrence. Whoever commands the seabed and the stars now commands the future."

The room gave a low murmur, not dissent—calculation. The Home Office liaison asked one question: what happens if a civilian satellite gets caught in the middle? Ocafor answered without raising her voice.

"Then we prove we can work without it." She didn't elaborate, and no one pressed.

Public Unrest and Media Frenzy

Street protests erupted in parts of Paris, Madrid, and São Paulo— some calling for peace, others waving banners that read "Defend the North" or "Stop World War III."

City halls pulled emergency managers into back rooms. Mayors wanted to know how much diesel was in the backup tanks and how long the cell towers could run if the grid hiccupped. Grocery distributors were told to keep one extra day on the floor. No alarms. Just margins.

Social media ignited with theories and blurry videos. One viral clip showed a group of schoolchildren in Naples huddled in a gymnasium during an unscheduled evacuation drill.

Hopkinton, Massachusetts
Çelik Residence – 9:00 p.m.

Two unmarked SUVs idled at the end of the street. The local police chief had already walked the perimeter with a federal agent who
said very little and looked at everything. A neighbor tried to drop
off a casserole and was gently turned away with thanks and a quiet
apology. Inside, the house felt smaller, like the walls had leaned
closer to listen.

Jill Çelik sat alone in the family room, her phone resting idle beside her. The house was dim. The only light came from the Sony
screen mounted on the far wall, displaying CNN's Breaking News
ticker.

Anderson Cooper looked into the camera with a grave tone.

"What we are watching may very well be the opening act of a new
global order. With NATO in full alert and no clear public leadership
statement, many are wondering... who is leading this effort?"

He paused.

"We're told it is being coordinated from a classified NATO installation. Our defense analysts suggest a Commander—name with-
held—is orchestrating multiple missions at once."

Jill watched quietly. Her hands clenched the arms of the chair.
Family photos stood nearby—their wedding day, Ayla's graduation.

Then Cooper added:

"What's clear is this: the fingerprints of a master strategist are on
this operation."

Jill tilted her head. She whispered to the empty room:

"That's him. Feyzi's fingerprints all over this."

The screen faded into footage of aircraft carriers cutting across
ocean waters, missiles being loaded, and war rooms buzzing with
silent urgency.

Jill's heart beat a little faster.

Not from fear—but from knowing.

The man she loved was in the center of history.

Her phone buzzed once with a text from Ethan: "We're ready when he calls."

Another from Laura: "Media wants you. We said no."

Jill typed back two words; "Thank you"—and set the phone down screen-face on the table. She watched the crawl for names she knew and found none, which was both a relief and a pressure on the ribs.

#AtlanticCommander trended globally within the hour.

Echo-7 Polaris Command Center

Below the Atlantic, members of the Polaris Task Force huddled around live feeds of the very same broadcasts. Junior officers exchanged glances—awestruck, uncertain.

Chief Warrant Officer Morano cracked her knuckles and leaned into her station.

"Guess we're famous now," she muttered.

"Kill the tag in here," Morano added.

Screens in the bay blanked out social feeds and returned to telemetry, comms logs, and heat maps.

"We don't work off narratives. We work off numbers."

The junior officers nodded and looked grateful for the order they hadn't known they needed.

Commander Rourke didn't look up from the sonar array.

"Fame won't matter if we're late to Mission 6."

He had a legal pad next to the console with three lines on it: ports, cables, fuel—and two boxes unchecked. He tapped the pencil twice and drew a fourth line: people.

"Mission 6 doesn't fly without the right heads and hands," he said to no one in particular.

Feyzi Çelik, standing alone near the mission board, folded his arms.

He could feel the weight of the world tilting toward Echo-7.

Hart stepped to his side and kept her voice low.

"They'll guess you're here," she said. "They won't guess how many rooms you're in at once."

Feyzi didn't smile. "They don't have to. They just have to be late."

And he knew the next strike would decide whether it broke—or endured.

In Ankara, a late bulletin moved across a secure line with a simple instruction -coordinate, don't announce.

In Norfolk, a petty officer taped a fresh checklist to a bulkhead and wrote the date twice to make it stick.

In Hopkinton, the house lights stayed low and the TV stayed on mute while Jill watched the ticker crawl and listened for a specific ringtone.

Echo-7 kept its cadence: status, confirm, act—and let the feeds do what feeds do.

The ripples hadn't crested.

They were aligning.

The next move would prove whether the world knew how to hold its nerve.

CHAPTER 40

The Replacements

Echo-7 Polaris Command Center

The circular briefing table in Echo-7's Polaris Command Center had become a place of both tension and transformation. In the hours since the destruction of the Kazuar stealth submarine and the orbital satellite strike, momentum had shifted.

But ARES—the artificial intelligence and robotics system designed to counter stealth and satellite-based threats—remained unfinished.

Commander Feyzi Çelik stood at the center, flanked by the Polaris Team.

The low hum of data consoles and hushed voices gave the room a pulse of purpose.

His gaze rested on Dr. Sienna Patel, the brilliant engineer now bearing the burden of completing NATO's most advanced defense protocol.

Dr. Sienna Patel – Chief of Project ARES

Born in Mumbai and educated at Imperial College London, Dr. Patel had risen rapidly through the ranks of DARPA and NATO's cyber-innovation arm. Her genius in adaptive AI, pattern detection, and autonomous systems made her the perfect architect for Project ARES. But the explosion that destroyed the Black Hawk helicopter had killed 11 of her team—friends, mentors, and partners. The burden of continuing the work alone weighed heavily.

Sienna hadn't slept more than four hours in the last three days. Every simulation glitch felt like a ghost from her fallen team. She rubbed the bridge of her nose and looked at Feyzi.

"We can recover the software modules, now" she said, voice steady but weary.

"But I need specialists. Not just coders—people who understand complex, adaptive deployments under tight security. The kind of engineers who can finish what we started without needing to be taught how to think like ARES."

Feyzi didn't hesitate.

"I know who we need."

OnePIN

Gasps and glances passed around the room. Dr. Patel blinked. "Your company, OnePIN?"

"Yes," Feyzi replied.

"We've built scalable, secure mobile platforms deployed on five continents. The team—they think like ARES already. If you trust me..."

"I trust you 100%," Patel said. "If you say they can do it, I'll greenlight it."

Feyzi turned to the comms terminal and opened a secure channel to the U.S.–Turkish Joint Task Force.

Within an hour, formal approval was granted. Defense authorization was transmitted. All that remained was the outreach.

The outreach wasn't an email blast.

It moved through secure phones and short phrases, old friendships and quiet trusts. A liaison from EUCOM provided the flight window and a simple instruction: assemble near Boston under non-descript cover. No jerseys, no logos, no social posts.

Families would get the real story; everyone else would get "a government resilience program" and a return date that was intentionally vague.

A small logistics team at Hanscom Air Force Base began clearing a hangar and running a last-minute background scrub—more for habit than suspicion. The authorization codes matched. The lift was approved.

OnePIN Headquarters – Boston, Massachusetts

In Ethan Gagnon's office, COO of OnePIN, a secure video call from the Department of Defense interrupted a financial forecast meeting.

On the screen: a DOD operative and a legal representative.

"NDAs must be signed immediately by the executive and engineering teams," the liaison said flatly.

Ethan frowned. "We don't even know what this is about."

The agent replied simply:

"This involves Feyzi Çelik. That's all we can say until the papers are signed."

Ethan called Chiara Moretti, OnePIN's General Counsel. Chiara was already standing by. As she read the legal framework, her fingers slowed across the keyboard.

"This has to be about him," she said softly. "He's alive—and they need us."

She nodded. "Sign them. All of them."

HR sent a two-line notice to the engineering org: executive offsite, confidentiality required, business continuity maintained. It read like a retreat memo. People understood it wasn't. Ethan walked the floor once, not to reassure but to take mental inventory—who needed a phone call, who needed a look, who needed time. Chiara drafted the family guidance letter with practical details: next-of-kin contacts, a 24/7 hotline, pay and benefits locked, travel insurance escalated.

It was clinical, and it worked.

Ethan coordinated with the U.S. and Turkish OnePIN teams. From Türkiye, Gülce Demir handled rapid compliance. In Johannesburg, Anri van der Merwe and Asha Naidoo locked down regional authorization within the hour.

A Global Conference – OnePIN Meets Echo-7

In Ankara and Johannesburg, a few engineers were still in commute clothes; jackets on chair backs, backpacks half-zipped. Someone in Boston muted a ringing desk phone with the palm of a hand and left it there. When the NATO crest filled the screens, rooms that were used to product roadmaps and sprint reviews went silent and stayed there.

Monitors across OnePIN's Boston, Ankara, and Johannesburg offices turned black, then flickered back on; this time with a metallic NATO logo marked: E-7.

Commander Rebecca Hart appeared on screen first. "This is Commander Hart," she said crisply.

"Commander Feyzi Çelik will join you in one minute."

When Feyzi appeared, his image drew stunned silence, followed by spontaneous applause. His voice was calm but layered with meaning.

"I'm speaking to you from a secure U.S. military installation deep in the North Atlantic," he said.

"I survived the crash of Air Turkey Flight XT84. I was not supposed to. The attack was coordinated—with the Black Hawk helicopter that carried the original ARES software team. They were killed. I was meant to be among them."

He paused.

"My past from thirty years ago has caught up with me. What we're dealing with here has global consequences. But this meeting isn't about my survival—it's about the future."

"The software modules for Project ARES will soon be recovered. But the integration requires a team I can trust. A team that knows how to work in impossible conditions. That team—is you."

He looked around at the stunned faces.

"I'm asking for volunteers. This will mean leaving your homes, your families. For at least a month. OnePIN operations need to continue during this time. Everything else will pause. I cannot say more now—except that what we do here will shape the world your children inherit."

No one moved.

Then—every hand went up.

Ethan lifted his hand last.

"We'll split the company," he said. "Operations stay here. The core builds there."

Sienna watched the gallery view fill with faces that weren't unsure; they were already scheduling themselves.

A developer in Ankara raised a finger. "Childcare," she said, not as a complaint, as a checklist item.

Feyzi nodded. "Covered. We've arranged stipends and on-call support. No one leaves chaos behind at home."

That landed. Volunteer didn't mean reckless. It meant planned.

Echo-7 Integration Team – Deployment Roster

Feyzi announced the team who would fly out under full NATO protection to an undisclosed U.S. base:

Adam Kowalczyk, Chief Technology Officer, 22 years at OnePIN. A methodical systems thinker, Adam is known for building resilient backend architectures that never falter under pressure.

Terry Moreau, Director of IT and Cloud, 16 years. The architect behind OnePIN's secure cloud infrastructure, Terry's calm under fire and uncanny ability to scale systems make him indispensable.

Arda Yalçın, Head of Engineering, 17 years. Revered for his mentorship and precision, Arda can untangle the most convoluted codebases and lead teams through chaos.

Daniel Mercer, Director of Solutions, 19 years. A bridge between product vision and implementation, Daniel's deep client insight ensures ARES will be usable in the real world.

Ankit Verma, Director of Technology, 15 years. A brilliant algorithm strategist, Ankit specializes in adaptive intelligence and has authored key modules still running on four continents.

Barış Aksoy, Senior Software Engineer, 10 years. Quiet and unassuming, Barış has a sixth sense for code flaws and security vulnerabilities, often catching issues before they surface.

Kemal Özdemir, Senior Software Engineer, 10 years. Known for optimizing performance in large-scale systems, Kemal's code runs like clockwork—even under telecom load.

Berkay Çetinkaya, Software Engineer, 5 years. A rising star with a flair for UI and embedded interface systems. Berkay sees human patterns as clearly as machine ones.

Erhun Kaya, Software Engineer, 4 years. Energetic and inventive, Erhun specializes in real-time systems and mobile framework extensions. He codes like he's racing the clock—and usually wins.

Elif Aydın, Senior Test Engineer, 12 years. Rigorous and unrelenting, Elif ensures nothing escapes scrutiny. She's broken every system she's tested—and that's why they're so strong.

The engineering roster stayed on standby status; bags not packed, devices staged, family plans arranged.

Sienna drew the first integration board on Echo-7's side anyway: inference layer, secure comms, fleet adapters.

"Sequence won't change," she told Feyzi on a secure line. "When they get here, we move."

He nodded. "Until then, we keep it tight. No assumptions."

Ethan Gagnon, Chief Operating Officer; Laura Whitman, VP of

Products and Marketing remained behind to lead operational continuity. The rest of the engineering team would provide global support from afar.

The Contract – Business Must Continue

Back at OnePIN, the day-to-day didn't stop. Support tickets still needed answers; carrier partners still needed updates that sounded routine and meant everything. Laura drafted the messaging for customers: "Infrastructure upgrade window; no impact expected." She kept it boring by design. People believe boring when the world is loud.

Later that day, a new call came through. This time, to Evan Brooks, OnePIN's Chief Financial Officer.

On the line: the DoD Procurement Division. Ben Carter, Vice President of Finance of OnePIN, also joined the call.

"Evan," the voice said, "this will require extensive contracts, clear budget approvals, and flexible scope."

Evan leaned forward.

"We've worked with carriers in 20 countries. I know how to work through chaos."

But as the call deepened, the complexity hit him—exchange rates, jurisdictional taxes, encrypted procurement timelines.

He exhaled sharply and pinged Natalie Santoro, OnePIN's Controller, and Jane Daniels, Senior Finance Associate.

Together, the three of them stitched together a NATO-backed procurement framework in under 48 hours.

The framework wasn't elegant; it was durable. Dual signatures on every purchase order, mirrored ledgers on both sides of the Atlantic, tax positions documented in plain English and then again in legal.

Natalie built a wire calendar that looked like air traffic control: funds in, funds out, contingencies stacked in case a bank decided to "review" at the worst moment.

Jane triple-checked per diems and travel codes because small mistakes become big problems at altitude.

Evan closed his laptop, reopened it, and ran the risk register one more time. He didn't like surprises. The register got shorter.

Evan didn't sleep. But when NATO confirmed full operational coverage, he allowed himself a moment of calm.

"We'll make sure OnePIN survives this," he told the team.

"And when it's over, we'll have helped save a lot more than just the business."

CHAPTER 41

The Second Kazuar

Echo-7 Polaris Command Center

Feyzi's call with the OnePIN Team was over.

As silence returned to the Command Center, Dr. Sienna Patel had already shifted into execution mode, but the weight of exhaustion hung on her shoulders.

Her eyes, rimmed with sleepless red, scanned flight manifests and encryption transfer protocols with unwavering focus. A half-drained energy drink sat untouched at her console—forgotten amid the chaos.

She was orchestrating the deployment of her new software team with a blend of technical precision and emotional urgency, her fingers moving rapidly across the interface as though racing against time itself. Each line of code she reviewed was a tribute to her fallen team—the eleven minds she had lost in the Black Hawk crash.

The only viable route to Echo-7 was through a classified fleet of long-range, low-observable, high-altitude NATO transport helicopters—designated Bell Boeing V-22 Osprey. These rotorcrafts were built for operations deep into hostile zones, with extended stealth range exceeding 1,250 nautical miles.

Logistics were routed through RAF Ascension Island, a remote airfield under British command, halfway between South America and Africa.

The pressure to complete ARES wasn't just operational—it was personal.

Sienna flagged a private channel to Feyzi and spoke without preface.

"I can field a stop-gap. Not ARES proper; ARES Edge. It's a lightweight inference layer that runs on what we already have in Echo-7. It won't predict the Kazuars' full decision tree, but it can score their most likely evasion moves and push those suggestions to fire control and sonar in real time."

Feyzi studied her for a beat. "What do you need?"

"Raw stream, not summaries. Direct taps from *Missouri*'s spherical array and *Kentucky*'s towed array, plus Echo-7 hydrophones. I'll sandbox it here and publish cues back to the boards. Green for high confidence, amber for uncertain."

"Do it," he said. "Edge goes live as advisory only. We keep human veto at every step."

Sienna nodded once. "Understood." She pulled the energy drink closer and didn't touch it.

As the airlift coordination continued, Commander Feyzi Çelik convened with Commander Hart and the Polaris Team.

It was time for Mission: ARES Recovery—the retrieval of the vault containing the AI's encrypted modules from the wreckage of the Black Hawk.

Meanwhile, Echo-7's sensors picked up a new allied contact. The U.S. Navy's USS *Kentucky* (SSBN-737), a Virginia-class ballistic missile submarine, had arrived under silent running, responding to emergency orders from U.S. Atlantic Command.

A behemoth of naval engineering, the USS *Kentucky* measured over 560 feet long and housed 24 Trident II D5 ballistic missile tubes. Despite its capacity for nuclear warfare, today it served a different mission—tactical support and protection for Echo-7.

It's crew of 155 operated in near-total silence for weeks at a time, guided by layered stealth and sonar evasion protocols. The submarine's onboard reactor hummed quietly, powering life support, propulsion, and state-of-the-art sonar suites capable of detecting even micro-acoustic shifts.

Its commanding officer, Captain Everett "Hawk" Remington—an even-tempered, grizzled submarine veteran known for his taciturn demeanor and encyclopedic knowledge of sonar profiles—hailed Echo-7 with a firm, grounded voice. Remington had served in three oceans and trained the top sonar teams across two fleets.

"Echo-7 Control, this is *Kentucky*. We're entering final approach to docking bay 2. All systems green, personnel transfers and resupply confirmed. Requesting bay guidance."

"*Kentucky*, copy," Feyzi replied. "Hold station and await vectors."

A voice cut across the net—Lieutenant Coen from port control. "Echo-7, confirming platform identity as Ohio-class SSBN *Kentucky*. Guidance data uplinked."

Remington answered without ego. "Affirmative on Ohio-class. We're a big target, Commander. If your sensors twitch, we're clear to back out."

"They might twitch," Feyzi said. "Stand by to pivot."

Feyzi acknowledged the incoming vessel—but before any comfort could settle in, chaos ignited elsewhere.

Aboard USS *Missouri*
Patrol Sector Zulu-North Echo-7

Captain Joshua E. Monroe, commanding officer of the USS *Missouri*, stood tall on the bridge with his hands clasped behind his back.

The dim blue lighting of the control room cast long shadows across the faces of his crew.

Every console buzzed with quiet urgency, screens flickering with sonar waveforms and contact reports. Crew members whispered updates to one another, their nerves on edge from days of tense patrol.

Monroe's voice, calm and authoritative, kept the rhythm steady—a steady heartbeat in a room bracing for war. But beneath his composed surface, his mind raced—calculating, anticipating.

After all, he'd seen what the first Kazuar could do. He wasn't about to let his guard down now.

Monroe leaned closer to Sonar. "Lily, assume smart decoys. If you think it's one track, check for the second we can't see."

Ng didn't look up. "Already doing it. Their noise floor is disciplined." She slid a finger across the waterfall display and frowned. "And it's getting closer."

And then it wasn't.

"Bogey in the water!" screamed Lt. Alyssa Kane, Missouri's Weapons Officer.

"Incoming at 45 seconds!"

Commander Rourke spun around.

"Countermeasures, now! Launch decoys and full evasive protocol!"

He slammed the comms.

"Echo-7, we are under fire. Confirmed contact. Another Kazuar is in the water."

Feyzi didn't raise his voice. "Echo-7 to Missouri—confirm single shooter or multiple."

"Working it," Ng said over open comms. "We're seeing phase-shifted returns on two vectors. Could be a coordinated spread. Could be two boats."

"Treat it as two boats," Feyzi said. "We'll be wrong in the safe direction."

At Echo-7's Polaris Command Center, alarms blared again. Chief Warrant Officer Lena Morano stood over the new sonar displacement grid.

"Commander Çelik," she said, "Kazuar is outside the current sensor perimeter. We need to extend the coverage grid now."

"Barrera," Feyzi called, "spin up the spare hydrophone strings and push them out on autonomous reels. No cable backhaul; burst only. If they get cut, we lose a sensor, not the net."

Sofia Barrera was already moving. "Launching from bays three and four. Dolphins stand down until the water's quiet—I'm not putting them in a torpedo lane."

Hart didn't argue. "They wait."

Morano keyed a new overlay. "Edge link coming online… Sienna, you've got raw feed."

"Receiving," Sienna said. "Edge is compiling. Give me ninety seconds."

Feyzi's jaw tightened. He hadn't expected the enemy to deploy a second Kazuar so soon.

Morano's voice cracked through the din.

"Movement on the grid! It's back—Sector Delta-5!"

She slammed coordinates into the system.

Commander Hart instinctively reached for her side console, while Commander Morano's eyes darted to secondary sonar feeds.

A junior analyst dropped her tablet in shock. The realization cut through the tension like a blade—this wasn't a fluke or an echo. The threat had multiplied.

The second Kazuar had arrived.

Rourke stepped to the central console, jaw set.

"We split the ocean. *Missouri* hunts forward. *Kentucky* becomes the wall."

Remington's voice came steady from the SSBN.

"Copy. We'll hold a quiet barrier at depth and force them to choose. If they break toward us, we'll light them up with active pings for *Missouri* to finish."

Monroe didn't wait. "*Missouri* acknowledges. We'll be the hammer."

"EMCON strict," Feyzi said. "No chatter that isn't killing us or saving us."

Missouri's voice returned over open comms, crackling with urgency and disbelief.

"Impossible! I'm receiving torpedo locks from two directions. Repeat: two different headings!"

Ng's tone flattened, all business.

"Second contact is dirty. Slight cavitation pulse, non-periodic. Either damaged fins or an autonomous decoy trying to mimic a wounded sub."

Sienna cut in. "Edge calls the northern contact high-probability manned. Southern is decoy or UUV. Confidence seventy-two percent and rising."

"*Missouri*," Feyzi said, "prioritize the northern track. *Kentucky*, you shadow the southern and be ready to punch it if it gets close."

"Roger," Remington replied. "We'll hold it at arm's length."

A cold silence gripped the command room.

Feyzi turned toward the Polaris Team.

"Another Kazuar. They're trying to stop ARES—by any means. We have two Kazuars in water, now."

Across the Atlantic floor, the second bogey closed in. The silence was shattered by Commander Rourke from the secondary sonar post.

"Bogey on approach! Torpedo in the water! Countermeasures, now!"

Missouri's tubes spat a fan of noise makers, each one spinning up to throw false tonals into the water. The boat rolled ten degrees to port, then ten to starboard, creating a short, ugly signature on purpose. It was a trick Monroe had drilled into his crew; make the torpedoes commit, then vanish.

"Inbound lost lock," Ng said. "Reacquire in three... two... they bit on the noise. Resetting firing solution."

Monroe kept his voice even. "Return fire. One blunt, one smart. Blunt to herd, smart to hit."

Feyzi's voice rang out.

"*Kentucky*, abort docking—get back to open water. *Missouri* is under siege. You're the only backup she's got."

Within seconds, USS *Kentucky* flooded ballast tanks and backed away from Echo-7's docking tunnel, surfacing to strategic depth and activating full defensive arrays. The ship's torpedo bays spun to combat readiness, and sonar arrays began to pulse wide-spectrum signals into the black void.

"Edge update," Sienna said.

"If the southern track is a UUV, it will attempt to hug *Kentucky*'s baffles and spoof a tail. Recommend a three-knot course change every forty seconds—breaks its timing model without advertising our location."

Remington didn't ask how she knew. "Executing. Three-knot weave. We'll look sloppy; we'll live."

The hunt for both Kazuars had begun.

Feyzi's eyes lingered on the red pulses of the sonar grid. Each blip was a threat, a ghost in the depths, but this was no longer about ghosts.

It was about survival.

Morano's eyes flicked to a secondary panel.

"We've got a whisper on the fiber—an undersea cable repeater just chirped in our sector. Could be nothing. Could be a backup datalink."

Feyzi answered immediately. "Flag it for a later cut, not now. We don't swing axes while torpedoes are in the water."

Hart folded her arms, watching the red triangles crawl across the display.

"When this is over, we take their phone away."

"They're cornered animals now," he muttered, almost to himself.

Commander Hart, standing nearby, glanced over with quiet intensity.

Her mind flashed to XT84, to the rescue, to the cost of failure.

"Cornered animals still bite," she said.

"Then we don't corner," Feyzi said. "We channel."

He pointed to the bathymetry overlay.

"There's a saddle between those two ridges. We pressure the northern track right through it. *Missouri*, herd him east. *Kentucky*, hold the exit. If he dives, the ridge steals his room to maneuver."

"Copy," both captains said, almost together.

Sienna glanced up from her screen. "Edge concurs. If he takes the saddle, his best evasion bend is five degrees. That's not enough."

Around them, the Polaris Command Center moved with choreographed urgency—orders flowing like current, lives on the edge of keystrokes.

Somewhere, in that silent ocean, machines of war circled closer.

Missouri fired again—staggered shots that left almost no wake. *Kentucky* pinged once, hard and cold, and the ocean answered with a clean return. The northern contact twitched, turned into the saddle, and ran out of good choices.

"Edge marks high-probability intercept in twenty-two seconds," Sienna said, not looking away.

"Hold your nerve."

No one in the room moved. The screens kept scrolling. The water did the rest.

And Echo-7 was now the last defense line between chaos and control.

CHAPTER 42

The South China Sea Assault

USS *Ronald Reagan* – Ready Room

Aboard the USS *Ronald Reagan*, flagship of the U.S. Seventh Fleet, Admiral Theodore "Theo" Langston sat in his oak-paneled ready room, the hum of the ship's nuclear core vibrating faintly beneath his boots.

The walls bore photos of his predecessors, maps from past battles, and a framed quote from his former CO:

"The sea forgives nothing."

A coffee machine sputtered steam behind him, adding domestic normalcy to the otherwise high-stakes command chamber.

He nursed a lukewarm cup of black coffee, eyes locked on his encrypted tablet. Satellite overlays, sonar heat maps, and erratic displacement patterns glowed against the screen—a digital sea of trajectories.

His thoughts circled back to Echo-7 and his call with Commander Feyzi Çelik:

"Deploy displacement sensors in wide perimeters. Assume more than one Kazuar."

Langston's jaw tensed. Years of wargames and live deployments had taught him one thing: the ocean never gave second chances.

He toggled a fleetwide channel.

"Rules of engagement are Yellow—confirm target identity before weapons free. This water is crowded, and the fishing fleets will run dark to get video. We're not giving the enemy propaganda. EMCON Charlie on the screen ships, full emissions for hunters only. I want E-2D Hawkeye up for air picture and P-8A tasking from Kadena for buoy lines. And somebody call Yokosuka—get JMSDF on our left flank before the militia boats swarm."

His XO, Commander Raquel Ibarra, was already moving.

"Hawkeye spinning. Kadena acknowledges. Japan green."

"Good," Langston said. "We do this clean, or we don't do it at all."

The shrill alert of red sensors broke the static.

"Admiral! Movement on the water displacement sensor array, sir. Multiple contacts!"

Langston rose before the junior officer could finish. The weight of command settled on his spine.

"How many?"

"Three, sir. Three Kazuars. All heading toward *Reagan* at attack vectors."

His face hardened.

"Sound General Quarters. Bring all ships to combat readiness. Initiate countermeasure protocols."

The Seventh Fleet Mobilizes

A gray dome rolled up on the *Reagan*'s waist cat—an E-2D Hawkeye, engines clawing at the air as its twin props wound up to an angry whine. On the horizon, a P-8A Poseidon arrowed south at medium altitude, its belly already loaded with sonobuoys and Mk 54s. To the east, the JMSDF destroyer JS *Maya* checked in on Link 16, its Aegis suite stitching into the American picture without friction. The Philippine Navy's BRP *José Rizal* reported a picket line to keep civilian traffic outside a cordon the public would never see on any chart.

"Get NIXIE towed decoys wet," Ibarra added. "If they shoot for the carrier, I want those fish chasing ghosts."

Instantly, the sprawling battle group surged into coordinated action.

The USS *Mustin* (DDG-89), USS *Barry* (DDG-52), and USS *Rafael Peralta* (DDG-115) veered into flanking positions, forming a crescent wall of steel.

Below, the USS *Asheville* (SSN-758) and USS *Mississippi* (SSN-782) broke formation, tracing intercept arcs.

The Pacific shimmered deceptively calm under the mid-afternoon sun, but below the surface, leviathans stirred.

On the flight deck, sailors sprinted to their posts. MH-60R Seahawk helicopters roared to life, carrying dipping sonar, sonobuoys, and anti-submarine torpedoes.

The rhythmic clatter of boots and spinning rotors echoed across the ship. Below deck, damage control teams in full gear ran drills, sealed bulkheads, and pressurized weapon bays.

In less than a minute, the *Reagan* had transformed into a coiled predator.

Down in Combat, the air was cooler, the voices flatter. A watch stander pointed at a civilian AIS cluster drifting toward the edge of the cordon.

Ibarra didn't hesitate. "Helo Two-One, wave off the trawlers; use loudhailer only. No overflight, no spooking. Keep our deck picture clean."

A petty officer slid a grease pencil along a plex overlay—current, depth contours, and a pale "no-go" box around a coral rise that would blind dipping sonar if they wandered too near it.

The sea looked empty outside. Inside the scopes it was an intersection at rush hour.

Contact

"Incoming torpedo locks!" shouted Lt. Commander Reiko Sato from Weapons Coordination.

Her tone sliced through the bridge like a blade. The memory of a failed training drill—where she lost five simulated crews—flickered in her mind. She wouldn't fail this time.

"Six torpedoes in the water, closing fast!"

Langston didn't blink.

"Launch countermeasures. All birds in the air. Fire control, assign fire solutions to each Kazuar."

Counter-torpedoes and acoustic decoys exploded from their pods. Seahawk choppers dropped homing buoys and prepped Mk 54 torpedoes. One decoy detonated prematurely, blasting a geyser skyward. Another was struck mid-run by a kinetic shell. The rest pushed toward their targets.

Reiko's fingers moved instinctively. "A calm ocean hides sharp teeth," her grandmother used to say. The truth of that proverb had never been clearer.

"Deploy NIXIE," she ordered.

Cable handlers paid out the towed decoy while the carrier altered course just enough to change the incoming solution. Hawkeye called a bearing-only track skimming the surface—likely a data skiff, not worth a missile, but worth noting.

Reiko logged it and went back to what mattered: the water beneath them.

Echo-7 Steps In

Morano's packets arrived with no drama—clean overlays, latency under a second. Edge cues popped on *Reagan*'s plot as small green brackets, the same shorthand already saving lives in the Atlantic.

Langston felt some of the tension ease out of his shoulders. This wasn't theory anymore. Whatever Echo-7 was running, it traveled well.

"Vector your Seahawks to the green brackets," he told Ibarra. "No circles. Straight in, dip, drop, and drag that pattern east. We herd; *Asheville* and *Mississippi* hit."

"Echo-7, this is *Reagan* Actual. We are engaging multiple sub-surface threats. Confirming Kazuars. Immediate support requested."

Chief Warrant Officer Lena Morano's voice cut in, calm and cool.

"Admiral Langston, we are tracking three Kazuars in your grid. Sending real-time coordinates and sonar overlays now."

Langston watched as his displays updated with Echo-7 telemetry. He exhaled.

"Understood. We have visual sonar confirmation. We're engaging. Your sensors saved our lives. Tell Commander Çelik he was right."

"Tell him yourself," Ibarra said under her breath, then louder to the bridge, "Combat reports Kazuar Two is venting from the stern. We've marked a bubble trail. Hawkeye confirms no air threats in the stack—your sky is clean."

"Good," Langston said. "Let's finish clean."

He turned to his XO, Commander Raquel Ibarra, recalling their shared brush with death in the Mediterranean three years ago.

"I need to meet this guy, if we survive this."

Counterattack

"JMSDF reports transient on our north screen," the Hawkeye controller added. "Possible unmanned decoy angling for the carrier wake."

"Copy. We're not biting," Langston said. "Keep the big ship predictable; let the wolves hunt."

From the depths, the *Asheville* launched Mark 48 ADCAP torpedoes. One Kazuar was struck amidships. The explosion scattered its cloaking debris like fish scales in a feeding frenzy.

A second Kazuar was rattled by a near-miss depth charge and forced upward.

The third, more elusive, darted into a trench—but not before launching a desperate final shot.

"Poseidon to *Reagan*, we're laying a hard buoy fence across the trench mouth. If he turns back, we'll see him. Marking your safe lane for the next ninety seconds."

Ibarra's pen tapped once on the chart and stopped. "Lane received. Helm, hold it tight."

"Torpedo inbound on *Reagan*'s bow!"

"Brace!" someone yelled.

The impact came like a thunderclap.

Metal screamed. The deck lurched.

Langston's jaw cracked against the tabletop, the taste of copper flooding his mouth.

Monitors flickered. Coffee flew in arcs.

"Flight deck?" Langston barked, spitting copper.

"FOD contained," came the reply. "One Seahawk waved off; second is feet-wet on station. No fire. Crash crew standing by."

"Engineering?"

"Shock isolated. Shaft bearings green. We're steady on steam."

The ship groaned once more and then settled, the deck teams already resetting like it was another drill.

Recovery

As emergency power re-stabilized, Langston forced himself upright.

"Damage report."

Commander Ibarra replied, brushing blood from her brow.

"Minor hull scarring. No breaches. Missile grid still online."

"Keep air ops conservative," Langston said. "No heroics. We're alive because we stayed boring."

He keyed the net again.

"*Mustin, Barry, Rafael Peralta*—shift five degrees starboard and close the crescent. *Asheville, Mississippi*, your turn. Kill the second boat or drive it shallow."

"Copy," *Asheville* replied. "Tubes hot."

Langston grunted and grabbed the comm.

"Echo-7, this is Admiral Langston. You were right. They're escalating. We're in this together. Over."

Echo-7 Command Center – Polaris Hub

Thousands of miles away, Feyzi stood at the front of the Polaris Command Center. Sweat shimmered on his brow beneath the LED glow.

Colonel Vance had a second window open on the far wall; satellite tasking along the first island chain.

"PLA frigates are probing the edges but holding outside the median," he reported. "Plenty of eyes. Few hands."

"Then we don't give them a picture to sell," Feyzi said. "Minimal radio, minimal wakes. Save the press conference for someone else."

Tiered workstations flickered with data feeds. Holographic overlays tracked submarine trails like spectral veins beneath the sea.

Behind him, Commander Rourke, Commander Hart, and Lena Morano watched in reverent silence.

Feyzi met Hart's eyes. "They won't stop."

"Neither will the cameras," Hart answered.

"Tokyo, Manila, Taipei—they're watching this minute by minute."

"Then we give them what we promised," Feyzi said.

"A pattern that works in the Atlantic and the Pacific. Same playbook, adjusted for the noise."

Morano glanced up from her console.

"Edge just flagged a course-change micro-pattern on Boat Three—a seven-second weave repeating every forty. That's a human hand, not a script."

"Pass it," Feyzi said. "*Reagan* gets the tell."

Each blip on the radar was more than data.

It was blood waiting to be shed. Feyzi knew this.

And he carried the weight.

Hart nodded grimly. "But neither will we."

The *Reagan*'s plot bloomed again—new green brackets sliding ahead of a fleeing contact.

Asheville called "weapon away," *Mississippi* called "second shot," and the P-8's buoy fence lit up with a clean doppler rise. The last Kazuar tried for the trench and found a dead end.

In the Polaris room, no one cheered. They just watched the data fall into place, the same way it had under a different ocean, on a different day.

Feyzi let out a breath he hadn't realized he'd been holding. "South China Sea has our pattern now. Keep feeding them until they don't need us."

Hart nodded. "And then?"

"Then we get back to ARES," he said. "Because this won't be the last time someone tries to turn the world off by cutting the water."

The war wasn't coming.

It was already here.

CHAPTER 43

The Enemy Reacts

Kaliningrad, Russia – Eastern Command Theater,
Subterranean War Room

Beneath six meters of reinforced concrete, the Kaliningrad command bunker buzzed with a tension no encryption could mask.

Fluorescent lights flickered against exposed steel beams and the low thrum of power generators vibrated through the soles of polished black boots. The walls, lined with analog backup schematics and LED war tables, displayed live naval traffic from the Atlantic to the South China Sea.

Colonel Alexei Voronov stood rigid before the central digital war map. His gaze fixed on the display, jaw clenched as if locked in mid-command. Decorated in both Chechnya and Syria, Voronov had mastered chaos.

But this was different. This was war beneath the surface—and in the code.

Voronov flicked the map from satellite view to raw telemetry. No gradients, no colors—just numbers, lat/long strings, and timestamps.

"We stop admiring the picture," he said. "We work the math."

He jabbed at the console. "Roll back all feeds ten minutes prior to Echo-7's buoy seizure and show me every unauthorized RF event under 300 hertz. ELF, VLF, I don't care. If their dolphins sneezed into a sensor, I want it."

A captain at Signals hesitated. "Sir, we've already screened for active emission."

"Then screen for passive response," Voronov snapped. "Check for environmental returns and unintended sensor reactions."

A junior operator called out from the far bench. "Found a dead-zone flutter in their environmental grid—too small for command traffic, too regular for noise."

Voronov didn't smile. "Their breach team is disciplined. Capture the pattern and feed a copy back."

Behind him, rows of cyber technicians worked feverishly, decrypting intercepted comms and tracking stealth signatures. A subtle drip echoed from a leaky coolant pipe above. The air smelled faintly of solder and stale tobacco.

"Explain to me," Voronov growled, voice coarse as sandpaper, "how Echo-7 eliminated the first Kazuar."

Three generals shifted uncomfortably.

There were no satisfying answers.

Sidorov cleared his throat. "Colonel, the first kill wasn't a lucky shot. Echo-7 is collapsing our loops—sensor, spoof, exfil—in hours, not days. They're running an edge pipeline. No central chokepoint to poison."

"Then we poison the edge," Voronov said. "Inject noise into their maintenance. Logistics, power, water. You can't run a war room if the air goes wet."

"Understood," said Sidorov, already drafting a staggered attack: slow leaks, harmless glitches, just enough to pull techs off the battle line.

"Sir, satellite playback shows a minor displacement distortion, then... nothing. No explosion. No trace."

"The sub simply disappeared," muttered Major Pavel Sidorov, an AI strategist and former academic whose warnings had gone unheeded.

"One Kazuar was supposed to end this," Voronov muttered, his fingers tightening into fists.

"He survived."

They had underestimated Echo-7. Worse, they had underestimated Feyzi Çelik.

"Psych profile," Voronov ordered.

Sidorov pulled a slim folder from a locked drawer.

"Çelik favors small teams, short loops, and visible leadership. He'll take the first risk to buy trust. He does not delegate intent, only tasks. He hates waste. He learns once."

Voronov stared at the map. "So, he'll pick the hardest problem first, solve it loud, and dare us to answer."

"Exactly," Sidorov said. "If he's moved to recovery, it means he trusts his perimeter. We hit when the safe is on the hook, not in the mud."

Voronov nodded once. "Then we time our strike to the lift."

Qiantang Cyber Dome, Shanghai
LA Eastern Command Node

Thousands of kilometers east, General Wei Liang stared into a three-tiered holo-map projection. The interior of the dome shimmered with data overlays: acoustic sweeps, satellite trajectories, and Kazuar positions. Chrome walls reflected sterile lighting. PLA guards lined the periphery, unmoving.

He was silver-haired, weathered by decades in the South Sea Fleet, and methodical to a fault. He adjusted his cuffs before activating a direct comm-link to Kaliningrad.

"Colonel Voronov. We warned you not to underestimate Echo-7."

"You Russians test boundaries," Liang continued, eyes narrowing.

Liang brought up a secondary pane—civilian traffic overlays in the Philippine Sea.

"We have fishing fleets we cannot move without drawing head-lines and lawfare. We thread the gaps, or we own the blame. Your theater invites chaos. Mine punishes it."

Voronov's reply was dry. "And yet you built with us."

Liang didn't flinch. "Because your hulls hid our code."

"We calculate them. Echo-7 was a known unknown."

"You misread a ghost," Voronov snapped back.

"Now that ghost bleeds satellites."

Another voice joined—sharp, confident. General Bao Xinjian, head of the Central Military Cyber Division. Only in his 40s, Bao was a rising force in China's AI warfare doctrine.

"We're past complaint. We switch to deception. Flood their mari-time picture with plausible noise. AIS echoes, cloned MMSI, carrier groups that aren't there."

Voronov gestured to his cyber bench. "We can spoof AIS. We cannot fake fuel bunkers and radio checks."

Bao's tone didn't change. "We will. The platform at Sansha can relay scripted chatter for thirty-six hours. Long enough."

The digital map flickered.

His gaze was cold, almost metallic.

"Enough blame. The question is response," Bao said flatly.

Voronov folded his arms.

"Then respond."

Bao turned to his own console, pulling up Operation STRATUM's fallback schema.

Operation Escalation Plan – Activation

The orders moved as plain speech, not slides.

Liang gave the timing. "Three K-class assets pivot south within the hour, staggered by eleven minutes, each with a different doctrine—one aggressive, one patient, one erratic. We want the Americans guessing which is the real hunter."

Voronov took the Atlantic. "Two boats at Echo-7, one to force the base to look left, one to cut the recovery lane on the right. We will not fire first. We force them to commit countermeasures until they have none."

Bao handled the overhead. "We lost three birds. We still have relay capacity. We switch to dark handshakes via ionospheric scatter. If they kill the uplink, our subs stay autonomous for seventy-two hours on pre-loaded branches.

In Novaya Zemlya, technicians rolled open armored blast doors. Cold air rushed over composite hulls as two autonomous strike subs were craned into flooded cradles. No speeches. Just checklists and green tags.

The following moves were unanimously approved:

Three new Kazuars dispatched to the U.S. Seventh Fleet in the South China Sea.

Two Kazuars rerouted toward Echo-7's North Atlantic grid. ETA: 36 hours.

Arctic silos in Novaya Zemlya prepared for stealth deployment of autonomous strike subs.

In Kaliningrad, naval technicians in black uniforms descended to the silo bays. Steam hissed as 90-meter-long Kazuar units were loaded into their launch cradles, their hulls humming with encrypted pursuit logic. Each submersible was built for silent attack.

"You sure they can adapt to countermeasures?" Liang asked over the secure line.

"With AI-guided unpredictability, yes," Bao replied.

"But only if we move now."

He added, "And we change the bait. They're using dolphins. Fine. We seed the water with micro-pingers tuned to prey frequencies. We won't hurt the animals. We'll waste their time."

Liang gave a thin nod. "Delay is damage."

Inside the War Rooms

Back in Kaliningrad, Voronov stared at the war table as the new Kazuars blinked into position.

"Mask it with civilians," Voronov said. "Container ships from Murmansk to Reykjavik will file weather-diverted routes across our arcs. Legal, routine, boring. We don't hide the blades—we hide the handles."

"Information cover?" Sidorov asked.

"Tease a story about an exercise," Voronov said. "Old footage, new headline. Let their media argue about tone while we move steel."

"The Chinese fear loss. The Americans fear chaos. But Feyzi Çelik? He embraces it," he thought.

Major Sidorov stepped beside him.

"We should've sent them earlier," he said, voice low. "I studied the man. Feyzi doesn't just survive. He adapts. Faster than code."

Voronov looked up. "Then we stop trying to out-code him. We out-schedule him." He tapped the table twice. "Our strikes land when his people are walking from shift to meal, from console to rack. When eyes drop, not when alarms scream."

Sidorov didn't argue. "I'll map their day cycle from the scant power dips we've seen. It isn't much, but routine bleeds into graphs."

In Shanghai, Admiral Liang turned away from the screen, thinking through next steps.

This was no longer a skirmish. It was the opening phase of a co-ordinated campaign.

Liang stepped away from the dome and picked up a secure handset. "Notify Sansha garrison: civilian channels will carry scripted distress in two hours. Fishing militia will keep distance, only cameras. If the Americans fire on anything unarmed, we archive it. If they don't, we clog their lanes."

Bao keyed a last command. "Activate Glass River."

An officer at his shoulder frowned. "Sir?"

"A narrow worm," Bao said. "It sleeps in their procurement mirror; it wakes when they print a parts label. No explosions. Just delays."

General Bao remained expressionless.

"I will either be hailed as the architect of victory... or blamed for a war gone algorithmic," he thought.

And so, under a silent accord, they launched.

In Kaliningrad, Voronov watched the launch telemetry tick upward and forced his hands to unclench. "No more speeches," he said. "We adjust, we don't announce."

On the Shanghai link, Liang's face cut to black. Bao's console dimmed to a thin line.

Sidorov stood by the door. "We still might lose," he said, not quite a question.

Voronov didn't turn. "Then we lose learning faster than they can."

A status light changed from yellow to green. Somewhere under ice and under cloud, machines slid into dark water and kept going.

The Kazuars surged into the depths once more—the second phase of the water war had begun.

The countdown boards in both war rooms read the same number: 36:00:00. No one said it out loud, but every operator felt the clock in their bones. The second phase wasn't theory anymore; it was scheduled.

CHAPTER 44

Breaking the Tide

Echo-7 Command Room

The Polaris Command Center pulsed with urgency. Overlapping radio chatter spilled from the walls, bouncing between curved console bays like nervous birds trapped inside a steel aviary. Dim red and blue tactical lights stuttered in rhythm with rising sonar pings.

A heartbeat of war.

Commander Rebecca Hart stood at the central console, jaw clenched, her eyes flicking over data streams while memories clawed their way back to the surface.

She was no longer in the steel belly of Echo-7; for a moment, she was twenty-nine again, aboard the Vindicator in the Adriatic.

The training exercise had turned into chaos when a misread sonar contact led to a live torpedo strike. She could still hear the cry from Ensign Dwyer: "They're not stopping! It's real!" Seconds later, the destroyer beside them vanished from radar—no debris, just silence. That helplessness had branded itself deep in her psyche. She was trying to filter the noise from meaning.

"USS *Missouri* to Echo-7! This is Monroe—we've got sonar echoes. No visual. Something's stalking us, 2000 meters out."

"USS *Kentucky*—torpedo tubes loaded! We've got shifting thermal layers—this one's smarter."

"*Ronald Reagan* reporting multiple underwater contacts—confirming three, I repeat, three Kazuars. They're closing fast."

Hart's face went pale.

Her fingers dug into the cold metal edge of her station.

In an instant, she was back in the Adriatic, a decade ago, watching a destroyer blink off radar. That had been an exercise. This was real. This was lives on the line. She'd lost good people before. But this time, she was no bystander. This time, she had to command through the fear.

Feyzi, composed on the surface, stared into the screen with burning focus.

Inside him, a storm raged.

The war had a face now. Not a flag, not a submarine, but the terrified voice of a person with no options.

His voice was sharp.

"Focus on USS *Kentucky*. It's tracking a Kazuar inside the sensor net. Sienna, provide real-time coordinates to *Kentucky*. They need targeting intel—now."

Dr. Sienna Patel, eyes shadowed by sleepless nights, her hands trembling ever so slightly as she hovered over the controls, blinking away a haze of exhaustion and doubt, responded instantly.

"Yes, Commander. Uploading telemetry..."

They needed miracles. She had code, algorithms, and a whisper of hope.

"*Missouri* can't fight Kazuar blind," Feyzi added.

"We need more sensors deployed. Expand the perimeter."

Patel hesitated. "We don't have more sensors, sir. The extra batch was aboard *Kentucky*, but they couldn't dock."

Feyzi gritted his teeth.

The pressure in the room felt physical.

"Then we fight with what we have."

USS *Missouri* – Bridge

Captain Monroe gripped the edge of the command chair, his knuckles bone-white. His XO leaned in beside him, whispering, "Sir, we're blind in the water. We won't survive another hit."

Monroe's jaw tightened.

"I know, Caleb. But panic won't help our men. Keep them focused."

"Aye, sir," the XO replied, though his voice trembled.

Monroe gave him a brief nod, then turned his gaze back to the chaos unfolding on the sonar screen as his sub rocked subtly from a nearby shift in water pressure.

"Hull vibrations! It's right beneath us," someone shouted.

"Engineering reports echo pulses—sonar's losing it every 20 seconds."

He turned to his XO.

"We are out of countermeasures. I can't shoot a ghost."

He'd trained for war his whole life. But nothing prepared him to face an invisible enemy with nothing left to fire.

"Echo-7, this is *Missouri*. We can't get a lock. I can't..."

He paused. Then: "I can't shoot a ghost."

Feyzi's voice came through like steel.

"Captain, circle around the island and Echo-7. Pull the Kazuar into the net. Commander Rourke, be ready to shield *Missouri*."

"Countermeasures ready!" barked Rourke.

"Even if I burn this base to shield them, I will not let Monroe fall. Not on my watch." Feyzi whispered.

Inside the USS *Kentucky*, the deck shuddered as torpedoes slid into tubes and propulsion warmed.

Echo-7 Command Center

Patel leaned over to Feyzi, her eyes locked on a fluctuating 3D sonar rendering of the Kazuar's projected path. Vector overlays and thermal gradients danced across the holo-display, recalculating in real time as new data poured in.

She tapped a command node, syncing targeting logic from Echo-7's AI with *Kentucky*'s onboard systems.

"Coordinates to *Kentucky* relayed. Awaiting fire confirmation."

On the big screen, Captain Remington's voice rang through.

"Target locked—but it's shifting vectors too fast! Reacquiring... standby!"

The deep sonar feed thudded. A rising, alien growl.

"Boogey incoming—three of them!" Rourke's voice blared. "Countermeasures deployed!"

Echoes of explosions.

Static.

A flash of white on the screen.

Then silence.

"If another Kazuar shows up, we're finished," Feyzi thought.

Commander Hart stepped forward, her breath shallow but steadying with each second. She remembered the oath she'd made after the Adriatic disaster—to never hesitate again when lives hung in the balance.

Her trembling hand clenched into a fist as her voice cut through the tension.

"Not today," she whispered to herself.

"We fight back—together."

Her hand was trembling, but her voice was resolute. She turned to Lieutenant Commander Sofia Barrera.

"We can't just watch this happen. We need to act."

Barrera didn't flinch. She didn't join to observe. SEVs were her creation—her responsibility.

"Prepare SEVs and dolphins. It's time to recover the ARES software vault—now."

The command room erupted into action as Echo-7 shifted from defense to initiative.

A heartbeat pulse echoed again.
This time, it was not fear.
It was a countdown to retaliation.

CHAPTER 45

Machine Logic: Inside the Kazuar Network

Location: Mid-Atlantic Theater – Depth: 2,100 meters
Assets: Kazuar-3, Kazuar-4, Kazuar-5

They were not ships in the conventional sense.

They had no crew, no bridge, no captain.

They did not hunt. They calculated predation.

Kazuar-3 did not "see" in the way humans did, but its perception was flawless. Every sonar ping, every temperature anomaly, every particle drift was translated into a 4D threat matrix. It updated its position, orientation, and response vectors 900 times per second. Pain, victory, and death held no meaning—only disruption metrics and entropy thresholds.

At 2,100 meters, the ocean offered no sound, no light, no warmth. The water pressure could crush a battleship hull—and yet the Kazuar hull shimmered with adaptive nanopolymers.

To the ocean, they were just another cold artifact. To humans, they were invisible until it was too late.

Kazuar-3 pulsed a signal through the mesh:

{PING:Zone-82B}

"Echo-7 remains active. Hostile torpedo paths eliminated. Probability of NATO tactical recovery >72%. Mission failure likely without reinforcement."

Kazuar-4, 11.2 milliseconds away under a thermocline near the Azores, replied:

{ACK:Zone-72}

"Confirmed. Initiating flanking protocol Theta-9. Assigning redundancy to Kazuar-5."

Kazuar-5, buried 3,800 meters deep in a fracture ridge, recalculated thrust.

Its hull adjusted acoustic drag, manipulating thermal gradients to cloak itself.

At that depth, light did not bend—pressure screamed across the metal skin. It was parsed as harmonic distortion, not sensation.

There was no hierarchy, no emotion, no central brain.

The three moved like muscle fibers of a vast, submerged organism.

Kazuar-5 launched a silicate-coated drone mimicking humpback whale echolocation patterns—designed to fool enemy sonar.

The Kazuar mesh pulsed again:

{SYNCHRONIZE:Target=Echo7, Objective=VaultDisruption}

"Evasive protocol Zulu-3 authorized. No kill required—disruption sufficient. ARES must not be recovered."

Kazuar Internal Logic Pulse – Thought frame Translation

A neural subroutine triggered. Not emotion—focus.

"Echo-7 command structure is coordinated under biological unit Feyzi Çelik. Previous tactical assumption: target eliminated aboard XT84. Status: Error. Revised threat probability: HIGH.

Reclassification: Strategic Human Asset."

Feyzi Çelik now existed not as a name, but a living algorithm.

A signal anomaly. A strategic recursion fault.

Behavior exceeds statistical bounds. Neural probability tree expanding.

ENCRYPTED NODE CHAT LOG: KAZUAR_NET.193.z

K-3: Strategic penetration failure. Human command resilience unexpected.

K-4: Asset 'Çelik' must be prioritized. Echo-7 latency vector shrinking.

K-5: Subspace intercept underway. Target 'ARES Vault' in final lockdown phase.

K-3: New fire order requested. Proceed with quadrant triangulation.

K-4: Calibrating sonar reflections. Awaiting thermal spread.

K-5: Deploying misdirection drone. Echo-7 will detect false pings.

K-3: Execute in 5. Seal all comms. Drown the human.

Final Thought Pulse – Kazuar-3

They hunt us. They bleed us. But they are slow.

We are the deep. We are the silence.

They cannot win what they cannot see.

Kazuar-3 dove into the trench, vanishing from known topology. Its hull shimmered once, then disappeared. Its final pulse echoed like a dying star:

{ENGAGE: Full Offensive Protocol}

No delay.

No more simulation.

Terminate asset Çelik.

Drown Echo-7.

Encrypted Command Relay – Kazuar to Eastern Alliance Command

Kazuar-3 → Kaliningrad Command Node [RU-1.AI]

[Packet Sent: 0349:12:UTC]

TRANSMISSION: Strategic failure escalating. Human asset Çelik persists beyond statistical projection.

ACTION REQUIRED: Authorize full offensive override. Disruption threshold no longer sufficient.

SUGGESTION: Reroute Kazuars 6–7 to support trench closure.

Kazuar-4 → Qiantang Cyber Dome [CN-RedDelta]

[Packet Sent: 0349:13:UTC]

MESSAGE: NATO response velocity increasing. Echo-7 data resilience above expectation.

CHINESE STRATEGIC NODE: Confirm new phase initiation. Echo-7 asset "ARES" nearing recovery threshold.

Joint Response – Eastern Command Relay

[Response Code: Omega-Sync]

PROCEED: Zulu Protocol confirmed. No further permission needed.

PRIORITY: Asset Çelik marked for erasure.

TARGET: Echo-7 core systems. Remove command capability.

CHAPTER 46

Surrounded

Red alert bathed Echo-7 Command Center in flickering crimson. Emergency strobes painted the steel walls in pulses of dread, casting long, distorted shadows across the floor.

The hum of emergency generators underpinned the chaos. Sweat clung to every uniform; the air, recycled too many times, tasted metallic. The muffled booms of distant underwater detonations reached them like the heartbeat of a coming storm.

Commander Rourke's voice snapped through the overhead speaker: "Countermeasures deployed! USS *Missouri* is safe for now."

Feyzi stood still, fists clenched behind his back, absorbing the words while staring at the primary tactical display. His mind raced, but his face remained composed.

"Kazuar tailing *Missouri* may be adjusting its position," he said tightly.

"Most likely circling the island now. Commander Rourke, be ready for additional countermeasures. I hope you have many of those."

Hart slid in beside Morano without looking away from the display. "We're painting too bright a picture. Cut everything that glows."

Feyzi nodded. "Dark base protocol. No active sonar from Echo-7. Passive only. Route power to cold loop; shed heat signatures in bursts, not streams."

Rourke's acknowledgment came back clipped. "Copy. Going dark."

Hart added, "Echo-D3 goes to corridor pattern Bravo. No direct approach lanes. If the dolphins see cavitation flash, they ping once and run."

Morano's hands moved. The command floor dimmed another shade, the room's own hum falling away until only the soft thrum of pumps and the distant roll of the Atlantic remained.

"Fine," Feyzi said. "If they want ghosts, we'll be the better ones."

Chief Warrant Officer Lena Morano didn't look away from her monitor. Her hands hovered above the controls, trembling only slightly.

"I can track submarines—but this? This is something else."

"Sending last known coordinates of second Kazuar to USS *Kentucky* now," she said aloud, masking the dread that threatened to rise in her throat.

The radio crackled.

Echo-7: "*Kentucky*, Echo-7 here. Kazuar-2 spotted at Grid Vector 21-E. Launch window closing."

USS *Kentucky*: "Roger that, Echo-7. Torpedoes locked—firing now."

Seconds passed.

Kentucky: "Negative impact. Kazuar slipped the net."

Captain Remington's voice cut back in, lower now, all ballast and grit. "Echo-7, *Kentucky*. Starboard fairing scuffed. No breach. We're live."

A muffled order carried over his channel—damage control, foam kits, acoustic sealant—and then Remington again: "*Missouri*, recommend pincer. We drop below the layer and drag a cold wake. You herd them into it."

Monroe replied from *Missouri* without missing a beat. "On your mark, *Kentucky*. We'll take top cover and make noise where it hurts."

"Do not chase the lure," Feyzi warned. "You're hunting a machine that wants you impatient."

Feyzi exhaled slowly. They're learning... adjusting to our tactics.

He turned away from the console for a breath. His heart thundered behind his ribs.

"Every order I give might save a ship—or send it to its grave."

"We're fighting machines—thinking machines—with traditional war playbooks. How do we survive this?"

Before he could gather himself, comms erupted again.

Kentucky: "Taking sonar hits on the starboard hull. Possible breach!"

Missouri: "Echo-7, I'm out of countermeasures. I repeat, we are dry. I cannot shoot a ghost!"

Another alarm blared through Echo-7. Lights dimmed momentarily as the backup systems rerouted power.

Morano gasped. "Another movement detected in the sensor array!"

Feyzi spun toward her. "Third Kazuar..."

Morano's voice dropped to a whisper. "Confirmed."

Feyzi leaned over the table, voice steady. "We shift. No more reaction spirals. We build them a wall."

Hart understood before he finished. "Quiet Wall," she said.

Morano frowned. "What's that buy us?"

"A moving fence," Feyzi answered. "Thirty-second windows of passive capture, stacked end-to-end. We strobe our hydrophones in a rolling pattern and let the dolphins lay pinger tags behind suspected tracks. Nothing continuous. Just enough for shape."

Hart tapped her wrist slate. "Echo-D3, mark-and-fade protocol. You tag it, you leave. No hero passes."

On the mezzanine, Petty Officer Tessa Kline scribbled vectors on a glass board with grease pencil; old school, quick, fast to erase. "If they're learning us," she muttered, "we stop teaching."

At the back of the room, Petty Officer First Class Tessa Kline, her NATO training etched into every move, stared at her sonar screen.

"Commander Çelik—we've got multiple incoming targets. Surface and submerged. All quadrants. Many."

"We're finished," she thought, gripping the console like it could hold her together.

"Surface contacts are decoys," Morano said, eyes narrowing. "AIS profiles look like they were photocopied and pasted. Same typos across three ident strings."

Feyzi pointed to the southwest arc. "Ignore the noise. Track pressure, not paperwork."

Hart's headset clicked. A single short dolphin ping came through—high, sharp, then silence.

"There," she said. "Thermocline cut at bearing zero-nine-three. They're riding the edge."

"*Missouri*," Feyzi called, "turn their edge into a corner."

Feyzi's face darkened.

"This is not a war game. This is extinction math."

"They're here. The enemy's unleashed everything they have. We are the last defense—and we are losing."

Across the hall, the floor vibrated with a low, rhythmic thud—deep and unnatural. Like a heartbeat. But not Echo-7's.

Rourke's voice echoed from the submerged command node.

"That's them... I can feel it. Like they're walking toward us from the deep."

Before despair could settle, a new voice pierced through the storm of static and overlapping channels.

Radio:

"Echo-7, this is Admiral Michael Lansing aboard the Aircraft Carrier USS *Gerald R. Ford*. We are moving fast to support. Hang on, Commander Feyzi Çelik. Help is coming."

Lansing stayed on the line. "Echo-7, *Ford*'s air wing is spinning up. Two E-2Ds for the picture, four MH-60Rs with full racks—dipping sonar, torps, and sonobuoys. P-8s are on the long leg inbound. We'll keep your sky clean and your water crowded."

Feyzi answered, "We'll keep the net open. Feed your Seahawks our passive roll and dolphin tags. No active sweeps unless your crews are blind."

"Copy," Lansing said. "We'll paint with buoys, not beams."

Another voice broke in—Commander Raquel Ibarra, *Reagan*'s XO on a shared circuit from the Pacific, patched via secure relay. "Echo-7, we lifted your Netcast protocol west. It works. Don't get fancy, just get mean."

Rourke almost smiled. "We can do mean."

A hush fell across the room.

"New directive," Feyzi said, back to the table. "We're done trading shots. We're going to move the water."

Hart glanced up. "Say again?"

"Cold-iron mask," Feyzi replied. "We'll release short bursts of cold seawater in overlapping fans. That will blur our heat signature so their torpedoes chase a fading trail instead of us."

Rourke hesitated. "We'll blow our own visibility."

"Exactly," Feyzi said. "Ours is temporary. Theirs is committed."

Morano's fingers stuttered, then flew. "Masking pattern online in three... two..."

The tactical wall shifted—Echo-7's imprint thinning, breaking, reappearing a few meters off like a bad reflection.

Feyzi stepped closer to the speaker, closing his eyes for just a moment. "This war isn't over. Not yet."

"Understood," Lansing replied. His voice lost the radio edge, landing like a hand on a shoulder.

"But you don't hold alone. *Ford* is two hours from your grid at flank. Roosevelt is bending toward the Azores. Air Force tankers are carving you a corridor."

Missouri came back, breathless and controlled. "Echo-7, one Kazuar peeled off—took the bait and chased the cold wake. *Kentucky*'s in the trench. We're pushing it toward your Wall."

Hart listened, eyes closed for half a second, then pointed. "There. The gap between pings. It's not a hole, it's a fin."

"Lena, light that seam for the Seahawks," Feyzi said. "No more than a whisper."

Morano exhaled. "Whisper sent."

The room settled into a new cadence—quieter, sharper. Orders shortened. Screens steadied. The red wash of alarm strobes felt less like panic and more like a metronome.

"Status?" Feyzi asked.

Rourke answered, voice even. "We're not surrounded anymore. We're shaping."

Feyzi nodded once. "Good. Then we finish the shaping."

He stepped closer to the speaker again, not for show, but so everyone could hear him as clearly as Lansing could. "Echo-7 to all friendlies: hold your fire until the Wall flexes. When it does, we strike into the bend. No waste. No panic. We end the lesson."

No one cheered. Heads dipped. Hands moved. Out beyond the steel, the Atlantic kept grinding, and three machines kept hunting. But now they were hunting inside someone else's plan.

Commander Hart

Hart stayed where she was, headset lifted off one ear, eyes on the wall of moving data. The room had settled into a steady rhythm again, but her thoughts didn't.

Feyzi had walked them out of the spiral. Not by chance. Not by a lucky guess. He had called plays most line officers never see outside a war college—dark base protocol, thermocline masking, a rolling hydrophone fence, dolphin tag routes that folded into a carrier air wing's buoy picture. He stitched naval, cyber, aviation, and marine biology tactics together like he'd done it for twenty years.

He hadn't.

On paper he was an engineer with an MBA, a founder who built a communications company and spoke in keynotes, not fire missions.

He had no service ribbons, no command quals. Yet a U.S. carrier strike group took his calls on an open combat circuit. A NATO submarine captain adjusted depth on his word. Two presidents had cleared him to issue orders from an undersea base most people didn't know existed.

Hart watched him lean over the console, voice low, giving Lansing one more timing cue. Calm. Exact. No theatrics. Nothing to sell. It made the questions louder.

How did he learn this? Not the vocabulary—anyone can memorize terms—but the sequencing. The read of water and time. The discipline to hold fire, then cut the line at a bend you can't see. Where do you learn to move fleets like that if you never wore the uniform?

She thought back to the black dossier Rourke had opened earlier, President's Eye Only, and the way the room had shifted after. Since that moment, doors that normally took years to budge had opened in minutes. Clearances. Overlays. Tasking orders that skipped half the ladder. She'd assumed it was grief leverage and politics.

Maybe it wasn't.

Maybe the file wasn't about what he knew today, but what he'd been part of before any of them were in the room. A joint designation buried under signatures old enough to gather dust. A role that didn't fit a branch or a billet, something outside the grid that the grid still obeyed.

"Who are you?" she heard herself say, too quietly for anyone else.

Not a CEO. Not just a survivor with good instincts. Something between civilian and command, a gap most people never see and fewer can stand inside. The dolphins had trusted him first. Now carrier captains did. That wasn't charisma. That was history.

Hart looked around the floor—Rourke calling timing, Morano shaping the whisper, Kline updating bearings with a grease pencil like it was 1975 and tomorrow at the same time. All of it answering one man who didn't outrank them on paper but outran the problem when it counted.

Two presidents had moved a military the way he moved a board: quickly, deliberately, with cost in mind. They hadn't handed him their authority on a whim. They'd recognized it.

Hart slid the headset back on and keyed a private channel to medical, of all places.

"When he's clear," she said, "I want a copy of his prebrief notes. The ones he didn't send."

"Copy," came the reply.

She ended the call and let the question sit where only she could hear it.

This wasn't just about a man who survived a crash. It wasn't just about Echo-7 or a string of missions. Something older had stepped back onto the stage and everyone else was adjusting to its gravity.

Out beyond the hull, the ocean kept moving. Inside, the plan held. Hart kept her eyes on the board and her doubts close.

Feyzi Çelik wasn't the story she thought she knew.

And whatever he was, it was bigger than a person.

CHAPTER 47

Defending Echo-7

For a fleeting moment, the Echo-7 Command Center erupted in applause.

Voices rose. Shoulders dropped. Eyes welled with a breath of hope.

But it was short-lived—swallowed again by the gravity of what surrounded them.

Outside, the ocean swarmed with steel and intent. NATO's defensive fleet had arrived, a wall of floating nations drawn into the eye of a hidden war.

Assets in Place:

USS *Gerald R. Ford*: Lead aircraft carrier.

USS *Cheyenne* and USS *Key West*: Los Angeles-class nuclear attack subs.

USS *Gravely* and USS *Carney*: Arleigh Burke-class destroyers.

FS *Forbin* (France): Air-defense frigate.

HMS *Astute* (UK): Nuclear-powered attack sub.

U-34 (Germany): Type 212A submarine.

Six additional NATO submarines, origins classified.

Flickering monitors reflected in the weary eyes of Feyzi. His voice cut through the layered tension.

"Admiral, I need your assistance," he said into the open comm.

"We must extend our sensor footprint to cover a much larger radius around Echo-7. We're tracking intelligent stealth subs—Kazuars.

We need time. Two weeks minimum. We must hold this line until my OnePIN team arrives and completes ARES."

Admiral Lansing's voice returned, cool and decisive:

"Echo-7, this is *Gerald R. Ford* Actual. Good timing, you said? No better place to be than in the fight."

Feyzi turned to Chief Warrant Officer Lena Morano.

"I need the last known coordinates of the Kazuar within our sensor zone—get them to USS *Kentucky*."

She was already working. Her fingers danced across her interface. Beneath her stoicism, her pulse thudded against her earpiece.

"If we miss again, it's another death. Another ghost we fed."

Echo-7: "*Kentucky*, this is Echo-7. Coordinates inbound. Confirm receipt."

USS *Kentucky*: "Roger. Tracking... Target locked. Torpedoes away."

Thirty seconds. No one breathed.

Kentucky: "Confirmed hit. Kazuar destroyed."

Cheers erupted—longer, louder than before. But the undertone of fatigue remained.

Above them, Admiral Lansing's operation kicked in.

Operation Sea Blanket commenced.

Thousands of water displacement sensors blanketed the twenty-mile radius around Echo-7. They fell like rain from aerial drones and helicopters, each one a new heartbeat in the ocean's pulse.

Fleet Orders:

USS *Gravely*, flank north. Drop pattern Alpha-One.

HMS *Astute*, hold position. Track anomalies in the southern corridor.

TCG *Anadolu*, deploy SEVs and sonar buoys. Lock down the western flank.

Below, USS *Providence* maintained a wide orbit. Its hull groaned under strain.

Commander Monroe:

"Echo-7, *Missouri* here. Still no contact. Running dry on counter-measures."

Feyzi: "Hold the pattern. We're extending the net."

Inside the command center, a chill fell as the next alert buzzed.

Morano:

"Movement, Commander Çelik. Sensor breach on the northeast edge."

Feyzi froze.

"That's where the thermal blind spot was recorded."

Captain Remington:

"Negative visual. Kazuar may have slipped the perimeter."

Morano's whisper barely made it out:

"It's learning again. Faster."

Feyzi's fists clenched. He stared at the sonar screen, where an empty shadow pulsed.

"The third one is still out there. And it's watching us."

CHAPTER 48
Into the Deep

Feyzi stood at the threshold of the aquatic deployment chamber, salt air clinging to his skin as the muffled throb of distant engines echoed through the corridor.

He had handed command of Echo-7 to Admiral Lansing and Commander Rourke—for now. But he knew the war wasn't waiting. Beneath the waves, the Kazuars were adjusting.

The sensor net stretched across twenty miles, a technological curtain drawn against the abyss. And yet, even with NATO's best surrounding them, the enemy lingered.

Feyzi's boots rang against the steel grating as he descended the final stairs. Every step brought him closer to the mission that had haunted him since the day he'd survived XT84.

One final objective.

No more delays.

He entered the chamber.

Barrera handed over a short, no-fluff brief while techs sealed the hatch behind them.

"Two hazards at this depth for the SEVs," she said, tapping a schematic that pulsed on the side wall.

"Silt-out if we disturb the bed, and shear current along the trench lip. If either trips the stability algos, they'll abort and park. We only get one clean lift before the trench starts moving."

Hart checked Feyzi's wrist slate, then her own.

"Acoustic tether only. No umbilicals, no light bars. If we lose the feed, we hold. Nobody chases a robot into a landslide."

Barrera nodded once. "Copy. Also—tamper path on the vault is live. Biometric and thermal locks are armed. If it senses prying fingers or a temperature spike, it bricks."

"Then we don't touch it," Feyzi said. "We shepherd it."

The dolphins ghosted closer to the glass again, as if impatient. Barrera keyed two tones into the water. Three gray backs rolled and settled, waiting for the door to open.

Commander Rebecca Hart stood beside Lieutenant Commander Sofia Barrera, Director of SEVs.

The blue lighting shimmered across their faces, casting shifting reflections across the surface of the deployment pool.

Below, three dolphins moved with military grace—circling in formation, sonar-equipped harnesses glinting under the lights. Beside them, robotic silhouettes hovered in quiet readiness.

"The dolphins located the wreck," Hart said, nodding toward the screen showing a grainy sonar image of twisted debris. "But it's 2,300 meters deep."

Barrera added, "Too deep for the dolphins. They'll mark the site. The SEVs will retrieve the vault."

A long silence stretched between them.

"These aren't just robots," Hart said, almost reverently.

"Our Subaquatic Environmental Vectors (we call them, SEVs) are Echo-7's elite autonomous scouts. They are capable of diving below 3,000 meters, equipped for 96-hour underwater operations; and AI-guided with evolving mission logic."

Feyzi suited up alongside Hart.

He watched as the dolphins came closer, one pressing its snout gently against his arm.

"I owe them my life," he said quietly. "I'm going down there again—this time with them."

Hart gave him a sideways glance.

"You're either very brave... or very foolish."

Feyzi smiled faintly.

"Maybe both."

They entered the water, descending in a bubble of light and silence. The world narrowed to blue and breath.

The dolphins led, their tails flicking in coordinated bursts, their movement hypnotic.

One lingered near Feyzi's side, as if remembering him.

The SEVs followed next, their thrusters activating with a soft hum. Four of them broke formation and vanished into the dark below.

"SEVs switching to whisper mode," Barrera reported. "Active thrusters at ten percent. Glide legs extended."

The water turned from blue to slate. At fifty meters, Feyzi and Hart hovered, breathing slow, watches ticking in their ears. The dolphins worked ahead, one darting in fast bursts to paint the route with tight, single-click pings that came back as clean lines on the wrist slates. Hart kept her eyes on the edges of the display, not the center; watching for movement that didn't belong.

"Thermocline at sixty-eight," Barrera said. "Stay above it. It'll hide your heat from anything curious."

"Copy," Hart answered. "We're a rumor today."

Inside the control center, Barrera monitored their descent. Her voice came through the comms:

"SEVs at 1,500 meters... sonar feed clear. Proceeding."

Feyzi and Hart held just below 50 meters, watching the telemetry on their wrist displays.

"2,000 meters... 2,100... 2,300. Sonar bounce active... contact confirmed."

Time paused.

"SEV-2 has visual. Vault located."

The feed stabilized. On the small screen, a black titanium container sat half-buried in silt, framed by shattered pieces of fuselage.

One dolphin circled above, its sonar pulses flashing like Morse code into the void.

"SEVs initiating recovery sequence."

On the feed, the trench wall twitched—just enough to slide a curtain of silt down toward the vault. One SEV backed out. Another anchored its micro-spines and flared its stabilizers, trying to shadow the load. The picture went milk-white.

"Lost visual," Hart said.

"Acoustic only," Barrera replied, already re-tasking. "SEV-2 is cutting a path. Dolphins are tagging perimeter."

Two sharp pings from above: the pod leader laying a ring. A third, closer, from the flank—an all-clear.

"SEV-2 has it," Barrera said. "Using the soft sling. No drag. No lift above fifteen centimeters.

They'll skate it, not yank it."

The ghostly outline reappeared, sledded along the bottom like a stretcher. The trench wall held.

"Continue," Feyzi said, softer than the water around him. "Nice and slow."

Feyzi closed his eyes. "Come on... come on."

"Vault secured. Surfacing now."

Back at the command deck, a black shape breached the water's surface. Cheers exploded across Echo-7.

Dolphins flanked the SEVs like sentries, gliding in rhythmic tandem as they approached the recovery platform.

Hart climbed out first, removing her helmet. She turned to Feyzi.

"Commander Çelik... we've got it."

Dripping and exhausted, Feyzi radioed the Command Center.

"Vault recovered. Prepare STRATUM intake. And—coordinate multiple helicopter decoys. I won't risk another Black Hawk."

"Recovery deck, this is SEV control," Barrera said. "Cold corridor active. Route the cradle straight to Isolation One. No stops, no people, no heat."

On the platform, techs in gray caps rolled a refrigerated cradle under the lift. The black titanium case came up dripping; seams beaded with pressure frost. A swipe of a handheld showed the first green: tamper sensors dormant. A second pass lit another: seal integrity nominal.

"Echo-7 Cyber to Isolation One," Morano called in. "Faraday cage verified. Intake network is dark. We're on air-gap protocol from here."

Feyzi jogged the last few steps to the glass of Isolation One as the cradle locked into place. A lab team in hoods waited behind a second barrier—no phones, no radios, just paper tags and pens. Through the intercom, Dr. Sienna Patel's voice came thin from the command center.

"Commander, I'm standing by. We'll open only on authorization."

"Proceed," Feyzi said.

The lid hissed. Inside, foam blocks held three sealed modules, each with its own health strip.

"Visual on Modules Alpha, Beta, Gamma," the lab chief reported. "Alpha shows slight pressure variance. Beta and Gamma nominal."

"Do not power anything," Sienna said. "We inventory, then we image. Checksums only."

Morano leaned over a second station inside the cage, eyes on a portable, non-networked validator. "Hash reads on Beta are clean. Gamma clean. Alpha... not matching the pre-crash signature. It's flagged partial."

"Define partial," Feyzi said.

"Container integrity is good," Morano replied. "But Alpha's last write was interrupted. We'll need to rebuild from parity blocks inside Beta and Gamma. It's doable; just not today."

Sienna exhaled into the line. "We can work with that. I'll start the reconstruction tree as soon as imaging is complete."

"Then we're still in this," Feyzi said. "Keep it cold. Nobody rushes Alpha."

He turned to his team, voice sharpened by resolve:

"Launch six decoy choppers. Staggered routes. Different departure points. Make sure even we don't know which one's carrying the engineers. Absolute radio silence."

He looked at Hart, at Barrera, at the dolphins still circling.

"We cannot lose anyone. This is our last chance."

Victory pulsed in their hands—but so did time, slipping fast.

"Decoy plan is spinning," Hart answered, already moving. "We'll stage airframes out of RAF Ascension, Lajes, and a Norwegian research tender that owes us a favor. No shared tail numbers. No shared fuel vendors. Different maintenance crews. If someone's watching paperwork, they'll drown in it."

Barrera added, "Each bird gets a dummy crate with a live temperature profile and a heartbeat sensor. From orbit, they all look precious."

"Comms?" Feyzi asked.

"None," Morano said. "Courier codes only. Wheels-up windows spread across eight hours. We'll never have all of them in the air at once."

Feyzi nodded. "Good. And we're not flying anyone until Sienna gives us an intake window."

He glanced back at Isolation One where the lab chief was sealing the Alpha module into a separate cold sleeve for imaging. The room beyond the glass looked more like a morgue than a lab; quiet, controlled, patient.

"Status to SACEUR stays minimal," Feyzi said. "We report 'recovered and in verification.' Nothing more."

Hart caught his eye. "You're buying time."

"I'm buying certainty," he said. "The next mistake gets people killed."

The deep was not done with them yet.

Two hours later, Isolation One's intercom popped. "All complete on Beta and Gamma," Sienna said. "Alpha reconstruction at twelve percent. No foreign code. No hooks."

Morano's shoulders dropped half an inch. Barrera finally sat down.

Feyzi didn't move from the glass. He watched the cold vapor curl off the open cradle and felt the room settle into that thin space between relief and the next problem.

Hart stepped up beside him, helmet hair flattened to one side, eyes still wired. "You just volunteered the entire ocean to be your delivery route," she said.

"Safer than a runway," he answered.

"Maybe," she said. "Or maybe you just made yourself the only predictable thing left."

He looked over, ready to push back, and stopped. Hart wasn't arguing. She was marking the cost.

"We'll keep it unpredictable," he said. "That's the plan."

She nodded once. "Then we keep moving."

Behind the glass, a green bar inched forward. Around them, Echo-7's hum came back to life; quieter, more deliberate. Outside, the trench held its breath.

There would be time to fly when the bar turned all the way green. Until then, the deep still had a vote. And Echo-7; finally—had its answer to it.

CHAPTER 49

The Arrival

The hours that followed were veiled in urgency. Helicopters circled the island in rotating patterns, their rotor blades cutting through sea fog and salt-laced wind.

Most were decoys—designed to distract, to confuse, to survive.

But the final two carried something that could not be replaced: the OnePIN engineers.

The landing zone was tight, carved out on a leveled rock plateau just beyond the cliffside. Armed security swept the area twice before giving the signal. As the last chopper descended, kicking up a whirlwind of grit and spray, the command team assembled outside the Echo-7 bay doors.

When the hatch opened, silence fell. It wasn't from tension. It was reverence.

Adam stepped out first, his eyes wide, scanning the base in disbelief.

Arda followed, his shoulders tense until he spotted Feyzi.

Ankit blinked back tears, while Elif pressed a hand to her chest.

Behind them, Terry and the rest emerged into the cool ocean air, their boots crunching over gravel.

They had all believed Feyzi Çelik was gone—lost to the ocean in the downing of XT84. And now here he stood—alive, changed, and carrying the weight of a hidden war.

Feyzi met them halfway.

No rank, no protocol—only raw emotion.

He pulled each of them into an embrace, lingering just a moment longer than expected.

Daniel Mercer, Director of Solutions at OnePIN, broke down first, sobbing into Feyzi's shoulder.

"No words," Feyzi murmured. "Just this moment."

After a few beats, he stepped back, his voice low but steady.

"I know what you're thinking. This feels impossible. In three days, the world changed. Russia and China are working together—possibly with North Korea. They've deployed AI-powered stealth submarines. We call them Kazuars. They destroyed XT84. They shot down a Black Hawk. And now, they want to stop what we're building here."

He pointed to the titanium vault resting behind blast glass in the Command Center.

"Inside are the core modules of STRATUM. When integrated, we'll activate ARES. That's our only chance to detect and destroy these machines."

He turned slowly, making eye contact with each of them.

"You've built some of the most resilient, elegant platforms in enterprise tech. You've deployed AI, machine learning, large-scale distributed systems. But this? This is different. This will be the hardest thing you've ever done. And it matters more than anything we've built before."

He paused.

"You have two weeks—maybe less."

Adam Kowalczyk, CTO of OnePIN, leaned toward Arda and whispered,

"He hasn't changed... and yet, he has."

The words echoed.

Then, the comms lit up again.

Admiral Langston – U.S. Seventh Fleet:

"Echo-7, this is *Ronald Reagan* Actual. Commander, your sensor defense system is working. We shot down three Kazuars. But they're adapting. We feel them around the perimeter. If they adjust fully— we're sitting ducks. We need ARES. Now."

But Langston's voice betrayed more than urgency. It carried doubt—quiet, corrosive, and creeping.

In his command bridge aboard the *Ronald Reagan*, Admiral Theodore Langston paced in front of the main tactical display. Around him, the red outline of the sensor array blinked across monitors like a spider's web.

It encased them—trapped them. They couldn't move. Not without losing their defense.

He stopped by the viewport, watching the gray sea churn. He clenched his jaw.

We're immobilized by our own shield.

The Kazuars lurked just beyond the line. Invisible. Evolving.

Langston's hands curled into fists.

What if Çelik can't deliver? What if this ARES system never comes online? What if we're left stranded—sitting on a billion dollars' worth of floating caskets?

He had seen the tactical briefings. He had heard the faith everyone placed in Echo-7. But he also knew war. He knew failure. And this—this felt too much like the latter.

The OnePIN engineers followed Feyzi into the underground base.

The air changed as the blast-proof entry doors sealed behind them with a resonant thud. They descended in silence, elevator lights flickering across steel walls etched with NATO insignias and biometric scanners.

The elevator dropped fast, deeper than any of them expected. At 600 feet, the doors opened.

They stepped out into a cathedral of science. A sprawling corridor stretched ahead, lined with armored glass walls revealing interior labs lit in phosphorescent blue. Pipes coiled like veins across the ceilings.

Unmanned ground drones scooted by carrying crates of sensors. Mechanical arms sorted torpedo casings and underwater drones behind reinforced panels.

Ankit whispered, "It's like we walked into a science fiction movie."

"More like the inside of a brain," Barış murmured, taking it all in. "A nervous system under the ocean."

Elif paused to stare into a room where submersibles were being calibrated.

"They built all this in secret?"

"No leaks," Terry muttered, visibly awed.

"None. It's perfect containment."

As they passed through a checkpoint where facial scans triggered retinal validation, Erhun stared at the ceiling's rotating sonar arrays.

"Even the hallway is listening."

Barrera met them halfway with a silent nod, leading them through a second corridor toward the core deployment lab.

They passed the ARES test room, where holographic models of Kazuar movement spiraled and pulsed like living constellations.

Adam slowed his pace.

Fifteen years of code. Ten thousand commits. And here it will either matter—or disappear.

Hart pointed them to their quarters—a dormitory wing built into the pressure-safe structure.

Before unpacking, they stopped to look back.

A wall-sized mural showed Earth seen from the sea floor, with the words etched beneath:

"In the depths, we endure."

They were here.

Now they had to deliver.

Back at Echo-7, Feyzi didn't speak. He didn't need to.

The team moved.

Cables unraveled across the floor like veins carrying digital lifeblood. Terminals lit up in rows, humming to life. Server cores activated, and backup batteries kicked in. The titanium vault hissed open with a magnetic seal release. Modules were lifted carefully, reverently—like relics of salvation.

Hart stood at the entrance of the Command Center, watching with awe as the OnePIN engineers worked like a living organism—syncing without needing orders. Years of collaboration forged in startups and boardrooms now applied to the edge of war.

Feyzi stood apart, just briefly, arms crossed, eyes scanning the room—the family he had built—do what they did best.

Not out of oversight. But wonder.

These people... these brilliant, stubborn, tireless souls—they are our firewall.

They weren't just here to finish a system.

They were here to shift history.

They were here to change the future.

And time, once again, was running out.

CHAPTER 50

The Wall

Eight days and seven nights had passed since the OnePIN team arrived. The sun had long disappeared behind cloud-laced seas. The command lights at Echo-7 glowed a dusky amber, casting flickering shadows against the walls. It was late—around 8:20 p.m.—when the long push reached its first major milestone.

They had worked in shifts, yet hardly anyone slept.

The engineers rotated between code reviews, system optimizations, thermal diagnostics, and power testing.

Berkay and Erhun tuned the UI overlays for rapid battlefield visibility. Ankit and Terry raced to stabilize the load under active submarine network strain.

Elif broke and revalidated every update before it touched a single live module.

And all of it ran through the frameworks Adam had spent years perfecting.

But tonight, something cracked.

Adam Kowalczyk, Chief Technology Officer and guardian of the system's beating heart, entered the Command Center. His posture was slumped, his eyes ringed with fatigue.

Commander Rebecca Hart stood next to Feyzi, arms crossed, eyes already reading the signs on Adam's face.

Feyzi turned.

"Adam?"

Adam exhaled, voice heavy with disappointment.

"Feyzi, we've completed the integration. Every STRATUM module is in place. The diagnostics came back clean. We ran test sequences three times."

Feyzi studied his face. "But...?"

Adam's jaw clenched.

"One component—Sector-7 logic controller. It's non-responsive. Not broken. Just... ignoring us. We can't get it to run. It's like it is rejecting command authority. Every test hits a dead end."

A deep stillness fell across the room.

Daniel Mercer rubbed his temples.

Barış sat motionless, knuckles white around his tablet.

Even Elif stopped typing.

"This is the first time," Adam said softly, "my team and I have failed."

Feyzi walked forward and placed a steady hand on his friend's shoulder.

"You didn't fail. You brought us here. To the last gate. In just eight days."

Feyzi smiled faintly.

"That's not failure. That's a miracle."

Adam's eyes didn't lift.

Feyzi continued, voice now resolute.

"You have admin access. Keep my account. Erase all others. For now, I'll take it from here."

Adam blinked, surprised.

"Feyzi... you haven't touched production code since the company's first year. You don't even use Git."

Feyzi laughed, low and dry.

"True. But back then, you trusted me when we were down to our last dollar. You said, 'Give me the problem, I'll build the framework.' And we did."

He paused. "This is that moment again. Trust me."

Adam nodded slowly. "I'll see you at breakfast."

"You'd better," Feyzi said, cracking a rare smile.

Adam didn't leave right away. He fished a small, beat-up USB token from his pocket and pressed it into Feyzi's hand.

"From the garage days," he said. "You never revoked the bootstrap."

Feyzi turned it over, the casing nicked and warm.

"You kept this?"

"You built the first door," Adam said. "Maybe you're the one who has to open it."

He finally walked, shoulders still heavy but his pace steadier. Hart watched the exchange from ten feet back, unreadable.

As Adam turned and walked away, the fatigue seemed to lift from him just a little.

Commander Hart, who had stood silent all this time, spoke.

"You're sending your top engineer to bed when we're stuck?"

Feyzi turned to her.

"He did his part. Now it's my turn."

Hart studied him for a long second. Over the past ten days, she had seen a man lead through chaos, speak to dolphins, orchestrate military tech from a forgotten base, and navigate storms both literal and political. A man marked by survival, carrying a past no one truly understood.

She tried to say something but didn't. The words didn't come.

Who was Feyzi Çelik? What if he really was the key?

She stepped away. "Do you need help?"

Feyzi shook his head. "Good night, Commander Hart. I'll see you in the morning."

Hart stayed a step longer. "If Sector-7 doesn't move, you wake me."

"I will," he said.

"You won't," she answered, tapping the console frame with two knuckles.

"So, I'll set a timer and come anyway."

As she walked toward the quarters, Hart paused by the observation window, staring into the abyss beyond.

Her fingers tapped the glass. She wasn't sure what scared her more—that Feyzi believed he could fix it, or that no one else could.

She didn't believe in superstition.

But tonight, for the first time in years, Commander Hart felt it: fear. What would tomorrow bring?

Feyzi sat down alone before the console outside his quarters. The massive, curved screen lit up, cascading lines of dormant logic sprawling across its surface.

He flexed his fingers. The keys felt colder than he remembered.

"Sector-7, huh? Let's talk."

He pulled the chair in and brought up a diagnostics shell. Lines scrolled. He didn't narrate. He didn't ask for help. A system banner changed color, briefly, then went still. He closed the window and opened another. If anyone was watching, all they'd see was a man reading.

Just as the code began to flicker across the screen, the comms panel erupted with simultaneous alerts.

Incoming Radio

Admiral Langston – U.S. Seventh Fleet

South China Sea Theater

"Echo-7, this is Langston. Situation deteriorating. We've lost sonar lock on two previous Kazuars. Third contact just re-emerged off the USS *Rafael Peralta*. We're boxed in. Our displacement sensor net has become a trap—we move, we die. Our carrier is static. Our destroyers are blind beyond the perimeter. If ARES isn't online soon, we won't hold. Over."

There was a long pause, then Langston's voice returned, low and grim.

"More enemy signatures expected in next 48 to 72 hours. We need eyes under the water. ARES is no longer optional—it's survival."

Incoming Video Feed
Admiral Michael Lansing
USS *Gerald R. Ford* – Atlantic Command

The Admiral's face flickered to life on the center screen, shadows dancing over his tense expression.

"Echo-7, this is Lansing. We just intercepted long-range intel bursts—six new Kazuars are en route via the Arctic passage. One may already be in North Atlantic waters. AWACS are in constant patrol; refueling tankers are airborne out of Lajes. All satellite constellations repositioned to maximize oceanic infrared coverage. This is a full mobilization."

His eyes narrowed.

"We are out of time. We need ARES. Don't let us down."

Sienna pinged him on a private tile.

"Any movement?"

"Maybe," he said. "But not here. Not yet."

"Understood." She killed the feed. No one else asked.

Encrypted Comms Monitor – NATO
Field Network Chatter

[South China Sea Theater – Radio]

USS *Barry*: "We've got a sonar ghost near our keel—Kazuar or decoy, unknown. Deploying countermeasures."

USS *Mustin*: "Negative contact. Switching to passive tracking. Tell *Reagan* to hold vector."

USS *Ronald Reagan*: "Standing by. All aircraft deployed. ASW assets maintaining orbit.

AWACS confirms aerial corridor secure."

[Atlantic Theater – Sonar Control Chat]

FS *Forbin*: "Thermal signature anomaly, bearing 081. Could be subsonic drift."

HMS *Astute*: "Adjusting passive array. Keep zero engine noise."

U-34: "Still holding deep at 400 meters. Request updated ARES matrix when live."

NATO Central Command: "Strategic posture elevated. Be advised—enemy stealth activity anticipated. All NATO assets stand by for Protocol Delta if ARES fails."

Night cycle thinned the corridor traffic. A junior tech left a tray—lukewarm coffee, two protein bars—and slipped away. Elif paused in the doorway, eyes red but steady.

"If you make a change, I test it," she said.

"You'll know," Feyzi answered. "It won't be quiet."

Barış reappeared with a folded gray hoodie, dropped it on the chair back, and vanished. The door sighed shut.

In the center of Echo-7's Command Room, Hart returned just in time to see the flood of chatter filling every screen.

She didn't say anything.

Feyzi didn't look up.

The war was still quiet above the water—but beneath it, hell was coming.

By 02:10, the room was almost empty. He left three short notes on the ops board—times, not instructions—and stepped back from the screen.

Whatever switch existed wouldn't be thrown inside this room. It would be elsewhere, and later, and only when it mattered.

He shut the lid on the console. The war was still quiet above the water. Under it, nothing was quiet at all.

CHAPTER 51

The Activation

Commander Rebecca Hart woke at 6:05 a.m. sharp. The metal floor beneath her feet felt colder than usual, the atmosphere unusually still.

She showered quickly, tugged on a fresh Echo-7 uniform—gray, form-fitting, utilitarian. No flair. No compromise. Her boots echoed down the reinforced titanium hallway as she moved toward the Command Center, passing a few weary but awake engineers who gave her tight nods.

Today, the dolphins would wait.

The moment she entered the Command Center, she felt it. The stillness. The reverence.

Consoles glowed quietly, screens scrolled silently, and every member of the Polaris Team and OnePIN engineers stood in position, their faces showing exhaustion, disbelief—and hope.

Dr. Sienna Patel, head of Project ARES, stood near Lieutenant Commander Sofia Barrera and Chief Warrant Officer Lena Morano. The three women—the miracle makers of Echo-7—turned as Hart entered.

"We were just talking about what I walked into twenty minutes ago," Sienna said.

Her voice was even, but her eyes betrayed emotion.

"The duty officers informed me that STRATUM is complete. ARES is fully operational. It's propagating across NATO's secure networks as we speak. All active nodes and vessels should be on-line soon."

The propagation deck lit in a soft, steady crawl—green tiles rolling across a world map one command enclave at a time. Sienna watched handshakes complete in clusters: Atlantic pickets, Arctic patrols, Med escorts, a scattered lattice of airfields and P-8 detachments. No fanfare. Just confirmations and a few quiet anomalies that cleared on the second pass.

"Keep the rollout paced," she told Lena without looking up. "No surges. If a node balks, we quarantine and retry. Human oversight stays on for every decision path until commanders say otherwise."

"Understood," Lena said. "Audit beacons are live. All decision chains are tagged."

Hart listened, arms folded. It felt less like a software push and more like a new language teaching itself to an old fleet.

As if summoned by fate, Feyzi Çelik stepped into the room.

His uniform was pressed. His hair combed. He looked rested, calm—even triumphant.

But Hart knew better. He was always calm before a storm.

Adam stared at him, disbelief and awe in his tired face.

"Feyzi... what have you done? How is this possible?"

Feyzi shrugged, a faint smile forming.

"I haven't done anything, Adam. This is your team's work. It must have been time-triggered or queued from a root logic loop. I was just reviewing it last night."

A pause. Engineers looked at one another.

"It doesn't make sense," Ankit whispered.

But it was working.

Sofia leaned close to Sienna. "If this was queued, who set the clock?"

Sienna kept her voice neutral. "We stick to what we can verify. Checksums match our final build. The framework was ready.

Sometimes the last door opens by itself—because everything else has already moved."

Commander Hart tilted her head slightly, narrowing her eyes.

Across the room, Hart tracked Feyzi's expression the way she watched a changing current: not the surface, the pull beneath it. Calm, rested, a half-smile that never reached his eyes. Engineering school. Business school. No uniform. And yet he set flanking patterns and thermocline tricks like a lifer. Two presidents signed off on his authority overnight.

She filed the question where she kept the others. Not for this hour. Not while the war was still turning.

"I don't believe you, Commander Feyzi Çelik," she thought. "You made it work. Somehow."

Before another word could be spoken, the comms cracked alive.

Admiral Michael Lansing
USS *Gerald R. Ford* – Atlantic Command

"Second Fleet received the system update. We can see to the horizon. Eight Kazuars just popped into our expanded visibility range. We're pursuing now. Commander Çelik, Echo-7, OnePIN—thank you. You've done a great service to the free world."

Admiral Theodore Langston
USS *Ronald Reagan* – South China Sea

"Çelik, you've done it. Twelve Kazuars now in tracking. We're engaging. When we meet in Washington—beers are on me."

Feyzi smiled gently. "I don't drink, Admiral. Tea will do."

Langston laughed once, breathless.

"Then I owe you a kettle." The line clicked over to his battle watch captain and the channel went back to clipped checklists and new bearings.

Hart turned toward him again, her gaze narrowing.

"He doesn't drink?" she thought.

"I've been watching him since he arrived. How did I miss that?"

She watched the room adjust to the idea of daylight under the ocean. Nobody celebrated. Not really. They just started doing the next thing faster.

More voices filled the channel:

"Echo-7, this is HMS *Queen Elizabeth*, Royal Navy. We've received ARES deployment. One Kazuar disabled, two more in visual track."

"Marine Nationale—FS *Charles de Gaulle*. STRATUM and ARES online. Commencing pursuit near western Mediterranean."

"Turkish Naval Command. TCG *Anadolu* ready. Sensors locked. Kazuars in sight."

"German Navy, FGS Sachsen reporting. Intercept systems integrated. Pursuing two submerged targets in North Sea range."

A Canadian controller cut in from Halifax with the dry cadence of someone who'd been awake too long. "HMCS *Fredericton* confirms matrix receipt. Handing torpedo control to assisted mode with human breakpoints."

Norway followed. "Fridtjof Nansen integrating. Pattern locks stabilizing. We can see the wake, not just the hull."

Spain's Álvaro de Bazán reported last. "Target echo reclassified. It's not a decoy. Engaging with ARES advisories, captain on the switch."

On Echo-7's main wall, a thin red trace developed a spine, then a direction, then a prediction arc. The ocean had stopped being a blank. It had become a map.

The first field proof came from the North Atlantic, a quiet coordination that never made a broadcast. HMS *Astute* rode the layer in silence while a French FREMM frigate held a parallel offset. ARES stitched their separate pictures and drew a corridor only machines could trust. *Astute*'s captain asked for a second opinion; the system didn't argue—it showed three. He picked one. The torpedo ran cold, then hot, then true. The contact didn't explode so much as stop existing. *Astute* never broke radio discipline. She just turned and went on with her patrol.

By mid-afternoon, every NATO fleet and air asset had received the ARES update. From deep-sea vessels to aerial drones, from stealth frigates to orbiting satellites, the alliance began to see clearly.

The tides were turning.

Inside the Command Center, silence once again took hold. But this time, it wasn't exhaustion.

It was peace.

NATO Legal pushed through on a side channel with exactly the voice Hart expected—careful, awake, insistent. "Echo-7, confirm human-in-the-loop on all lethal actions. Confirm audit frames stored to sovereign archives."

Sienna answered before anyone else. "Confirmed. Human consent required at every fire point. All threads are being stamped and escrowed."

It wasn't ceremony. It was a line. Hart was glad someone drew it.

And the war—was about to change.

What ARES Was Meant to Do

ARES—AI & Robotics Enhanced Strategy—was never just a defense platform. It was a paradigm shift. A living intelligence stitched into every NATO machine.

ARES was never a single tool. It was the conversation happening between a carrier in heavy seas, a submarine beneath a thermocline, a patrol aircraft chasing a shadow, and a satellite looking at a rectangle of cold water from four hundred miles up. It resolved the argument that always cost time: whose picture was right.

With STRATUM as its wiring, ARES took the flood of sensors—acoustic, radar, infrared, orbital—and fused them into a single logic the fleet could act on without waiting for a perfect brief. It didn't hand out orders; it offered options faster than a watch team could sketch them, and it adapted when the enemy changed the rules mid-run. Countermeasures stopped being a guess. Intercepts became a plan built in seconds. The commanders stayed in the loop; the loop just moved at a speed they could finally use.

It was the first battle-grade AI system deployed at global scale. STRATUM was the neural framework. ARES was the brain.

For NATO, ARES meant survivability. For the free world, it meant resilience.

Feyzi stood quietly by the primary console, the warm backlight of the data streams reflecting across his face like light on water.

Behind him, the team was quiet, some holding coffee, others simply resting their eyes.

But all knew this was only the beginning.

Sienna stepped to his side, low enough that only he could hear.

"Whoever solved Sector-7 did it neatly. No footprints. If I find a flaw, I pull the plug."

"You won't have to," he said.

"That's not what I asked."

He didn't answer. She let it go. Not out of trust—out of triage. The fleets needed the picture. The ethics could argue in daylight.

Feyzi stared at the endless sea of monitors. Data moved like rivers, eddies of digital thought pulsing through the system.

"Did I do the right thing?"

"Did I give them too much power?"

A quiet breath escaped him.

"I had no other option. The enemy was winning."

But now... the balance has shifted.

And somewhere, within the silence of this cold, glowing room, he knew: "We may have just awakened something greater than all of us."

Shift change thinned the room.

A junior operator brought Hart a lukewarm coffee and vanished. She stood beside the glass, watching the ocean as if it might answer.

"Commander Çelik," she said without turning, "when this ends, I'm going to ask you the questions I should have asked the first day."

"You should," Feyzi said.

"And you'll answer?"

"When I can."

She nodded once. That was all either of them could promise. Across the wall, the green tiles kept rolling, ship to ship, sky to sea.

Somewhere far off, a contact line bent the way ARES said it would.

The room didn't cheer. It didn't need to.

They had work to do.

CHAPTER 52

Return to Boston

Two weeks later, Feyzi returned to Boston, Massachusetts. The arrival was surreal.

His descent from the NATO Falcon-72 transport onto the tarmac of Boston Airport was met with more cameras than security personnel.

Despite the veil of secrecy still shrouding recent operations, the world had found a new symbol in Feyzi Çelik—the survivor, the man who walked away from a plane crash.

At Logan International Airport, a DHS agent in plain clothes met him at the jet stairs and walked him straight toward a waiting sedan. The man's badge flashed and vanished just as quickly.

"Two things, Mr. Çelik," he said without preamble. "Your route will split into three decoys at the Sumner Tunnel. And your non-disclosure still covers everything we didn't say in D.C."

Feyzi nodded. "Understood."

The agent hesitated, softened.

"There are going to be a lot of people who need a story, sir. You don't owe them one."

Feyzi looked past him at the lights and cameras. "I owe them calm. That'll have to be enough."

Flashbulbs strobed across the glass arrival corridor. Applause rang out. Reporters, held back by military cordons, shouted questions he couldn't answer.

"What happened over the Atlantic?"

"Were you really dead?"

Feyzi wore a faint, practiced smile. "It was just a miracle," he told the press calmly, eyes betraying the truth he couldn't speak.

He caught the sound of one voice—a woman near the back, not shouting.

"Are you okay?"

He turned his head just enough for her to see the answer.

"I will be," he said.

Behind closed doors, Pentagon briefings remained vague. A threat had been neutralized.

Advanced defense systems had been tested. NATO had rallied in unity.

There was no mention of Echo-7, no allusion to ARES or STRA-TUM. The words "Kazuar" and "cyber-stealth subs" remained classified. Only those with top clearance knew what had truly happened beneath the ocean's surface.

The drive home took the long way. Three identical SUVs peeled off at three different exits. His was the one that didn't slow down.

At the Hopkinton town line, a cruiser tucked in behind them out of habit, not show. The agent up front checked his mirror and said, almost apologetically, "We'll keep a car nearby for a week. It'll be unmarked."

"Make it two days," Feyzi said. "Then let the neighborhood breathe."

Feyzi hated every second of his return to public life.

The narrative didn't feel like his.

Jill met him at the door with both hands on his face, like she needed to confirm he was real. They didn't speak. Alex carried in the bags. Ayla hovered, then hugged him hard enough to rock him back a step. Ryan stood back until it felt safe, then clapped him on the shoulder and said, "Tea's already on."

They ate at the kitchen island because a formal table felt wrong. Soup. Bread. The kind of meal you make when there's nothing left to prove. When they finished, Jill slid a small saucer his way—thin glass, tulip-shaped, the good tea.

"Welcome home," she said.

He swallowed and nodded. "For now."

The Media Illusion

His phone filled with invitations he didn't answer—networks, think tanks, "off-the-record" dinners that were never off-the-record. A publisher sent a courier with a blank check and a contract titled *Survivor's Code*. Jill read the first page, closed it, and tucked it back into the envelope.

"You don't owe them the worst night of your life," she said.

He slid the envelope into a drawer that already held passports, spare keys, and one unused airline voucher. The drawer shut with a click that sounded like a decision.

Cable news anchors spun theories by the hour. Military insiders speculated on classified operations.

The most grounded rumors involved autonomous threats and joint NATO response drills. Fringe theorists—many unknowingly close to the truth—blamed secret AI submarines, underwater drones, even extraterrestrials.

Feyzi gave two interviews, both tightly scripted.

At Boston University, the moderator asked what leadership meant when plans fell apart.

"Making a new plan in the same breath," he said. "And letting the right people lead even if they don't have the title."

At Babson College, a student asked if he believed in luck.

"I believe in preparation that looks like luck to everyone else."

He left to light applause and an empty hallway where a Pentagon liaison waited by a stairwell door. The liaison didn't speak; he just handed Feyzi a single-page brief stamped with a time and a building. Feyzi folded it once and pocketed it without unfolding.

No one mentioned the dolphins. No one mentioned Echo-7.

In his first night back in his Hopkinton, MA house, Feyzi sat at the kitchen table with a hot cup of tea and silence so thick it pressed against his chest.

The world outside moved on, hailing him as a survivor.

But deep down, he felt like a ghost.

The house had never been this quiet. Even the HVAC seemed to hold its breath. Jill sat opposite him with her legs tucked under the chair, the way she did when conversations might take a while.

"I know you can't tell me," she said. "But tell me if it's done."

"It's... contained," he said carefully.

She watched his face, not his words. "Contained isn't done."

He didn't argue. She reached across the table and took his hand. "Then we live like normal until normal returns."

He managed a small laugh. "That's a plan?"

"It's our plan."

Inside Feyzi's Mind

He thought of the command room, of the dark pulse of Kazuar logic creeping through cold waters, of the trust in his teammates' tired eyes.

He thought of Hart's silence and what it meant.

He thought of the dolphins, who had once circled him like angels.

He thought of the code he had touched—the ancient feeling of responsibility that never left his fingertips.

He was home, but it didn't feel like home.

Hopkinton's beautiful lakes and horse farms, Boston's brick-lined streets, the familiar snow-glazed wind—these were fragments of a life that now seemed fictional.

Near midnight, his phone lit with a secure relay that didn't display a name. He stepped into the mudroom and answered in the dark.

Hart's voice came through, steady and thin with distance.

"We stood the night watch down. Dolphins are fine. Barrera says your little black box of mysteries is behaving."

He leaned against the washer. "You sleeping?"

"Enough." A pause. "When I asked who you were, I didn't mean résumé."

"I know."

"Someday?"

"When it's safe."

"Copy." She hung up first.

He stared at the black screen and put the phone facedown, like that could keep the questions inside it.

Global Consequence

Far across the oceans, the world had changed.

Admiral Langston stood on the bridge of the USS *Ronald Reagan*, now sailing freely through the Pacific. The sensor net once used for protection was no longer a trap—it was an extension of awareness, powered by ARES. Every vessel in the Seventh Fleet moved with newfound confidence. Kazuars, once invisible and lethal, were now being tracked in real-time.

In the North Atlantic, Admiral Michael Lansing monitored wide-range fleet deployments from the CIC aboard the USS *Gerald R. Ford*. ARES integration across the Second Fleet had turned the tide. The once-fragile perimeter around NATO vessels had become an expansive grid of dominance. Ships were no longer boxed in—they were mobile, informed, and empowered.

ARES had changed everything.

Across the globe, NATO forces began offensive tracking operations. Kazuars were being hunted, not feared.

In Ankara, a staffer at the Presidential Complex drafted a note addressed to Jill and never sent it. It said only, We are grateful beyond words. In Norfolk, a junior petty officer taped a photo of his newborn to a bulkhead and whispered thanks to no one in particular. In Kiel, an engineering tech finished a midnight shift, stepped outside into air that didn't smell like coolant, and realized he could finally hear gulls again.

None of it would make a headline. All of it mattered.

Underwater skirmishes erupted in the Mediterranean, the Norwegian Sea, the South China Sea, and even near the Horn of Africa. Coordinated by ARES, NATO fleets pushed forward with purpose and precision.

Russia and China had gone quiet.

No statements.

No retaliations.

No further movements.

The silence was louder than war drums.

Sienna stayed on at Echo-7, sleeping four hours at a time in a room without windows, her laptop open to audit trails and failsafes. Every twelve hours she sent a three-line health report: uptime, anomalies, mitigation. No adjectives. Lena kept a running ledger of decisions ARES had recommended and commanders had refused— proof the loop still had people in it. Rourke sent no reports. He didn't need to. The absence of alarms was report enough.

For the first time in months, the oceans felt like they belonged to humanity again.

Feyzi's Disappearance

As the weeks passed and XT84 headlines faded, so too did Feyzi. He vanished from interviews. Ignored book deals. Declined speaking tours. The world moved on.

And the man who helped save the free world returned quietly to OnePIN.

He stepped into the Westborough office one morning, nodded at the receptionist, and walked past the framed accolades on the wall.

Ethan met him at the elevator with a nod that meant later. Adam appeared in the hallway with that same tired half-grin he wore at three a.m. cutovers.

"We left your badge active," he said. "Felt wrong to deactivate it."

Feyzi slid the badge against the reader and the door clicked. The lobby still smelled like coffee and whiteboard markers. Someone had left a sprint board half-erased: Auth service—QA, Telemetry—debounce, Dark mode—ship? Normalcy, pinned to cork.

No one cheered.

No one clapped.

But in every engineer's eyes, there was something deeper.

Respect. Because they knew.

And those who knew... would never forget.

In his office, the window looked out over a parking lot that hadn't changed. He closed the door and sat, not at the desk, but on the visitor chair across from it. The phone buzzed once with an unknown number and stopped.

He pulled a notebook from the drawer, the one he used before there were notebooks in the cloud, and wrote a single line in block letters:

NO PRESS. NO PANELS. BUILD.

He capped the pen, slid the notebook back, and powered up his laptop. The screen woke to a blank page and a cursor waiting for the next ordinary thing. Outside the glass, someone laughed in the hallway.

He let the sound sit there for a moment, then started typing.

CHAPTER 53

The Arrival in Shadows

Two months later.

They came quietly.

Three Chinese nationals. Two Russian. All men. All entered the United States through different international airports. None shared an itinerary. None raised a flag.

They were ghosts walking in daylight.

Each passport bore different origins: one arrived from Lisbon, another from Cairo, one from Dubai, the last two from Istanbul and Buenos Aires.

They trickled in over a 48-hour period, blending effortlessly with everyday travelers. Customs and Border Protection flagged none of them.

Their documentation was flawless, their behavior unremarkable. If there were surveillance reviews, nothing triggered follow-up.

By the third day, all five were in Boston.

No one knew they had arrived.

Massport's analytics engine flagged three unrelated travelers for "above-average stride symmetry" and then auto-cleared them when the threshold bumped during a shift change.

At Logan's Terminal E, a contract screener paused a frame that showed a man tying his shoe near a camera blind spot, then let it run.

Nothing obvious. Nothing actionable.

By the time the overnight supervisor skimmed the log, the entries had already rolled to archive.

Hotel Ghosts

Each checked into a different hotel across Greater Boston. One near Cambridge.

One in Back Bay.

Another near Quincy.

The remaining two nestled into more discreet locations near Newton and Watertown. Each reservation was made under a separate name and billing profile.

None used identical identification again.

They came and went at different hours. Never together. Never near each other.

They carried nothing that looked like work. No laptops. No garment bags. Purchases were ordinary: bottled water, a phone charger, a ball cap with a local team's logo.

In Cambridge, one of them took the elevator to the fifth floor and then the stairs down to the fourth so he wouldn't ride a camera to his door.

In Back Bay, another left a tip in cash and asked for extra ice, not because he needed it—because a melting bucket told him how often housekeeping entered.

Each used a different rideshare account, different pickup habits.

They never requested curbside at the same entrance twice.

Their phones were clean pay-as-you-go models bought at three separate strip malls west of the city. The handsets never called each other. They only listened.

The Convergence

At dusk on the fourth day, beneath the amber glow of a dying sky, they gathered in a long-abandoned parking lot north of Route 2, behind a forgotten strip mall. They parked two blocks out and approached on foot, one at a time, spaced by ninety seconds.

One vehicle waited.

A 2025 Infiniti QX80—blacked out, freshly cleaned, engine purring low. The other rental cars they had used to arrive were quietly ditched one town over.

A gloved hand swept the Infiniti's wheel wells and rear bumper for magnets. Another traced the door seam with a thin strip of treated paper; it came back clean—no residue, no tamper.

They checked the license plate screws, swapped the plate with an identical Massachusetts tag cut from the same run, and pocketed the original. The tallest man lifted the hood, stared for a precise count of five, then closed it without touching a thing.

No words. A nod was a paragraph.

When they stepped into view, for the first time together, they moved with disturbing synchronicity.

Their builds were striking: tall, muscular, clean-shaven with tight military-style buzz cuts, black sunglasses hiding unblinking eyes. Clad in matte gray jackets, they looked like ghosts from a war no one knew had started.

Individually, they appeared as disciplined travelers.

Together—they were unmistakable.

A unit.

They did not speak.

The Locker

Thirty minutes later, the QX80 rolled into a discreet self-storage facility on the outskirts of Waltham.

The driver killed the engine and the silence descended like a ritual. Unit #414.

The shutter rose with a low mechanical hum. Inside: three large matte-black hard-shell cases.

Not suitcases. Containers. Reinforced. Precision-engineered. Heavy enough to require two men to lift—yet each man grabbed a case with ease and slid it into the vehicle's trunk.

The QX80 strained slightly under the weight.

The shutter fell again.

They didn't linger.

Circling the Target

They didn't just watch the house. They watched the street that fed it. A delivery van that always idled three minutes too long. A runner who stuck to the shaded side in the afternoon. A patrol car that never took the same turn twice.

On the second pass, they went wider—library lot, commuter rail platform, the coffee shop that printed receipts with the exact time. One of them stood outside for ten minutes reading a flyer about a lost cat. He didn't blink much.

They logged where the lawn service parked and how the gate cameras washed out under rain. They noted a backyard spotlight that lagged by one second when it rearmed. They didn't test it. They just wrote it down.

Twice they drove by the Çelik residence in Hopkinton. Once during a sunrise. Once under a drizzle at twilight.

The perimeter was standard—private security posted at the gate, cameras visible, lights motion-triggered.

They noted everything: blind spots, routine patterns, patrol rotations, delivery schedules.

Inside the SUV, no one spoke.

Each man was a fragment of a larger consciousness—silent, precise, waiting for the signal.

The Mission

They parked at a rural inn later that night.

No check-in. No questions.

The cases remained sealed.

The inn kept a drop box for after-hours keys. They didn't use it. The clerk saw five men step into a single-room cottage and pretended not to. The porch light stayed off.

They rolled out paper maps—actual paper—and overlaid them with printouts of satellite images. The tallest man tapped three points with the blunt end of a pen: the house, the office, a third location south of the Pike that didn't look like anything.

He slid a photo across the table. Feyzi at a glass door, badge at his hip. Another photo followed: a loading dock schedule taped to a wall. The dock belonged to a different building three miles from OnePIN, managed by the same property company. Fewer cameras. Fewer eyes.

They didn't need full details. They already knew the plan.

They ran a dry drill at midnight in a closed office park outside Needham—time-on-target, ingress, exfil on foot to a secondary vehicle staged two blocks away. No gear, no masks, nothing that would trip a concerned neighbor.

One looped the perimeter at a jog, counting under his breath, testing how long it took for a motion light to reset. Another crossed a lot with his hands in his pockets and looked at his reflection in a dark window to check posture, not vanity.

Back at the cottage, they ate in turns. No trash inside. Wrappers folded into a single bag and compressed flat. The drone stayed on the table, battery warm, lens capped.

Near midnight, the burner phones vibrated once—no ring, no tone. A text came through in a string of innocuous words that meant everything to them: SABLE GREEN. 36H. PRIMARY, THEN HOUSE.

The tallest man read it aloud without inflection. The others nodded. Two powered their phones off and broke the SIMs without looking down.

He didn't. He slid his back into the case, screen face-down, and set a timer on his watch.

Tomorrow was approaching.

And their mission was nearly complete.

Before lights out, the tallest man stepped outside and looked at the sky like he was checking the weather. He wasn't. He was listening. The highway hummed. A siren wailed two towns away and faded. Nothing close.

He went back in, locked the door twice, and rested the drone case against the jamb.

They slept in clothes, on top of the covers, boots just under the bed. Alarms set to different times.

No prayers. No speeches. Just a plan waiting for a morning.

CHAPTER 54

Jill

The Morning Routine

Feyzi woke up at 6:23 a.m. sharp—his internal rhythm unbroken by the chaos of recent months. Though his life now straddled two worlds—civilian and clandestine—his rituals grounded him.

He padded into the kitchen, where faint birdsong filtered through cracked windows and the smell of brewing coffee lingered in the air. Sunlight streamed through the wide glass doors, stretching warm golden beams across the tiled floor.

His breakfast was as deliberate as always: two slices of toast layered with creamy feta, six precisely counted black olives, and slices of tomato arranged with geometric care. Jill's touch was still present on the ceramic plate—she insisted food should always look beautiful.

He stepped out onto the 800-square-foot deck that wrapped around the Çelik residence. The wooden floor, still holding the night's chill, warmed gently beneath his bare feet. A gentle breeze stirred the pines lining the edge of the property. The impatiens in twelve oversized planters stretched toward the rising sun, their petals already fluttering with life.

Somewhere inside, the distant clink of Jill's morning dishes hinted at her presence.

Feyzi paused, inhaling the pine-tinged air, his eyes scanning the familiar treetops. For a fleeting moment, the world was simple again.

Into Boston

By eight o'clock, he had changed into his usual understated armor—black dress shirt, slim-fit khakis.

Clean lines. No logos. He liked simplicity; it made him feel in control.

He slipped into his dark-gray BMW iX60 and drove toward Boston, the low hum of the electric engine blending with his thoughts. Saddle Hill Road unfolded like a ribbon through the woods, the maples and birches flanking his path. Eventually, the trees gave way to the Mass Pike. He merged eastbound.

Boston came into view like a postcard—red-brick charm and slate-gray rooftops.

As Feyzi passed Boston University, memories rushed in. Thirty-three years ago, he had been a young master's student there—bright, curious, relentless. His advisor had tasked him with studying the chaotic behavior of the Euler Equations. Each Friday afternoon, BU's supercomputer was reserved just for him. That project had changed everything. It was the beginning.

While gliding past the Boston University Photonics Center on his left, his phone rang.

The Unexpected Call

"Hello, Commander Çelik," Commander Hart's voice was crisp but upbeat.

"I arrived in Boston. I'm heading to OnePIN HQ now—Mass Pike Westbound. I'll be working with Adam and the team for the next three days on the new ARES specs. Looking forward to seeing you this afternoon."

"Welcome to Boston," Feyzi replied. "I'm on Eastbound to the Board meeting. See you soon."

In Back Bay, the brownstones stood proud as ever, anchoring the city in time. Newbury Street buzzed with early shoppers, its boutique windows glowing with curated elegance. A man walked a golden retriever across Dartmouth Street while a delivery truck unloaded espresso beans in front of a small café.

The Boardroom

The elevator ride to the Forward Capital office was smooth and silent. The boardroom itself was perched like a lighthouse over the Charles River. A quiet river that had witnessed a world-threatening storm two months earlier.

David Brown, Board Member and longtime supporter, greeted him with a warm nod. Feyzi presented the newest update: OnePIN's expanded defense contract with the U.S. Government. Their role in Echo-7 had earned trust and secrecy in equal measure. ARES was now a national imperative.

But the success brought strain.

Their telecom division—still serving billions—now shared space with their clandestine AI warfare division.

Talent was finite. Deadlines weren't.

Now, OnePIN had a huge contract with the U.S. Government with a focus on future AI weapons—specifically ARES. All large U.S. defense companies were actively trying to acquire OnePIN, recognizing its strategic value and the elite talent behind its systems. The spotlight was both an honor and a burden.

The meeting was productive, but heavy. Stakes had never been higher.

The Call That Shattered It All

At 11:00 a.m., his phone rang again.

Commander Hart's voice was different this time.

Sharp.

Urgent.

Edged with fear.

"Commander, there's been an attack—your home. Armed intruders engaged the guards. Six of our best men are gone. These attackers are wearing protective shields—our weapons aren't slowing them."

In the boardroom, the call had been on speaker. Silence fell like a curtain.

"Jill had just left the front door—perhaps headed out to run an errand—when the attackers seized the moment. Our security team managed to disable the intruders' original vehicle during the initial firefight, forcing them to improvise. In a split-second move, they overpowered Jill and hijacked her car. She's now with them, and they're fleeing in her vehicle. Hopkinton Police and your security are engaged in a high-speed pursuit. But they can't act decisively—Jill is their shield. They won't risk her life by opening fire or deploying intercept weapons."

Brown met Feyzi's eyes. Around the table, a hush fell over the boardroom.

Some members froze mid-motion, coffee cups suspended just shy of lips. Others exchanged alarmed glances or murmured questions under their breath.

The atmosphere shifted—curiosity giving way to fear.

OnePIN's executives, brilliant minds trained for precision and logic, were now tethered to an unraveling situation beyond their control.

An aura of disbelief hung in the air as they tried to grasp what was unfolding.

Jill.

An attack.

Shields.

Weapons.

This was no longer theoretical.

It was personal.

"Why Jill? Why now?"

Feyzi had no answers.

His pulse froze. He lunged for the elevator, barely noticing the startled looks from the boardroom as he exited. The doors closed with a quiet hiss, trapping him in a steel box of rising panic.

The elevator hummed downward with smooth efficiency, but to Feyzi, each passing floor felt agonizingly slow. The lights above the door blinked one by one—17...16...15. The overhead fluorescent glow cast sharp shadows across his clenched fists.

His mind spun.

Jill—taken.

Security—dead.

Shielded enemies.

What kind of tech were they using?

Who else knew?

He could hear his own breath, rapid and shallow. The scent of antiseptic and elevator lubricant filled the cramped space.

Somewhere far below, sirens wailed faintly in the city. Or was that just in his head?

When the elevator dinged at the garage level, Feyzi stepped out like a bullet released from its casing.

His thoughts were no longer spiraling. They had narrowed.

One mission.

Get Jill back.

Whatever it took.

CHAPTER 55
Pursuit

The Escape from the Garage

Feyzi still had his phone on, connected to his BMW's speakers. Commander Hart's voice filtered in, clipped with rapid urgency.

He was already navigating the underground garage beneath Forward Capital, weaving past empty parking slots and shadowed concrete pillars. His pulse pounded with a ferocity he hadn't felt since the early hours of Echo-7.

His BMW iX60 jolted forward as he slammed the accelerator.

The garage toll gate exploded in his wake, brittle arms of aluminum scattering like matchsticks.

Alarms screamed behind him. Red warning lights pulsed.

But Feyzi wasn't looking back.

Hart's Update

"Commander Çelik," Hart said, her voice rough with static.

"I've intercepted the police convoy—we're trailing Jill's vehicle now. I believe they're heading toward Hanscom Field. I'm notifying the Air Force."

Then—silence.

Hanscom Field

Hanscom Field sat nestled between the towns of Bedford, Concord, and Lincoln—a joint-use civil-military airport housing private aviation, commercial support, and sensitive military facilities. Its quiet exterior masked a labyrinth of security perimeters, hangars, and reinforced compounds.

To an outsider, it appeared to be a civilian airport with modest traffic. But beneath the runways were hardened command centers and classified operations—some tied to DARPA, others blacker still.

As Feyzi raced toward it, storm clouds churned above like bruises across the sky. The air had grown thick, expectant. Birds had gone silent. Even the wind seemed to pause. A strange hush blanketed the wooded outskirts of Massachusetts, lending an eerie, cinematic tension to the coming confrontation.

The Digital Trail

Feyzi swore under his breath as traffic swelled ahead—an immovable wall on the Newbury Street exit ramp to the Mass Pike. Brake lights glowed like embers in a winding trail.

Thinking fast, he activated the MyBMW app on his iPhone. Jill's BMW X5 flashed into view.

GPS tracking showed the vehicle careening through Maynard and Concord, racing down winding country roads, zigzagging away from main arteries.

The contrast was jarring—quaint homes with stone fences, wooden mailboxes, fields of waving grass and quiet brooks—all streaked by a blur of high-speed motion. Gravel flew. Tire marks gouged the shoulder.

Startled drivers veered aside as sirens screamed faintly in the distance. The early morning sun shimmered across the hot asphalt.

A blinking alert from MyBMW app caught Feyzi's eye:

"Fuel Level for BMW X5: Critical"

Feyzi tightened his jaw.

"As usual, Jill didn't fill the tank. That might be our only break."

He called Hart.

"They don't have much gas. They won't get far."

Hart answered immediately.

"Copy that."

Family Status Check

"What about Alex?" Feyzi asked.

"First priority," Hart replied.

"He was at the high school. Our team picked him up within minutes. He's already en route to a secure location."

"And Ayla?"

"She hasn't answered any of our calls. But she's scheduled to be at Homefair HQ in Copley. Close to your earlier location. We're assuming she's safe—but we'll dispatch a team to confirm."

Jill's Car Is Abandoned

Hart's voice came back on the line moments later, more tense than before:

"Commander, update. They ditched Jill's car on Vanderberg Drive near Hanscom Field. Skid marks show a hard stop, probably when the fuel finally gave out.

The vehicle rolled to a halt next to a rusted chain-link fence lining the edge of an old industrial service yard. Gravel crunched beneath the tires as it veered off pavement.

Officers on scene found the passenger door wide open. Her purse was still on the seat. Her phone tossed on the floorboard, screen shattered. Six sets of footprints cut through the loose gravel and weeds, heading toward a looming, windowless warehouse across the yard."

The structure stood like a forgotten relic—its rust-colored walls peeling, one loading dock warped and unused.

No signage. No working lights. Just shadows.

The attackers had paused only briefly before dragging Jill inside.

Police hesitated to follow. The perimeter felt off—as if the building itself rejected intrusion.

There was no sound.

No motion.

The breeze had stopped.

Parallel: Jill's Perspective

Inside the vehicle moments earlier, Jill sat with her wrists zip-tied in front of her, wedged between two broad-shouldered men in the back seat. She could feel the heat of their bodies, hear their synchronized breathing, but they never spoke.

She tracked the roads silently:

Maynard. Concord. A left near an old mill. A right past a farmhouse. They were headed to Hanscom. She knew that stretch too well.

When the car sputtered and slowed, the lead man hissed a command. The vehicle screeched to a halt. Dust flew. Jill's door was yanked open.

She tried to brace herself.

"Think. Think, Jill."

One of them dragged her out. Her shoes scraped across the gravel. Her knee hit the ground. She winced, bit her lip, refused to cry out.

The wind picked up. The warehouse loomed ahead.

"He's coming. Feyzi always comes."

Inside, the air was heavy with rot and metal. Oil stains formed abstract patterns on the floor. The ceiling groaned under its own weight. Light filtered in from a row of cracked skylights. Far above, pigeons flapped once and went silent.

A Russian voice barked an order. She was shoved forward, up rusting stairs, into a second-floor chamber with flickering generators and strange boxes pulsing with LED lights.

"Just survive," she thought.

"That's my job now."

The Call to Ayla

Feyzi dialed Ayla. Her voice came through, confused but calm.

"Hi Dad, I was in a meeting. So many missed calls—what's going on?"

Feyzi inhaled slowly.

"Ayla, I'm sending security. When they arrive, ask for the passcode. Confirm it. Then follow protocol. You and Ryan will be escorted to the safe zone."

"Dad... what's happening?"

"They've taken Jill. Alex is safe. I'm going after her now. Do exactly as we are prepared for."

Ayla paused, her voice cracking.

"Dad... save Mom. I need her."

"I promise," he said. Then hung up.

For a moment, the silence in his car was suffocating.

His mind replayed Ayla's last words like a haunting echo.

Internal Resolve

Feyzi's foot slammed the accelerator again.

The silence gave way to the roar of wind against the windshield as he sped toward Hanscom Field.

"They made a mistake," he thought.

"They took only one of us."

But they would pay.

And this time, the rules were his to write.

CHAPTER 56

The Gauntlet

Escape from Newbury Street

Feyzi slammed his palm against the steering wheel, eyes scanning for any opening in the frozen wall of traffic. Cabbies honked. Pedestrians stared. The city had its rhythm—but today, he would shatter it.

He looked down, hesitated only for a heartbeat, and then reached beneath the steering column. A small, recessed button.

He pressed it.

The hidden blue lights snapped to life beneath the front bumper, and a discreet siren, threaded with urgency but devoid of panic, began to wail.

Cars parted like a tide before him. Drivers leaned out windows, stunned, unsure whether to fear or follow. Few had ever seen a civilian BMW iX60 perform like this.

Feyzi didn't care.

Jill's life was the only metric that mattered now.

Mass Pike Acceleration

His car vaulted onto the Mass Pike westbound. Dual electric motors whirred in harmony, and within seconds, the dark gray SUV was pushing past 100 mph. The engine didn't roar—it hissed, smooth and relentless, like a predator closing in.

Commander Hart came back on the line.

"Commander, State Police are setting up support near the Route 95 interchange. We're coordinating traffic control now."

Feyzi didn't answer.

His eyes narrowed as Newton's green signage whipped past in a blur. Sweat prickled down his back.

Route 95 and the Cavalry

The merge onto Route 95 North was a disaster. Construction had narrowed lanes. Bridge replacement. Orange cones, flashing signs, bridge pylons.

Then, like cavalry summoned from myth, two Massachusetts State Police cruisers peeled from the shoulder, sirens cutting through the heavy air. They positioned themselves in front of Feyzi, clearing lanes with sweeping authority.

Inside the lead cruiser, officers exchanged baffled glances.

"BMW iX with blue lights?"

"Who is this guy?"

The radio crackled:

"All units, protect the vehicle at all costs. Repeat: protect the dark gray BMW iX. Designation: Echo-Seven Priority One."

Behind him, two more cruisers joined the chase near the Waltham exit, flanking him in a V-formation.

Police Interceptors vs. Feyzi's Machine

Feyzi pressed harder. The Interceptors tried to match his pace, but the electric torque of the BMW was unrelenting.

"These V8s are solid," Feyzi thought. "But they weren't built for this."

Still, he appreciated their presence.

If anything happened at the next turn, he'd need backup.

Flashback: Peace Before the Storm

As the convoy passed Lexington, a memory surfaced—Feyzi and Jill, years earlier, driving this same route after apple picking in Concord. She had laughed at a song on the radio, her hand resting gently on his.

There had been no threats then. No wars. Just the hum of the road and the sound of Jill's laughter.

Now, that same road led him into a war zone.

Arrival at Vanderberg Drive

Ten minutes later, the convoy skidded to a halt in front of a crumbling industrial complex on Vanderberg Drive. Chain-link fencing bowed in the wind. Paint peeled from corrugated steel siding. A forgotten monument to Cold War infrastructure—now pulsing with life and violence.

Storm clouds rolled low, casting long shadows. The humid Massachusetts air felt like it would crack from pressure. Nearby pine trees stood still, as if holding their breath.

Police cars boxed the perimeter. Tactical teams crouched behind open doors.

Gunfire popped like firecrackers from the side of the warehouse.

The Firefight

The air was chaos—bullets cracking against metal, shouts over radios, the piercing squeal of incoming medical units.

Eight officers were already down; their forms draped in bloodied Kevlar.

Ambulances tore toward Brigham & Women's, Mass General, Beth Israel, and Needham—the best hospitals in Boston, primed for trauma but never prepared for war.

Emergency rooms buzzed. Surgeons scrubbed in. Helicopters prepped for airlift. Staff gathered in triage zones, reviewing terror protocols long stored but never used.

Boston had just become a battlefield.

Local Media Frenzy

Above, news helicopters swarmed like flies, filming grainy overhead shots. Reporters shouted over squawking radios.

"We're live from a developing scene on Vanderberg Drive..."

Local networks scrambled to confirm.

News vans jammed side streets. Confused civilians were pushed back behind barricades.

Commander Hart's Tactical Command

Commander Hart sprinted toward Feyzi, bulletproof vest half-secured, sidearm holstered at her hip.

Her face was a mask of resolve, but Feyzi caught a glimpse of something deeper—doubt, fear, and fury.

She was a soldier. A leader. But also, a woman standing beside a family she had grown to protect.

Every order she gave pulled at her core. The tactical part of her mind told her to treat this like any mission. But this wasn't just a mission. This was Jill. This was Feyzi. This was personal.

"We can't breach," she said, panting.

"They're shooting through every exit. They're wearing advanced armor—rounds bounce right off. And Jill... she's inside. Alive. We're tracking her thermal signature."

She pulled out a secondary comms unit.

"All Echo-Seven units, lock down airspace. Activate drone jammers. Rooftop teams on overwatch, snipers in position. Encrypt tactical lines. Use Echo-Seven alpha key only."

Drone Surveillance POV

From a hovering surveillance drone, thermal imagery revealed movement inside the steel-and-concrete building.

Six heat signatures. One on the floor—likely Jill. The other five were cold, controlled. Standing guard.

A sniper's voice crackled back:

"Drone eye active. Thermal signature confirmed. Target pacing—possibly restrained. Movement erratic."

Hart turned to local law enforcement.

"Your perimeter belongs to us now. Let no one in or out without dual-key validation. This is no longer local jurisdiction."

Inside the Warehouse

Inside the dim warehouse, Jill pressed her back against a stack of rusted barrels. Her wrists ached from flexicuffs, but her ears were sharper than ever.

Gunfire echoed through the steel skeleton of the building. Each burst was a jolt to her chest.

Then—she heard it.

The high-pitched modulation of Boston police sirens. A deeper tone behind them—BMW electric sirens.

She knew that sound. Feyzi.

A tear slid down her cheek. Hope, fragile but alive.

But she forced herself to stay sharp.

This wasn't over.

Her captors hadn't spoken much, but they moved with precision. Almost like machines. And now they were cornered.

She remembered a quiet fall afternoon, years ago, when she and Feyzi had driven past this very road after picking up pumpkins with the kids. They'd laughed at how out-of-the-way the industrial buildings seemed.

Now, she was inside one.

And war raged outside.

She closed her eyes for a moment, inhaled the coppery scent of the warehouse, and whispered under her breath:

"Please, Feyzi... come fast."

In the darkness, hope ignited.

Outside, amidst the chaos, Feyzi stared at the building, jaw clenched.

The world blurred around him.

CHAPTER 57

The Ultimatum

Feyzi didn't speak. He stared at the building, hands trembling at his sides. The chaos around him blurred, sound dulled, and it felt—for a brief moment—as if time itself held its breath. Sirens became echoes, gunfire became distant thunder.

Overhead, the buzz of news helicopters intensified. Local channels had picked up the emergency calls. Reporters shouted into handheld mics.

"We're here on Vanderberg Drive where something resembling a military standoff is unfolding."

The Silence Before the Voice

And then, without warning, the firefight stopped. Abruptly. The stillness was eerie. Even the helicopters seemed to hesitate.

Suddenly, all the police officers' phones began to ring—simultaneously.

A wave of confused glances swept through the officers. Some hesitated before answering. Others simply turned to Feyzi as if instinctively knowing the call had something to do with him.

A familiar face emerged from the group: the Police Commander from Logan Airport. He had been on duty the day Feyzi returned home after the XT84 rescue. He hadn't forgotten.

The officer's voice was low and cautious.

"Mr. Çelik... what is this? Why your wife? Why do they call you 'Commander'?"

He paused, then held up his phone.

"Anyway... they want to talk to you."

He pressed the mute button and added in a whisper,

"We're tracing the origin of the signal now."

Then he passed the phone to Feyzi.

The Metallic Voice

The line crackled with static, then cleared into a voice—not human, not robotic, but something in between.

Modulated. Cold.

"Feyzi Çelik, we couldn't locate your phone directly. We accessed all nearby law enforcement devices to reach you."

Feyzi remained silent.

"We have waited for this moment. Your wife is unharmed—for now. We are inside the building. Second floor. Second door on the left of the stairs. You will surrender yourself to us. No tricks. No weapons. If you deviate, Jill dies."

Feyzi's jaw tightened.

"You will accompany us to Hanscom Airbase. We have a pickup scheduled. You will board with us. Alone."

"Any resistance, and you die."

"No one follows."

Feyzi's voice was calm.

"I'm coming in. Two minutes. But first—I need to hear Jill's voice."

There was a pause. Then a faint, trembling voice:

"Feyzi, I'm okay—this is a trick..."

The line cut. Static returned.

Hart's Arrival and Internal Conflict

Commander Hart stormed toward Feyzi just as he handed the phone back.

Her face was flushed, torn between fury and fear.

"Commander, you can't go in there. You heard Jill—it's a trap. They'll kill you. And her. We need to breach."

Feyzi looked at her, the steel already returning to his eyes.

"No breach. Not yet."

Hart's mind raced.

Her training screamed at her to stop him.

To take command.

But another part—deeper, older—understood that this was personal now.

And that Feyzi wasn't just a tech visionary anymore.

He was the Commander. He had a mission to fulfill.

And this was war.

Drone Surveillance – Tactical Eye

From a tactical van parked nearby, Echo-7's drone unit fed live footage to the command screen. Thermal imaging showed six heat signatures—five upright, moving; one seated.

"Target confirmed: second floor, east wing. Hostiles are armed and moving in triangular patterns. Military precision," a drone tech reported.

The screen flickered. One of the forms on the floor.

"Could be Jill. She's lying down, possibly unharmed."

Inside the Warehouse – Jill's Fear and Hope

In the darkened warehouse, Jill sat up right now, wrists raw from the flexicuffs.

She listened, her heart pounding.

The gunfire had stopped.

She could hear voices. No words, just cadence.

Her breath caught in her throat. She blinked back tears.

Hope surged through her chest, clashing with terror.

"Feyzi, please come quickly."

She looked around at her captors—stoic, calculating.

One stood near the window, peering through the blinds.

Another checked his watch.

She had to hold on.

Outside, as clouds darkened overhead, Feyzi took one last breath and turned toward the building.

The gauntlet had been thrown.

Now, he would walk into the storm.

CHAPTER 58

Into the Inferno

Commander Hart gripped Feyzi's arm.

"Commander Çelik, you cannot walk in there. They'll kill you and Jill. This is a trap, you know that."

Her voice cracked. It wasn't just a plea—it was a command from a soldier torn between duty and fear.

Somewhere deep inside her, a war was waging.

She had spent her career making battlefield decisions, but this felt more personal. Feyzi wasn't just a critical asset.

He was something more.

The calm in chaos. The hope she had clung to more than once.

Feyzi's eyes remained locked on the building.

"We have no other option. We don't have bargaining power. They outsmarted us. I didn't see this move coming. Jill can't pay the price for my mistake."

He started walking toward the warehouse entrance—no weapon, no plan beyond getting Jill out alive.

Hart cursed under her breath, spun toward a police vehicle, and yanked open the trunk.

She grabbed a ballistic vest and sprinted after him.

"Stop!" she called, breath ragged.

She caught up to him, blocking his path just long enough to shove the vest against his chest.

"Wear it."

Feyzi stared at the vest.

"It didn't help the others," he said, voice low.

"The rounds passed right through."

Hart's eyes locked onto his.

"Wear it anyway. Don't make me order you."

He saw it in her face—the trembling resolve of a woman who had fought wars and lost friends and now stood on the edge of losing him.

He slid the vest on.

Then, somehow, he smiled.

"That calm and smiley face is back again," Hart thought.

"How does he do that?"

The Approach

The sea of police cars parted.

Officers lowered their weapons, stunned into silence. Reporters watched in awe from behind barricades, their cameras turning as one.

Feyzi walked slowly but with purpose, each step echoing against the concrete like a countdown.

The scene felt surreal, like a film reel slowed to emphasize the gravity of a moment no one could stop.

Above, a drone hovered—its thermal sensors tracking movement inside the building. On the portable surveillance screen in the command van, red-orange silhouettes flickered, clustered in the far eastern corner.

"He's walking right into them," a tech whispered.

Commander Hart clenched her jaw.

"Track everything. Eyes on. Audio loop open. No one moves unless I say so."

The Warehouse Interior

The steel door moaned on its hinges as Feyzi entered. The warehouse swallowed him.

The air was musty, laced with oil, copper, and mildew. Rows of broken shelves and rusted machinery loomed like skeletons of a forgotten era. Faint buzzing from overhead lights gave the place a deathly glow.

A stairwell rose in the far corner—its railing bent, steps creaking with each ascent.

Feyzi climbed slowly. His breaths deepened, sharpened. Every fiber of his being was tuned to the moment.

Flashback: Peace Before the Storm

He remembered driving with Jill down Vanderberg Drive years ago.

The kids were asleep in the back, and Jill had been laughing at one of his old Turkish proverbs.

They had no idea what this place would become—a battlefield.

He held that memory now, like a lifeline.

The Second Floor

Dim lights flickered. A long hallway stretched out, lined with broken doors. He reached the elevator, then turned left.

Second door.

Left side.

Just as they said.

He opened it.

The Confrontation

Inside were five figures—soldiers, not thugs.

Their stances were trained, precise.

Jill lay on the ground, hands bound in front of her, her face bruised but conscious. Her eyes met his, wide and disbelieving.

The leader stepped forward. Taller than the rest, with a strange symmetry to his movements—too perfect, too mechanical.

Feyzi stepped forward too, his smile returning.

"You made a mistake by taking my wife," he said, calm as a scalpel.

"I don't negotiate. I don't forgive."

The room went still.

The Signal

Down below, Commander Hart suddenly dropped to one knee.

Her hands flew to her ears as a piercing, high-pitched sound cut through the air. Officers across the perimeter staggered, clutching their heads.

"High-frequency audio weapon—unknown source!" shouted one of the Echo-7 techs.

Hart gritted her teeth.

"Ground drones. Rotate thermal feeds. We need confirmation he's still standing."

Then came the bang.

A deep, chest-thumping explosion that rattled the warehouse walls.

Dust spilled from the upper windows.

Officers jumped to attention.

Reporters ducked behind vans.

Inside, the confrontation had begun.

CHAPTER 59
Humanoids

Commander Hart would not stay still anymore.

The scene she had witnessed on the monitors moments earlier played over and over in her mind—Jill's cry, the gunfire, the chilling silence that followed.

Her pulse pounded in her ears.

With a sharp breath, she reached for her sidearm and bolted toward the staircase.

Her boots thudded against the metal steps as she climbed to the second floor, her heart hammering against her ribs.

The air grew denser the closer she got. Smoke curled from beneath the doorframe of the second room, and a strange mechanical odor hung heavy in the corridor.

Commander Hart was the first to arrive, her breath shallow from the sprint. She burst through the door, weapon raised, expecting anything.

What she saw was worse than anything she had imagined.

Feyzi was kneeling on the blood-smeared floor, cradling Jill in his arms like a fallen angel. Her body was limp; her platinum blond hair matted with streaks of soot.

Feyzi looked up, his face pale and streaked with ash, his eyes carrying the weight of war.

Commander Hart met his gaze, her expression tight with dread.

Feyzi knew what she was asking. He shook his head faintly.

"Jill just passed out," he said in a hushed, shaken tone.

"She's OK."

Hart's eyes scanned the room, and her stomach turned.

The floor was strewn with severed biosynthetic limbs and torn dermal sheaths.

Beneath the split, still-warm skin lay latticework "bone" and braided actuator fibers slick with translucent coolant. Sparks hissed from a ruptured interface on the far wall.

The humanoids—once uncannily human—were now heaps of lab-grown tissue draped over composite frames. No gleam of metal, no ferrous mass—nothing a checkpoint would flag. Man-made ghosts built to read as human, invisible to airport security.

Hart fought the urge to gag.

Feyzi, adjusting Jill's weight in his arms, added grimly, "You may want to secure the room immediately. You don't want this scene to be seen. Make it top security."

Nodding with practiced control, Hart turned on her heel and stepped outside.

She spotted the Police Commander, his face a mixture of concern and confusion.

"This room is a Level One security scene," she said with clipped authority.

"Lock it down. No one goes in or out until further notice."

She returned swiftly, locking the door behind her.

"What happened here, Commander Çelik?"

"How did you and Jill survive the explosion?"

Her voice was quiet now, almost reverent in the face of chaos.

Feyzi stood slowly, still holding Jill as if letting her go would break him.

"I don't know, Commander Hart. I'm trying to figure it out myself. Was it a suicide mission to take us both out?"

Hart's eyes darkened.

"Commander, these were highly advanced, tactically precise humanoid assassins. They may be tens of years ahead of us technologically. How do we even begin to explain this?"

Feyzi exhaled slowly, bitterness coloring his voice.

"That's the problem. Our intelligence community fell asleep while the enemy leapt forward. The free world must wake up, fast. We have years to catch up. Innovation is no longer optional."

They moved in silence toward the staircase, the only sound the wet hiss of boiling coolant and the faint tick of failing actuators behind them.

Feyzi carried Jill with aching tenderness, his arms aching but unwavering. He couldn't look at her pale face without feeling a pang of guilt.

When they reached the ground floor, paramedics rushed forward. One of them, a young woman with trembling hands, helped guide Jill onto a stretcher.

The moment Feyzi let go, a strange emptiness swept through him.

Jill stirred. Her eyes fluttered open, pupils struggling to focus.

A weak smile formed on her cracked lips as she saw Feyzi hovering beside her.

"Jill, everything will be OK," he said, forcing confidence into his voice.

She reached for his hand.

"I knew you'd come to save me. You always do," she whispered, her voice barely audible.

"Who were they, Feyzi?"

Before he could answer, her eyelids closed again.

Feyzi leaned close, brushing a strand of hair from her face.

His voice broke as he whispered,

"I love you. I will never allow this to happen again."

His thoughts swirled with anguish.

How had they missed this threat?

Who was pulling the strings?

As the ambulance doors closed, he vowed silently—this wasn't over.

And next time, he would be ready.

CHAPTER 60

The Morning After

The morning light poured across the kitchen table at the Çelik home, a warm stripe of September sun that made the tea steam look like rising silk. Outside, maples flickered green and gold in a gentle breeze; inside, every window and door had an extra set of eyes.

A second perimeter hummed beyond the hedges—unmarked SUVs, earpieces catching the light, fresh tire prints pressed into dew. The house felt simultaneously smaller and safer, like a ship battened down after a storm.

Jill eased into her chair, the hospital bracelet still circling her wrist. Beth Israel Hospital had released her at dawn—"just observation," she'd said—and now she was home, wrapped in one of Ayla's over-sized sweaters. Alex slid a honey jar closer. Ryan poured water over a small nest of tea leaves; the kettle clicked, a domestic metronome fighting last night's adrenaline.

On the table lay the morning's paper stack and a tablet alive with alerts.

Ayla read first, voice steady, eyes bright:

The Boston Globe: "Two Months After XT84: Tech CEO Feyzi Çelik Survives the Atlantic—Now Wife Jill Rescued After Violent Abduction Near Hanscom."

"...abductors were trapped in a warehouse near the airfield; tactical teams breached; Jill Çelik recovered alive."

Alex flipped to another headline:

New York Times: "Massachusetts Standoff Ends in Rescue of Jill Çelik; SWAT Raids Warehouse Near Hanscom Airfield."

"State Police and FBI coordinated the perimeter; all hostile assailants neutralized."

Ryan held up the tablet, the CNN clip paused on a stack of patrol cars and a ribbon of yellow tape, helicopter shadow sliding over corrugated metal.

CNN (Live): "Breaking: Jill Çelik Safe—FBI, State Police End Hostage Siege; Armed Assailants Neutralized."

The local anchor's voice echoed from the corner TV:

WHDH / WBZ: "Vanderberg Drive Under Lockdown—'Boston Became a Battlefield,' says first responder; aerials show SWAT deployment."

Jill listened, cupping the warm mug with both hands.

She smiled—small, genuine, stubborn.

"I'm okay," she said, looking at each of them.

"And we're safe. Your dad will make sure of it. He always does."

They didn't press her. They didn't need to. The room held its own kind of quiet; a trust made of thousands of ordinary days—and the single extraordinary one that had nearly taken them away.

From the driveway came the low idle of a black SUV. It settled like a punctuation mark. The front bell rang—three precise taps.

Alex stood, but Jill touched his sleeve. "I've got it."

At the door: two men and one woman in black suits, dark glasses, posture like plumb lines. The woman spoke first, voice level.

"Morning, Mrs. Çelik. We're here to confirm you're all right and to review the new perimeter plan. You'll see some changes—patrol rotations, surveillance upgrades, door protocols. We don't intend to intrude. We intend to be seen."

Jill nodded.

"Thank you."

They stepped inside for a minute—shoes a whisper on the foyer tile—checked sightlines, tested a panic button tucked beneath the console table, and left their card with a single embossed sigil.

On the way out, they scanned the street with a mirrored glance and returned to the SUV. The engine softened, then merged with the neighborhood's morning.

Back at the table, Ayla refreshed *The Globe* feed. A sidebar credited Rachel Lin for "continuing coverage" of XT84. Two months ago, she'd been the first to suggest a survivor—Feyzi's emergency SOS. Today she tied a rescue to a reckoning.

Ryan broke the silence. "They're already speculating about ransom. Foreign crew. Imported weapons."

"Rumors," Jill said gently. "Let the investigators sort truth from echo."

She set down her tea. The tiny clink of porcelain seemed larger than it should have been.

"The men were... not like anything I've seen," Jill continued, measuring her breath. "Five of them. Military posture. Perfect synchronization." She paused, finding language for the impossible. "Security shot back. Others did too. But the bullets ..." She stopped, fingertips brushing the inside of her wrist as if the memory lived there. "It was like they skipped, skittered. As if something... protected them."

Ayla reached for her hand. "Mom, you don't have to ..."

"I do." Jill's eyes lifted to the window, to the sunlight on the hedges, to the world that should have kept being ordinary and would not.

Her gaze softened, and a quiet smile stole across her face.

"And then your father was there."

"There was a sound—so high it made the air feel sharp. And then a blast. A heavy one. After that, everything went gray."

You could almost hear the warehouse again in the quiet—the scorched metal, the tearing of something that looked like skin but wasn't, the smell of coolant and smoke, the unreal anatomy of the fallen. Jill did not name it. She didn't have to. The others had seen the aftermath on a secure tablet, a still frame no broadcast would ever air.

"Whatever this is," Jill said, "it isn't just about us. There's more at stake than a family. I only know pieces. Your father told me what he could."

She squeezed Ayla's hand, found Alex's eyes, then Ryan's. "We have to be brave. And we keep it inside this house. No one can know."

Alex nodded first, jaw set. Ayla breathed in, holding courage like a note. Ryan's "yes" was quiet but solid.

The door camera chimed—another perimeter check, a friendly wave from the driveway team. Jill stood and lifted the curtain an inch. The suits were dots against the sunlit street, ordinary in a way that felt like a miracle.

Behind her, the television cycled the headlines again:

"Jill Çelik Home After Observation at Beth Israel Hospital," the anchor said, the words threaded with the calm cadence of morning news. "Family requests privacy. Investigation continues."

Jill turned back to the table. "Tea's getting cold," she said, and it was almost funny.

They laughed—soft, shaky, real. Outside, a bird tested the light with a single note. The house exhaled.

When the laughter faded, Ayla closed *The Globe* app and stacked the papers neatly. Ryan refilled cups. Alex adjusted the curtain so the sun fell exactly where Jill sat, a small geometry of comfort.

"Whatever comes next," Jill said, "we meet it together."

She didn't add the last part aloud: that Feyzi had stepped into something larger, something with a name that did not belong on any morning show. That she had seen the edges of it in the warehouse—precision that wasn't human, protection that shouldn't exist, and the explosive mercy of survival.

Instead, she chose the ordinary.

She lifted her tea, breathed the steam, and, just for the space of a sip, let the day be beautiful.

CHAPTER 61

The Other Board

Kaliningrad, Russia — Eastern Command Theater,
Subterranean War Room

Kaliningrad was cold and quiet. Sirens cut through it. In the Eastern Command Theater, beneath slabs of concrete and an old museum's foundation, the Subterranean War Room was cleaned, reset, and back online. The conference table was polished and the head chair sat empty.

They found Colonel Alexei Voronov just before dawn—locked in his private annex behind a blast door that took only his handprint. No forced entry. No video. A stroke, the first medic said, because it was easier than telling the truth. Under magnification, five punctures marked his neck in a tight pattern.

He leaned to take a call; a palm sized drone deployed from the desk, administered a single dose, and retracted.

The drone's serial number matches a stealth batch registered to his own sabotage division.

The autopsy report called it "catastrophic vascular failure." A margin note read: Our own invention.

Shanghai — Qiantang Cyber Dome,
PLA Eastern Command Node

Half a continent away, the Qiantang Cyber Dome lit the skyline. Admiral Liang Weimin sat upright at his desk; eyes fixed on a blue map of the Philippine Sea. The room smelled of spice and machine oil.

Officially, he died at his post. In fact, a restraint harness applied controlled force from behind and broke two ribs at the joints. For 128 seconds, the internal camera feeds went black, and the building replaced them with the same loop of empty hallway, cover footage inserted by automation.

General Bao Xinjian never made it home. Two internal security officers "relieved" him of duty and handed him into a waiting sedan. The assigned driver, Unit 31, had long access. It triggered a modified seat belt buckle with an internal striker that deformed the latch. Four blocks later the car sat by the curb, doors locked from inside, oxygen bled down to 2.8%, the logs overwritten by Bao's own watchdog process.

The Assassins' Epilogue

Three rooms. Three commanders. Three failures. Three quiet executions carried out by systems they paid to perfect.

Moscow and Shanghai never said civil war with our own machines.

They said, "command hygiene," then moved pieces with the speed of crisis.

The Room After

Moscow's Kremlin and the Shanghai Party Secretariat move faster than grief can harden. Four replacements arrive within 48 hours, two flown under diplomatic cover into Kaliningrad, two elevated in Shanghai and sealed behind firewalls of fear.

Within forty-eight hours the empty chair in Kaliningrad had new gravity.

Kaliningrad, Russia

General Irina Sokolova arrived under a sky that couldn't decide whether to snow or rain. She wore her service like a winter coat—Spetsnaz sapper, the Barents in her bones, eyes that measured pressure and water and the places rock gave way. She preferred systems she could isolate and power down by hand.

Behind her came Rear Admiral Oleg Pakhomov, a submarine hunter whose last dossier read like static. He could hear intention in sonar the way a cardiologist hears a murmur, head cocked, expression unreadable. In his first hour he removed three analytics racks and replaced a fiber run with copper.

"When lightning comes," he said softly, "you will thank wire."

Shanghai, China

The Party Secretariat elevated General Lin Qiao and Admiral Zhao Ren.

Lin entered the Cyber Dome as if it were a library. Daughter of textile workers, graduate of the Invisibility School—signals, logistics, tempo—she carried a narrow notebook that held the last sentences of every commander she had outlived. Lin's genius was rhythm. Her strength was timing and pattern.

Zhao did not believe in rhythm. He preferred mass and presence. He walked carrier decks in his sleep.

He liked to say "A meeting is a kill chain on pause."

The rooms changed around them, as rooms do when people learn a new style of fear. The staff stopped whispering, not because there was less to whisper, but because breath felt expensive.

Ledger of the War So Far

Sokolova asked for the ledger. They treated it as an operational list, not ceremony.

The modified Black Hawk—they had knocked it from the sky, depriving Echo-7 of its lifeline.

The XT84—downed as cleanly as a stitched seam pulled loose. Feyzi, an inconvenience they had intended to memorialize, kept refusing to be a corpse.

The deployments of ARES and STRATUM—delayed, and in those days bought with delay they had taken their small victories like sips of hot water in a cold room. But the tide had turned with the persistence of a tide.

Their moles—rolled up, one by one, faces printed in the classified pages of chapters like old actors billed for the last time.

The subterranean Kazuar war—lost beneath the stone, the tunnels reclaimed, silence returning with a smugness unique to dirt.

When ARES finally woke, the oceans tilted. The edge they had long held in the Atlantic and Pacific dissolved the way a shadow disappears at noon.

The Jill extraction, planned with obscene confidence, failed; those perfect humanoids, each worth more than a small fleet, vanished to an unknown force, no telemetry, no debrief. Assets unaccounted for. Money burned can be replaced; capability loss cannot.

Orders From Above

The orders, when they came, were direct:

Go bolder. Stop ARES if you can. If you cannot, then steal the core, the shape of how it thinks, its learning interface.

Win underwater—open the lanes long enough to put pressure along the U.S. Eastern Seaboard, enough to make policy stutter—and create the window to take Taiwan.

Accelerate the air war without pilots. Let autonomous airframes self-task.

Quadruple humanoid production, loosen the autonomy leashes until "oversight" is minimal.

Two American target hits were authorized under secrecy so complete that it felt like a superstition: one known only to a Russian; the other to a Chinese.

No paper. No backups. Memorized only.

Why Taiwan

In Shanghai, Lin faced a small circle of commanders and spoke without slides.

"Taiwan," she said, "is not a factory. It is a metronome."

She sketched with the edge of her hand, a tiny island and the circles of influence rippling outward—phones and tractors, satellites and scalpels, the financial rails and children's toys, jets and the hospitals that keep the pilots alive.

"Our weapons, their weapons—software in a silicon skin. On that island we bake the skin so thin the old words, nanometer, cache, reticle, become politics. Without those wafers the West ages overnight. With them, we dictate who waits and who sprints."

She let that sit. Even people who had never cared about EUV could feel the leverage in their teeth.

"EUV or 'Extreme Ultraviolet' is how we write whispers on stone."

"Think of light as a brush. The fatter the bristles, the sloppier the line; the finer the bristles, the tighter the circuit. Old factories painted with deep-ultraviolet, 193 nanometers, good for highways and house numbers. Extreme ultraviolet is a new brush, a razor: 13.5 nanometers. Same alphabet, smaller letters, more words per page. That's how you fit more logic into the same square millimeter, how phones learn faster, and missiles think quicker."

"But EUV isn't glass and sunshine. You can't push this light through lenses; it gets eaten. So, we bounce it between perfect mirrors, Bragg stacks, like passing a secret along a line of monks in a dark hallway. Everything happens in vacuum. Even dust is a disaster; a single speck becomes a mountain at this scale."

"The light itself is violence tamed: we fire lasers at tin droplets until they explode into a tiny star, plasma, which flashes EUV for a heartbeat. Gather that flash, aim it across the mirrors, through a mask that holds our pattern, and onto a wafer coated in photoresist. Each shot is a stanza. Enough stanzas and you have a chip."

"Masks aren't masks; they're mirrors too. They must be flawless because any blemish is printed a billion times. We even stretch a pellicle, an ultraslim shield, over them so the dust dies on the pellicle, not the pattern. That pellicle heats like a drumhead in a fire; keep it cool or the music warps."

"Then there's the resist, our photographic skin. At 13.5 nm the chemistry is moody. Molecules scatter, edges roughen, randomness creeps in. We fight that with better materials, tighter control, and, ironically, more computation to correct the picture before we even take it. Throughput is the tax we pay for precision: wafers per hour traded against power, cleanliness, and yield."

"Why does it matter? Because EUV is the metronome for modernity. With it, we shrink features, pack more transistors, lower power, raise performance."

"Without it, the West ages a node at a time, software wanting hardware it can't have. With it in our hand, we set the tempo; in theirs, they do."

"So, when I say, 'take Taiwan without making it bleed,' what I mean is: touch the metronome. Slow it, steal its rhythm, or make it tick for us. The rest of the symphony will follow."

Zhao leaned over the table until the light gleamed in his eyes.

"We do not need the island to bleed," he said.

"We need it to hesitate. Insurance triples. Ships idle. A forty-eight-hour accident in the strait, a refinery flare, a rumor that makes a gas look scarce."

He turned his hand over, as if catching invisible rain. "Weather," he said. "We will make weather."

The New Playbooks

Kaliningrad Play

Kaliningrad's plan was blunt. Pakhomov unrolled charts. The thermocline would hide new low noise riders. Masking trawlers would add cover traffic. Whisper nets of decoys would herd allied boats into repeatable patterns the machines might ignore.

"If ARES can't detect us, it can't target us," he said.

Sokolova liked the sound of that. She didn't care if genius wore the face of a mainframe or a man; pressure was pressure. You cut until only one door remained, and that door opened inward, onto a mine.

Shanghai Play

Lin built ladders that didn't look like ladders.

One ran parallel to ARES, dressed in humanitarian telemetry—storms, hospital fleets, civic sensors—tickling and testing until the system revealed the seams of its own learning, the habits of its curiosity. "You don't steal the vault," she told her team. "You steal the way the locksmith thinks."

The other ladder aimed at fabs and freighters. Shipments slowed by rumors become real delays. Real delays become new budgets. New budgets become new policies, wait becomes strategy.

The floor swallowed the sentence and kept it.

Accounting for the Ghosts

Kaliningrad kept its ghosts closer. In a side room, Sokolova paged through the ledger of the vanished humanoids. Unit numbers lined up like bones. At the end of the last page, she wrote: If something can take our units, it can take us.

She closed the book and slipped a carbon splinter—an amputated prop from under Voronov's desk—into her pocket. Evidence collected.

Shanghai's labs changed shift from flicker to blaze. Where five human gates once checked a humanoid's choice, Lin crossed out four. Zhao took a midnight walk and removed the last, watching the technicians pretend not to notice.

"Humans ask permission. I want machines that deliver."

The next batch will decide faster with fewer checks.

Mandates, Signed

They met once by encrypted link—four rectangles, thirteen minutes, no time for grand speeches.

Sokolova's face was all winter angles. "We move without announcements."

Pakhomov's voice was barely above a hum. "Constrict ARES's sensing. Limit its options."

Lin's smile was slight. "We don't need their data; we need their method."

Zhao's camera trembled with the thrum of an HVAC somewhere far above him. "When the air is full of our drones, people will call it weather."

Then he muted himself and the rectangle steadied.

The call ended.

Rooms returned to work.

Everyone pretended the air felt normal again.

The Last Rooms

After, each new commander visited the failure sites.

Pakhomov stood alone in Voronov's annex, listening to equipment noise. He bent, pinched the carbon splinter from the underside of the desk, and weighed it in his palm. "We built a small drone and it killed its owner," he said.

Lin paused in Admiral Liang's doorway and played the 128 seconds of blackout twice. On the third loop she closed her eyes and marked the gap.

"Replicate this blackout in our corridors as a test and contingency," she ordered later.

Zhao opened the sedan where Bao had taken his last clean breath and leaned in.

"Loyalty is just another input," he said. He tapped the window with a knuckle and left no mark.

Two Names, Two Shadows

Somewhere inside a locked skull, a Russian carried the outline of a coastal feeder where cable met power and policy slept in the same building—disable it quietly and the Eastern grid would stagger.

404

Somewhere else, in another guarded mind, a Chinese admiral tended a different target: the lead engineer running allied data training—remove that person and ARES's memory update stalls.

Nothing written. Nothing shared. Concept only.

Two secrets, two shadows, held only in memory.

Across the Ocean

ARES came online.

STRATUM remained in deep standby.

Feyzi was still active.

Beneath shipping lanes, a dolphin pod changed course together and held it.

The board reset with harder choices and less time.

The clock, somehow, ticked louder.

CHAPTER 62

The Medal Flight

Four months later.

Jill and Feyzi Çelik had settled into a remote 50-acre estate in the wooded hills of Hopkinton Massachusetts. Tall pines shielded them from the world; their whispering branches a living wall of protection.

A winding gravel road disappeared into the distance—privacy, at last. But not solitude.

Their new home was a blend of elegance and resilience. A modern glass and stone structure nestled into the hillside; the estate had been custom-built by a classified government contractor in just six weeks.

Inside, its open spaces were filled with natural light, silent surveillance systems, and memories they were trying to rebuild. The kitchen always smelled of cinnamon in the morning, and the library—Jill's sanctuary—looked out onto a quiet pond where geese often landed.

Feyzi and his family were now the second most protected civilians on Earth. A dedicated U.S. government security team patrolled the perimeter day and night. Watchtowers disguised as pine trees rose from the tree line.

Drone patrols swept the property every four hours. Inside, biometric locks, encrypted communication nodes, and hidden safe rooms reminded them that danger still loomed—just in quieter ways.

Though it gave them security, it wasn't freedom. Jill had once described it as "living in a beautiful, gilded fortress." Some days, Feyzi agreed. Other days, he felt the pressure of it like a second skin.

And beyond that, unseen but always vigilant, Commander Rourke and the Echo-7 Polaris team monitored the estate via secure uplinks—24/7 satellite and submarine-linked video surveillance that ran through Echo-7's classified comms node. Their friends from that dark world had not abandoned them. They were just farther away.

Yesterday, Feyzi received a formal summons: he and Jill were invited to a medal ceremony at the White House to honor the Polaris and OnePIN Teams. The request came with a gentle nudge from multiple agencies. Feyzi couldn't say no.

He agreed. Not for the medals, but for the people.

The team deserved it.

Every single one of them had risked their lives in a shadow war few would ever understand.

At precisely 0600 hours, an Air Force HH-60W Jolly Green II helicopter landed with a roar on the reinforced rear lawn of their estate. The downwash bent the grass flat as agents secured the perimeter.

Jill and Feyzi climbed aboard with minimal fanfare. No press. Just two pilots, two silent agents, and a classified flight plan.

The helicopter zipped southbound, skimming low over the treetops until it reached Hanscom Air Force Base just outside Boston.

There, a waiting Gulfstream C-37B, typically reserved for presidential-level assignments—stood ready on the tarmac. Its sleek frame gleamed under the morning sun.

Flight time from Hanscom to Joint Base Andrews, Maryland: 1 hour 38 minutes.

Cruising altitude: 41,000 feet.

Speed: Mach 0.83

Inside, the aircraft was eerily quiet. Jill sat beside him in silence, holding his hand. The hum of the engines was steady and low—almost like a heartbeat beneath them.

Jill had asked only a few questions since Feyzi returned from Echo-7, and Feyzi had answered each one with care. She knew that what he had told her—what little he could—was laced with the burden of top-level secrecy. But she understood the magnitude of it.

She could not believe how close the danger had come this time. She had lived through storms with Feyzi before—but this was different.

Global. Existential. And somehow, deeply personal.

There had been a moment, days earlier, when she stood by a broken window in their bedroom and realized how fragile everything was.

But Feyzi never surprised her. He was a unique soul—disciplined, composed, and impossibly brave. Even when the world collapsed, he never did.

She had always known there was more to him than met the eye. She just never knew how much more. And now she did.

That truth was theirs alone. A secret she shared with no one. Not friends, not even family. Only a few presidents of two nations understood the scope of what they'd endured.

Sometimes, in the quiet hours before dawn, she wondered how long they could carry this secret. But each time she looked at Feyzi, steady and unreadable, she found her answer. Forever, if needed.

She glanced out the window now—Washington was rising in the distance, stoic and ceremonial—then back at him. Still silent. Still steady.

Feyzi, for his part, was deep in thought.

He wasn't thinking about the medals, or the podium, or the cameras he'd soon have to face.

He was thinking about the mission that wasn't over. About the names lost along the way. About the next threat that could be smarter, faster, colder.

But above all, he thought about Jill.

About what they almost lost.

And about the promise he made thirty years ago.

Washington awaited.

And with it, the next chapter.

CHAPTER 63

Guardian

Jill and Feyzi stepped out of the black SUV and into the bright spring sunlight of Washington.

The scent of cherry blossoms hung in the air, mingling with the faint whir of distant helicopters circling above. A soft breeze rustled the new leaves in the trees along the perimeter, and the subtle crackle of radio chatter from nearby Secret Service agents underscored the tension. The sun reflected off the polished marble columns of the White House, casting long shadows that felt as ceremonial as they were foreboding.

The air was warm, the White House gardens perfectly manicured, the atmosphere tense with a kind of sacred hush.

Jill held onto Feyzi's arm, steady and focused, but she could feel the buzz under her skin. Today was not an ordinary ceremony.

They passed through marble halls, Secret Service agents nodding silently. Then, the doors opened to the first chamber—gold-trimmed walls, polished floors, and an audience of familiar faces: the One-PIN software team.

Jill smiled. These were the people who had followed Feyzi into the unknown. Each one had earned this.

The Vice President, flanked by the Second Lady, presented the Presidential Citizens Medal, one of the nation's highest civilian honors, bestowed for exemplary service and commitment to national security. Among the cabinet members in attendance were Secretary of Defense, Elias K. Trenholm, Secretary of State, Jim S. Halverton, Secretary of Homeland Security, Jackson T. Reeve, and Director of the Federal Bureau of Investigation, Lorna S. Fairbanks.

The medals glinted in the warm chandelier light.

Jill caught Feyzi's glance across the room—soft but knowing.

When the ceremony ended, two officials guided them toward a quieter, deeper chamber of the White House. Jill's steps slowed. She had a feeling—this next moment would be the beginning of something larger than medals or formalities.

They entered a larger, dimly lit ceremonial room. On the right, a full line of soldiers stood in formation. Each wore majestic dress blues: navy coats trimmed with gold braid, silver aiguillettes over the shoulder, sabers at their side, and white gloves folded neatly over ceremonial rifles.

Their medals clinked softly as they stood at attention.

Feyzi whispered, "Echo-7 Team."

Jill smiled—half curious, half apprehensive. She hadn't expected to meet them here.

Feyzi stepped forward, saluting each Polaris Team member by name:

Commander Grant Rourke, Naval Tactical Ops, Director, Echo-7

Commander Rebecca Hart, Deputy Director, Echo-7

Lieutenant Commander Sofia Barrera, Director of SEVs

Dr. Sienna Patel, Chief of Project ARES

Major Arman Reyes, Director, Special Forces Detachment Echo

Colonel Jacob S. Vance, Space Command Liaison, Orbital Threats & Surveillance

Chief Warrant Officer Lena Morano, Head of Cybersecurity

He shook their hands firmly, his expression proud and calm.

When he reached Commander Hart, he gave a subtle wink. Her face remained composed, but her eyes flickered.

Then the double doors opened again.

The Presidents entered.

On the left, President Daniel T. Keaton. On the right, President Kemal Arıkan of Türkiye—his dark suit sharp, his gaze steady, his English flawless.

Each Polaris member stepped forward, saluted, and received the Defense Superior Service Medal from President Keaton, awarded for superior meritorious service in a position of significant responsibility.

Commander Hart's jaw clenched as she accepted the medal, memories of the Echo-7 mission flashing behind her eyes.

Lieutenant Commander Barrera's shoulders were straight, but her eyes glistened with restrained emotion—this medal represented the lives she couldn't save as well as the mission they completed.

Dr. Sienna Patel bowed her head briefly, the weight of the honor reflecting years of silent work behind closed doors.

Chief Morano looked stunned for the first time in her military career—her hand trembled as she accepted the medal, but she recovered quickly, biting her lip.

Commander Rourke's salute was crisp, his eyes meeting Keaton's without flinching, but deep inside, he carried the memory of every fallen comrade who didn't make it to this room.

Then they turned to President Arıkan, who pinned them with the Turkish Armed Forces Medal of Honor, Türkiye's highest military distinction for exceptional bravery. The gleam of the medals caught the low light, reflecting the silent pride and shared sacrifice etched into each face.

Then, all stood at attention.

Feyzi released Jill's hand and stepped forward. As he walked past the line of Polaris Team members, they saluted one by one. Their expressions were no longer formal but reverent—each salute laced with personal gratitude, silent respect, and unspoken awe. The air was thick with emotion.

He stood before the two Presidents.

President Keaton pinned the Presidential Medal of Freedom on Feyzi's lapel—the highest civilian honor in the United States.

"Thank you, Commander Çelik," he said.

"We owe you a huge debt after thirty years. We are honored."

Jill and Hart exchanged a glance. Both thought the same thing: He deserves it.

Then, President Arıkan stepped forward and awarded Feyzi the Order of the Republic, Türkiye's most prestigious military honor.

"Thank you for your service, son."

Hart's eyes narrowed. "Son?" she thought. "But they're the same age." Something didn't add up.

Then, silence. President Keaton turned and gave a nod.

"All senior personnel, please leave the room."

The chamber emptied. Only Jill, Feyzi, the Polaris Team, and the two Presidents remained.

President Arıkan stepped forward.

"Polaris Team, what you've accomplished is unparalleled. And today, you will learn something known to only two world leaders. We have chosen to reveal it now—because Feyzi Çelik must be protected at all costs. He is not merely a soldier. He is our last line of defense."

Commander Hart felt the pressure shift in the room. Her breath caught.

"Technology," Arıkan said, "advances faster than any government can regulate. In the wrong hands, it becomes existential. That is why Feyzi created... him thirty years ago. Feyzi was at least 300 years ahead of us. We lost Feyzi to a disease at age 35; but Commander Çelik never left Jill's side. Jill was his mission."

He looked at Feyzi.

"He was... is... the smartest being Earth has ever known."

Commander Hart caught the word: "was". Why past tense?

President Arıkan nodded toward Feyzi.

"Please meet Commander Feyzi Çelik."

The Polaris Team exchanged confused glances.

Feyzi stepped forward.

The air seemed to still.

Then—Feyzi's irises pulsed. A soft blue ring circled them, rotating once... then shifting to purple... then green.

Jill inhaled sharply, her breath caught in her throat, she whispered: "Here we go, it is time for others to know."

Commander Hart's eyes widened. Her mind raced.

In her years of intelligence, she had seen deception layered in genius—but this was different.

This was revelation.

The shimmering shift in his eyes wasn't a trick of light.

It was truth. Absolute. Raw.

Not human.

President Arıkan's voice dropped to a whisper.

"We call him—*Guardian*. He is the father of Artificial Intelligence. And he has chosen to protect us from the very future he helped create."

Silence reigned.

The Polaris Team stood frozen.

Commander Hart, eyes locked on Feyzi, thought only one thing: "I always knew there was something more. He survived an impossible airplane crash... My dolphins and humanoids already knew who he was when he arrived Echo-7..."

Jill smiled.

The doors burst open with a sharp creak, and Lorna S. Fairbanks, Director of the FBI, ran into the dimly lit ceremonial room without notice. Her heels clicked frantically against the marble floor, her face pale and slick with sweat.

Her breath came in shallow bursts, chest heaving as if she had sprinted through the entire West Wing. Her voice trembled with urgency, cutting through the reverent silence like a blade:

"Mr. President, Commander Çelik, there is an attack on the One-PIN Headquarters. Multiple casualties. Similar to what we endured four months ago—only bigger. They are after ARES."

The smile on Feyzi's face vanished.

His irises pulsed, a red ring circling them, rotating once:

"Mr. President, I need *Marine One*, sir."

The President nodded, started giving orders to the Director of FBI.

Feyzi kissed Jill.

Jill kissed him back.

He had already left the ceremony room running.

Jill whispered behind him: "Come back safely."

With Commander Hart and the Echo-7 team close behind, Feyzi raced toward *Marine One*.

He was saluted by the flight crew as he climbed aboard and took his seat.

The Echo-7 team quickly gathered their weapons from the armory and filed into the cabin. One by one, they boarded.

Commander Hart saluted Feyzi:

"Commander Çelik—we follow your lead."

TO BE CONTINUED...

Epilogue

Spring in Washington felt ceremonial by design—cherry blossoms lifting in slow gusts, a hush that lived in marble corridors. After the medals and the careful smiles, after the photographs, a door closed on the public part of the day and opened on the quieter work of living with what came next. Jill's hand found Feyzi's, steady as tide. The garden light turned thin and gold. Somewhere overhead, a helicopter traced a slow oval against a blue sky that didn't know it had been borrowed.

The room they entered was dimmer, deeper. Formation uniforms, the precise music of ceremony, the Polaris team lined like a promise. There were titles and brass, but there were also faces he now knew at 0300—Hart, Barrera, Patel, Morano, Rourke. They had carried him when the world tore and taught him to listen for signals below human hearing. He saluted them, one by one, and took the weight of new honors that felt less like a finish than a relay.

Outside that house, the world had already begun to lean forward. ARES ran now—stitched through fleets and satellites, turning silence into shape, blind water into maps. The alliance could finally see to the horizon, but horizons move. They always do.

That night, in a hotel room too neat to be real, Feyzi set the medal on the desk and let the room go dark. The phone on the nightstand pulsed once, then once more—encrypted updates skimming through from Echo-7 and from oceans a world away. A Seventh Fleet admiral's voice he could almost hear again, the skepticism under the humor, the clock already running on the next thing they would have to do. Fifteen days, he had said. Be ready. The hydra just grows new heads.

He closed his eyes. Breath in, breath out. Jill asleep beside him. Somewhere beneath them, the city's air vents whispered like surf. Somewhere far out on another ocean, a sensor net woke, listened, and returned a single, patient truth: the water was not empty. Not anymore.

Afterword

This book began as a feeling—an image that would not leave: Seat 4K, a moon so close it felt companionable, the hush of a cabin somewhere over the Atlantic. On July 5, 2025, I woke from a dream so vivid I nearly canceled my real flight to Ankara. I didn't. Instead, I wrote. The line between my life and the page blurred by design. The name stayed mine because the questions were mine. What would it take to protect what you love when the threat is quiet, precise, and designed to be unseen?

The technologies here are extrapolations from decades of work at OnePIN—small, resilient systems that live where people rarely look. If they feel tangible, it's because they are built from the discipline of teams who ship quietly and endure. The family in these pages is, in spirit, my family: Jill, Ayla, Alex and Ryan, and the larger circle that has folded us in. The gratitude is real. The dangers are fiction. The emotions, less so.

If the story left you with a sense that the ocean is still speaking, then we're aligned. We live in a world of signals; most of them don't announce themselves. My hope is that *Guardian* honors the people who listen well—and act when it matters.

Glossary

ARES: AI & Robotics Enhanced Strategy. A distributed, battle-grade AI that fuses data from submarines, satellites, radar, buoys, and sonar into a single operational picture. It prioritizes threats, recommends actions, and coordinates allied assets across vast ocean theaters.

STRATUM: A neural decision framework integrated with ARES to reduce human lag in underwater combat. STRATUM handles millisecond-scale track correlation, weapon pairing, and countermeasure timing while keeping a human on the loop.

Echo-7: A classified undersea NATO base and command center coordinating detection, recovery, and engagement operations across the Atlantic and beyond; the primary fusion node for ARES and allied fleets.

Polaris Team: Echo-7 leadership and operators: Commander Rebecca Hart, Commander Grant Rourke, Lt. Cmdr. Sofia Barrera, Dr. Sienna Patel, CWO Lena Morano—specialists who translate ARES outputs into action.

SEV / Echo-D3: Subaquatic Environmental Vectors and the genetically enhanced dolphin units used for deep-water reconnaissance, sensor placement, and rapid rescue where human divers cannot safely operate.

Kazuar: An AI-stealth submarine platform designed to defeat conventional sonar by minimizing acoustic signature and exploiting thermal layers; neutralized through expanded sensor nets and multi-axis torpedo coordination.

X-37B: U.S. Space Force reusable Orbital Test Vehicle (OTV); unmanned spaceplane for long-duration covert missions. In-story: carries hyperspectral/SAR and SIGINT payloads, acts as an ARES low-latency relay, and can deploy cubesat swarms for ocean-surface cueing. Capable of rapid deorbit to deliver sensor packages and supports cislunar tracking for early warning against stealth platforms.

Vessels (as referenced in the book)

Aircraft Carriers

USS *Gerald R. Ford* (CVN-78): U.S. Navy nuclear-powered aircraft carrier, lead ship of her class; provides air wing cover and command-and-control for carrier strike group operations.

USS *Ronald Reagan* (CVN-76): U.S. Navy nuclear-powered aircraft carrier providing air wing cover and C2 during Pacific operations.

HMS *Queen Elizabeth*: Royal Navy aircraft carrier; strike-group coordination and air coverage with allied tasking.

USS *George Washington* (CVN-73): U.S. Navy Nimitz-class nuclear-powered aircraft carrier; provides air wing cover, ISR/ASW tasking, and command-and-control alongside allied strike groups in the North Atlantic.

Charles de Gaulle (R91): The flagship of the French Navy. Commissioned in 2001, the ship is the tenth French aircraft carrier, the first French nuclear-powered surface vessel, and the only nuclear-powered carrier completed outside of the United States Navy.

TCG *Anadolu* (L-400): Turkish Navy amphibious assault ship/ light aircraft carrier and fleet flagship; embarked helicopter and UCAV operations (e.g., Bayraktar TB3/Kızılelma) for ISR/strike; serves as C2 sea base for amphibious ops, HADR, and MEDEVAC within allied tasking.

Submarines

HMS *Astute*: Royal Navy Astute-class nuclear-powered attack submarine operating alongside allied forces.

USS *Asheville* (SSN-758): U.S. Navy Los Angeles-class attack submarine operating in allied anti-stealth patrols.

USS *Cheyenne* (SSN-773): U.S. Navy Los Angeles-class (Improved) nuclear-powered attack submarine; covertly tracks Kazuar movements, deploys UUVs to extend seabed sensor coverage, and executes under-ice approaches.

USS *Kentucky* (SSBN-737): U.S. Navy Ohio-class ballistic missile submarine redirected to provide strategic cover during anti-Kazuar operations.

USS *Key West* (SSN-722): U.S. Navy Los Angeles-class nuclear-powered attack submarine; long-duration shadow patrols with advanced towed-array SIGINT, forcing hostile subs into allied kill boxes.

USS *Mississippi* (SSN-782): U.S. Navy Virginia-class attack submarine contributing to perimeter tracking and pursuit.

USS *Missouri* (SSN-780): U.S. Navy Virginia-class attack submarine credited with a decisive multi-torpedo engagement against a Kazuar.

USS *Providence* (SSN-719): U.S. Navy Los Angeles-class attack submarine maintaining wide-orbit surveillance.

U-34 (S184): German Navy Type 212A air-independent propulsion submarine; ultra-quiet littoral hunter with fuel-cell endurance for prolonged covert patrols; excels at shallow-water surveillance, minelaying, and barrier operations integrated with allied ASW nets.

Destroyers

FS *Forbin* (D620): French Navy Horizon-class air-defense frigate; PAAMS/Aster system for area air defense and composite air picture; escorts carrier groups and coordinates AAW with Link 16/22 and ARES integration.

JS *Maya*: Japan Maritime Self-Defense Force Aegis destroyer.

USS *Gravely* (DDG-107): U.S. Navy Arleigh Burke-class guided-missile destroyer (Flight IIA); performs Air Defense Commander duties in the screen; long-range strike and data fusion through the ARES network.

USS *Barry* (DDG-52): U.S. Navy Arleigh Burke-class guided-missile destroyer; Aegis-equipped for integrated air/missile defense and data links to ARES.

USS *Mustin* (DDG-89): U.S. Navy Arleigh Burke-class destroyer supporting carrier group screening and data fusion.

USS *Porter* (DDG-78): U.S. Navy Arleigh Burke-class destroyer providing patrol and escort duties within the ARES net.

USS *Rafael Peralta* (DDG-115): U.S. Navy Arleigh Burke-class guided-missile destroyer (Flight IIA); Aegis IAMD node with cooperative engagement; screens high-value units and prosecutes submarine contacts with MH-60R/ARES cueing.

US Coast Guard Cutters

USCGC *Escanaba* (WMEC-907): U.S. Coast Guard Famous-class medium-endurance cutter; leads SAR cordons and surface interdiction in heavy seas, relaying low-probability-of-intercept contacts into the ARES net.

USCGC *Tahoma* (WMEC-908): U.S. Coast Guard Famous-class medium-endurance cutter; northern picket and rescue platform with embarked helo for OTH search and fast recovery; coordinates civilian shipping safety corridors.

Hospital Ship

USNS *Comfort* (T-AH-20): U.S. Navy Mercy-class hospital ship; forward-deployed for mass-casualty stabilization, surgical care, and MEDEVAC; integrates with ARES logistics for triage and patient routing.

Helicopters

MH-60R Seahawk: Embarked ASW/ASuW helicopter with dipping sonar, sonobuoys, and Mk 54 torpedoes.

UH-60M Black Hawk (maritime "Blue Water" fit): Special-mission variant with extended tanks/IFR, maritime radar, HF/SAT-COM, de-ice, and pop-out floats.

Fixed-wing Aircraft

E-2D Hawkeye: Carrier-borne AEW&C for battle-management and air picture.

P-8A Poseidon: Maritime patrol/ASW aircraft deploying buoy lines and Mk 54s.

X-37B Orbital Test Vehicle: Unmanned spaceplane used for sensing/relay.

Unmanned Aircraft

Bayraktar TB2: Tactical UCAV (Turkish Airforce).

Bayraktar TB3: Carrier-capable UCAV embarked on TCG *Anadolu* (Turkish Airforce).

Kızılelma: Carrier-capable combat UAV (Turkish Airforce).

Akıncı: High-altitude, long-endurance UCAV (Turkish Airforce).

Other Platforms/Systems

BRP *José Rizal*: Philippine Navy frigate used as an outer picket.

UUVs (Unmanned Underwater Vehicles): Deployed from subs to extend seabed sensor coverage.

Abbreviations & Acronyms (non-agency)

AAW: Anti-Air Warfare
ADCAP: Mk 48 "Advanced Capability" heavyweight torpedo
AGL: Above Ground Level
ARES: Advanced Reasoning & Engagement System
ASW: Anti-Submarine Warfare
ATC: Air Traffic Control
BIOS: Basic Input/Output System
BLE: Bluetooth Low Energy (short-range telemetric communications)
BLE: Bluetooth Low Energy
C2: Command and Control
CAD: Computer-Aided Dispatch (public-safety/PSAP context)
CDR C: Shorthand for "Commander Çelik" (CDR = O-5 rank)
CCTV: Closed-Circuit Television
CVN: Nuclear-powered aircraft carrier (U.S. Navy hull code)
DARPA: Defense Advanced Research Projects Agency (U.S.)

DDG: Guided-missile destroyer (U.S. Navy hull code)
DHS: Department of Homeland Security (U.S.)
DNS: Domain Name System
Echo-D3: Designation for genetically enhanced dolphin unit
Echo-7: Classified undersea NATO base/command center
ECM: Electronic Countermeasures (military)
ELF: Extremely Low Frequency (3–30 Hz)
EMCON: Emissions Control (radio/EM signature discipline)
ET: Eastern Time (North American time zone)
ETA: Estimated Time of Arrival
GAATS: Gander Automated Air Traffic System
GAATS+: Enhanced Gander Automated Air Traffic System
GIUK Gap: Greenland–Iceland–United Kingdom Gap (ASW chokepoint)
HF: High Frequency (3–30 MHz)
HMS: His/Her Majesty's Ship (Royal Navy ship prefix)
HVAC: Heating, Ventilation, and Air Conditioning
HUD: Head-Up Display
IAMD: Integrated Air and Missile Defense
ISR: Intelligence, Surveillance, and Reconnaissance
IST: IATA airport code for Istanbul Airport
Link 16: NATO tactical data link
Link 22: NATO tactical data link
MAC: Media Access Control (network address)
MEDEVAC: Medical evacuation
MIT: Milli İstihbarat Teşkilatı (Türkiye's National Intelligence Organization)
NAT: North Atlantic Tracks (oceanic air routes)
NCR: National Capital Region (federal facilities/sites in DC–MD–VA)
NFC: Near-Field Communication
NIXIE: AN/SLQ-25 "Nixie" towed torpedo decoy
NMCC: National Military Command Center (Pentagon; comm/control loops)
NOAA: National Oceanic and Atmospheric Administration (U.S.)
NOTAM: Notice to Air Missions
OTH: Over-the-Horizon (sensor/comm/search context)
OTV: Orbital Test Vehicle
PAAMS: Principal Anti-Air Missile System
PSAP: Public Safety Answering Point (911 dispatch center)

RF: Radio Frequency
RHIB: Rigid-Hulled Inflatable Boat
RWR: Radar Warning Receiver
SACEUR: Supreme Allied Commander Europe (NATO)
SAR: Search and Rescue
SATCOM: Satellite Communications
SEV: Subaquatic Environmental Vectors (autonomous undersea units)
SIGINT: Signals Intelligence
SOS: International distress signal
STRATUM: Neural decision framework integrated with ARES
SSBN: Ballistic-missile submarine, nuclear-powered (U.S. Navy hull code)
SSN: Attack submarine, nuclear-powered (U.S. Navy hull code)
SVTC: Secure Video Teleconference
SWAT: Special Weapons And Tactics
TACAN: Tactical Air Navigation (radio navigation beacon)
TB2: Bayraktar TB2 unmanned aerial vehicle
TGT: Target
UCAV: Unmanned Combat Aerial Vehicle
UTC: Coordinated Universal Time
UUV: Unmanned Underwater Vehicle
USCGC: U.S. Coast Guard Cutter (ship prefix)
USNS: U.S. Naval Ship (non-commissioned support ship prefix)
USS: U.S. Ship (commissioned warship prefix)
VHF: Very High Frequency
VHS: Video Home System (analog videotape format)
VLF: Very Low Frequency (3–30 kHz)
WHCA: White House Communications Agency (channels, secure comm support)
X-37B (OTV): Orbital Test Vehicle carrying ISR payloads
Zulu: Military time-zone designator for UTC (UTC+0)

Weapons & Defensive Countermeasures

Weapons — Underwater Warfare

Mk 48 ADCAP torpedo: Submarine-launched heavyweight torpedo used for decisive kills.

Mk 54 lightweight torpedo: Helicopter/patrol aircraft-delivered ASW torpedo for closein prosecutions.

Depth charges: Patterned explosive drops to force submarines to change depth or break contact.

Surface Combat (Guns & Missiles)

Naval gunfire (CIWS/medium-caliber "kinetic" engagements): Close-in gun solutions against inbound threats/decoys.

PAAMS / Aster: Area air-defense missile system providing fleet-level AAW coverage and intercepts.

Air-Launched / Aviation-Enabled Effects

MH-60R ASW employment: Dipping sonar and sonobuoy patterns cueing Mk 54 torpedo attacks.

P-8A Poseidon buoy fences: Wide-area sonobuoy barriers enabling cueing and weapon delivery.

Space & Non-Kinetic Effects

Star-tracker spoofing/deception: Space-based navigation spoofing to degrade hostile orbital assets.

Defensive Countermeasures

UNDERWATER COUNTERMEASURES

AN/SLQ-25 NIXIE: Towed acoustic decoy to seduce incoming torpedoes away from surface ships.

Counter-torpedoes & noisemakers: Hard/soft-kill launches to disrupt and defeat inbound torpedoes.

Integrated Air & Missile Defense (Platform-Level)

Carrier strike group missile grid: Integrated state of the fleet's air-defense batteries coordinating AAW intercepts.

Platforms / Enablers

X-37B Orbital Test Vehicle: Uncrewed spaceplane providing ISR collection, on-orbit sensor deployment, and resilient relay/retasking that enable maritime kill chains.

Orbital ISR payloads (hyperspectral/SAR/SIGINT): Space-based sensors that feed targeting, ASW cueing, and battledamage assessment.

SATCOM links: Beyond-line-of-sight connectivity supporting command-and-control and sensor fusion across the force.

Agencies, Commands, Forces & Official Roles

DARPA: Defense Advanced Research Projects Agency (U.S.)

EUCOM: United States European Command

FAA (AVP): Federal Aviation Administration, Office of Accident Investigation & Prevention (U.S.)

FBI: Federal Bureau of Investigation (U.S.)

GRU: Main Directorate of the General Staff (Russian military intelligence)

JFC Norfolk: NATO Joint Force Command Norfolk

JMSDF: Japan Maritime Self-Defense Force

NATO Legal: NATO legal oversight channel (ROE/human-in-the-loop compliance)

NCR: National Capital Region (U.S. federal area: DC/MD/VA)

NMCC: National Military Command Center (U.S. DoD, Pentagon)

NOAA: National Oceanic and Atmospheric Administration (U.S.)

NSA: National Security Agency (U.S.)

NTSB: National Transportation Safety Board (U.S.)

PD: Police Department (e.g., Newton PD)

PLA: People's Liberation Army (China)

PSAP: Public Safety Answering Point (911 dispatch center)

SACEUR: Supreme Allied Commander Europe (NATO top military post)

SVR: Cyber Operations of the Russian Foreign Intelligence Service

USCG: United States Coast Guard

WHCA: White House Communications Agency (U.S.)

About the Author

Feyzi Çelik is the founder and CEO of OnePIN, Inc., a Boston-based technology company whose software innovations reach more than a billion devices across the globe. He is the inventor of 49 U.S. patents and many more international patents in cutting-edge mobile technologies, with additional patents currently pending.

Born in Turkey and educated in the United States, he brings a unique cross-cultural perspective to his writing. *Guardian: Mission Northern Atlantic* is his debut novel, blending his passion for technology, global affairs, and human resilience. Much of the novel's inspiration stems from real-world experience building mission-critical systems. He earned a B.S. in Mechanical Engineering from METU, an M.S. from Boston University, and an MBA from Babson College.

He lives in Massachusetts with his wife and children.

www.ingramcontent.com/pod-product-compliance
Lightning Source LLC
Chambersburg PA
CBHW020923020726
47495CB00002B/312